THE AFFINITY BETWEEN US

Book 1 of THE AFFINITY BETWEEN US Series

Melissa Sweeney

This is a work of fiction.
Names, characters, places, or incidents are either products of the author's imagination or are used ficti-tiously. Any resemblances of people, living or dead, is entirely fictional.

ISBN 978-1-7338679-6-2 (pbk)
ISBN 978-1-7338679-7-9 (eBook)

For me,
past, present, and future

1

Kevin

He tried to defend his innocence from those who called him a monster, but a gun pressed between his wings and threatened him to keep moving.

Lightning cracked in the humid sky. Just a few hours ago, he'd been with Nikki and Derek, heading to Morgan's for after-school ice cream. Today wasn't supposed to end like this.

The guard led Kevin up the stairs leading to the Asilo, the group of large government buildings making up their Líders' headquarters. He'd only been this close during school field trips glorifying their Líders' lineage. He never expected to be led here for his own execution.

"E-excuse me," Kevin said.

The guard, paying him no mind, shoved him through the automated doors.

The fluorescent lights stung his sensitive eyes. The tiles were too shiny, the walls too white. Signs pointed to doctor offices and meeting rooms.

A group of idle guarddogs watched Kevin get dragged through the foyer. His makeup was smeared from the struggle. His wings, ten feet each of feather and bone, were streaked with rain and blood.

If he'd seen himself, sobbing while evading authorities, he too would've called himself a criminal. He'd heard it on their earpieces: He was the prime suspect in Derek's murder.

But that wasn't the case, and he needed to explain everything as soon as possible. His hyperventilation was doing him no favors.

His guard brought him to a set of elevators. "This way," they said.

"No, please," Kevin begged, but he tripped getting in. He hadn't been in an elevator before. He wondered how it worked.

The guard hit a button on the wall for the top floor.

"No." He tried to struggle, but the moment he moved, the guard grabbed his shoulders and restrained him against the wall.

He let out a gasp in pain. This wasn't right. He was a good kid. He had a part-time job at his family's coffeehouse. Things like this didn't happen to people like him.

Tears he'd been trying to suppress let go, and he sobbed into the cold, sterile wall. "I'm sorry," he said. "I'm so sorry, I didn't—I didn't mean—"

The words kept popping in his throat. The explanation for what'd happened to Derek, he couldn't get it out.

The elevator shuttered to a stop, and the guard half-walked, half-dragged Kevin down a new hallway. It was windowless and smelled of bleach and blood, with the faintest hint of salt. The taste of his tears, maybe.

The guard walked up to a random door and used something on their wrist to open it. They unveiled a small room with an operating table in the center, medical equipment, and a lonely chair. Two other guards were waiting, one with a clipboard, the other putting on a pair of medical gloves.

Delayed panic sparked in Kevin's heart. He knew it'd make him look more guilty, but he couldn't stop himself from struggling. His flight instincts had been berating his over-worked brain for hours. He was becoming desperate.

"Stop it!" the guard yelled, and something rammed into the back of Kevin's head.

Sky dots burst in his vision. He slumped forwards. Real, physical pain he wasn't used to vibrated from his head down to his tail feathers.

The guards sat him down on the chair. His wrists were tied behind his back and wings. No, *chained*. Two *click-clicks* and he was immobilized. His wings, too tired to take flight, wilted like trodden flowers.

A quiet moment. Soft beeping and the guards discussing something important. His ears were clogged. Slowly, his mind caught up with his thoughts. The reality of his situation was not good, and he was too stupid and scared to fix things. He felt himself quickly giving up.

Tears dripped off his freckled nose. He wanted Derek back. He wanted Nikki to console him. Mom, to pet his hair like she used to and Dad assuring him that he'd take care of everything. Because that's what they did. They were a family. They took care of each other.

The guard with the clipboard studied the words written on it.

"P-please," Kevin said, "we need to find my sibling. He didn't die when he touched the Barreira, he fell through—I couldn't believe it when I saw it, but it's true."

The guards looked at him like he was becoming what he feared: a disillusioned bird with blood on his hands for a crime he must've committed because no other answer made sense.

He swallowed. "He isn't dead," he confirmed. "I didn't kill my twin."

The guard frowned. "That's a case nobody's gonna believe you on, kid."

Two heavy knocks struck the door like bullets.

The guards snapped upright, tails alert. They straightened their uniforms and hair to appear ready for company. "Yes, your Líderships."

The door slid open. The newcomers were silhouetted in harsh, yellow light, making them appear dream-like. And that's what they were to them, especially to Kevin. Surely, he wasn't in front of the world's leaders. He hadn't done anything to warrant this type of meeting.

Nadia and Mikhail, the two Líders who held the world in their hands, stood before Kevin Harrow.

He stopped breathing. He'd never seen them so close up. Nadia, a timber wolf crossbreed with hair cropped to a sharp point. Mikhail, a dog with a smile you wore when committing a crime. Their families were descendants of the first leaders of Raeleen when it was birthed from dust and decay, the howling canines who rose up to remake the world.

Kevin bowed, offering them the back of his neck.

The two Líders stared him down. Their eyes almost glowed with intensity.

They gave the room a beat. Then Nadia asked, "Why're you still here? Get out. Now."

Kevin went to move, but guard boots shuffled to escape the room instead.

When it was just them and Kevin, Nadia said, "Zantl, come in now, sweetie."

Someone came in. Kevin saw boots, the flow of black, shiny hair that reached the floor, and a tucked-in, black tail that contrasted their parents' bold postures. To be polite, Kevin lifted his head.

Zantl stared disgustingly down at Kevin, and Kevin nearly threw up. Nadia's and Mikhail's child, a genderless heir, born and adopted sometime during the winter months.

Kevin was perhaps the first Raeleenian not part of the Guard to have seen Zantl in person like this. Unlike their parents, who came out for assemblies and gave monthly radio speeches, Zantl was an heirloom hidden from the public. Very few even knew what they looked like. This was per their parents' requests.

Zantl was said to be special beyond birthright, or adoption-right. Schoolyard rumors that jumped to the adults' lips. Supposedly, they had "powers." Mysterious, deadly powers that could hurt people. Kevin hadn't seen it in person, but his parents had, once.

It was when the Líders had come out and publicized that they'd adopted an heir—a dog and a wolf couldn't bear adequate children. On the steps of the Asilo, the infant now known as Zantl cried so hard that the reporters documenting the event exploded from the inside.

Kevin had been two at the time, but those in attendance—his family, who were interested in politics—had witnessed it. They still couldn't talk about the blood that pooled in the canals that day.

And Zantl had come out of hiding.

Today.

For what Kevin had done.

"Sit up."

Kevin did as ordered. He didn't know where to look.

Zantl's upper lip curled in disgust. They kept a hand near their chest as they tried to physically get away from Kevin.

"Okay," Nadia said. "Now that we all have a good look at you, tell me: What in the *fuck* is going on here?"

So informal. Kevin was speechless.

A sharp *whack* and he was seeing sky dots again, but this time it was more precise against his right cheek.

Mikhail lowered his walking cane. "She asked you a question. It'd be right of you to answer her."

Kevin went to wipe away the sting, but his hands were still bound. He used the elbow of his wing.

"Father."

Mikhail turned eagerly. "Yes, Zantl?"

Zantl folded back their ears. "Don't hit him. Don't make him mad."

Kevin looked up. Merciful, an act of good faith for someone innocent?

Or fear that Kevin was more unhinged than initially thought? From the look in their eyes, Kevin guessed the latter and needed to fix that. "I won't hurt anyone," he promised.

"Ugh, yeah, right," Zantl said. "I don't want to be near him any longer. I'm leaving."

Mikhail's ears drooped. "Of...course, Zantl. Whatever you'd like, we shall grant."

"No, wait," their mother said. "What's wrong? What're you feeling?"

Zantl left without another word.

Mikhail sighed and leaned back on his cane. "Ah, well. We'll get back to them once they're in a better mood. So, little bird, why have our guards brought you here today?"

Kevin didn't know where to start. Wasn't he already dead by going up to the Muralha? That itself was a punishable offense. "I, um, don't know."

"It's been all over our earpieces. Clamor about two ospreys attacking the Guard, about shooting one in the *face*."

The bloody memory flashed behind Kevin's eyes. "That wasn't us. That was...that was..." He felt sick. All that blood...

"Don't try to lie now. We saw photos of the body. We're having trouble identifying it. And then we have reports of you flying up and up and *up*..." He pointed above them. "*All* the way up to the Muralha."

He and Derek *had* flown to the Muralha, the thousand-foot wall surrounding their city, but they didn't have the whole story yet.

"And then," Nadia continued, "whatever occurred on that slate of granite, only one of you came down."

"You, covered in scratch marks," Mikhail added.

"And crying like a *child*," Nadia finished.

Mikhail knelt down to get a better look at Kevin. His teeth were naturally sharp. "Whatever excuse you're going to come up with, you better make it compelling, because your case is *not* looking good."

Even if it was impossible, what'd happened, Kevin had to do this right. For his sake. For Derek's.

He lifted his head a little higher, just a little. "My sibling and I were picking up our younger sister from school. He was a little energetic, and it was my fault for not reining him in. He was kicking rocks down the road and hit a guard with one. We tried to explain how it was an accident, but then Derek got scared and ran off holding my hand. Nikki stayed behind. She has nothing to do with this."

"Oh, how noble of you, defending your little sister."

Kevin gulped. "A-and then we ran. I didn't know what he was doing. We were cornered by the Guard, and then..." He readied himself. "We heard a voice."

Nadia's eyebrows raised. "A voice?"

"Your conscience?" Mikhail teased.

"It was a little girl's voice, a voice both of us heard that I don't think the guards did. It was like she was talking directly into our minds."

Mikhail tilted his head. His eyes opened in wonder. "And what did this little voice say?"

"We couldn't understand her, but she did something to the guard that killed him. Then it was like..." He bit his lip. "She told us to go to the top of the Muralha, and it was like we couldn't stop ourselves. She asked us to follow her, so we did. She said she was trying to save us."

Both Nadia and Mikhail looked at one another, having a conversation with their sharp eyes and not tongues.

Kevin's knees began to shake. He couldn't do this. There was no logical explanation for today, let alone what happened next. He'd rather die than describe it properly.

"The girl," he continued, "well, her *voice*, was really worried about us. She said the Muralha was crumbling and it *was*. I don't know if you know—well, of course you do, of course—but the Muralha doesn't look good. Pieces of it are falling into the valleys and forests beneath it." He picked a large piece of skin from off his thumb. "She wanted us to go through the Barreira."

That was the most illogical part of the story. The Barreira was the invisible eggshell over the Muralha that kept everyone in. Nothing could pass through it other than clouds and rain. From that alone, he sounded like he'd lost his mind to madness.

Hurried footsteps ran back down the hall. The guards outside jumped in surprise as Zantl ran back in, hair flying up and boots skidding to a stop. "She did *what*?" they demanded. "Are you serious? She got one of you *out*?"

"Zantl," both of their parents gasped.

"Shut it!" Zantl pushed both of them into medical equipment. "What else did she say to you?" they asked Kevin. "What does she know?"

He stammered, "I-I don't know. I don't even know what she looks like. I tried telling her that it was impossible, but then something grabbed Derek's ankle and tried taking him through. I tried to stop her. I tried to save him, but—" He sniffed. Derek's nails, digging into Kevin and pleading that he not let go. He'd tried, but the rain had been too strong and the girl was so determined to...

Zantl backed away. "That's insane," they whispered. "She's insane. She *killed* him."

"No, he's alive," Kevin sobbed. "He has to be!"

"She's crazy. She's crazy." Zantl pushed back their long hair. Their parents waited for what they'd say next like true dogs.

Kevin choked on another sob. "I'm sorry. I know it sounds crazy. It doesn't make sense, but I tried everything to stop it from happening. I didn't kill Derek." He dared a look up, a pitiful glance for forgiveness.

Nadia's and Mikhail's jaws had dropped. Zantl was pacing and muttering to themselves about this supposed girl they knew, but she'd been just a voice in Kevin's head. She hadn't been real.

"Her name," Nadia asked. She was trying hard to keep her voice level. "Did she tell you her name?"

Kevin hadn't said. He thought the whole story was too unbelievable, who cared if this girl had a name?

She did have one, though. "Maïmoú," he said. "She said her name was Maïmoú."

Kevin watched Nadia's heart fall through her ribs and hit the floor in shock.

Horror.

"Fuck," she whispered.

"Fuck," Mikhail agreed. "Zantl—"

"Fuck this!" Zantl ran out of the room again. "Keep him away from me! I'm not to be within a hundred feet of him, do you hear me?"

"Wait, Zantl, what should we do with him?" Nadia called out. "Tell us."

"Enlighten us, please," their father begged, but Zantl was already gone.

Kevin felt the room's temperature drop. His story should've sent him to a psych ward, yet they were acting as if this was an extremely normal and dire story beat.

Nadia snapped at her guards. "Lock him in a room. Post a guard...no, bring the Marcos Unit in."

The guards rushed in to free Kevin. Others tidied up the space, feigning disinterest to world-altering news.

Kevin moved with them. Was his execution delayed? They usually did it in the streets, publicly shooting someone and broadcasting it on the radio. Had the story changed?

"My," Mikhail said, watching the room thrum with life. "What a fascinating day this has become."

"What's happening?" Kevin asked. "Am I—?"

"Are you going to be killed?"

Him saying it so nonchalantly made Kevin rethink everything he knew about the world. Sure, the Líders were cruel. What Líder hadn't been? They had an awful task with running the world. But to play with Kevin's life like this, it was demented.

"No," Mikhail answered for him. "You aren't. Not now. You're too valuable."

"Why? Because of that girl?"

Mikhail grinned, but it was off, like he was about to start crying.

The Líders had always sounded so wise on the radio. They were all-knowing and knew how to keep the city functional. But today, Kevin had gotten a personal look at their hidden lives: two adults, both irritable loons, who clung to every word spoken by their teenage brat.

"Can...can I call my family?" Kevin asked. "Can I tell them I'm going to be alright? They were so afraid when I was taken away. I don't want them to worry."

"Oh, you don't have to worry about them any longer."

"Why?"

"Because you're going to be living here, with us, in the Asilo, for the rest of your life."

An empty numbness spread through his hollow bones like an irreversible plague. He stood a thousand feet above the world, atop the wall known as the Muralha. Its grey stone was chipped underneath his heels. His family had been right. It was ready to give any day.

"Kevin."

Tears clouded his already cloudy vision. Around the Muralha bubbled the Barreira. You usually couldn't tell it was there unless the Sun's rays hit it just right, but a few feet in front of him, it oozed and shifted like dark, wet sand. He'd heard the stories. It looked like the night sky, sparkling with sky dots.

Nobody was able to pass through it. Everyone knew that, but still, those tried. Birds flew up here to search for a break. Kevin had daringly pressed his hands into the ink. It was like trying to pass through solid concrete, a fool's errand.

"He'll be okay."

He searched the stormy sky. He'd been hearing that voice for nearly thirty minutes. That's how long it'd taken for his world to permanently change course. "Why'd you do it?" he asked, too shocked to ask more. "He was my sibling."

The girl didn't answer, but Kevin knew. All that lay outside the Barreira was the sky, sky dots, the Sun, the Moon. Eternal emptiness where souls went to die.

She'd killed Derek.

"I didn't mean to."

Another gust of wind ruffled his feathers. He looked back into Raeleen, his home, their home.

In the distance, sirens wailed for his execution.

2

Nikki

Nikki stared at the new hole in the wall, eyes half-lidded, thinking about what to break next.

Blood rounded off her scarred knuckles. They were old wounds she thought she'd put an end to after being adopted. She'd had the childish notion that life got better when you had a family to die for.

But life hadn't gotten better. The scars had only reopened.

Her ears flicked. Wet, heavy footsteps plodded up the stairs towards their apartment—her parents were home.

Nikki surveyed her wrecked bedroom. She'd promised her parents that she'd finally clean up. Ever since the incident, she'd let her room fester with her heart. She was ignoring the mold in her cups and the rain leaking in from her window. It hadn't stopped, the rain.

Nikki nudged dirty laundry behind her mattress. It'd been there for days. She was in the same baggy sweats and hoodie she'd changed into after school that day, and she hadn't done anything with her hair. Kevin used to style it for her.

The front door opened. Keys hit the counter and shoes were kicked off. Her parents started a muted conversation.

Nobody came upstairs. Nobody told her they were home. Nobody acknowledged anything.

She dug her nails into her palms. She had her fists and her bat was somewhere underneath the trash. She had so many options to mar the world to show that she was still here despite everything being taken away from her. But her fists couldn't do it for her anymore—they only left behind scars that hurt others more than they hurt herself.

She flung open her bedroom door. One of its hinges was loose and thwacked against her sandbag in the corner. Whatever her family had been talking about, they'd stopped and listened from downstairs, waiting for Nikki to act out like a child. She *was* a child, damn it, and she was taking this far better than any of *them* were.

Refusing to look at Derek's and Kevin's bedroom across the hall, Nikki trudged downstairs to greet her remaining family.

Her father was untying his apron while her mother was grabbing the milk delivery out front. She was with Vanna, holding his fifth or sixth coffee of the day. Nikki hadn't heard him come in. Damn him and his soft footfall.

Her mother and father were Derek's and Kevin's birth parents, so they, too, were ospreys of brown and grey, not black rats like Nikki. They were both beautiful in her eyes, but their freckled faces now reminded her too much of her siblings.

"Hey," her mother said, looking vaguely in Nikki's direction. "You should've seen the lines at Morgan's today. Some boar threw a cheesecake in her face and Del had to toss them out. It was a mess."

"Vanna handled himself well," her father said. "Didn't you, Vanna? He's starting to get better at handling customers."

Vanna looked away, pretending to unacknowledge Nikki right when he had. This bastard of a boy was Nikki's cousin. He often came over unannounced to eat, clean, hang out. He was a lynx, tall and lanky and rarely able to make a strong impression, yet he somehow had a way of pushing Nikki's buttons.

Unlucky for him. All of her buttons had been pressed for days.

"Are you hungry?" her mother asked. "We nabbed some leftovers from Morg's. We got cake and your favorite buttered pasta."

Nikki's small body seized, a spring ready to jump. She wasn't hungry. She hadn't eaten a full meal since Derek disappeared.

"Disappeared," because there was no way the murder reports were true.

"We should finish up the leftovers in the fridge," her father recommended.

"And you got an extra bottle of milk," Vanna said, counting the glasses of milk. Nikki had heard them deliver it but couldn't leave her room.

"Wait, so how many bottles did we get today?"

"Seven."

"How did they even fit an extra bottle in the holder?"

Nikki's chest shivered in loss. She couldn't explode, but—

"Oh, Nikki," her mother said, "did you hear another piece of the Muralha fell?"

Nikki punched the closest wall as hard as she could. She clipped the corner and chipped the peeling wallpaper with her bare, bruised knuckles. "Why're you all acting like this? Why're you acting so weird? What's going on?"

Everyone other than her lowered their heads.

"Why're you ignoring what happened? For All That's Above, two of your kids are gone and you're acting like you lost a pair of socks at the laundromat!"

When none of them said anything, she continued stoking the flames. "Are we accepting it, then? Are we seriously gonna believe the Líders, that Kevin pushed Derek off the Muralha? That doesn't make any sense, and it's unfair of you to act like you're not upset by this."

She'd turned that day over in her mind. She'd gotten out of school with Vanna late. Vanna left to study in the library, as if he wasn't the top student in their class. Derek and Kevin had picked her up to go to Morgan's. She told them they didn't have to, but they always did. Derek had been stupidly kicking rocks and hit a guard with one. Derek *was* stupid, but ever since Nikki had been adopted, she hadn't known him to act that recklessly.

The guards had cornered them. The one he'd hit, a poodle just out of the academy, was crying, but only in the way when you popped an eyebrow pimple—he'd hit her between the eyes, it wouldn't leave a scar. She'd insisted that it wasn't a big deal, but her pack hadn't been so kind. Nobody could hurt the Guard and get away with it. Someone had to be punished.

Instead of apologizing, Derek had taken Kevin's hand and fled, leaving Nikki to defend herself against three angry guards.

One had gone after them. One had escorted her home. The hurt poodle went between them both, trying to keep everyone at peace.

An hour or so later, Kevin returned home soaking wet and covered in scratch marks, crying about the Muralha crumbling and a voice and Derek, Derek, Derek. Derek went through the Barreira and he didn't know how but they had to help him *now*. Nikki had never seen her brother so frantic.

She always stood up for Kevin. She saved him from bullies and helped him gain a confidence she'd fortified when she'd been homeless. He was an innocence she needed to protect.

When she'd seen him in the living room, screaming nonsense, she hesitated, not because she thought him guilty of any crimes, but because she'd been thinking over the ways she could've prevented this from happening.

That night, they'd taken him away. They said he'd killed a guard before throwing Derek over the Muralha. They said he'd be executed for his felonies.

Nikki had argued it. Without knowing the truth, she'd fought, bitten, and clawed at the officers for his honor, but it'd been no use. He was taken from her, and hours later, they'd received a phone call saying that Kevin had been tried and committed to death for unnatural acts against Raeleen.

And Nikki. Did not. Take that. There was *no* way on this cruel Earth that her brother would've ever done *anything* to hurt Derek. The boy didn't even kill bugs in their room, Nikki had to do it for him.

She needed answers for what really happened that day. She wanted action. She wanted her best friends back.

And her parents. Looked away. And acted like this was all a bad dream.

"There's no use stirring things up," her father had said.

"Please, Nikki, we don't want to lose you, too," her mother had said.

"Nikki, stop fighting," Vanna had said, "and let it go."

She glared at all three of them, rat tail flicking. She was going to die on Kevin's innocence. Even if she lost her family's respect for acting out, she'd find a way to bring *both* of them home.

Her father set down his work bag. He always wore a stern expression even when making jokes, but after this week, he'd become more jagged. The bags under his eyes were more present. "Nikki, please. We can't do this right now. We need to let it go. I know you're upset."

"I'm *upset*?" She gagged. "And *you're* not? *You're* not?" she asked her mother. "Kevin's dead, Mom. He's not coming back!"

Her mother covered her eyes from the truth.

Nikki didn't understand. Why wouldn't they let themselves mourn? Why was she being seen as too emotional?

Nikki, out of options, turned to Vanna for support.

Vanna took a sip from his coffee mug in avoidance.

Nikki stormed over to him. At least she could justify her parents being emotionally distant from shock, but Vanna wasn't like that. He cried when he got too upset or happy, he'd laugh so hard, he'd snort. He couldn't hide his heart from her.

She rammed him up against the wall, knocking the coffee out of his hand. He was too tall and she was too short, but she easily pinned him with his stupid scarf. He always wore it, this checkered, tattered piece of fabric, even before they'd met as little fourteen-year-olds. It smelled like him: coffee stains and bookmarks.

She glared into his green eyes. Pointy nose, white skin, and orange hair that was striped brown. Everything about him was the opposite of her. In any other life, they would've been strangers, perhaps enemies.

He met her gaze, grimacing in pain or something else. He sucked in his thin lips with something to say.

"What?" she demanded. How she hated him like this. Let him say something hate-filled and callous. Let them argue for hours until their voices went. She just needed to hear him speak. This distance, it was so lonely.

"Then talk to me!" Nikki yelled. "Tell me what's going on with you! It's like none of you even care that they're gone!"

"Because we can't," her father stressed. "If the Líders saw us acting up over this, we'd be watched. The Guard would always be at our doorstep, our bank cards would be limited—"

"Is *that* all you care about?" she exploded. "Your *bank* cards? Derek and Kev are gone, Marshall! Kev's been—" She couldn't say it. "You're never gonna see your kids again if you keep acting like this makes sense, or if it truly happened in the first place!" she added, because something inside her told her that through these convolutions, her siblings were alive. Why weren't the Líders looking into this "break" in the Barreira? Why hadn't they executed Kevin in the streets?

She knew denial was part of the grieving process, but all this secret-keeping made her secretly hopeful for a happy ending.

"Nikki, that's enough," her mother finally said.

"Oh, shut up," Nikki spat, and pushed off of Vanna to head outside.

"Nicole!" her father shouted. "Nicole Lenore, how dare you—"

She slammed the front door on them. They lived on the second and third floor above a tailor shop, so to keep away from everyone, to keep from her flighted parents and cousin with a keen scent of smell, Nikki climbed up to the roof.

Her sneakers gripped the shingles as she made her way up. From here, she saw most of Raeleen. This rainy city of derelict buildings that morphed into industrial complexes the closer they got to the Asilo. Palm trees grew from the sidewalks. Children played with nicked balls in the alleys. This was her home, safe from the violence she'd been born into.

After this week, nothing felt like a home. She had a broken family. She'd lost her heart.

Her parents began whispering again, not even trying to make an effort to come up and check on her. Not that she expected them to. She was eighteen, it wasn't like she was a baby in need of being coddled. She'd once taught herself to never rely on anyone for anything, especially love. They'd find a way to hurt you with that weakness. She'd buried away that big part of herself.

Then this family decided to give her a home from the rain, and for a few years, things got better.

And now she was broken because of it. Stupid. So stupid.

A low roar echoed across Raeleen, like a multi-car car crash or avalanche in a nearby mountain.

It was the Muralha again. She didn't live far from it, but at this height, she could make out its horizon line through mangos and telephone wires.

A dust cloud poofed off the wall. She saw no damage—her eyes weren't *that* good—but she knew what'd happened. Another piece of the wall had broken off.

It happened, just like the rain and every hardship you faced in life. Ever since her parents' parents' time, the Muralha had been breaking. Sometimes, it was a few crumbs. Other times, the chunks were bigger than her apartment complex. When breaks like that happened, the Guard would be sent to patch it. People would talk about it for a few days, it'd have a five-minute segment on the radio, and then they'd forget about it, the world ignoring itself.

What would happened when it fully cracked in two? Would they fall into the sky? Would the world collapse in on itself? Nobody knew. The Líders said not to worry about it, so they, in theory, didn't.

Unable to deal with any more conspiracy theories, Nikki lay on her back, watching the dark clouds go by. The rain let up until patches of yellow broke through the storm.

She closed her eyes and timed her breathing. In, out. In, out, each breath slower than the first. It was a technique Kevin had taught her. She wondered if he'd implemented it that night.

"...lo?"

Her eyes snapped open.

"Hello?"

It was farther off that time, the voice, but the question was clear in her mind.

She sat up and repositioned her rat ears. It sounded like a little boy asking for directions. It reminded her of Kevin, but she'd never heard this voice before. "Hello?" she asked no one. "Who's there?"

Only the wind replied.

3
Derek

He didn't know where he was or what'd gone wrong. All he knew was that he was certainly, most assuredly, fucked in the ass.

He was face-planted on the ground, that much he knew, and he'd been here for some time. His body hurt and his head pulsated from a bad hangover, so he kept his eyes closed. He did hear waves pulling in and out near him. Birds cawed at each other above. And he had the strangest taste in his mouth. Like sand. Salty, wet sand. Tasted like shit.

He coughed, and realized the taste was actually sand. He was eating sand.

He spat it out and tried rolling over. Something was on his back, preventing him from getting comfortable.

A wave of icy water crashed into him. He choked on the salt threatening to drown him and fumbled for dryer land.

When he opened his stinging eyes, he had two answers.

He was either:

1. Actually still asleep, just kidding, or
2. Certainly more fucked than he thought

He awoke to water. It started at the horizon line and kept *going*. Like, it merged with the skyline and pooled around this strip of sand he was stranded on. It was flooding the world.

He'd never, *ever* seen so much of it before. It was vast and looked empty yet was full of ripples and waves that moved with the wind. It was dominant and peaceful at the same time, like a sleeping creature able to eat you in one gulp.

He checked behind him. Attached to his back was a pair of wings, heavier than they looked and striped with muddy brown and white feathers. The inside feathers were fluffy and pale while the back feathers were coarse and dark. Some of them were missing. His tail feathers were bent.

His clothes, a black shirt with tight pants, lay in tatters across his sore body. His hair, matching the colors of his wings, reached down his back in mats. He looked and felt like he'd narrowly survived an attack.

"Fuck," he said. "What happened to me?"

He actually needed someone to answer that for him, because he had absolutely nothing in his brain. No name, no goal, no memories of what'd gotten him here. He was just *here*, and he really had to pee.

"Oh, my goodness!"

Two figures were standing down the strip of sand, watching him. The taller one wore a cape while the smaller one wore a pink dress with bows in her hair. He could tell that they were rich and probably blood-related in some way, like siblings or cousins. They wore jewel-toned clothes and had the same worried lines creasing their eyes. They looked mature for their ages.

"Pray tell us," said the little girl, "Do you need help?"

"Cellena, don't get near her," the older boy warned. "You don't know what will happen."

"But she's hurt."

"But you don't—Cellena, listen to me!" the boy shouted, but the girl was already rushing towards him.

Was "he" a "she" now? Based on the cock and balls hanging between his legs, he figured he was a "he," but who knew, and who cared? He went along with it, his head becoming fuzzier. "Hey," he greeted, "uh, where the fuck am I?"

The two siblings stopped a few feet away from him. The boy kept looking at his wings, the girl at his body, specifically the parts that hurt most. He didn't like that, their staring.

"Hey," he said again, trying to stand up with his wings, "can you, like, help me or—?"

His knee cracked. His vision spotted. Standing was way harder than he expected. Falling was so much easier.

He fainted in the endless sea of water, drowning for the second time that day.

4

Kevin

If he'd been Nikki or Derek, or if they'd been with him, he would've acted differently. After the Líders told him he'd be living in the Asilo forever, he should've asked why. Why wasn't he being executed? Why couldn't he phone his family? Why was he being kept a prisoner?

But he was alone, a cowardly boy who tried his best and usually failed. While Nikki would've fought back and Derek would've charmed his way out of trouble, Kevin, the oldest in the family, was a baby.

He wiped his red face with his newly freed hands. He couldn't even defend his story anymore—the Líders were already gone. His confession had cast them away.

"Kevin Harrow."

Standing outside the door was a boy waiting to escort him to his room. He looked about Kevin's age, though Kevin knew from rumors that he was decades old.

He was known as the Marcos Unit, a servant that followed the Líders' family everywhere they went. He was something called a robot, termed by the Líders to describe a machine built to resemble a crossbreed, and a bad omen that announced a Líder's presence. Such technology was too advanced to be real—aside from the lack of any animal characteristics, you couldn't tell he wasn't a real person. He stood statue-still, not breathing, his blue eyes focusing and unfocusing underneath a sweep of blond hair.

"I-I'll be right there," Kevin said, and went to fix his skirt. Most clothing in Raeleen had zippers or buttons sewn into the back for tails. His had been torn from being handled too roughly.

"Normally, people confined in the Asilo are given Asilo-assigned clothing," the Marcos Unit said. "Your case is...different, so I'll see to it that you are given appropriate clothes within the week."

That felt extreme, to cast aside his entire wardrobe from home, but that's what it'd come down to, at least for the time being. Perhaps he could have another hearing with the Líders when things calmed down.

It'd sounded like they hadn't believed his story until he mentioned the voice in his head: Maïmoú, a girl who'd dragged Derek through the Barreira and off the Muralha before disappearing. It should've labeled him as delusional, but the Líders had taken it at face value. Were they as crazy as the story? He knew his family thought very little of the government, but he'd expected them to be smarter than this.

As Kevin went to leave, Marcos blocked his path with his body. He looked down at Kevin's shoes. "We ask that inmates refrain from wearing shoes within the complex," he said.

"What?"

"It tracks in dirt."

He did as told. He should've expected weirder by now.

His shoeless gait sounded so light compared to the weight of an entire robot walking beside him. His arms didn't move. He turned the same way every time. Both alive and mechanical, this thing. Or person.

They turned to a set of elevators. Marcos pushed to go up. They waited in silence as the walls creaked and lifted the metal box up to the sky.

Kevin dug his nails deep into his finger beds. This abrupt silence after ceaseless trauma made his head pang with a headache. He felt like he'd been caught in a lie that wasn't true. Why wasn't he saying anything?

They descended down, past the foyer into unnamed levels. They must've had basement levels, too, just like at Morgan's place.

Kevin watched for the Marcos Unit to breathe. He looked so authoritative, like he could massacre an entire room of people without breaking a sweat. He probably didn't have to, sweat.

He took his shot. "You're younger than—"

Marcos flinched and raised his hand to defend himself. Inside his wrist unsheathed a thin yet deadly knife the length of a ruler. He pointed it directly at Kevin's face.

Kevin stepped back. "I'm sorry! I—sorry. Sorry."

Marcos, evaluating that there was no real threat in this elevator, sheathed his weapon and returned to facing the wall.

Kevin peeled off a crescent of dead skin from his thumb. Was he that much of a criminal to these people? He'd be sure not to make such a mistake again. No talking. He could do that.

"I apologize for startling you," the Marcos Unit said, not looking at Kevin. "I've been informed that you're a high-risk inmate."

"I shouldn't have been so startling," Kevin said.

The small room lurched and the doors opened. They continued down the new hall. Kevin made sure to stay far away from the robot.

The lights down this hall were exceptionally dimmer than the ones a few stories up—cobwebs covered up the needed light—and the locked rooms looked more sinister. The locks were more apparent as chains and bars. Down four-way intersections, he saw abandoned gurneys and dried IV stands. The whole floor felt both sterile and dirty.

He'd heard rumors pertaining to the Asilo. From backdoor broker deals to unethical practices done on crossbreeds. Some went as far as to say that the Líders were creating new breeds in secrecy, like insect crossbreeds, something that didn't exist, or new breeds entirely, ones that didn't have animal equivalents.

He wasn't a huge conspiracy theorist like the rest of his family was. The simplest forms of corruption frightened him, and he liked being a model citizen to balance out his family.

But knowing that the Líders knew about a voice in his head made his mind wander into darker woods.

"What was it," the Marcos Unit said, "that you were going to say?"

Kevin manually calmed down his breathing. In, out. In, out. "Just that you look younger than you do in the paper. You really look alive, like you could've gone to school with me and my siblings. And cousin. They're younger than me, but we were all in the same school for a few years."

The Marcos Unit continued on his path.

Kevin clamped his mouth shut. He'd *just* promised to keep quiet, too. He couldn't help but overshare when it came to his family. He had to be careful with *that*, too, his family. He had to keep most of his opinions to himself because of them.

The Marcos Unit stopped at a door that looked as scary as any other door they passed. He lifted his palm to the handle. The mechanisms inside the wall clicked and slid open. The doors here didn't even have hinges. What a feat.

The room was about the size of Nikki's bedroom back home, but he wouldn't call this room a bedroom. A twin-sized cot in the corner. A wall-to-ceiling mirror on the right. White walls. Barren floors. That was all that was given to him.

"You will be kept here for the foreseeable future," the Marcos Unit said, seeing Kevin in. "Your dinner will be brought up to you in two hours. I read that you have no allergens to speak of, so you will be given the standard meal that is appropriate to your breed's diet. Your meals will be delivered to you at six, noon, and six in the evening, with bathroom breaks allotted five times a day between your meals. We expect you to keep your room clean at all times and that you obey every rule given to you by a guard or Asilo official. We also ask that you give us blood and urine samples that will be taken in the next hour. Do you have any questions about these rules so far?"

"I...don't think so," Kevin said, even though he had thousands. "Can you tell me why I'm being held here?"

"I cannot," he said, "however, if you have any more information about the disappearance of Derek Harrow, you are allowed to vocalize them to me, as my memories will be replayed to the Líders so they can better understand the situation."

"So they're not ruling it as a murder anymore?"

"We have not recovered a body, so this's still technically a missing person case. Until the Líders tell me otherwise," he added, "this is a missing person case."

Kevin watched the robot's movements more closely. The way he spoke was mechanical in nature, and his diction sounded like Raeleenian was his second language, even though Raeleen only had one language.

But something about the way he was staring at Kevin was different, like he was waiting for Kevin to say something not so that he could record it, but for his own learning. Maybe that's how robots worked. He imagined cars acting the same way if they had intelligence.

"I'll keep that in mind," Kevin said, "thank you."

"So you have nothing left to tell me?"

"I'm sorry. It's hard to think clearly right now, so I don't want to give you any wrong information. Is that okay?"

Marcos' head twitched to the right, trying to come to terms with Kevin's shift in attitude. "That…is fine," he said, forced. "Is that all?"

Kevin nodded.

"Well. I'll. Get your food ready. Then." He lowered his head, almost showing his neck like Kevin was someone beneath him, and left.

Kevin waited for his footsteps to fade, but the room was vacuum-sealed. After the door shut, he was barred from the rest of the world.

He collapsed. He gripped the sheets as if he'd sink through the tiles and let himself cry. For Derek's alleged death, for the very real idea that he might never see him or his family again, to the thought of being experimented on as punishment.

He breathed in the harsh scent of mildew from the sheets. He bundled them up and breathed. In, out. In, out. Normally, he faked being emotionally strong for his family. He could control himself in front of them only to lock himself in the bathroom and cry so hard, he'd puke. Everything terrified him, everything could and would end terribly.

He was now in a den of wolves who only saw him as a murderer. They didn't care that he was spineless, he didn't have every piece to this puzzle. If he was to survive, he had to be stronger than this.

He just didn't know how, and he had no one to lean on here. What was the appropriate amount of time to grieve a loved one that might not actually be dead? A week? Forever? Neither felt like enough time. Did he have enough tears for a year's worth of grief?

Wiping his cheek on his cold sheets, Kevin checked how awful he looked in the mirror.

The hair on the back of his neck stood on end.

There was someone watching him, in the mirror. A little girl, maybe thirteen. No tail or ears, no markings or fangs discerning a breed. She had fair skin and long, blonde hair, long enough to reach the floor. Her white dress, beautiful and youthful, was stained in a concerning amount of black sludge. It came from her mouth and nose like vomit and puddled the ground.

She pressed her stained hands against the glass, her forehead cracking the pane. She was talking to herself, but Kevin couldn't hear her. He could only see her through the mirror and nowhere else.

Kevin fixed his skirt over his knees. "Hello?"

The little girl looked up. She exhaled slowly like an injured animal. Strung around her neck was a long, hidden necklace with a crescent moon dangling at the end. It, too, was stained by darkness.

"Are you alright?" he asked, "and, also, not as important as the first question, are you real?"

The girl drooped her shoulders, stunned at being perceived.

"Because you look like you're hurt, but if you're not real and I'm imagining you..."

The girl took a step forward through the glass. Then another. All of her weight fell onto each step.

"I wouldn't know...what to do..."

The girl dropped to her knees in front of him, wrapped her arms around his head, and hugged him so fiercely, his shoulders almost dislocated.

He took in her scent of gunpowder and cooked meat. Her body was warm, real. He did what felt right and patted her back. He felt every bone poking out on her spine. "Are you okay?"

She choked on the darkness inside her and pulled back to cough. A dollop of black sludge splattered to the floor like gelatin.

Kevin turned to his room's locked door. "Excuse me—"

The girl slapped her hand over his mouth. A feral look flashed in her blue eyes. She shook her head, looking between him and the door.

He did the same. *"Sorry,"* he muffled into her hand.

She pulled back and asked him a question. Her lips were moving, but he didn't hear her speak.

"I'm sorry, I can't hear you," he told her.

She said something under her breath, likely a curse, and got up.

"Wait," he said, "do you need help? Are you trapped here, too? You're not wearing shoes."

She pulled a face, then looked at her feet. They were calloused from living a life shoeless.

"Are you real?" he then asked. The girl was trembling the way older people did, a leaf about to fall from a dead tree. He wanted to make sure she was okay. He needed to. "I don't know if I'm seeing you because I'm freaking out or what, but if you're hurt, I can try to help..."

His fingers curled back. His mind, it'd been warped from anxiety and the threat of being killed multiple times. He knew he wasn't thinking right.

But now, the jagged pieces of the puzzle were falling into place, and he was a fool for not putting them together sooner.

He scooted back. "You—" He swallowed. "You're the girl, aren't you?"

She didn't say anything.

"Y-you brought us up to the Muralha. You sent Derek through the Barreira." He kept scooting back. The power this little girl had bested the Guard *and* the Líders. She'd pushed someone through the *Barreira*.

"Maïmoú," he said. "That's your name, right? Where's Derek? He's okay, right? You didn't do anything bad to him, right? He's okay?"

Maïmoú didn't answer, eyes unmoving, face cold as stone.

Then she nodded once, twice, and mouthed a sentence that took Kevin a moment to decipher.

"I would never hurt either of you."

And just from that, Kevin believed her. A cooling energy pooled through his body and soothed him. Through whatever magical powers she possessed, Kevin would always believe this girl's motives to be genuine and kind.

It scared him how easily his brain persuaded him to believe that, and that he didn't have a choice to contradict the thought. She was a little kid, how could he blame her for anything she may or may not have done?

"Who are you?" he asked. "*What* are you?"

She coughed again. A gallon of darkness emptied from her stomach. She pointed at the ceiling and mouthed a single word: *"Deity."*

"Deity?" he asked. "Is that what you said? What does that mean?"

She laughed at his naivety at a concept he didn't know, then lost her footing and fell into the mirror.

It shattered to a million pieces. Fragments of glass spiderwebbed to every corner until a giant piece fell out of place. It phased through Maïmoú's body like a magic act. She gave Kevin one last look, saying something only she knew, before the piece snatched her away and fractured on the floor.

The Marcos Unit ran in, blade unsheathed. He scanned the room for what could've caused so much damage in so little time.

Kevin tightened amidst the shards of glass. He waited for Maïmoú to return and explain herself.

She didn't return.

Days passed during his confinement, and she, this "Deity," never returned.

5
Nikki

Mornings lost their sweet charm without Derek and Kevin around. No more Kevin running up and down the hall to complete his pretty outfits. No more Derek waking up late and hogging the bathroom to get ready. Nikki always helped get their acts together while their mother and father made breakfast for their busy family of five, sometimes six or more if Vanna's family was visiting.

Waking up to silence felt wrong.

She pinched the bridge of her nose, trying to subdue the headache waking with her, and turned on her shoulder.

She met Vanna's coffee-stained breath. He was asleep at the edge of her bed, knees tucked, his wristbands nudging his cheeks. His nose twitched from dreams he wouldn't tell her about.

Even though he frustrated her to no end, Nikki didn't hate Vanna. He was her closest friend who pushed her to what *he* knew she could achieve.

In the past, Little Nikki survived on primal instincts. She taught herself how to make food last a week and which abandoned buildings were safest to sleep in. Attending school was idiotic in theory, until she saw Vanna's and Kevin's aptitudes for it. The two used to study at each other's houses for hours. Their parents beamed whenever a 50/50 came home.

The red that streaked Nikki's face when she scrounged up a 19/50 almost made her drop out day one. She was already delayed in education, and being taught with literal toddlers wasn't motivating. But Vanna had persisted. He'd sat her down with her and hadn't fallen asleep until she understood every branch of arithmetic. They'd overtake Nikki's dining room, textbooks bookmarked with colorful tabs courtesy of Vanna, and study until he was satisfied with her results.

Her 35/50s still depressed her, but Vanna, almost in tears, would flatten each exam and place them in a special folder he kept at his desk. Her parents' smiles forever burned in her brain, reminding her of what she left behind. If the school board decided to take in a rat like her at that age, then she knew she couldn't disappoint anyone else.

Then she lost Derek and Kevin and she was back to square one.

Stretching her back, Nikki leaned over and flicked Vanna's ear.

It twitched like a real kitten's. He awoke with a sharp inhale and blinked away eye crust. "Way to wake a person up."

"Way to break into someone's room without permission."

"Your door was unlocked, and don't give me that look," he said, interrupting her formatting a response. "You only do that when you want someone to talk to you. I know you, Nikki. Don't start." He checked the time on his watch. "It's time for school."

"I don't think so."

He stood up, still dressed in his school uniform from the previous night. "Get dressed."

"I'll go back eventually."

"I've worked too hard for you to quit now."

"You say that like I wasn't involved." She referred to her writing desk. Her stack of late assignments were piling up.

Vanna picked up her limp hand and played with her fingers. Bandages were taped over her scarred knuckles. Another courtesy of Vanna and his personal medical kit.

Her chin fell to her collarbone. Someone had laid out her uniform at the foot of her bed, ready to wear for the day. She hated wearing it.

"Please," Vanna begged. "I want you to get better."

"I'm fine."

"No, you're not. Look, I don't—I *can't*—talk about what happened yet. I know you want answers about their disappearance. I know you want justice. But we don't get those in this world. The more you ask of the government, the more you'll get hurt, and I won't lose you, too, Nikki. I can't."

"But what're we gonna do? Do you really believe the reports?"

"Of course I don't, but if I learned anything from my moms, it's that you shouldn't put all your cards on the table thinking you know how the game will end when there're seven other players who've played the game longer than you have."

She arched a brow. "I don't play cards."

"You get what I mean." He struggled for a better metaphor. "We should wait for a better time to act. When we're this broken and emotional, we become rash. Your parents are emotionally distant. Mine are, too. We're the only two who wear our hearts on our sleeves."

"You cover yours up," Nikki noted, watching him fiddle with his wristbands.

He dropped his hands. "I'm on your side," he finished with. "I believe everything you do. Just keep your head down, alright? There've been more guards driving around your neighborhood. They're suspicious of us."

Nikki gazed out the window. A lazy fog slept in the alley, perfect weather for unwinding with her bat.

This week had been the worst week of her life, but the weather was still perfect.

She poked Vanna in the chest. "I *will* go back to school, for you, so don't crap your pants about it."

"Thank you, but—"

"*But* I'm not going to school today, and you're dumb for thinking you can get me to go back on a Friday when the weekend is right there. I'll go back when I'm ready. I won't leave you alone."

Vanna placed a hand on his hip and glared at her.

"Vanna, I swear to the Above, if you give me any more sass."

He threw up his hands. "Okay, fine. No more fighting. I'll take it. Thank you."

"Good. So. You're playing hooky with me."

"Uh, no, I'm not."

"Uh, *yeah*, you are. I don't trust myself to be alone right now, and Mom and Dad are already gone. I heard them leave."

"Probably an early day at my moms' place."

"Wouldn't have hurt to say goodbye," she grumbled.

"They wouldn't have wanted to wake you. They know you're taking this as hard as all of us, Nikki. They're not against you."

"Yeah, yeah." She got up like she had an extra hundred pounds weighing her down and got dressed in clean clothes. Not in her school uniform—the shit-brown plaid made her want to shoot herself. Just her sweats, tank top, and hoodie she liked leaving unzipped, otherwise she looked like a kid wearing their mother's clothes.

"Where're we going?" Vanna asked.

She picked up her metal bat from off the floor. "The park."

Giving in too easily, he unzipped his bag and took out his mitt.

Nikki smirked. "*Oh, I want you to go back to school with me*," she mocked in Vanna's nasally tone. "Liar."

"My voice isn't that high."

"Sure, and it doesn't crack when you're nervous. Change out of that stupid uniform so you don't get busted by the Guard. There're some of your clothes on my closet floor."

As Vanna got changed, Nikki stared at her door, prepping for the hallway. She'd been avoiding it all week, the other side, though she wanted nothing more than to cuddle into either of their beds and relax in their down feathers.

She stepped out of her room and came face to face with Derek's and Kevin's bedroom. She read the crudely drawn name sign the siblings had drawn when they were younger.

Her feet, betraying her heart, walked her inside.

Two matching closets, two desks, two twin beds with matching end tables, and two lamps. The morning they'd disappeared, Kevin had made his bed while Derek's looked as unkempt as Nikki's. Kevin's guitar sat up against the window. Derek's radio still had his favorite album in it.

This side of the house had never been so quiet.

Vanna tugged on her hood. He'd changed to his regular clothes of tight black and studded jewelry. "Come on."

Nikki took another minute for herself, then kissed her knuckles and pressed them into their names.

Unfazed by the darkening weather, the world continued on. Unschooled kids kicked rocks into gutters as street vendors sold mangos and bananas they'd picked the day before. Behind Nikki's house was a dried stream, tangled telephone wires, and apartment complexes more broken than hers. Over the decades, kids with too much free time had graffitied the boarded windows with paint. Nikki thought it artistic. The Guard thought it vandalism. Neither, in Nikki's opinion, were wrong.

They left her neighborhood, Nikki on foot, Vanna on his bike, and headed north, parallel with the Muralha.

Depending on where you stood in Raeleen, sometimes it was string-thin, almost invisible, and sometimes, it stood tall enough to block out the Sun. As a vagabond, Nikki had once bet old friends that she could climb it. She'd pound her chest and point at the wall, promising a better life beyond the Líder's eyes.

Vanna followed Nikki's line of sight. "My mom said another piece of the Muralha broke off. Somewhere in the south."

"I saw, back when...I lashed out yesterday."

The memory of that boy's voice came back to her. She'd almost forgotten it. She'd checked her surroundings, but there'd been no one around. And she'd *heard* that voice, as if she'd had an earpiece in.

She stuffed the thought back into her subconscious. People heard voices when they were grieving. Maybe the voices were always *that* clear.

"She said she saw guards running up and down the street all night," Vanna continued. "She said to anticipate an assembly."

"An assembly? The Líders didn't even do that for, you know." She didn't say their names for Vanna's sake. "They only do that for serious stuff, and the Muralha's been crumbling for years."

"I'm just saying, we should take her word and plan ahead. They take up the whole day, I swear."

Kids were taught about the Muralha in school. Nikki had missed those formative years, but it didn't take a genius to understand the concept. It contained Raeleen, and everything beyond it was the sky. You couldn't leave because of the Barreira, all of it was built before their time by unknown hands, and sometimes the wall crumbled, but it wouldn't fall. That's what the Líders said, so that's what they had to accept.

Nikki was a generally defiant person, especially when it came to her family, but she didn't know enough about the world to refute the logic. She, like everyone, had to run with it as fact.

Everyone, but Vanna's mom. He had two moms, one soft-spoken—Nikki's mom's sister—the other a wild, chaotic mess that was Morgan Owens. She was the owner of Morgan's Delicate Sweets and Drinks, the coffeehouse her family worked at. She knew all the dirt the Asilo swept under the rug and sniffed out the deeper rumors with skills akin to a guarddog. Nikki didn't know the depth of what her aunt knew, but she wouldn't have put it past her knowing the true builders of the Muralha and Barreira.

As they reached Main Street, two guards slipped out from a dark alleyway, touching their earpieces and whispering their concerns about the youth thinking too hard about their world.

Nikki flipped up her hood and walked Vanna onto the sidewalk. "C'mon."

Vanna, ears folded, turned his back on them.

Nikki had known Vanna for years as a good kid, but his mothers held a deep-seated hatred for dog breeds. Generational ignorance poisoned kids' brains into hating people they didn't even know. She didn't think it'd affected Vanna because he was smart, but she still had her doubts. He never looked guards in the eyes.

But some people chose to have birth children, twisting their hands into courting certain lovers. Dogs with dogs, cats with cats. Some families had expectations to continue the family tree by blood. Her family, while having birth children, had also adopted her, and Vanna's moms had adopted him out of guilt.

Derek, he'd had no preference. Since Nikki had known him, he'd been with a bear, a ram, a fox, and a few dog flings that lasted as long as a special at Morgan's. He'd tried his best at finding his forever person, but the people he'd slept with treated him like dirt. Cheated on him, mentally and emotionally abused him. Nikki had consoled him break up after break up.

She walked over a short bridge that crossed over a hidden canal. Most streets had deep canals cut near the sidewalks that you needed to be cautious of. Being as wide as a car and just as deep, falling in would've sent you to the hospital. Nikki didn't know what they were meant for. They'd controlled the flow of rainwater before moldy cracks made them structural hazards. Storefronts were built down there, but most people avoided them. A lot of the homeless stayed in these parts, and since no breed could breathe underwater, one bad storm could wash you away.

"Wanna take the trolley?" Vanna asked her.

"You have a bike," she said.

"Yeah, but you don't. C'mon, my treat."

Before she could argue that he was wasting his money, a trolley pulled up to the nearby trolley stop. A stern-looking guard eyed them from the entrance.

"I don't have any money," Nikki reminded him. "My bank card's still frozen."

"That's why I said it's my treat." He hovered his red card over the slot.

Not a lot of teens were on this ride, freeing up their favorite spot: the back. When Nikki was homeless, she'd hop on to the back of these things and hold her breath that nobody narked on her. She had no place to go, it was just to feel the wind in her hair, to free herself from rainfall.

Vanna parked his bike in the bike rack and enjoyed their ride through town. The city awoke with them. Shops opened for the day, families biked or drove to school and work. Bird cross-breeds flew above the rooftops as herds of deer mingled on city lawns with their neighbors.

They had to pass the purebred districts to get to school—districts known to only house dog breeds—and the guard academies. Packs of purebreds jogged as one and practiced firing at wooden targets. Nikki looked away as they hit their marks. She didn't like guns, even as a means of self-defense.

Vanna peeked at the trainees before pretending like he hadn't.

"You're not getting like your moms, are you?" she asked.

His thin brows furrowed. "Why would you say something like that?"

"I'm just making sure."

"You know me, Nikki. When have I ever been like that? The Guard frightens me, that's it, but it's not because they're dogs."

"You've been..." She let it go. There was no use starting up another argument with him.

"I've been what?" he asked.

"Different, but I don't know what that difference is yet. It's like you're not telling me something."

"Don't be crazy," was all he said, and kept his eyes on everything but the academy.

Nikki kept hers on her cousin. They'd made up, but that rift between them was shifting. Not increasing, but the edges were crumbling, and soon, one of them was going to have to jump across the chasm to save the other.

Five minutes later, they arrived at Nikki's favorite park. Adults were battling around the basketball hoop in derive competition. The jungle gym was full of kids and old folk were strolling the gated area. She spotted all kinds of beings here, from horses to panthers to a few birds perched in the trees. There were makeshift benches for them across the sturdier trunks.

She always envied bird breeds gifted with the ability to fly. Derek had once said it was the same as running, but Kevin had told her that it was like running uphill on the hottest, most humid day. It took everything in you to fly, and their bones were more brittle than other species. A wrong landing would break your leg. Derek had rolled his ankle the second month Nikki had been adopted and she'd been stuck caring for him. She'd learned a lot about bird species that month, and how Derek liked to joke around even when bed-ridden.

But she always wondered what it felt like to detach yourself from Earth. Existing in weightlessness sounded nice regardless of how depressed you were.

She took practice swings at nothing as Vanna mounted the pitcher's mound. Her father had gifted her the bat a few years ago when they'd discovered Nikki's love of the sport. It felt right, hitting something not to break it but to have it soar across the sky as an achievement.

She squeezed the tape around the grip. "Ready."

The first ball bounced into the gate and startled the bird crossbreeds. Vanna jogged for it and threw an even faster ball.

Nikki shouted as it made contact with her bat. A loud *click* took it into the sky. Vanna walked in circles, nose up, and caught it.

"Again!"

He stumbled from the catch, then threw an even harder ball.

She swung with enough force to break a femur. She spat into the dirt when she missed and threw the ball back, almost losing her footing. "Again!"

Sweat dripped down their backs as they played into the day. Nikki bit her tongue when the hit connected and cursed when she missed. Locking herself in her room had made her weak. She was a little girl again, cooped up in a wet canal, wasting away while growing hungry and sick. Taking those feelings to her bat was the best remedy, though she preferred if it was the knees of those who took Derek and Kevin away.

She swung her bat and sent the ball into the clouds. It landed in a palm tree, shaking its branches without falling. The birds near them didn't make an effort to help.

Nikki immediately touched her pointer finger to her nose. Vanna waited for the ball to fall, then flicked his ears and looked at Nikki, his finger quickly raising to his nose.

45

"You," she said.

He flattened his pointed ears. "Nikki, I'm not as agile as you."

"And I'm not as tall as you. Scoot."

He sighed, losing the game of "who's it," and jogged for the tree.

Nikki, feeling lonely, followed him to the tree and slouched against the scratchy bark.

"Hey, just so you know," Vanna said as he climbed, "your parents aren't out to get you. You really hurt their feelings last night. Your mom was really sad."

Nikki dug her shoe into the dirt.

"You can't hold this against them. Everyone deals with loss differently. You know they love you. And Morgan loves you, and Del loves you. They all care about you. And yes." He reached for the ball. "*I* love you, even if you make my life a thousand times harder, so don't go quiet on me. Don't leave." He kept reaching. "I can't have you leave, too, okay? Promise me that."

She looked up at the wrong time. The second she gave in to this side of Vanna she didn't often see, the ball dropped right on her nose, blinding her senses and making her brain think she was being attacked. She swatted at it like a bug. "Ow, Vanna! Warn me next time."

Vanna was clinging to the tree, pupils slit like a true cat. He was staring over the fence into town.

Nikki, curious, stood on her tiptoes to see what he saw. A couple guards near the embankment, a family of capybaras. "What?"

He squinted. "It's the robot."

The robot. That word, or idea, impossible by every metric. The public knew very little about him. The Líders kept him in arm's reach as their personal assistant. Those who saw him looked away—they didn't want to be recorded by him.

She spotted his unnaturally blond hair hiding between two buildings a block away. He was wearing all black, trying to look inconspicuous as an undead boy wearing clothes not meant for warmth.

And he was staring right at them.

He touched his ear, said something Nikki couldn't pick up, and ran.

"Oh, shoot," Nikki said, because before she could check in with Vanna or her brain, before she could process how stupid this was, she hopped the fence.

"Nikki, no!" Vanna called out. "Don't chase it!"

"He's connected to the Líders!" she explained. "He might have information about Derek and Kev!"

"Nikki, no!"

She'd already lost him, but his heavy footfall kept her on the chase. She ducked underneath walkways and bridges, cut through backyards and abandoned plots of land. She ran onto a main road and almost got hit by a trolley. They didn't go fast, but it took them longer to hit the brakes. Nikki skidded over the hood and got honked at.

"Wait!" she called out to the Marcos Unit. If she had one chance to get answers to her questions, she'd leave it be. She'd go back to school and act like everything about their world was normal. She just needed to know one thing:

Had Kevin confessed to murdering Derek?

If he gave her that answer, even if it was fake or cleverly bypassed to not actually contain the truth, she'd stop fighting, because her family had been through enough. She just had to hear it from this robot's mouth, because despite being a terrible liar herself, she could rat out someone's lie like it was nothing.

She turned a corner too sharply. He'd taken her down a tight alley and over a short bridge slick with rain.

Nikki's foot slipped in a puddle. She went to grab the railing or a jutting brick, but nothing was available. Her back grated against the brick, and she fell into the canal.

She hadn't been born a cat or a crossbreed with exceptional landing. She was fast and quick on her feet and mind yet lacked any sort of awareness when it came to consequences. Thinking she could cushion her fall, she landed hard on her back and saw sky dots.

She rolled to her side. Her eyes were spinning. Her hands were vibrating. Her knees burned with scratchy blood.

The Marcos Unit jumped onto the bridge railing. He had one boot on the ground as he surveyed the situation like a hawk.

"I'm *fine*," Nikki groaned. She hated when people looked down on her, literally. "Go away, I'm fine."

The Marcos Unit opened his mouth to speak, then examined her injuries with a keener eye.

He turned something off in his ear and reached out to her. His fingers clicked into place as he held on to a light post to get to her. If Nikki stood up, she would've been able to touch him.

His free hand clamped down on his offering one. It appeared like two programs were fighting to gain control of his motor functions, wanting to do what was right and knowing it was wrong. His legs forced himself back. His deviating hand still made an attempt to help her.

"I'm...sorry," he said, and disappeared, his unsure steps echoing into the city.

6

Derek

A distant bell tried its hardest to wake him up. He'd been ignoring it, hoping to catch a few more hours of sleep to douse out this hangover, but the light was too bright and he could no longer ignore the world.

He awoke in a room decorated like he was important. Crystal chandeliers hung above him, with gold melting down the white walls. A fireplace had been lit and was warming the room, but it still smelled like perfumes in here, tingling his nose.

The bed he was on was plump with feathers in which he melted cozily. At his bedside was a ginormous window. Outside, a forest of pine trees went on forever. He was high, wherever he was, and saw over the treetops easily. Across the land were mountains blurring into the horizon line. They had white tips like frosting. He didn't know why.

As he sat up to see farther, he winced and sat back down. Someone had bandaged him up and changed him into silky, white pants and socks. He was now wearing a beaded necklace around his neck. It had a pendant at the end of an upside-down T that had two horizontal lines instead of one.

He held it up to the morning light, reflecting himself in the polished gold. "Pretty," he said absentmindedly, because everything in this place was. Inside and out, this world glittered with abundant wealth. Like that watery place, back before he fainted. He'd never seen waves catch the Sun like that.

Another flicker caught his eye, and he craned his neck to the bedside table. His old clothes were folded up with a small book, more bandages, and a bottle half-filled with something smelly.

"Oh, fuck me." Wiggling like a slug, he forwent the bandages and snatched up the bottle. He uncapped the top and sniffed. It tickled his nose hairs. He grinned and took a swig.

He forced the drink down. The stuff hit *hard*, like drinking snake venom. He laughed as he wiped his lips. Was this even alcohol, or had he just drunk medicine?

The door across his room unlocked. It was the little girl he'd seen from before.

"You're awake!" She ran in, her dress raised to keep her from tripping. "Oh, my goodness, I'm so happy you're alright. You *are* alright, aren't you? Do you need anything? Do you need anything to drink? To eat? We've had breakfast, but I'm sure the cooks can make you anything you want."

A man entered his room next with a bow. He was dressed in metal and brandished a metal stick at his side. "Be at ease, Your Highness. He just awoke."

"But he's awoken! Brother said he wouldn't wake for another day, but I had a feeling you'd awake today."

"I mean, I *think* I'm awake," he, still without a name, said. "Maybe give me some time to wake up with this."

The little girl looked at the bottle in his hand. "Oh. Oh, dear. Did you drink that?"

"Was I not supposed to?"

"It's meant to help heal your wounds. You weren't... necessarily supposed to drink it."

He blinked. The little girl blinked back at him.

Then she snorted and immediately covered it up with her gloved hands. "Forgive me."

"Ha! You snorted."

That made her laugh harder. "Don't tell my brother, he hates when I laugh so uncouthly."

"Uncouthly?" He finished what was in the bottle and set it aside. "By the way, who are you, and where am I?"

"Oh!" She backed up and curtsied. "My name is Princess Cellena Wueng of the Drail Kingdom. My older brother and I found you on the coastline severely injured from your fall, so we brought you to our castle and have been taking care of you. It's a pleasure to finally meet you."

"I fell?"

"From the sky," she said, "from the Heavens."

"*Haven*?" He compared her accent with his. "Where's that? Hey, how come you don't have any animal features like me?"

"I'm not sure I follow. You're not an animal. You're an angel."

"A what? Wait, does that mean you hear out of your ears?"

She pulled on one of her lobes. She wore these pretty, golden hoops he wanted to try on. "I do. Do you?"

"No." He palmed his head and found a small hole above each of his normal ears. He could finger them, but it tickled. "Weird."

"Cellena!" The boy he'd seen near the water came in after his sister. "What're you doing here? Nero, why didn't you stop her?"

"I had no control over her," the Metal Man—Nero—said, "you know that."

"See, Jabel?" Cellena said. "I told you he'd wake up by Sunday."

"That doesn't—" Jabel straightened up at the sight of him and bowed. "Forgive me, Your Grace, for this impertinent waking."

"Imper—I don't know what you guys are saying." He rolled out his shoulders, shaking off his blankets to reveal his wings. "This place's whack, ain't it?"

Jabel gagged and quickly looked away. Cellena awed at the wingspan.

"C-cover yourself!" Jabel ran to one of the wardrobes and dug out some clothes. "You're in your *underwear*, your Grace."

Did they consider pants underwear? What prudes. "Anyway," he said, "is that my name? Grace? Do you know who I am?"

"You're an angel." Jabel came back with a white dress shirt as fancy as his own. The cuffs were embroidered with blue diamonds. "Let us excuse ourselves while you change."

"Don't be crazy, it'll only take a minute." He re-dressed, careful about his achy bones. Someone had cut holes in the back for his wings. They slipped right through. "So, is my name Grace?"

"You don't know your own *name*?"

He pulled a face at Jabel. Why was he giving him so much sass? "No. I don't remember anything before waking up at that watery place."

Cellena looked over at his folded clothes. She began unfolding them.

"So you can't remember anything about the Heavens or our God?" Jabel asked. "Nothing about the other angels or what our God has told you about our dilemma?"

"I literally don't know what half of those words mean." He held his head. *Were* all his memories gone? While he didn't know his name or age or who he was, he did know how to breathe. He knew how to walk and that these two siblings were rich given the way they presented themselves. He just didn't know where he'd come from or what his name was.

He wanted to say it was Kevin.

"What about this?" Cellena lifted up the collar of his old shirt. "Our scholar couldn't decipher the writing. Can you read it?"

"What material is it even made of?" Jabel questioned, eyeing it as Cellena passed it to him.

He shrugged and popped open the collar.

DEREK HARROW

"Derek Harrow," he said. "Huh. Guess that's me."

"What a lovely name," Cellena said. "It's nice to meet you, Derek."

"It's nice to be alive." Derek looked out the window. It was such a nice day. Cool and blue. He figured that was his favorite color by how it attracted him.

"Well, now that we have you," Jabel said, "allow me to introduce you to the Drail Kingdom. I am Jabel Wueng, firstborn to the twelfth king of Drail, King Hatten, and our mother, Queen Channity. We've been dealing with a threat lurking in our forests and have been seeking guidance from our God to help us. Demonkind, as you must've been aware of prior to losing your memories, have been with us since the world was created over 500 years ago, and we need you to..."

Something creaked on the roof, spiking Derek's heart rate. Something was above them and he wanted to see it. Like a child smelling their favorite candy, hearing something unknown filled his childish, animalistic heart with intrigue.

"Your Grace?"

Ignoring whatever Jabel was talking about, Derek flipped around, flapped his wings, and pushed his body straight out the window.

"Your Grace!"

Instincts took hold. His bird brain didn't know much, but it knew how to fly. Careening straight down, his wings pivoted at the last second and arched him into the sky.

"Wow!" Cellena stuck her head out of the window, followed quickly by Jabel. Their astonishment was swept away by the wind.

Derek opened his mouth to taste the salty air. His tail flared out as it worked with the beat of each wing. They flapped in tandem, keeping him rising. Impulsive action freed his pained body. He felt like himself.

This "Drail Kingdom" was hilly. Deep craters that could fit houses dotted the land. He saw farms around boulders and hills that swiftly turned to those mountains dipped in white. Ice, he guessed, as puffs of white left his mouth. In the distance, he saw some type of town in-between the hills. The "castle" or wherever he'd woken up in was right on the edge of a white cliffside.

And the watery place. He hadn't gotten a bird's-eye view of it until now. It went way, *way* farther than he could've imagined. It curved around the world and reflected the heavy clouds above. Was it part of the sky, a mirror of the blue and white smears above them? Little black things bobbed in and out of the water, and out in the distance, things with white flags sailed towards the Sun.

"What the fuck," he said. His mind was snagged on the sight, so mighty, so fucked, that he turned his left wing to map out where the water ended.

He dipped. Absolutely plummeted like a rock from a bird's ass. His body tried to save him, but he was too mesmerized by this world he'd supposedly fallen into.

His short life flashed before him. Cellena's smile, the smell of salt, waves crashing over his body, a mirror image of himself, reaching out to him with tears in his eyes, a young girl's voice...

Before he splatted, a pair of strong arms wrapped around him, and he blacked out for a quick second before landing on cold ground.

His brain was a smoothie in a blender. It wasn't a life-threatening land, nor a painful one. Just surprising—his heart hadn't caught up with his brain telling him that he was, in fact, alive.

Grass tickled his cheeks, and above him, spitting out feathers from his mouth, was his savior.

He was tall, and big. *Big* big. Six-foot-something big, muscles bulging from his shirt big. He was maybe a year older than Derek, and his skin was whiter than Derek's hair. Grey shadows angled his already angular face and pointy ears. Soft, concerned eyes looked down at him through a thicket of black curls.

Something hit Derek's ankle—a tail, wire-thin with a tuft of hair at the end.

This boy was part-animal, like him, or part-angel.

Nearby, the same bell he'd heard when he'd woken up chimed through the land.

Derek pushed back his bangs. "Hey. How'd you do that?"

"Huh?"

"How'd you catch me?"

"Oh, uhm..." The boy sat up, but his hands didn't want to leave Derek's body. They, unlike his pale face, were completely black, like he'd dipped them in soot all the way up to his elbows. "I—uh...I'm sorry."

"You're sorry for saving me?" Derek sat up slowly, hoping not to spook the poor dude. He was so nervous and for what? "You okay? You can chill out now. I'm fine."

"That's good. I mean, it's not good that you fell. You're still injured, I see. Are you hurt?"

"Yeah, but it's no big deal. What are you?"

"I'm...I'm a demon, sir. I mean, Derek. Uh—" His face was going red. "I'm sorry. I'm not sure how to address you. I've heard maids call you many things. N-not that I've been listening!"

Derek took him in again, this time making his ogling more apparent. He pinpointed everything he liked about a person in him. He even had horns, two points that stuck out above his eyes.

"Derek?" the boy asked. "Are you alright?"

Derek's heart, more specifically his cock, took over. "You're really hot."

The emotion in his face drained into the grass. "Huh?"

"You're hot," Derek repeated. "Like, handsome? Pretty? You're really pretty. Do you have a lover?"

The boy's brain didn't register what Derek had said. He stared straight through him, frozen.

The blush beginning at his ears dyed his whole face a deep red. Shocked by Derek's declaration, he jumped back and floated into a landing. Big as he was, he was still able to float without wings.

"Woah," Derek said. "That's cool. Hey, thanks for saving me. You saved me, right? From falling to my death?"

Mouth still agape, the boy nodded once. "I...saw you. Fall." He pointed at the castle rooftops. "From there."

"Why were you on the roof?"

"Uhm..." He double-checked behind him like he thought the castle wouldn't be there.

At the top of the roof poked out two pointy ears. Not like the boy's fleshy ones, but furry, cat ones. A girl, who was hiding behind a pillar of stone, peeked down at them. She had long orange hair striped brown and white. Her tail, just as colorful, flicked as she watched.

"Who's that?"

"Oliver!"

The boy flinched and disappeared in a puff of black smoke. Jabel, Cellena, and Nero had run all the way down from the top floor and were now sprinting across the yard.

Oliver reappeared next to the cat girl still on the roof. He said something to her, hugged her, and the two of them disappeared for good.

Derek looked around for them, wondering how they could do that and if that blush had meant he was single. Probably, right?

"What happened?" Jabel asked Derek. "What did he say to you?"

"Are you alright?" Cellena asked.

"Are you hurt?" Nero added.

Derek touched the back of his head. That guy's hands were huge. He still felt his fingers threading through his hair.

An excited smile tickled his lips. Screw whatever these people were talking about. He wanted to learn more about this Oliver guy. He probably worked out a ton. Above, he was horny. When was the last time he'd jerked off?

"What on Earth was he doing?" Jabel asked himself. "He knows better than to get so close to the castle."

"Who was he," Derek asked, "and how old is he? You said his name is Oliver?"

"Oliver Solos. He's a demon, the beings my family has been trying to slaughter for generations. He knows better than to get so close to us. What was he doing?"

"He normally keeps his distance," Nero noted. "He must've been interested in seeing the angel."

Derek leered into the forest. The pine grew heavier with every step in, until you couldn't see past ten feet.

"We should leave," Cellena said. "Father won't like that we're outside of the castle."

"I know," Jabel said, and went back to the castle for safety. "Derek, Mother and Father wanted to see you when you awoke. If you're well enough to fly, let's get things over with."

"Your Highness," Nero said, scolding him.

"They're going to have our heads when they find out what happened. Nobody say a word about this, alright?"

When Derek didn't move, Cellena offered him her hand. "Are you alright? You would've died if Oliver hadn't been there to protect you. I was so frightened."

"You're right." Derek licked his lips. "I should thank him properly."

7

Marcos

Marcos' right hand wouldn't let go of his left until he ambled into the Asilo District.

He flexed his distrustful fingers. He'd accomplished his task with exactitude: Follow the family of Kevin Harrow, track their movements, and keep his distance. This family was "different." Not "dangerous," not "illegal," from what the Líders told him. Just that he and select members of the Guard had been issued to watch them for the past twenty years. Marcos didn't understand the instructions, but when he was ordered to carry out a mission, he physically couldn't disobey. It was in his programming. Whatever the Líders wanted, it was done by his hands.

But he'd failed. He'd been a street away and Nicole Lenore had *still* spotted him. He'd tried to keep himself concealed, but with his recognizable face and lack of animal features, he stood out. And absence of tails and ears wasn't uncommon—some people even docked them once they reached adulthood—but everyone knew Marcos for the worst reasons. He was the stoolie who kept tabs on the populace and reported every misgiving to the Líders. He'd heard the rumors that he was immortal and had heat vision and the ability to crush a person's skull with one hand. He couldn't feel emotions. He couldn't think for himself, didn't want to.

He wasn't alive.

He wasn't a person.

He was a machine.

He kept his head down as he walked through the streets he protected. So rarely was he able to go out on his own like this without the fanfare of the Líders or their child beside them. The stares were more manageable that way. Alone like this, the public looked down on him like he was a disease from which they had to scrub their hands clean.

He hopped on the quickest tram to the Asilo. Though trapped in every sense of the word, he was given free, complimentary rides on any tramline. Not for his own free time, but for missions and assignments. At least it gave him a false sense of freedom as the wind messed up his synthetic hair.

His eyes fell on the travelling tracks. He sat farthest from the rest of the passengers to make everyone feel more comfortable. He still felt them staring at him and let them.

A child began crying towards the front of the tram, and Marcos almost turned to it. He prided himself on many things outside of the Líders' control, and childcare was one of them. There was a patience only a robot could have with children, and despite what Nadia and Mikhail said, he knew he was good with kids.

Programs embedded in his brain forced him to turn away and ignore it. He wanted to help. That was all he wanted to do. He wanted to be there for people and receive praise. He didn't want to be so hated.

"Please, see me," he wanted to shout. *"See me and know that I'm worth more than this."*

But he couldn't, because his brain wouldn't allow it. Nadia had wired his brain to obey, not to live.

He held down that hand again. It'd disobeyed his programming to help Nicole Lenore. He'd been ordered to watch her movements specifically to "find out information" on Derek

Harrow's disappearance. He was told not to engage with her, as she was a "catalyst."

But his hand had gone beyond those orders, somehow, and reached out to her. Perhaps it was due to the strong likelihood that she'd snapped her wrist from the fall. He always wanted to help those who felt physical pain.

Something beeped inside of his brain, and a code of text floated into his vision.

TEST SUBJECT: ZANTL
HEART RATE: 125 BPM since 2:25pm

Check in with SUBJECT: ZANTL immediately to ensure safety and health.
Recommendations: snack of choice (see document 2.1), one (1) glass of cold water, a 30-min neck massage

If possible, Marcos would've rolled his eyes. Zantl didn't exercise past a heart rate of 100 beats per minute. Expectations for an heir like them were to be smart and to shut up, so when their heart got this way for an extended period of time, especially after their second breakfast, it was most likely from them pleasuring themselves.

And Marcos did *not* want to invade their privacy like that. That was a special time for beings to be alone, or with their partners. It always sounded like there was always another person in the room with them, but he didn't know for sure. When Marcos had to forcibly open their locked bedroom, they'd act like they were hiding someone in the shadows. It had to be either a guard or an Asilo worker. Marcos did *not* like the odds that they were sleeping with someone much older than them. Zantl was only eighteen years old.

He hurried off the tram and took the Asilo steps two at a time to get this check-in over with. Nadia and Mikhail were very strict about Marcos taking care of their precious heir. While, yes, they were to inherit the entire world after Nadia's and Mikhail's rule, it wasn't because Zantl was their child that they fawned over them. It was because they were special.

"Special." A connotation for either incredibly lucky or devastatingly cursed. Marcos had listened in to every conversation and document he was allowed to take in, and he still didn't know which one Zantl was.

The Líders kept everything tightly under wraps between them and their child. He didn't know the extent of their powers, but he had an inkling. Through context clues, he figured Zantl's abilities were connected to their mind, and that no one else had these gifts. All knowledge came and stayed with Zantl, who abused their power and strung along their parents like puppets against their wills.

And the Líders didn't care, for it meant that Raeleen was in powerful, albeit mysterious, hands.

Marcos took an elevator to the top floor where their bedrooms resided. It was the quietest floor. His footsteps echoed down each intersection. He watched the shadows for movement. Any moment and he could walk straight into one of the Líders and be talked into another highly illegal escapade. The less time he spent with them, the better for everyone.

As he came up to Zantl's room, he cringed. He could already smell the bodily sweat seeping out from underneath the door.

Still, per the instructions in his head, he knocked. "Zantl?" he called out. "Zantl, it's Marcos. Are you alright?"

Subdued moaning dwindled to heavy breathing.

He tried again. "Zantl, I need confirmation that you are alright. Can you please open the door? You know I will have to open the door by force if you don't respond in—"

A quick *whoosh* of air and the door zipped opened. Zantl was glaring at Marcos, their exposed chest covered by their blanket. Their room was pitch-black, but before Zantl pushed Marcos back, Marcos caught it: the blur of glowing, yellow eyes sitting atop their bed.

There was someone in there with them.

Zantl shoved Marcos into the hall. To keep them from breaking their wrist, Marcos let himself be pushed.

"Get *out!*" Zantl demanded. Their cheeks were still flushed. "You know I'm fine. Why do you have to be a freak and check up on me when I'm like this? Leave me alone."

"Your parents insist that I—"

"I don't *care* what my parents want. Tell them that if you check up on me like this again, I *will* break you, and I mean it. *God,*" they cursed as they walked back into the darkness. "You're such a *freak.*"

The door shut in Marcos' face unnaturally hard. Zantl must've just used their powers to make their anger clear.

Marcos fixed his collar. He didn't know what he'd done to be so hated by Zantl. Growing up, Marcos had cooked them meals, sung them to sleep, bathed them, changed them. Zantl had loved being around him.

When Zantl became a teenager, their dynamics changed. Now, Marcos was the villain for following orders he couldn't ignore.

He held his unloyal hand at the foot of the door. He had no other obligations to complete at this time, aside from reports he'd give to the Líders about Nicole Lenore once they asked for him.

To kill his valuable free time, Marcos chimed for the elevators again. Should he check up on Kevin Harrow? His dinnertime was soon, and his allotted bathroom break wasn't for another twenty-five minutes.

Feeling a bit embarrassed, Marcos nixed that plan. He did so many things for the people living in the Asilo, but something about Kevin and his eyes, the way he smiled, asked him how his day was going...

Marcos slammed his finger too hard for the button to take him down. Kevin Harrow was a kind person, born into an even more caring family that made him pure, and Marcos had a horrible habit of putting too much thought into people like that. Kind gestures were simply that. Kind. Marcos had read the reports on Kevin's life thoroughly and he'd been kind to everyone, so his demeanor wasn't unusual or something to read in on, aside from his cracked mirror that the Líders had written off as a faulty screw placement.

Marcos had taken the time to research Kevin's dating experience. Even with a lack of lovers, Marcos had concluded that Kevin would most likely not be interested in someone like him.

Feeling even more abandoned by his own feelings, Marcos made his way to the bottom levels of the Asilo. You needed several access keys to be led down here, all of which were embedded inside of Marcos' wrist. He, the Líders, and high-level guards and scientists were given permission to be down here. No one else knew the secrets beneath the earth. Not even the general public knew about these subterranean levels. They housed the deepest kept secrets, and the most important people.

The pressure levels dipped. Seconds swam by and he still continued dropping down, floor by floor, 700 feet down to the lowest levels, where his little girl lived.

He pulled up her file in wait. She was nine months old and had been born in the Asilo just like he'd been. Normally, people kept in the Asilo despised Marcos based on his connections. Children, especially babies, had yet to have their minds poisoned by prejudice, so Marcos was drawn to them, especially to her.

TEST SUBJECT: ALEXI

Marcos smiled as her name crossed his sight. Alexi, a baby who always made him smile. She'd blow bubbles in her water and laugh when Marcos pulled the ridiculous faces he used to pull with Zantl. Marcos wanted to protect people like that for as long as he could.

Alexi's feeding time was a half hour ago, but Marcos didn't trust most of the guards who worked down here. Every week there were more reports of mistreatment and abuse he sought to correct. This led him to taking over most of the burpings, feedings, changes, and general care that was so often ignored.

The elevator doors opened. The lights to the hall flickered on. The atmosphere was dense and wet and smelled of salt.

He passed by top-level doctors wearing surgical masks. He avoided the operating rooms and testing labs they worked in. Nothing could be done there. He couldn't stop what the Líders wanted done.

Blocking out this world, he entered the room that housed Alexi. The walls appeared blue by how the water in her tank shone through the fluorescence. There were no toys here for a baby's enrichment, only an empty room with a chair in the corner, a refrigerator that kept her food cold, and a tank that sank through the floor and connected to the other tanks around this level.

Stripping off his clothes, Marcos donned one of the waterproof slips that hung on the wall and took out a bowl that'd been Alexi's dinner. Like he'd guessed, someone had forgotten to feed her.

He opened the locked hatch atop the tank, tested the water's salinity level, and plunged into the darkening water.

8

Derek

Derek didn't know what a king or queen was, but he was kind of excited to meet them.

As he was led back into the castle, Jabel's and Cellena's demeanors flipped. Their backs got stiffer, Jabel kept retying his ascot even though it was already tied. They were off to meet their parents *knowing* they'd done wrong by letting their angelic godsend near a demon. They were shitting bricks.

Derek didn't know why that was a bad thing. The leader of these alleged "demons," this Oliver boy, was anything but scary. Derek was still riding on the high he'd given him. Straddling him in public like that, saving him like a hero. And he had no business being as hot as he was, fidgeting and blushing with those muscles.

Derek fixed his silk pants. He had to chill out.

The castle interior was nuts. The halls were two stories tall, making everything appear bigger. Every ten feet were life-sized paintings and crystal chandeliers. Not one inch of this place was bare. It was like a fairy tale Derek could wander through for hours.

Well, until he got bored and needed a new outlet to explore.

"Mother and Father should be in the church," Jabel muttered to himself. "They had a meeting with Father Alec today."

"Where?" Derek asked, eyes now fixed on the ceiling. How had they painted something way up there?

"It was the building to your left when you crash-landed."

"There was a building out there?"

Cellena ran up and glued her side to Derek. "Do you think they saw us?"

"I'm sure they'll be lenient," Jabel said, "once they see him."

"But we shouldn't have let him out of our sight in the first place."

"I know. Two minutes awake and he's already met with demonkind." Jabel sighed. "This's going to be awful."

"I'll defend you," Nero said, his metal bodysuit clanking away. "I saw everything. I'll be your backup."

"They'll only believe you if they're in a good mood."

Derek, whose eyes started travelling back to the castle architecture, was pulled back to the present. "Are your parents, like, shitty?"

"What? No," Jabel said. "And language, my God."

"They expect a lot from us," Cellena said. "Sometimes I think...No, we're supposed to be royals. We're expected to take the throne."

"And I will be the next king." Jabel tried to say that confidently, but he looked sicker the closer they got to "church."

Two metal people were guarding its entrance with those knife-looking weapons. The doors were made of wood and looked a billion years old. Derek found a story carved within the wood about snake-looking lizards. Fire spewed from their mouths, their talons as long as the humans fighting them. He tried to catch more—there were forests and that ocean place— but the metal people opened the doors for them.

Derek immediately felt light-headed. Like, no joke. This building was arches and slanted roofs and windows of colorful, painted people. Everything was aglow with candles and the morning light entering semi-transparent windows. A dozen benches were compacted into the space with people sitting shoulder to shoulder in them. At the front was some type of altar with a statue of the upside-down cross, and everything was gold. Gold and bright and shimmering.

And so, so, *so* cramped. Too much so. He didn't feel like he belonged in such a place.

Two people were standing near the front of the room. They looked like Jabel and Cellena, with their jet-black hair and fair skin. They were speaking to a balding man surrounded by twenty or so others, but when the door opened, all of them stopped and stared at him, at Derek.

Unable to take another step in, Derek ducked out of the doorway and flapped his wings to give him an extra foot of distance.

"Derek?" Cellena asked. "Aren't you coming in?"

"Are you alright?" asked someone else.

"What's wrong?"

He had no clue. His heart was pounding and he couldn't breathe, as if something was on his chest that he couldn't scratch away. The church just had too much in it, like they were compensating for something larger than themselves.

"Your Grace?" One of the men came up to him. "It's an honor to meet you, Your Grace. I wasn't aware you'd arisen. My name is King Hatten. Are you feeling alright? Do you need anything?"

"What lovely timing," one of the women said. "Pleased to meet you. Are—"

Derek held his head. He didn't know what was happening, but he hated everything about this. The crampedness, the lack of exits, their eyes, judging him.

"It's, uh, cool and junk," he said, "but I, uh, can't stay here. I have a thing with tight spaces and, uh..." He wiped his face. "C-can we get out of here? Now?"

The king and queen retracted their hands and joy.

"Of...course," the king said. "My apologies, Your Grace. We hadn't meant to overwhelm you."

"Derek," he corrected. "Just Derek."

The king looked to Nero, then to his own children, who stood closer together for protection. "Let us leave, then. How about we—"

"Go somewhere else!" Taking the lead, Derek spun on his heels and started walking nowhere. "This castle, I mean, *wow*, am I right? It's such a...marvel. That's a fancy word, ain't it? W-where's the bathroom in this place? I'm sure ya'll have dozens of bathrooms here."

"Would you like a tour?" the queen asked. "We'd be more than delighted to shepherd you through the Castle of Wueng."

"We can show you our church another time," the king said, dejected, but who cared? Instincts told Derek to take care of himself, and right now, he couldn't be trapped.

He pretended to be interested in their talk. The king and queen went off about everything under the Sun. They started off with their family, which was a super long and boring family tree, then about the world they governed and all their duties Derek didn't care for. They explained how the king's great-great-great-great something had built the world up with the help of "dragons." They talked about something called a Barrier.

"Do you know of them, Your Grace?" the queen asked, bringing Derek back. "The dragons?"

"Huh?"

That made them stare at him again, and he hid in his wings. "Uh, no," he said. "Not really."

"He lost his memories," Jabel explained. "He didn't know his name until he read a label on his shirt."

"His name is Derek Harrow," Cellena added, looking at her mother who still called him by the wrong name.

"How unfortunate," the king said. "Do you recall anything from your time before meeting us?"

"No. Sorry," Derek added, seeing the hurt on their faces.

"We should take a tour of our library," the king then said, "that way, we can teach you about demonkind. To summarize, Your Grace, this world we've come to cultivate as our own was first birthed by the dragons. They were mythic beasts who carved the earth and rivers with their bodies, who heated the sky with their fire and formed the oceans with their tears. From the beautiful darkness above us to the vile darkness bubbling beneath us, they created our world from nothing, and we must pay them our respects."

He rolled up his sleeves. Rounding his forearms were tattoos of a slithery serpent tail, the start of a taloned claw. "They were magical creatures who disappeared long before humans were born from their wombs. The men in my family honor them by getting their likeness inked across our bodies."

Jabel rubbed down his own arms, refusing to show off his draconic tattoo.

Derek looked up at the ceiling again, a comforting gesture to escape their eyes. It hadn't been lizards carved in the doors, but *dragons*. He saw more of them now, like uttering their existence brought them out of hiding. They climbed up the white pillars and wrapped around the railings. They had sharp teeth and talons, colored red and black and white, rainbows of violence.

To each their own, but if Derek was devoted to anything or anyone, he wouldn't have gotten them inked on his skin. Maybe a rose or a sunrise. And didn't they hate darkness? Now it was a good thing?

The king kept talking. The queen chimed in sometimes. Derek blocked out most of it. Something about that church place had knocked him off his feet, and not in the way the humans had expected.

When he came back to the world, they were in a music room. The queen was trying to get Jabel and Cellena to play for Derek, much to their dismay.

Derek looked out the window for security. Beneath them was a beautiful garden growing pink flowers and the start of that forest. He wondered if he stared long enough, would he have seen Oliver?

"Why're the demons so bad?"

It slipped out without thinking. The humans' eyes were back on him. Jabel and Cellena exchanged sibling glances.

"Who are they?" he clarified. "My memory, you know."

"They're horrible creatures," the king said. "Devilish beasts born from the soot of the Earth's fire who tempt us into misery. We've killed most of them, but there're nine left who're immortal like yourself. They have powers of flight, teleportation, and abilities that disregard all of our core beliefs."

He held his head higher with pride. "The Wueng family has kept peace in the Kingdom since its creation. The wars you've seen illustrated throughout our castle paints us a valiant victory over demonkind."

Derek saw. "How many of them have you killed?"

"Thousands. They used to litter my kingdom with their foul children. My forefathers eradicated the races decades ago, aside from the nine who cannot be killed."

"Why?"

This time the whole Wueng family, even quiet Nero, turned to him.

"I mean, what've they done to hurt you?"

"They're demonic," the king said plainly. "They're demons, from the Underground. We're not meant to be near them."

"So who created them?"

"Our God, of course."

"The person you devote your lives to?"

"Yes. Our God is All. They created everything."

Derek's brain was hurting. "So your God created evil things?"

"They created All," the king repeated, pissed but hiding it well, "but demons were created from *our* darkness. Every cruel action a human makes fuels a demon's primal instinct to cause chaos. To eradicate them, we shall be free of darkness."

"Darkness that your God created?" Derek wanted to ask, but that sounded mean. He didn't have all the facts to make a solid decision on this. He didn't even know what made up "darkness."

"You must be faint from falling down to us," the king said. "Fear not, Your Grace. I shall fill you back in on demonkind."

"I—"

"The demons left on our island reside under one roof in the Temno Forest. Their manor's located somewhere between here and the Kavka Mountains. They're shifty. When one of my knights find their location, they pick up and disappear. They live resiliently."

"...What does 'resilient' mean?"

The king gave him another one of his pitiful looks.

And Derek nearly snapped at him. These looks were seriously getting underneath his skin. Was he really stupid? Maybe it was because of his missing memories, but he was starting to feel shitty about himself.

"It means they're a durable race we cannot kill, and they're deadly. Some can breathe fire. There're two grey-skins who can teleport into our minds, one of whom is their elected leader, Oliver Solos."

Derek piqued. Cellena and Jabel acted like they didn't know him.

"Then there're two vicious siblings, winged like bats who can breathe the hottest flames. They're both deeply broken, body and mind, but don't let their disabilities fool you. There's also a heinous couple who brews magical potions with their child. Those ones sicken me the most. Demonkind has this way of coupling that forces an individual to fall in love with them. They call it 'mating'."

"Dear." The queen held her lover's arm. Her two kids were red-faced in embarrassment.

"I won't bring up the details in front of my family," the king said, "but it's something I wish to see an end to post-haste. There's also a woman whose mind is lost, featuring many qualities of a real-life house cat. She poses little threat to us. And then—" He actually shivered. "The waterborne one."

"Uh, Father," Jabel interjected. "I believe Derek has been made well aware of who these people are."

"The Angel needs to know of our ordeals, Jabel. Please forgive my son, Your Grace. He had an incident with the water demon a few months back which nearly cost him his life."

Jabel huffed at the passing walls.

"Three months ago, he was wandering alone and unsupervised *as he often does*. He wasn't prepared for a sudden attack to leave him defenseless on our very shores. Left to die, soon the water demon emerged from the waters and brought him back home."

Derek waited for more. "So, what did the water demon do to him?"

"Why, he attacked him."

"Like, with a club?"

"Oh, no, Your Grace. It seems we have quite a lot to catch you up on. Demonkind has been attacking our minds for upwards of twenty years. These attacks damage our hearts and leave us at death's door. At times, they're little more than headaches. Other times, especially in the last few weeks, they've been especially burdensome."

"Maxwell saved me that day," Jabel muttered. "If he hadn't brought me back here and called for someone—"

"My *children*," the king interrupted, "as you see, do not fully grasp the perils of demonkind. They are liars and cheats who will stop at nothing to get into our hearts and sway our judgements. They cannot be reckoned with, Your Grace. Remember that."

Derek didn't say anything. What in the flying fuck had he flown into? He didn't want to be a part of this fucked, unfair war. What was he supposed to do for them? Save them? From *what*? Mind powers?

These humans, they had issues, and that was fine. He had them, too.

But why dump them on *him*? Was an angel supposed to fix everything? Everything that, supposedly, their creator had created?

"Well, I can see that you're a bit overwhelmed," the king said. "Enough talk of these beasts. We needn't worry about them now that an angel has finally heard our prayers."

"Oh, great," Derek said, and felt a little sick with himself.

The next place on the shit tour was the library, which Derek pictured wildly differently. He'd seen another tight room with an old man carrying dusty, yellowed books. Perhaps that was his warped sense of a "library," a place, he guessed, he'd never willingly entered before.

This library was unnecessarily gigantic. Two stories tall, hundreds of bookshelves with hundreds of books per shelf. It was like a small city, something Derek also guessed this kingdom didn't have.

"We have three thousand books, scrolls, and documents for you to peruse," said the king. "Everything from novels to history books to journals from renowned travellers, all of it resides here. In fact, where is our historian? Nero, where is your wife?"

Their knight stood at attention. "I'm not sure, Your Majesty. She said she'd be working on the first floor."

Derek looked over the railing. He found more aisles and windows, opening up the already open library. This was the best place in the castle by far. Hardly anyone here and quiet enough to jerk off in a corner and not get caught.

A woman screamed. Nero didn't unsheathe his "sword," so Derek kept from flying out the window, but fuck. It was so loud, and sudden, like someone had seen a rat scurry across their feet.

Someone ran up the stairs. Her dress bounced as she ran to meet them, her petticoat acting like wings. She was a smiling woman with skin tanned by the Sun, who wore glasses that matched her long, red hair. Derek was instantly drawn to her as he was with Cellena, the two people who'd broken away from this place's stuffiness.

"How wonderful it is to see you, Your Grace, Your Majesties, Your Highnesses." She gave each family member an informal bow. "I've been *so* excited to meet you. I was jealous to hear that Nero was assigned as your knight. Oh, my name is Runa Alswhite. A pleasure."

"I'm Derek. Just Derek," he reiterated.

"Oh, you have a name now! How splendid. My, I had no idea I was going to meet you today. What an impression you must have of me."

"Trust me, you're fine."

Runa's enthusiasm died down. "That's good to hear," she said.

"She was greatly interested in learning about you," Nero said. "She loves learning about everything she can get her hands on."

"Oh, you flatter me," she teased, "but yes, I do have a habit of getting lost in research. I haven't been able to control myself when I found out our Highnesses found you lost on our shorelines. I have so many questions for you."

"Now, Runa," Nero said, reeling her in. "He's just woken up and his memory is hazy. We must give him and Their Majesties some space."

"Oh, of course." She curtsied to the king. "My apologies."

"Not a problem, my dear. We came here hoping you'd be able to shed some light on our angel to our kingdom."

"Oh, yes!" Runa said. "Where to begin?"

Everywhere, apparently, because Derek was lost on practically everything that made up Drail. He told them that he didn't know what "royalty" stood for or what "demons" or "angels" were. He didn't understand the concept of "oceans" or "snow," though the last one sounded fun to play in. Farms he got—they were an outdated concept in his mind, but he got them nonetheless—but their towns, fantasy villages with windmills and waterwheels, none of that registered with him.

He also couldn't read. The words didn't make sense. The letters had extra swirls and lines through them, some which were completely new to him. Which was great, really helped him feel smart in front of these people.

The maps, however, were the strangest things here.

He found one on his own. It was tacked on the wall between two windows, a hand-drawn, figure-eight pattern colored blue, green, and white.

The ocean hugged the south. The forest and mountains were in the north. Encircling it all was a label he guessed read "The Barrier," like that was so mundane, knowing that a type of barrier surrounded this world.

As well.

Because in his life...

Before waking up...

He was used to a barrier keeping everything in.

Keeping them out.

A little figure popped up beside him. Cellena was holding a book on star navigation that "boats" used. "Hello."

"Hey," he said.

"Are you alright?"

He traced the edge of the map. "There's a barrier here, too."

"Was there a barrier in the Heavens?"

"Something like that. It's the only part of your world that's made sense."

She traced around the land. "We have about 200 miles of land and fifty miles of ocean to use. Waterfalls dip off around the ocean, preventing us from leaving by boat, and we can't cross the Kavka Mountains. Not even the demons can cross it, but my father…" She searched for him. She lowered her voice. "He believes that demonkind is keeping the Barrier up. He believes that if he kills the ones left in the forest, the Barrier will fall and we'll finally be able to explore the rest of the world."

"The rest of the world…" Derek drew his finger up towards the north, to the Heavens. A drawing of an angel was blowing wind over the world. "What if there's nothing past it?"

"What?"

"On the other side. What if it just ends?"

"I wouldn't want that to be the case. That'd make me feel quite lonely. Is that what you want?"

He didn't know. He wanted time to himself right now, or with her. She was becoming the exception in this backwards world.

Cellena went to pick up another book, but as soon as her fingers grazed the edge, she yelped in pain and held her heart.

Around the library, he heard it. The aches. The humans clutching their hearts and doubling over. It hit them in a wave, all but Derek.

"Woah," he said. "Hey, are you alright?"

Cellena opened one eye as she contorted her face to hold back the pain. "Yes. It's not as bad as..." She winced again. "I-it's not as bad this time."

"What isn't as bad?"

The King stumbled to them holding his own heart. "Y-you're not affected," he said to Derek. "That's good. Good."

Derek tried supporting him so he didn't take a header. "What the fuck's going on?"

"This's what the demons do to us. They attack our hearts with poison. This never happened up until a few decades ago. They're becoming more frequent."

"Why're they doing this?" He looked backed to Cellena. She was already standing up straighter.

Jabel came out from around the corner holding a book about poetry. His knees were knocked. "They aren't...the ones doing this."

"*Enough*, Jabel," the king spat out. "Honestly, this isn't the time for your hypotheses. You're meant to be king, you can't talk about these beasts as people."

"But we have no proof that they're the ones doing this."

The king caught the book his son was holding and slapped it out of his hands. "Put that away. I told you not to read effeminate rot."

Jabel, through strain, bent down and dusted off the book. "You ask for my opinion—"

"When it is helpful," he rephrased. "Leave us."

Hurt, Jabel looked to his sister, who hadn't been asked to leave. Blinking hard, he left, unwanted.

The King fixed his ascot as he sat up tall. He sighed. The "attack" seemed to be over. "Please forgive him, Your Grace."

"For what?" he blurted out, and when the king looked up, he said, "Never mind, it's okay," but he didn't know what he was pardoning. "What were you saying?"

"That this is the demons' doing. Oliver swears that neither he nor his family are the ones doing it, but you can't hold their truths to heart."

The King cleared his throat. "I'm sure you'll be able to get to the bottom of this for us," he said. "We're putting our trust into you."

Derek smiled and nodded, not having the heart to tell him that he *did not care* to be involved in this.

When the king left to check up on his "wife," Cellena wiped the new sweat from her brow.

"You alright?" Derek asked.

"Are *you* alright?"

"Yeah." He faked a smile and ruffled her hair. "Cellena, between you, me, and the books, I don't think I know as much as I should, you know? I think I'm stupid."

"Don't say that. You're very kind and carefree. And you lost your memories. No one would fault you for not knowing our ways."

"Your dad seems to."

She didn't disagree.

"I think my head's screwed on wrong." He peeked around the corner. On the other side of the library was a door partly ajar. "Hey, can you keep a secret?"

She nodded without question.

"Good," he said, and led her away.

Cellena gasped and looked back down the hall. They'd escaped down a narrow corridor without windows. "Where are we going?"

"Outta here." He pushed open two double doors. "I *hate* reading, Cellena. Like, seriously."

She chuckled. "Even I enjoy a book every now and again."

"What are you, thirty-five?" He opened up his wings and tickled her sides, and she burst into a high-pitched squeal that almost blew their cover. He covered her mouth as they descended down a short staircase into a new, spacious corridor.

They took off through the castle like two teenagers drunk on stolen freedom. The corridors begged to be run in, and how could they *not*? Derek even tried to fly when the halls opened to grand staircases.

"We're going to get in trouble!" Cellena said, laughing.

"Good! Above, this place is so *stuffy*!" To make his point, Derek flew to the highest chandelier and flapped his wings at it. Dust blew out the tinier candles.

Cellena laughed and covered her head until Derek landed. "What does that mean?"

"Huh?"

"Above. I think I heard you say that once before. Is it a curse?"

"Like, For All That's Above? I don't think it is. It just means the stuff above us."

"Like the sky?"

"Yeah, and the sky dots."

"Sky dots?"

"Oh, don't tell me that's another thing I don't know. My brain's too full."

"If you're questioning anything, don't hesitate to ask me. I won't make fun of you. I have trouble remembering important dates, and Jabel isn't good at giving speeches or making his points clear. He and Father butt heads about it quite often."

"Yeah, I can tell."

Their detour ended at a dead-end of paintings. They were of the landscapes he'd seen while flying over the kingdom, of farmlands and mountains. To their right was a wall of windows that showed off the steep cliff into the ocean. He heard the waves crash against the rocks hundreds of feet below.

Someone else had taken to this quiet corner of the castle. A boy no more than thirteen floated a foot above the ground.

He had dark hair like the royal family but was wearing a fancy robe, nothing like what they wore. He also had a tail, one too big for his body, and pointed ears and horns.

Another demon.

9
Kevin

Living in the Asilo was okay.

It wasn't bad.

He wasn't dead. That's what he kept telling himself. And he was being cared for, that had to count for something. He wasn't being starved, even if the food was blander than actual bird food. His family was alive, and Derek, under Maïmoú's word, was still alive.

And he believed her, in the way a naive child believed their parent.

What a strange girl she was. He had a soft heart when it came to people like her. He trusted instantly, forgave too quickly. He always saw the best in people because he couldn't do the same with himself. It helped, wanting to help others.

Maïmoú was a whole separate entity. The way she rewired his brain scared him as much as it titillated him, and he didn't think it was because of his imprisonment. She was real—she'd broken his mirror—and he wanted to know more about her.

He related it to wanting to know about a catastrophe.

His first weeks in the Asilo passed quickly and methodically. He had neither a clock nor window to measure the time, but the Marcos Unit—Marcos, his name was Marcos—kept him on a rigid schedule. Breakfast of the same oats and beans, a shower every morning in the communal bathrooms, his bathroom breaks, lunch and dinner the same as his breakfast. Marcos had brought ten outfits from his home and washed them every Tuesday, and he was offered to shave under Marcos' watch every Wednesday. Routine, routine, routine. He didn't know how Marcos dealt with it.

He took blood from Kevin. He calmly drew his blood, swabbed his mouth, and gave him medicine every morning. Kevin hated that the most. When he complained about his anxiety, boom, the next morning, sedatives were mixed in with his oats. He hadn't realized it until he'd woken up nine hours later unable to move his body.

"You said you had trouble sleeping," Marcos had said, "so I gave you a sedative."

"But I hadn't asked for one," Kevin had said.

"It's in my programming that I sedate any subject with unusual levels of stress or anger. I apologize for this inconvenience."

"Am I a subject now?"

Marcos hadn't said. He didn't disclose information like that. The vials of blood they were taking from Kevin weren't privileges he got to know about. It irked him, but he didn't protest. Neither of them had a choice here. It was up to Kevin to be a conformist.

And not a boy with a thousand secrets, one of which was a half-dead girl who spat up the night sky and broke glass with her fingertips.

"Your new mirror has been installed with more permanent restraints," Marcos said. He was taking a new vial of blood. Kevin pretended not to see the needle burrowing into his vein. "Are you sure you have no idea as to why the first mirror cracked?"

Kevin dragged a heavy hand across his face. These sedatives were really kicking his butt this morning. "I don't know why," he lied. "I thought I saw someone's reflection next to me, but when I got a closer look, it cracked."

Marcos, just like the first time Kevin had told him this, showed no emotion to his unbelievable answer. He said, "And this person—"

"Had blond hair," Kevin said, "a lot of it."

He closed his eyes, then opened them. "May I ask you a question pertaining to the vision you believe you saw?"

As if he were making it up. "Of course."

"You said you haven't had hallucinations before this?"

"Correct."

"And you haven't been involved in any violent altercations at home, work, or school?"

"I believe so, yes."

His eyes dilated and sharpened. "I see." He pressed the cotton swab against Kevin's skin.

"Did you put sedatives in that?" Kevin asked. "Is that something you can tell me?"

"You've had your daily limit for the day."

That didn't make him feel any better. "Why are you giving them to me? I don't need them."

"I cannot tell you classified information." He set aside the blood sample on his rolling medical table. "I hope you understand."

"How does that work? Is this how Nadia programmed you to act?"

He hesitated. "...Yes," he said. "I apologize. I didn't know that was declassified information until now. Nobody has ever asked me how I was programmed."

"I think it's interesting. Were you built like that?"

"I don't know. Nadia didn't create me."

"Really?" he asked, feigning surprise. He'd learned about that from his aunt.

"She said I was found and that it took multiple generations of Líders to get me to function. I don't believe they had the proper technology to turn me...turn on my processors. She had to rewrite multiple lines of code to make me work, and I've been programmed to follow her and Zantl ever since."

"What's Zantl like? You never see them out in public, and I feel like I met them on a bad day to get a read on their personality. If they're to be the next heir, I thought I'd get to know them a bit better."

Marcos blinked three times. "They are..." He touched his throat, straightened up. "Zantl is a difficult individual to describe. They have lived through many hardships with their parents. They expect many things of Zantl, but Zantl has little interest in...people. They often keep to their room for days at a time, talking to themselves. These past few days are the most I've seen them emote in months."

"I thought you didn't leave their side. Wouldn't you know more about them as their friend?"

"I don't believe Zantl and I have that type of relationship. If anything, it's more akin to a coworker and their boss. They don't confide in me the way I see other people do, only when they're upset with their parents and need a wall to talk at. I don't know their favorite songs or their favorite season. That's not our relationship."

"Oh. I'm sorry. I didn't mean to make you feel sad."

"I don't believe sadness is in my programming, but based on what I've observed, I deduce that it makes me more upset than anything, like I've failed them as a...friend."

"Do you ever wonder who created you?" Kevin asked. "Whoever did that must've wanted you as their friend, right?"

"I have," Marcos said, "thought about it. Quite a lot. Nadia doesn't know about that yet, so she cannot tell me to stop."

"I wouldn't want you to. Thinking like that makes you look more alive."

Marcos busied himself on the rolling table, then caught Kevin staring at him and looked away. "I," he started, "do... have a person who I might consider a friend. She's more of a...I'm not sure what our relationship could be considered."

"Like a lover?" Kevin guessed.

"Oh, no," he said quickly. "She's an infant. Her name's Alexi. She's always excited to see me and looks at me when I speak. I value that in a person. I notice you do it with me. I'm sorry," he added. "I don't know why I'm telling you this."

"Don't be." Kevin leaned in. This was a better breakthrough than he'd hoped for. "So she's a baby? Who does she belong to? Do you get to visit her often?"

"I can't speak about declassified information, but I visit her about once a day for checkups. She's learning to take her first steps and her personality is so authentic and bold. I enjoy listening to her babble. I think I like children."

"That's good!" Kevin said. "So you wanna be like a caretaker or babysitter? I can see you being really good at that."

Marcos took hold of his own hand. "Why are you asking me so many questions? You know I'm to analyze your psyche and report it back to the Líders."

"I was curious. There've been so many rumors about you and Zantl...that I've heard," he added, because he didn't want to say he'd heard most of them from school. Somehow, schoolyard rumors hit worse than regular rumors. "It's nice to finally get to know the real you."

Marcos rolled the portable working station toward the door, then stopped. "Thank you. I know most people don't trust me straight away."

"I trust you."

He looked up.

"I do," he said, lying but not really. He didn't distrust him the way his family did, who hated the concept of an autonomous, crossbreed-like boy who could kill someone in a single breath. He simply didn't know him that well. What was his favorite color? Did he have any hobbies? Could he taste food? There was no chance of asking him now without making it sound forced.

"Well then," Marcos said, "if you see this vision again, or if it starts to speak to you, not that it will, I—" He almost dropped the vial of blood. "Thank you, firstly. For what you said. That you trust me. That means a lot to me."

"Of course. Out of everyone here, I trust you the most. You've been the kindest to me."

Marcos locked his hands behind his back. "I read in your file that you were kind-hearted. I didn't think it resounded like this."

"I just like trying to keep the peace. The world is falling apart. Why make things more meddlesome with negativity?"

"Hypocrite," the pessimistic voice in his head said. He ignored it.

"That's an exemplary trait to keep," Marcos said. "I'll try to make your stay as positive as possible. If you hear or see anyone else in this room, please alert me immediately. I can give you medicine for mental stability."

"Oh," Kevin said. He thought he'd just broken through with him. Why bring back up the medicine?

Marcos shifted his heavy weight from foot to foot. "Do you need anything else from me?"

"No, thank you," Kevin said. "I'm quite tired from this morning's blood thing." He picked at his bandages. There was already a dark bruise bleeding through his skin.

"Of course." Marcos bowed. "Good evening, then. I'll be up with your dinner shortly."

"You can skip that, and my bathroom break. I'm not hungry."

Marcos, who'd started opening the door, paused. "Are you sure? You lost about twenty percent of your normal blood volume in less than forty-eight hours. You need your—"

"I'm honestly just tired tonight, Marcos. I'm sorry."

"Of...course. Good night."

Kevin kept his back to Marcos as he closed the door. He didn't like that. He thought Marcos was different, that the threats Morgan said he carried weren't true. No emotions, just following rules without remorse. And rumors sucked. Back in school, Kevin's classmates had made fun of his makeup, his particular interest in the cute and the pink. They'd called him childish for enjoying things that reminded him of a happier childhood, and he'd downplayed it into his twenties. Simple jeers like that messed with a person.

Not that his childhood was bad. It never felt right to compare it to, say, Nikki's homelessness, but his parents had fought. They'd hit, screamed. Mom had once had a dependency on alcohol that'd seeped into Derek's adolescence, and Dad got angry easily. Many nights were spent under the covers with Derek close by. Even before Nikki, when things got tough, they'd always had each other to confide in.

Tears welled up in his eyes. He had to stop thinking about his family, but what more could he have done? Maïmoú hadn't returned, Marcos was suspicious of him. No Mom. No Dad. Was Nikki taking this well? Probably not, and that was his fault. He should've been doing better, acting better. He was the oldest.

He curled up in bed to sleep off the sedatives. He wanted his old life back.

He wasn't allowed a radio to fall asleep to. Nothing to read, no one to talk to. He was alone even when he slept.

Whatever time it was, he decided it was time for bed, and made up a dream fantasy to fall asleep to instead. Back at school, he'd find a girl his type—soft-spoken, kind to him in ways he couldn't be to himself—and she'd like him despite him being so submissive. He didn't care what breed she might've been. Some people valued others based on breed similarities, but Kevin had no preference.

They'd meet for coffee at Morgan's place. Derek would tease him for finally finding a lover, Nikki would fend off Morgan trying to show off Kevin's baby pictures. They'd share a plate of warm cookies and order two drinks, but Morgan would only make one, forcing them to share. They'd end up leaving and going on a stroll, and then he'd walk her to her doorstep before flying back home, giddily smiling at the thought of seeing her again.

That's what he wanted, in the end. No high-risk situations with people who didn't care if he lived or died. He wanted love and freedom in the simplest forms.

It astounded him how hard that was to get once you grew up.

He lifted his sleepy head in a yawn. It was bright, too bright for the Asilo, and something smelled nice.

He wiped spit off of his chin. He'd fallen asleep at someone's kitchen table. It was a primitive place made of clay and wood and smelled of roasted wood from a fire.

The Sun was warm on his back. His wings were gone. Tail, too—he was a whole new person here. His hair was short and black. His skin was a shade tanner, and his face felt longer. He had dirt underneath his fingernails. They, like his own, were scarred from ripping off the skin.

He got up and examined the kitchen. It was extremely prehistoric, with no lights or plugged-in appliances. They had a fireplace instead of an oven. The table had been carved by hand

and the floorboards were each a different color. There was an anvil out back. A chicken was sitting atop it.

He looked behind him, out the windows into a field of yellow. A wheat field the size of a parking lot grew in the back-yard. It smelled of farm life and burned in the hot Sun.

His fingers traced the worn wood on the table. He'd never been on a farm before, but he was nostalgic for this place. It smelled like home.

His foot grazed something underneath the table. It was a wooden string instrument with a carving of a Moon at the bottom. It looked pretty and easy enough to play, so, enjoying this perfect day, he got comfortable and began playing.

Songs flowed out of him like the wind through wheat. Happy melodies reminding him of Derek, of the life of this carefree, nameless man he'd become. The instrument had a lower tune than his guitar back home, but he didn't mind it. There was something beautiful to its melancholy.

Someone opened a door in the living area. He stopped play-ing, hoping for a loved one. "Hello?" he called out.

The door closed. Two feet ran into the kitchen, stopping abruptly in the archway.

She looked better since the last time he'd seen her. She wasn't coughing or choking on that black stuff. Her white dress was clean, wrapped around her body in a new way, and her hair was done up like a mother had styled it.

"Maïmoú," he said, breathing out her name like a sigh of relief.

Maïmoú stepped back, then took a step forwards, unsure of where to go. She looked around the kitchen for someone or something else.

He said what felt most natural. "It's okay," he said, "I'm—"

"Dang it!" Maïmoú cursed at the ceiling. "What the hell is wrong with you, you—" She broke off into a language Kevin didn't know and pointed at herself, then at him, then at the ceiling again. She stomped her shoeless feet like an elephant.

"Maïmoú." Kevin set aside the instrument. It was called a lute. He didn't know how he knew that. "Maïmoú, are you okay?"

"Why do you look like that?" she asked, not looking at him. "You shouldn't be—God, as if this *freaked* situation wasn't bad enough, now I gotta talk to you like *this*."

"I don't understand. What's going on?"

"You're in my Void, but—" She pushed back her hair. "Are *you* doing this? Are you projecting your old life into my brain? Is that why I feel better?" She touched her bare arms, making sure they were there. "That's nuts. I didn't know you could do this."

Kevin watched her animate with her arms. This Maïmoú and the one he'd first met were like night and day. Back before, she was puking so much, she couldn't speak, tremoring from an unknown illness. Now, she looked like an ordinary girl in need of getting her questions answered.

Unfortunately, he was the same way. "Is this a dream?" he asked.

She exhaled and came back to herself, actually shaking out her head like a wet dog. "No. Uh, I don't know exactly what's going on or how I'm gonna fix this, but I'm breaking you out. Right now."

"Huh?"

"From the Asilo. I can't believe you haven't broken yourself out yet. What're you doing? You're just like Hassan."

"Who?"

She motioned to his body. "You. Him. From before."

He reexamined himself. "I don't follow. What're you talking about?"

"Okay, uh—" She rolled on her heels. "Keep up with this, because I don't know how long this place is gonna last, and I need to condense this down the best I can."

She inhaled. "My name's Maïmoú. It's a nickname I'm never changing. I'm technically a thirteen-year-old girl who's been alive for thousands. I'm a Deity, which's kinda like a person powered by a certain thing called a Domain. I used to be powerful. I *am* powerful," she corrected. "I've just been weakened. My Domain was a group of people called humans who I thought had died out 500 years ago. The Others hated me for being strong and tried to kill me off but *failed* because they're *stupid* and *dumb* and *weaker* than me, and now the whole world's screwed up because of them, and *I* am out here doing my best," she said, pointing to her heart, "half-alive in this purgatory all because my humans were so great. And Shào's been freakin' MIA for the past half millennia—I have *no* idea where he is— but his crossbreeds are stuck here with me, which means he's corporeal to some extent, like me, which means my humans are somewhere out there in the world. And I need to get back to them, but I need to save you first, because you're my dad. Well, used to be, before you died."

Kevin crossed his legs as he listened to her, but just as he got comfortable, she was done. She was giving him this blanked stare that said, *"That's it. What else do you want from me?"*

"Oh," Kevin said. "Okay."

"Don't," she warned. "You always said that when you were like this. *'Oh, okay, that's fine, Maï-Maï. Everything will be fine. You're okay'.* But I know you're scared of me, so I need you to wake up so that I can fix all of this and save you."

Her voice was picking up, something that didn't sound right coming from such a young girl.

Kevin sat up. "Maïmoú."

"Come on. I need to hurry."

"Maïmoú."

"Wake up."

He hugged her.

And that warmth he'd once felt from her filled him with love. This little girl, this child he wanted to protect and watch grow up, she was so small, too young to be feeling like this.

Maïmoú's hands slowly reached around his wingless back. It was an odd feeling, having someone touch the contours of your shoulder blades. It was like they held your whole being in their hands.

"I don't understand what's happening," Kevin told her, "and I don't know who you are, but I feel like you're taking on much more than you can handle right now, and that's not good for someone your age. You shouldn't be fighting this alone."

She exhaled like she was laughing at him. "I can handle anything."

"I have a feeling that you're lying, but why do I know that? Who are you, really?"

She dropped her head deeper into his chest, nuzzling him. "You're a soulmate."

"What does that mean?"

"It means you're connected to a Deity, to someone like me. When someone dies, their mind doesn't shoot up into the sky to become a sky dot like your people believe. When you die, you get reborn into a new life. Sometimes you're a different race, different breed, but your insides—your *soul*—stays the same. Some people are born to meet each other, and we call that a soulmate. And if your soul is connected to a Deity, that means you're *our* soulmate. You're able to see us, love us. An instant connection bonds us together."

"What's a soul?"

"It's like if your brain and heart had a baby. It's what makes you you."

She backed up and picked a fuzzy from off his tunic. She pulled it back to reveal a long, red thread connected to his chest, inside of him. He felt the tiniest tug when she pulled it taut. The other half materialized through her, into her very own heart.

Kevin looked down at her, at his new body that felt similar for being different.

"You were a human being named Hassan, back before," Maïmoú explained. "You were...like a dad to me, some 1,500 years ago. You and Derek."

"*1,500* years ago?" He didn't know time went that far back. "Wait, with Derek? Is he here? I-is he alright? You said you'd never hurt us—"

"He's alright," she said. "His thread hasn't been severed from me." She lifted her arm, and another thread materialized through her. It didn't connect to Kevin. It trailed through the house and out the window into the field of wheat. "He's somewhere out beyond Raeleen, but he's alive."

"Why did you do it?" Kevin asked. "You pushed him off the Muralha."

"Because I need to leave this prison and get back to my humans, but I need to get both of you out with me, too. You were, for me..."

She dug the balls of her hands into her eye sockets. The red threads tangled between her fingers. "You're my soulmates. You were like a dad to me, before, and Derek was my mom. You two adopted me when nobody else cared. Nobody loved me but you."

"Oh," he said, and touched his heart. He heard it beating through the string. "That's why I felt so strongly about you when we first met. That's why I heard you as a voice. Was I just remembering you?"

"I hope so. It'd been so long, I didn't know if you'd remember me before this."

"Before you...got weakened?" Kevin asked, trying to keep up. "Who hurt you?"

"The Others. It's what I call the other Deities. It's why I look so broken in the real world. They tried killing me."

"So there're more people like you who're invisible? More Deities? How many are there?"

"Seven, including me, and they all hate me. I'd nearly lost hope for this world, but then you and Derek were reborn as twins, and my drive was relit. I needed to live again, and I've been doing everything I can to become physical and save you two."

"Because you were invisible when I first saw you, on the Muralha," Kevin said, grasping for more understanding. "You're hurting yourself to become visible. Is that why you're choking on darkness?"

"It doesn't matter. I need to save you."

"From what?"

"Don't worry about it. It'll only make you nervous-pick." Seeing him reach for his nail beds, she slapped his hand down. "Right now, I need to break you out of this insane asylum. I'm getting you over the Barrier the right way and I'm bringing you to Derek."

Hearing that swelled Kevin's heart. To see his twin again, to hold him in his arms...

"Wait, but what about the rest of my family?" he asked. "My mom and dad, and Nikki and Vanna. They all need to be saved, too."

Maïmoú frowned like she'd tasted something rotten. She tightened her grip on Kevin's thread.

"Right?" he asked.

"I'll do what I can," she promised. "Now, wake up. I can't lift you out or Sphere you away, so we're running."

"Wait, what?"

Kevin almost awoke with his eyes open, his body lifting without his permission. He pivoted his wings and tail feathers that were back on his body to get him moving, but another force was lifting him now.

Maïmoú, holding both of his hands, was pulling him vertical. Her dress was stained black again from a nasty-looking nosebleed.

Kevin blinked back the sleep from his eyes. He couldn't tell if he'd been asleep for five minutes or five years. "A-are you alright?" he asked. "What's going on?"

She tried to speak, then coughed and splattered up poisoned ink. Giving up, she turned to the locked door and balled her fists. "We're leaving," she grunted, and headbutted the metal, obliterating it.

10
Nikki

"You're an idiot. You're the biggest idiot in Raeleen and I'm revoking our statuses as family members."

"Oi." Nikki shoved Vanna against his bed frame.

"I'm not talking to you," he muttered. "Hold your breath."

She did as instructed, and he pressed a damp rag of hydrogen peroxide to her cheek.

They were in Vanna's bedroom. His house was built right above his family's coffee house, so everything smelled like freshly brewed coffee and sugar. His room was small because of this, like hers, but unlike hers, his was clean. Books stacked neatly around homework done three weeks in advance. Even his CD collection was alphabetized.

"Your parents will find out about this, you know," Vanna said. "You can't hide anything in that house."

"I tripped. What do you want from me?"

"Maybe you shouldn't have been chasing a *robot*, Nikki. You have to stop running into trouble. You have a family to take care of. What if he was leading you into a trap? What if you got hurt?"

"I thought he'd give me information on Derek and Kev."

"He wouldn't have been able to. I'm pretty sure divulging secret Asilo documents isn't in his programming. You need to be more careful." He placed a bandage over her cheek. "This's the last time I'm doing this for you. I'm done swooping in and patching you up every time you act out."

"I never ask you to."

He merely rolled his eyes and put away his bandages.

He probably could've been a doctor if he wasn't so afraid of blood. He'd had his medical equipment back before they'd been introduced. Back in the day, Nikki was more of a bastard, biting people and starting fights. Her instincts had overtaken her and she'd broken teeth without remorse.

It'd taken Vanna to change her. One day, she'd come to the coffee house after being sent home for starting a fight. She'd run out with a lost tooth, blood everywhere, and he'd actually cried for her. Not because she'd been sent home with a detention— he had perfect attendance—but that she'd have a missing tooth that'd cause her pain. It'd taken seeing another person upset *for* her for her to understand her self-worth. Her fights didn't start and end with her, it affected others.

And she was still mucking things up for those who still cared.

Vanna turned around and started clearing up his room. Nikki watched. His ears were folded down.

She froze. While he cleaned his bedroom of blood and mud, her sharp eyes caught his bony wrists. His wristbands usually covered his wrists wholly, but that evening, whether from playing baseball or from worrying about the only cousin he had left, one had slipped down his freckled skin.

"'Ey, you're bleeding."

Without looking at her, Vanna immediately covered up his wrists. "Huh?"

"You're ...your wrists," she said. "What happened? Was that from playing baseball?"

He didn't answer. He wasn't even looking at her.

Nikki's ears fuzzed up. While fretting over herself and relationships, she'd unknowingly stepped into territory she wasn't equipped to handle.

"Those...aren't recent," she said, knowing how scars worked. "What happened?"

"It's nothing," he said.

"But..." Her mind was both blank and reeling from questions. "What did you do?"

His ears flattened hard. "Look, you take your sadness out on your family, I do this. You have no right to judge my coping habits."

"Coping—Did you make those cuts on *purpose*?"

He stayed quiet.

"Vanna!"

"Look, what does it matter to you?" he snapped. "It's something I do, and both my moms *and* your parents know already, so you have nothing to hold against me."

Nikki fell back, appalled. Not against him. She had self-destructive tendencies to deal with her own emotions. She'd made holes in walls to give her anger a mark on the world.

But she never hid it. She never pretended like everything was fine when her life—their lives—were falling apart.

She thought she was accessible to her family's feelings. She'd tried so hard these past few years to be approachable, to show her love when it was so hard for her to do so.

She stepped back from herself. This wasn't about her. She needed to help him, now, right now, even if he didn't want it. "Why're you hurting yourself?"

"It's none of your business."

"Is it because of Kev? Is work too hard? I'll talk to your moms for you, I can—"

"Nikki, stop." He caught himself from raising his voice. "Stop talking about it. Don't bring it up. It's not—"

"Of course it's a big deal! We're family. You could've talked to me about this."

"I *couldn't* talk to you about it!"

"Why not? We're all dealing with Derek and Kev in our own ways!"

"This isn't *about* Derek and Kev!"

Timed knocks hit the door. Before Nikki could devise a cover-up for their argument, Vanna's moms walked in.

Morgan stood smiling with two hands on her wide hips. She was a golden monkey crossbreed who always had on a smile even when a customer was screaming in her face. She wore thick glasses due to her poor sight and a hearing aid in one ear due to an injury from her youth.

Vanna's other mother, Del, was Nikki's mother's sister, the connection that bonded them by blood. She had the same brown and white wings as Derek and Kevin but had her hair chopped short to her scalp. She had to keep it at that length— she worked in the kitchen, baking all the storefront pastries.

"Pulling an all-nighter for a test?" Morgan asked. "You two have quite the competition brewing. Heard you all the way downstairs."

Vanna fixed his wristbands back over his wrists.

"That it, then?" she asked. Like Nikki, her voice strained to be emotionally supportive. They both knew they weren't the best at dealing with their loved ones' feelings. "Everything fine?"

"Yeah," Vanna said. "Sorry, for shouting."

"You don't have to apologize," Del said. She was tall, over six feet, with a deep voice that made her sound wise despite her not saying much.

"Take a breather, yeah?" Morgan said. "Your mom and I will be free later tonight. If you're both still up, we can tune into a program. I'll make crackers." She nodded to Nikki. "Guess you're staying over, yeah?"

She couldn't go home with a bandage over her cheek. All of them knew that.

"I'll ring your mother, then." Morgan pushed Del out with a smile. "Nice cheek," she added to Nikki, and left.

Vanna kicked his bed frame. "Thanks," he said, "now they have even *more* to worry about tonight."

"Vanna, come on."

He hit shoulders with her and exited seconds after his mothers.

Nikki didn't get families, especially Vanna's. She liked them, and they were nice to her and offered her family jobs at the coffee house, but they were odd. What kind of parents acted this way? If she'd found out that her child was hurting themselves, she would've done something. She would've shown that she was emotionally available, and if she couldn't, well, then she wouldn't have taken on a whole child to raise. Why didn't they care, and why didn't Vanna want to talk about it?

Kicking her feet, she followed Vanna downstairs.

Morgan and Del had closed the coffee house for the night. Pink stools balanced on top of turquoise tables. The menus had been collected and filed behind the cash register and the checkered tiles had been scrubbed. The croissants, muffins, and strawberry cakes they were known for were now in dark fridges, ready for tomorrow's open.

Nikki peeked around the staircase into the living room. Their first floor was connected to the sales floor by way of two swinging doors. It was dark on this side of the house. The radio was silent. "Where'd Del and Morgan go?"

Vanna ran his hand over the counters.

Clicking her tongue at the silent treatment, Nikki squatted to the customer fridge and stole her favorite order: a bowl of premade buttered noodles and an iced mocha frap. This combo usually did the trick for her, but not tonight. Shoving her chair into the window, she crushed the drink in her hand and slammed her noodles down hard enough for them to spill out. She wanted to throttle Vanna sometimes, she swore to the Above.

Vanna kept busy by reorganizing the fruit basket in front of the register.

Nikki's lips touched her lid. "Where'd your parents go?"

The cash register closed. Off in the distance, Nikki's ears perked to the sound of machinery overworking in the kitchen.

Vanna's stubby tail pressed up against the counter. "I'm going to bed."

"So why'd you come downstairs?"

"I don't know."

"I don't know either, that's why I'm asking."

"Why'd you do it?" he then asked. "Why chase after someone as risky as Marcos? Do you do it because you want people to notice you, whatever the cost?"

"What does that mean?"

"I mean, it's the only explanation I can come up with. You act out *knowing* it's going to get you in trouble. You *want* the attention. I thought you'd outgrown this phase."

That hot knife he was carving into her back stung.

"Is it because of Derek and Kev?" he then asked. "Is that why you lash out? Is that why you're *always* angry *all* the time now?"

She abandoned her food on the table. "I'm sorry, okay? I'm sorry for trying to show you that I care. I'm sorry for taking out my anger by trying to find answers to questions none of you bother answering."

"So you grieve by running after robots and lashing out at your parents? Is that how you want to mess up your family's life?"

Nikki slammed her fist on the table. "I just want Derek and Kev back! Why's that so bad? Why don't you *care*?"

His face splintered between anguish and anger. "Because they're not coming back, Nikki! Above, why can't you understand that? Why can't you think about what you have now!?"

She lunged for his stupid scarf. "Because all I have left is you!" she screamed at his face. "You're all I have, and you treat me like I'm this *burden* you're forced to carry because we're family! Just because..." She couldn't stop herself in time. "Just because you didn't love them as much as me doesn't mean you get to dictate how I grieve!"

Vanna cracked the fruit basket against Nikki's head. Fresh fruit bounced over the tiles and skidded underneath the tables. One piece hit her in the eye and caused her to loosen her grip on Vanna, giving him enough room to escape.

He fled upstairs, not bothering to hide his crying. Their vehement conversation ended when the last piece of fruit rolled against Nikki's sneaker.

Nikki covered her eyes, digging her short nails into her forehead. What was wrong with her? She hadn't meant that. That was the build, the anger that was burning her away to her most based element. There was no way Vanna would open up to her now. She'd be lucky if they were on speaking turns come January. That was so like her, the problem child ruining everything without the means to fix it.

She left out the second-floor window, keeping quiet as she passed Vanna's locked room, and climbed up to the roof. Luckily, the sky looked clear enough to sleep up here—it was all she deserved after tonight.

The twilight air fondled her injured cheek as she made her bed. Bunching up her hoodie, she made a makeshift pillow and gave in to a few hours of rest, trying to forget about her disjointed life for a few hours.

Lí was thankful for many things in his life, but he was immensely grateful that tonight's forecast wasn't rainy.

He completed his breathing exercises through the night air. Just ten minutes of breathing. That's what his therapists told him he needed to do. Just ten minutes a day to himself, wherever he found peace. Tonight happened to be on one of Pangea's rooftops. His duties, meetings, conferences, existential nightmares about how he didn't deserve anything good in his life and that living was the most selfish choice he could make—

Inhale.

Tonight was good. The stars were sparkling and the traffic outside the city was palliative. He should've been asleep because he'd have to be on a plane in a few hours and fly halfway across the world for a UN meeting—

Exhale.

He was okay. He was helping people and doing good because the news said so. They called it imposter syndrome, the feeling of feeling like shit even though you were doing your best. But his best should've been better. He'd only saved, what, hundreds of people from the radiation zones? When billions were suffering? .0001% of nothing.

Great job, Lí, *said the voice in his head,* You're doing jack shit.

At least Tai had finally gotten to bed. Lí had waited until his husband had passed out before he'd escaped to the roof. They'd been on and off planes and trains for weeks. Tai needed his sleep. Lí didn't, didn't deserve it.

He lifted his left hand to the Moon. Around his fingerless gloves was his wedding band tightly secured on his ring finger. It shone silver, dazzling.

His hand dropped. He blinked.

Nikki, she blinked, watching through the eyes of a boy she didn't know.

She looked left, then right. Blinked again. Breathed.

She patted her chest, her flat, masculine chest, wearing clothes she didn't own in a body that wasn't hers. No tail. No ears. This boy had stubble and unkempt hair, a lighter skin tone. He was the same height as her and had similar cuts in his fleshy ears, but...

She rubbed these hands she now controlled. However she fell asleep, she could *always* control her dreams. She could morph nightmares into pleasant dreamscapes and meet friends and family as she pleased.

This wasn't a dream. She was too conscious, living in a moment she couldn't place.

This person, whoever they were, was living a life she couldn't control, and he was real.

She covered her—his—mouth, and looked past the roof to see where she was.

Her arms turned to jelly. She was up way too high, at least a hundred stories so. Skyscrapers shot up around her, shiny, glass structures with trees growing from their rooftops. Their designs didn't make sense and bent and formed differently from the standard skyscrapers she knew. There was a full tree growing next to her, part-industry, part-nature-preserve. Below, when she dared to look down, she saw parks and ponds and roads for tiny cars or people—a future city.

She fell back behind the railing. She wasn't in Raeleen. Nothing like this was fathomable in Raeleen.

The sky rumbled above her like it was thundering. She saw sky dots—stars, Lí had called them—and the Moon before something flew across it.

Nikki ducked. A machine bigger than her house soared through the clouds. It was shaped like a mechanical bird. It was big and metal and loud, *so* loud that she had to cover her fleshy ears instead of her absent rat ones.

She shuddered, unable to move from her vulnerable position, until the nameless contraption flew over this unnamed city.

But it wasn't unnamed. Lí had a name for it. She was in a place called Pangea, a one-of-a-kind city that housed thousands of important people. And that bird-like contraption was called an airliner, a type of airplane used to bring people all over the world.

Nikki pinched her cheeks, trying to wake herself up. She'd somehow extracted those details from the boy's brain, but she could've easily been making all of this up. None of this could've been real. She was dreaming the way normal people did.

The longer she spent in this body, the more she learned. It was unfocused, like remembering a dream you'd just woken up from. He was twenty-six. He was a Taurus—whatever that meant—and had the same birthday as her.

He liked buttered noodles, just like her.

And baseball, same as her.

She looked back at his—her—hands. "Lí?" she called into the night. "That's your name, yeah? What's going on?"

The boy's body didn't answer. Course.

She stood up, careful so as not to fall even though there was a railing. She needed to get to ground level and talk to someone. Maybe that Tai person? She felt the wind on her body—*his* body. This couldn't have been a dream.

"Lí?"

She turned, hair tousling in the wind, and found all of her answers.

She didn't know what to look at first. Floating in front of the city was a boy of about thirteen years old, and he was unlike anyone she'd ever seen. He was wearing a strange robe of red and black, with gold lining the edges. He had a long, red tail with yellow fur at the end, and stubby horns with pointed, fleshy ears. She didn't know his breed. He was one of a kind, able to fly without wings.

The way he was staring at her, it was like *she* was the odd one out, as if he wasn't the one defying physics.

"*Lí?*" the boy repeated. "*Lí, is that truly you?*"

"*Yeah,*" Nikki found herself saying. They were both speaking in the language Lí had been thinking in. Nikki knew it, somehow.

The floating boy took in the nighttime city like Lí had done, calculating his position in the dream. While turning, Nikki noticed a small birthmark underneath his right eye, but she'd always known it was there.

The boy floated in closer, closer than Nikki would've let someone get to her. She stepped back, but he kept coming. His normal hand cupped her face and, before she could push him away, he floated to her level and hugged her.

She locked up. She couldn't think. She couldn't kick him off or slap his face, because the Above knew this boy didn't hug her with ill will, and when they were together, he hid nothing from her, from him, from them.

Lí closed his eyes. Shào, like usual, emitted a soothing aura that helped Lí cope on his missions around the world. But he needed to get back to his room. He needed to make a call to the border commissioner to make sure his team had clearance to enter the radiation zone tomorrow morning. He couldn't get wrapped up in another issue. He had people he needed to protect.

He was one of the few, rare people that were unaffected by the radiation.

Shào hugged Nikki tighter. "Oh, Lí, how I've missed you so."

A sickening feeling infected Nikki's chest, and she jumped back, swallowing hard to feel spit go down her own throat. His voice, while nice, made her feel too uncomfortable.

When they separated, she switched back to her true body. She made fists with her bleached, gloveless hands and rubbed her rat ears through her curls. She was back to herself. Lí, for the time being, had relinquished his power over her.

Nikki stood her ground with the floating boy, who was neither friend nor foe because she didn't know what on Earth he was. He seemed more startled that she'd returned to her real self than she was. He floated a foot back.

"Who are you?" Nikki asked. "What's going on?"

The boy gasped. "You speak the same language the humans do?" he asked. "Who *are* you?"

"I asked you first," Nikki said. "I was just sleeping on my aunts' roof when I woke up here. Where am I? This isn't anywhere in Raeleen."

The boy looked down to the streets below. "Did you arrive with the osprey as well? Are you in the Drail Kingdom?"

"Stop asking questions about me. Where am I?"

When the boy didn't say anything, Nikki gave up. "I'm making myself wake up."

"Don't!" He grabbed hold of her arm, actually afraid of her leaving. His grip was strong for his age. "Please, don't leave. I'm sorry. I haven't conversed with someone in hundreds of years. I'm simply perplexed by this meeting and who...you are."

Nikki braced for the worst.

Sensing her reaction, Shào loosened his grip but refused to let go. "What's your name this time?"

"This time? Nikki," she said. "Nicole Lenore."

Shào attempted a hurt smile, and those feelings Lí had once felt refilled her. "What a prepossessing name. Nicole Lenore..." He closed his eyes. "I didn't think this was feasible, for you to return."

"Return where?" She tempted another look over the railing into this strange city of Pangea. The view made her go jelly again.

The boy laughed to himself. His voice cracked. "How do I explain—I've gone over this conversation a thousand times in my head, hoping to one day speak to someone.

"Firstly." He bowed. "My name is Shào Kai, and it's a pleasure to remeet you. I am what you might call a God, or a Deity, or a creator, depending on how your culture views creation. There've been many names for us, but I am a being with immense powers that's been cursed time and time again by fate. I was trapped here in this purga…in this prison of consciousness centuries ago, meant to live out eternity in my own head. I thought I was surely dead and had gone crazy from loneliness."

He took in the scenery in a longing gaze. "I knew you in a past life, as a boy named Lí Naranbaatar."

"A past life?"

"A life you lived before this one. When a person dies, they're reborn into a new body. Sometimes you'll be reborn instantaneously, sometimes it takes hundreds of years for the connection to be made, but your soul remains yours."

Nikki didn't even try to comment. She kept her questions to herself, getting all the information she could before questioning his logic.

"And there're some souls connected to us Deities," Shào continued. "They're extremely rare. We call them our soulmates, as crude a placeholder that may be."

He touched Nikki's cheek, and Nikki didn't—couldn't—pull away.

"You were *my* soulmate," he said fondly. "My courageous, helpful Lí Naranbaatar, and I have waited so many years to find you again."

There was a connection, she felt, between them, like meeting an excited puppy for the first time and wanting to play with them.

But she didn't know if he could snap and bite her, and she didn't want to cross either of their boundaries to find out.

She stepped back from his touch.

Shào curled back his fingers. "I apologize. Lí had warned me that I often went too far with him. I can't handle myself when I'm near you. You cited a place called Raeleen. Is that your homeland? Is that where the fledgling came from?" He crossed his legs in midair and leaned in with his hands underneath his chin. "What is your world like?"

She thought about it for two seconds. "Bad," she said. "Our leaders suck and our government's corrupt. There're guards everywhere, watching us. There's a lot of homeless kids who get ignored by the majority of the world, and the schools aren't funded well."

Despite calling out her world's faults, Shào's face brightened. "How incredible. And there're others like you? Are my other crossbreeds with you?"

"*Your* crossbreeds?"

"I'm the Deity who governs crossbreeds. I control them. Are there any humans where you live? Do you know what that word means?"

"I don't, but...Lí was one, yeah?" She'd gathered that from his memories. "He didn't have any animal features, and I think I tapped into a few of his memories. Or thoughts?"

Shào covered his mouth in glee. "How wonderful. This's all so incredible, Nicole. I thought I'd never be able to return to this odious world, but I can. I can come back."

"What do you mean? How can I help?"

"Oh, Nicole." He hugged her suddenly. "I admire your selflessness. You've become such a charming young person this time around."

"Thanks?" she said, but it didn't feel right. If she were to believe anything he was saying, they'd technically just met.

He smiled that little smile again, one barely visible if she wasn't standing inches away to see it. "I've only met you moments ago, Nicole, yet you've made me the happiest I've been in my life, and I thank you for this."

She wasn't used to this. Being fawned over like she was someone to be admired. This boy didn't know anything about her, yet he still acted like she was a good person. It felt dirty, thinking of herself so highly.

But she didn't hate it. This one boy was making her feel so beloved. Her parents did their best and Derek and Kevin showed it at times, but Shào was something—someone—more.

She just hoped he wasn't in "love" love with her, otherwise she'd be sick with disgust and break his heart.

She hid her hands in her pockets. "No problem. So you know me, or you know someone who looks like me. This Lí person, yeah? Who was he?"

"Oh, he was sublime, Nicole. Such a kind boy. He helped so many people out of such a dangerous situation."

"What happened to him?"

Shào's animated face fell, reminded of something he'd wanted to forget.

"Shào?"

He went to open his mouth when his pointed ears flicked. Alerted, he floated up and searched the city with a high-strung gaze.

His eyes went to slits. The shaved hair on the back of his head stood up. "She's here," he whispered.

"Who?"

He floated back to Nikki. There was a new grimness in his face. "Nicole, forget what I said. You need to wake yourself. You need to leave. She's coming."

"Who?"

111

"I—" He whipped his head around, digging his talon-like nails into Nikki's shoulders.

Far out into the city, standing atop a skyscraper's antenna, was a young girl. She had long, blond hair and a white dress that turned in the turbulent winds. She was staring right at them. Once their eyes locked, she jumped off the building and floated as Shào did.

"Shào?" she called out. "Shào!?"

"Maïmoú." Shào's hand pawed for Nikki, and once he found her, his grip could've splintered bone.

Time must've stopped with how long he stared at Nikki. They'd only just met, but his eyes screamed they'd have to part, and that he'd do anything to keep that from happening.

He gritted his teeth. "Shit. I can't teleport you from here. How ineffectual I've become."

"Shào, who's that girl?" Nikki asked. "Why're you so afraid of her?"

"I'm sorry," he said, and disappeared only to reappear by the floating girl. Before a second passed between them and their reintroduction, he punched her into the building.

A bright light detonated from their impact, and the building cracked and tilted into a fiery ball.

Nikki shielded herself from debris. Windows shattered and blew out like bullets. Gas tanks erupted and engulfed rooftops. Shào and Maïmoú were eaten by the explosion, but their attacks jumped from building to building, following them. Each building fell like dominos.

Maïmoú spun out in circles from the fiery smoke. She coughed out something black like tar and held her head until she got her senses back.

When she noticed Nikki through the flames, every drop of blood in Nikki's body coagulated.

Nikki had never seen someone so angry at her before. Nikki, locked in a dream beyond her control, had just been given a death sentence by a Deity whose glare said she wanted her skinned alive.

Screaming threats in a language Nikki didn't know, Maïmoú transported herself across the city and went to shatter Nikki's skull with a single punch.

Shào teleported in from her left and kicked her in the head with enough force to sever it from her neck. She flew a thousand feet back, her body clipping building corners.

Shào flinched and held his head in the same place he'd just kicked Maïmoú. His feet curled in pain.

"Shào?" Nikki called out. "Shào, are you alright?"

A second explosion sent a pile of shingles over Nikki. Through the flames, Maïmoú grabbed Shào by his collar and launched him across the city into a park. His impact left a sizable crater amongst many others.

The building Nikki was on shifted. Something during their fight had blunted the structure. She was going down.

The sky went from clear to covered as Maïmoú, stained in black, clasped her hands around Nikki's throat and squeezed. The air keeping Nikki alive snuffed out like a wet candle.

"Keep *away* from him!" Maïmoú screamed in her face. "All you did in your past life was hurt my Shào, you don't deserve him as I—!"

Nikki blinked awake. Gone were the fire and flames from the fight between Deities. She was back atop Vanna's home. The night was quiet.

She got up, processing what'd taken place in her dream, Shào's words, Maïmoú's wrath, before the coffee house exploded in smoke and knocked her off the roof.

11

Derek

For the first time since arriving in Drail, someone ignored Derek's presence. The floating boy didn't gawk at him. He didn't notice him at all. He stared out the window with drool on his lip, eyes crossed. He looked half-there, half-alive.

"Who's that?" Derek asked Cellena. "Someone we should worry about?"

"Who?" she asked.

"That demon kid."

She looked everywhere but at the kid. "Who?"

"What, can demons go invisible? But then why can I see him?"

Cellena double-checked that they were the only three in the hallway. "Are you seeing someone in front of us?"

"Yeah, right here." He waved his hand in front of his face. "Hey, you good?"

A soft moan oozed from the boy's lips.

Cellena tugged on Derek's sleeve. "Derek, are you alright?"

Derek got in front of the boy. He looked like Cellena and her family, with rich qualities to boot. Wipe that drool off of him and he'd be a royal kid. "Who *are* you?" he asked him.

"*Maïmoú.*"

Derek hitched his breath. That name, and feeling, *that* was what he wanted. Fuck the church, fuck obligations. For a split second, all he cared about was that person and their name.

Melting into the rug, Derek touched the kid's shoulder. "What'd you just say?"

His knees instantly gave out like a puppet with its strings cut. His eyes rolled back, his head drooped. The last thing he tried to do was grab Cellena and tell her to run, because touching this boy was like poison to his body.

Something unnatural, like what the king had said. He'd called it "demonic possession."

When he awoke, he awoke in darkness. It was nighttime and the grass in which he lay was dewy upon his cheek.

He pulled himself up. He was no longer in the castle. He was in a pitch-black meadow near a pond emitting a lazy fog. Trees lined the perimeter, and into the sky shined thousands of sky dots.

Derek shook himself off and got up. Inside the pond were these animal-looking things with fins. They were tear-shaped and kind of creepy looking. Derek wanted to eat one.

As he leaned over the pond to better watch the animals, he heard someone come up behind him. Their hand grabbed the back of his collar.

"Hey—!" Too late. Derek lost his footing in the soft earth and got pushed face-first into the water.

It was that drooling boy, though he wasn't drooling now. He was now fully coherent and smug as fuck that he managed to push Derek into the pond.

"What in the absolute *fuck* is going on?" he demanded from Derek. He was still floating, able to hover over the pond. "Who are you? What's happening to the world?"

Derek scrambled out of the pond. Just like the church, being in water panicked him, even if it was only ankle-deep. "Uh, what the fuck?"

"Pray tell," the boy said, "assumed angel to humankind: Which one are you?"

"*Huh*?"

"Which reincarnation do you *derive* from?" he reworded, ticked off by Derek's lack of understanding. "Who were you to us last time round? My name is Shào Kai. Is that name *au fait* with you? I certainly know you're not Lí, as I'd just met with him, so you therefore mean quite little to me, though I'm not familiar with the Others' soulmates to get a read on your personality. So I ask again: Who *are* you?"

"I have no idea what you're talking about." He shook his wings of the smelly water. "What the fuck is your problem?"

"Ugh." Shào floated to his back and placed a hand over his eyes. "I *hate* talking to you souls. You're always so emotional and probing. What number are we on now? First Holly Bennett, then Nicole Lenore, and now *you*?"

Derek didn't know what a hollied bennet was, but that second name held a stronger connection to him. He tried to hold on to that feeling for as long as he could, but like that other name Shào had mumbled, a loving memory came and slipped away.

"I mean, it's getting *excessive* now," Shào went on. "Is it going to be like last time when there were, Christ, *five* soulmates running around the world? I can't imagine such a fate."

"I, uh, don't know what you're talking about," Derek said. "Well, like, I don't think I do. Is this angel business?"

"Oh, God, no. Spare me a religious sermon." He rolled to his belly and stirred his finger in the air. Feet away, the pond water began stirring with his movement. "Do you have an inclination to water? Have you ever felt pulled to it like you'd find true happiness submerged in the bottom of the sea? How about the

116

Earth? Do you feel grounded when you're shifting your hand through blooming peonies or fresh soil? What of fate itself and how it ties us together yet makes us feel lonelier than the farthest star in the most distant galaxy? Do you crave death?"

Derek sucked in his lips. "Is this, like, a test?"

"Oh, *Lord*, you don't even know of the seven Deities." Shào pushed his bangs from his face. "I forgot how *taxing* communication is with someone who gives me no meaningful purpose. How about the question we all wish to know: Why are you here? Nicole had mentioned that crossbreeds are thriving in a place I haven't the faintest clue how to find. Did a Deity send you here?"

"I-I have no idea. My memories are busted. Look, are you a demon? I won't tell nobody you were in the castle. To be honest, I don't agree with most of the humans' beliefs, so I can keep this a secret. No feathers off my wing."

"*Demons.*" He said it like a bad pun. "No, I am not a *demon*."

Derek looked at his tail, horns, pointed ears. "Then what are you?"

"Nothing more than an ancient echo lost to a forgotten world."

Derek blinked at him.

Shào frowned back. Maybe he actually *was* a child and wanted Derek to play along with his boastful smartness. "I am a Deity. Shào Kai, Deity to crossbreeds. The pleasure is all yours."

"What's a crossbreed?"

"It's what you are. Part-human, part-animal. Well, it's more of a 90/10 cut in your DNA, but these humans haven't gotten that far in genetics."

Derek looked around the meadow. "And where am I?"

"My mind, a torturous replay of all of my past mistakes."

"Ew, I'm in your *brain*?"

"Is it that shocking at this point? Yes, these are my memories, and no, I cannot let you out. I'm too weak to use my powers. You must've just touched me and I was lost in thought and accidentally lured you in. It's something you soulmates can do. You find us like fish to a dangling worm."

"What's a fish?"

"What's a—?" He sighed. "Never mind, I haven't the energy to process that. God, I knew someone like you from my past. I dare presume you and her are somehow related. Curse the world if that be the case."

"Do you mean that Nicole person?" For some reason, that name sounded so nice to him.

Shào smiled. "No, because the world is a more blessed place with her in it."

"Then are you talking about Maïmoú?"

Shào lost the tension in his tail.

"You said that name right before we got swept up here. I feel like I know it somehow. Oh, is *she* an angel? The humans said they have these crazy mind powers or something. Are *you* an—"

Shào barreled into him, knocking him back into the water, and strangled him in a chokehold.

Words abandoned Derek. Shào had gained the strength of twenty knights, cutting off his blood supply in a single move.

"Don't fret," Shào grunted. "Death is quite a serene experience. Let us pray a being can die in a Void. What a turn if you become trapped in this purgatory dungeon with me as a ghost. What a turn," he added, squeezing harder, "that I became acquainted with one of *her* soulmates."

"What?" Derek choked.

"Congratulations. You're a damned soul connected to a Deity who has more blood on her hands than I do. You are Maïmoú's love, her heart, the reason she exists. You are connected to her, mind and spirit. You will always love her and

118

defend her actions until the day the world stops turning, and I *deeply* sympathize with you."

The choking feeling doubled. Derek gagged on his own breath. "What...did..."

"What did you do?" Shào asked. "Nothing. I told you, you had no choice in this, just like I have no choice in killing you to *spite* that vicious creature built of flesh and bone. Oh, how I will get immense satisfaction from seeing one of her soulmates perish by my hands. An eye for an eye, 'ey, fledgling? It's what she *deserves* after all the *suffering* she's put me through."

Derek closed his eyes. Whatever. Maybe the humans would find a better placeholder between their fight with demonkind. Surely it didn't have to be him if he couldn't fight off a kid demon. Deity. Whatever.

Like being shoved down a dark pit, Derek's body slipped away from Shào, and he fell into a warm and heart-pounding chest.

He coughed and held his throat. He was back in the castle, Shào was gone, but he could still feel the phantom hands on his throat.

Someone gasped and jumped back. Watching over him in the hallway wasn't Cellena or Shào, but that girl he'd seen hours ago atop the castle.

The cat girl sat on her hands and knees, watching him like a cat did a toy. She really was part-animal, that 90/10 split Shào was talking about. Furry ears and a tail, flicking with curiosity as to how Derek got back to the real world.

A crossbreed.

"How—" He coughed. His throat really hurt.

She creeped up to him. Her amber eyes were unnaturally wide, unblinking.

She sat back and searched inside one of her pockets. From it fell out red berries and twigs, little buttons she'd collected over time. She then pulled out a notebook on a key ring. She opened it to an old, bookmarked page and held it out for Derek to read. It had flower doodles around the border.

My name is Holly Bennett.
I'm a 21-year-old girl who cannot speak, but I understand a lot of what you say.
I'm afraid of loud noises and men, and my development is that of a child.
Please be forgiving of me.
I wish to be friends.

Derek read that twice to make sure he got it right, then forced himself up. Shào was nowhere to be seen.

"Did you save me?" he asked her. Shào had said something about a Holly Bennett being like him. "Who are you?"

Holly flicked one of her large cat ears, judging him. Then her eyes went wide and she opened her mouth, a silent freeze-frame.

"Uh—"

She jumped. Clambering to one of the—now open—windows, Holly hopped straight out of the castle to her death.

"Woah!" Derek fell into the curtains. His body was all sorts of messed up, but if he flew quick enough, he could save her.

It was a straight shot down, with only a few feet of grass separating the castle from a watery death.

Holly was there, tiptoeing over dandelions. She stopped to pick and place one behind her ear when she saw Derek staring at her.

His hair whipped in the wind as they caught each other's eyes. "You're insane," he exhaled in relief. "Add that to your fucking notebook. Crossbreed cat girl. Soulmate. Insane. *Fuck.*"

Holly slowly stuck out her tongue, her only way to communicate, and disappeared down the coastline.

Derek clutched the curtains. His body wasn't feeling good. Knowing Holly was okay and off doing whatever the fuck she did, he fell to his knees and aired out his fancy shirt.

Shortly later, Cellena, with an entourage of her family and knights, ran in to save him from nothing.

Derek massaged his swollen neck. He was back in that bed he'd woken up in that morning. A fire was going to keep him warm for the night.

The royal family cancelled all the meetings they'd planned for him. They'd bandaged him, nursed him with medicine and funky-looking soup that tasted like pure salt, and put him to bed, hoping their angel hadn't been harmed by another "demon" attack.

He'd tried to tell them about Shào and how he said he wasn't a demon, but they disregarded everything in lieu of him getting better. They told him that demons were known for their lies and to continue distrusting them.

Cellena sniffled at his bedside. "I'm just so glad you're alive."

"Okay, *why* are *you* still sniffling about me?" Derek teased. "I'm fine. Anyway, isn't it past your bedtime?"

"I've never seen an attack happen so suddenly before. You were talking to an invisible person, then reached out for something and just collapsed. I thought you'd died. Your breathing was so weak and your heart barely beat. I thought..." She dabbed her bloodshot eyes with a handkerchief. "I thought the worst."

"Hey." He brushed back her hair. "Quit it. I ain't dead yet."

"My mother always says I take on setbacks like a king."

"You'd make a great one." His left wing got pins and needles from sitting on it wrong. He turned to better face her. "King Cellena, born to rule and honor her kingdom!"

Cellena finally laughed. "Are you okay?" she asked. "I should call the doctor and have him tend to you."

"Don't. I'll be fine."

"But aren't you in pain?"

"I just need some space from people right now. I need to turn off my brain and take in everything."

"Oh." Her smile fell. "I'll leave you be, then."

"Hey, look at me." He took her face in his hands. "This isn't your fault, okay? You did everything fine."

"But—" She sniffed again. "I should've been more mature about this."

"You're, like, ten. Nobody should expect you to act like an adult when you're not even a teenager yet. Now get." He playfully shooed her away. "Your parents are probably wondering where their rambunctious little prince went."

"Princess," she corrected, and curtsied. "Derek, I'll...I'll research everything you need to know about Drail. I'll make it concise and easier for you to read. And if you don't want to read, I can memorize it all and relay it to you. I'll help you."

"You don't gotta do all that."

"I want to. You're my friend."

"Course," he said but lacked the conviction Cellena needed. Even memory-less, he knew he didn't have close friends. He wasn't that type of person. Just family and lovers he could hopefully call friends if they kept him long enough.

"Okay." Rejuvenated, Cellena darted to the door. Behind it waited Nero, Derek's personal knight for the night. "Goodnight, Derek. I'll check on you in the morning, okay?"

"Kay," he said, and waved both of them off.

The temperature of the cool, lonely night settled into his hollow bones. He heard the creaks of the castle walls and the wind rustling the forest pine outside. He was finally alone, away from the responsibilities of being known.

He held up his necklace, feeling the edges cut into his palm. He was an angel, a prophet, and now also a "soulmate." Once he was ready, he'd have to ask the humans about that last part. He couldn't imagine anyone having those types of answers, let alone him. Ties to a God? Sounded rough.

A yawn escaped from his mouth, and he rubbed his eyes. He wasn't even tired, he just needed to close his eyes and not be him for a night, so he could reset his factory settings.

Did the Drail Kingdom even have factories? Probably not.

"Derek?"

He opened his eyes.

"Derek, are you there? It's Maïmoú. Answer me."

Derek tried to sit up. He'd heard that voice before, from a time long past. It was young, like Cellena, innocent, dreamlike. But it hadn't been Cellena. This was coming from his brain, like a little mouse was whispering into his ear.

And she sounded bad. Like, real bad. Voice cracks and coughing between words. He felt compelled to ask if she needed help, but he didn't know where she was in the world.

"Uh, hello?" he called out, hoping for a response.

His door opened. Nero was holding his head, panting slightly. "A-are you alright?"

Derek looked over his bed frame. "Huh?"

"It's another attack. It's small, but—" He composed himself, already feeling better. "You really aren't affected by them, are you?"

"...Don't think so," he said. He was still waiting—hoping, praying—to hear that girl's voice again.

"Alright, then. Forgive the interruption. Goodnight."

Derek dropped his body back into bed. Was *that* demonic possession? Holly was a demon, right? Had she done something to him when she'd saved him from Shào?

No, Holly couldn't talk, and that voice had said her name was Maïmoú.

Maïmoú. Like that Nikki name, it pulled a string on his heart, lacing up a hole he hadn't known he had.

Derek moaned in annoyance. Too many people. Too many powers. Angels, demons, Deities, soulmates. Too confusing. Did *not* care.

He needed to jerk off. Put something inside him and neglect his duties to strangers. Finishing off and sitting in a warm pool of your own mushy feelings? That was better than sex. Well, maybe. A night with Oliver could change that.

Stuffing a hand down his pants, Derek got to work with Oliver in mind.

Tapping rapped on the windowpane next to Derek's bed.

"Fuck—" Derek parted his red curtains and was met with darkness. The dark sky dyed with the distant blues and purples. A thousand sky dots lit the sky tonight, and the trees were all dyed the single color of pure darkness.

"...Maïmoú?" he called out.

A shadow formed around the night. A head of curly hair, two pointed horns, a fidgeting, wire-thin tail.

Oliver floated from nothing into the window. Derek couldn't believe how he did it without wings, how the Earth levitated these people between the ground and sky. He appeared lighter than air, even though he was taller, bigger, and stronger than Derek was.

Biting his lower lip, Derek unlatched the window lock. "Hey."

"Hello. Uh, evening, I mean. Good evening." He cleared his throat. "I was wondering if you were feeling better?"

"Do the bandages give it away?"

"Oh, uh, I...suppose they do. I meant from what happened to you this evening. I heard you were attacked, and I had a feeling you were..." He started over. "What happened to you, if you mind me asking?"

Was he trying to turn Derek on? All that mumbling and stuttering, you would've thought he was in front of an audience. "I think I met with a God."

Oliver's pointy ears stuck out from his hair. "Really?"

"I think. I don't know." He flopped down into bed, making a point to spread his legs and air out his crotch. "I don't know nothing about this place. I don't even know what a demon is. Are you part-animal? Something different altogether? It's batty. Pun intended. Because, you know, bats. Oh, I met with your friends earlier today," he added. "One of them was the cat girl. Holly?"

"Oh, yes. Did she show you her notebook? She finds herself in, uh, predicaments, on top of roofs and underneath logs and the like. Once, I found her in a cave miles into the Kavka Mountains. She was out there for days." Catching himself, he bowed to Derek. "Forgive me. I ramble when I...when I'm—"

"Scared?" Derek guessed. "Don't be. I met another friend of yours. Two, I think. Shào and Maïmoú. What's their deal?"

Oliver repeated the two names slowly. "I...don't think I've met anyone named that before. What did they look like?"

"Well, one's obviously a demon, though he says he's not. He's got a long, red tail with fur at the end, with horns and ears like you. The other was a voice I heard. Said her name was Maïmoú."

"I'm sorry. I've been around for hundreds of years, and I don't know anyone named that. No demon has those abilities, either."

"You don't look hundreds of years old."

"Our brains and bodies don't age. We're stuck at these ages for eternity, never advancing."

Derek raised a brow. "So how old are you, mentally?"

"I'd say...about your age. Maybe a bit older."

Derek felt himself biting his lip again. He placed pins in Shào's and Maïmoú's names for later. They *must've* been Gods, then. The humans were going to have a field day knowing that their beloved person up in the clouds had to share the spotlight.

"Well, I'm glad you're alright," Oliver said. "I should be heading back."

"No, stay." Derek made a grabby motion with his hands. "You can spare a few minutes for me, right?"

Oliver looked over to Derek's locked door.

"A knight's guarding it," Derek said.

"Is it Nero?"

"Yeah."

He relaxed and floated into Derek's room. "He's a friend to demonkind, he and his wife. They give us fresh fruits and vegetables, as well as supplies that we run out of."

"So they don't think you all should burn in fire for existing?" He'd meant it as a joke.

Oliver didn't laugh. "No, they don't."

"Right. Sorry. I'm still getting used to things here."

"They say you lost your memories."

"Word travels fast."

"We learn fast. It's what we have to do to survive. Every step the humans make, we have to be six steps ahead."

Derek didn't know if he'd ever thought *two* steps ahead about anything. "Hey, could you stop, like, hurting the humans? At least stop hurting Cellena? She doesn't deserve that. She's a kid."

"We're not the ones hurting them. I don't know what's been afflicting them these past decades, but it hasn't been us. None of us even have the power to do that."

Derek rocked on his butt. So *intense.* It got him hard. "Got it. That's just what the humans have been telling me. So you don't have heart attack powers. Can you read minds?"

"No. Well, we have this sort of, uhm, mating process." He looked away. "We mate for life, and when we meet our mate, we have an internal bond with them. It's like an explosion of information. You instantly know their wants, their needs. We share part of our soul with them forever."

"Woah. That sounds pretty serious."

"It is. It's the most important relationship a demon has in the world."

"So, does it only happen with demons? Can humans do it? Can you mate with a human?"

Oliver played with the end of his tail. "No. It's only with demonkind." Then, "The bond...*can* happen between a demon and a human, but it'll only be one-sided on the demon's end. If the other partner reciprocates the feeling, then it's the same as human love, we're just the love-struck fools bent on adoring them forever."

Derek worked his warm tongue in his mouth. That kind of bond might've put some people off, but to Derek, lovesickness made him feel special, but not in an angelic way. More like a special person way.

Concealing his boner in the blankets, Derek nudged Oliver's foot with his wing.

He flinched.

"Hey," Derek said.

He looked at Derek's nose rather than his eyes. "...Hello."

"You should, like, come in. If you'd like."

"I shouldn't."

"But do you want to?"

He licked his lips and gave Derek another needy look.

His bed was big enough for the two of them, but Oliver still crawled along the edge like it was a twin and held himself small. His tail wrapped around his boots.

"You alright?" Derek asked.

"Yes. No."

"Yes, no?"

"I don't know what to say at this moment."

Derek smiled at his stuttering. "So."

"Yes."

"You know where I am at all times."

He nodded.

"You know how I'm feeling like it's sonar attached to your brain."

He nodded more urgently, which made Derek beam.

"You've *mated* with me," Derek teased, "haven't you?"

Oliver curled more into himself, hiding his face, his hands, the truth pouring from the pores he tried so hard to hide. A nervous twitter fell to his toes, and he curled them in his boots until it looked like he was dancing.

Derek laughed. "You're an awfully good liar, aren't you? It's okay."

"No, it's not. I shouldn't be like this. You're a man."

"I'm not a man."

He looked up. "Oh. How old are you?"

"I don't know, but I'm not male."

The look he gave Derek was that of disbelief, like an answer to a math problem he hadn't been expecting. "I only assumed...the maids who'd bathed you had said..." He clammed up, thought on it. "Should I...should I call you something different?"

"I don't think so," Derek said. "You can still call me a 'him', I'm just not *fully* a him. It's like something else is tacked on to me. It's kinda hard to explain, but that's me. A problem child through and through."

You could still see Oliver processing the words Derek had said, but once he stopped talking, he immediately said, "I don't see you as a problem child."

"You don't know me well enough to know. Above, *I* don't know anything about me."

Oliver moved closer to him on his own. "Uhm, while this's something new to me, it's not—what do you call it—a dealbreaker. I don't think badly of you for being something I

128

hadn't expected. It's something I'll learn about, from you. If you'll let me."

"Sure," Derek said with a shrug, but his heart was pounding. He hadn't told any of the humans about this. They must've all regarded him as male. He wished they would've asked, but they still had trouble getting his name right. They still thought it was Grace.

"Thank you," Oliver added, "for telling me that. I feel like I know you a little better."

"And I still don't know shit about you."

"I'm Oliver."

Derek broke and laughed. "Above, you're cute."

Oliver shivered through his own laughter. It was high-pitched and churned something in Derek's stomach. This was like talking to Cellena but different. He didn't care that he was an angel. He hadn't even brought it up once. Throughout the day, Derek been fighting to breathe, and now he got it. All that he needed was to be choked in the good way.

"I say what's on my mind," Derek said, "and I said it. You're hot. You should try it sometime."

"I couldn't. I'm so afraid about people hating me, I tend to keel over at the slightest inconvenience."

Derek understood. He felt like he knew someone like that from his past. "Well, I don't hate you. In fact, I especially like you right now. You better keep that up by being cute."

"I-I'm not—"

"Don't try denying it. Are you blind?"

"But I'm not. I've let myself go these past few years. I've gained weight and my nose is too big."

"I'm not hearing anything that'll make me *not* want to make out with you. Try again."

Oliver moaned and used both arms to shield himself from the truth. "Please, stop. You're embarrassing me."

"It's how I show my love. I like to tease." He grinned. "Do you?" he asked.

"Do I what?"

"Wanna make out?"

Oliver sucked in his grey lips. "Well." He gulped. "That, uh…"

"We don't have to."

Grasping on a lifeline, Oliver's ears shot up to hear every word.

"Yeah, we don't have to." Derek stretched out his legs, knowing he wouldn't be getting anything tonight. "You're probably the type to take me out on a nice, candle-lit date before we have any fun."

"Would you not like that?"

"I feel like I've never gone on a proper date before."

"Well, I can always be your first." Oliver smiled at the naive thought. Then, when he played it back in his mind, he hid his red face in his hands. "I'm—forget I said that. I didn't mean it that way."

"Wait, what was that now?" Derek tried to pry away his hands. "I'm gonna be your first, huh? First in what?"

"Nothing."

"*Nothing*? I'm your mate, ain't I? What other firsts can I take away from you?"

Oliver squealed and tipped over, curling up and kicking his legs.

And Derek had no choice but to annihilate him with tickles.

12

Kevin

He was running before he found his feet.

"Come on—!" Maïmoú coughed. She was still visible to him but struggling. She yanked his arm to move him faster.

But he faltered. Alarm bells were ringing up and down the hall. Electricity was sparking from the ceiling. Maïmoú had destroyed not only his door but the whole wall, which was made of solid metal, with her head.

She lugged Kevin over the debris and out of the room he'd been quarantined in for weeks.

"Where're we going?" He tripped over his own feet. "Maïmoú, the sedatives haven't worn off yet. What're you doing?"

"They *sedated* you?" She snarled. Her teeth were animalistic, but not like a crossbreed's. Hers were larger, sharper. "I'm gonna *kill* them."

It was weird, escaping for your life, knowing that every officer in this building had weapons able to kill you, with nobody actually chasing you. The alarm sounded like something from Morgan's basement, but nothing was being said. It was blaring for Kevin to stop breaking the law.

He held his stomach as he kept with Maïmoú's pace. He didn't want to do this, but he didn't want to disobey. He didn't want to get hurt, but he didn't want to hurt others. He didn't want to be ostracized. He didn't want to be here. He wanted to leave.

He wanted to be with his loved ones.

A door somewhere down the hall opened up. Two men yelled for him to stop.

"Kevin!" Maïmoú grabbed him by the sleeve and forced him to keep with her. "Come on!"

But he couldn't. They were at a dead end. There were no stairs, only the elevators you needed a keycard to access. And the guards were coming in closer, closer. A gun was cocked and aimed.

Maïmoú cursed and waved her hand at the inbound officers.

A sudden force of wind shot through the hallway, and the guards running towards them were thrown into the wall. Their bodies made imprints in the metal as they hit and collapsed.

Kevin covered his mouth. "Maïmoú."

Maïmoú wasn't looking at him, instead diverting her energy into opening the elevator. Using both hands, she ripped open the double doors and gained them entry. She shoved Kevin inside and stumbled in afterwards.

Kevin, shaking, went to the elevator keypad. He didn't know what was up and what was down. Should they go to the foyer? The bottom floor? That would've been a parking garage, right? Or a shelter?

He picked at his thumbs. Time was running out. All of those guards, they'd only been following orders.

Maïmoú hovered her hand over the broken doors and shut them upon her will, but the force shuddered the tiny room and knocked her off her feet. Kevin moved just in time to catch her and fall to the floor with her.

The ground rumbled. The room lurched down, hopping his knees.

"No." Maïmoú banged on the floor. "Up, up."

But slowly, they descended. With each floor they passed, Kevin watched the door, expecting a platoon of guards to come storming in. Each floor sentenced him to a graver death.

Maïmoú turned away from Kevin and coughed up more blackness. "I would've...would've flown you out the windows—teleported you—but I didn't wanna risk dropping you. I have just enough strength to stay visible right now. Kevin, click the...the top button. The foyer."

"Are you alright?" he interrupted. "Honestly. I need to know."

She wiped her lips. "Head feels broken."

"...Mine, too."

She burped on a laugh. "Not the same. Have you ever woken up with a migraine? Multiply it by a plane of existence you can't mentally comprehend, then by a hundred. Perks of being a Deity. You feel pain nobody else can." She groaned. "God, I sound like a kid I used to know. Forget I said that. I'll be fine."

"Why're you doing this for me?"

"Because you're my dad."

That memory he'd dreamed up warmed his heart with color. "Were you serious? That man, he was me from a past life?"

She nodded. "You and Derek are my everything. I'm not losing you again."

But you're overworking yourself to death."

"I have to. The damn world's falling apart, and if I don't work faster, it's gonna crack..." She trailed off. "Don't worry about it. Kevin, the foyer."

But he *would* worry. She was dying because of him. Who wouldn't worry about a child hurting themselves? "What's going to crack? Do you mean the Muralha?"

She glared up at him, and he let her go.

"The Muralha's been falling apart for years, Maïmoú. There's nothing you can do to fix it. Not even the Líders can fix it."

She tried standing up on her own. Kevin hovered his hands over her. "It's not gonna fall," she mumbled to herself. "I won't let it."

Kevin didn't know the beginnings and ends of what being a Deity meant. He saw Maïmoú and all the work she was putting into "saving" them, but it was destroying herself in the process, and for what? To save them from what?

She dug her bare hands into the side of the elevator. Her nails left claw marks down the metal as she focused on the floor. "I...will not...let it fall. I...will not...fail."

Kevin watched her intently. "Maïmoú," he said, "are you...keeping the Muralha from *falling*?"

She cleared her throat of darkness. The beeping went faster and faster, floor by floor.

"Maïmoú."

"As long as I concentrate on holding it up," she said quickly, "it'll be fine for, like, another month."

"*What*?"

"And if I get you out soon enough—"

"Wait, you're holding up the Muralha? All by yourself? *Mentally*? Now? How? Why's it falling?"

"I can handle it. I may be dying—"

"You're *dying*?"

"No—ugh, listen to me!" She held Kevin by the shoulders. The lights above them flickered with impatience. "I'm *not* gonna die. I've been alive for 3,000 years and I *will* not die. I *will* keep the Muralha up and I *will* get you back to Derek and I *will* find my Shào even if I have to drain the oceans to see him! You can't keep him away from me!" she addressed the ceiling. "You hear that, you jerks? You can't keep me locked in here! I've found Shào! I know he's out there, and when I get out of here, I'm gonna—!"

The girl, who fought to keep positive for Kevin, who pushed herself too far to make sure he could escape safely, heaved over and emptied from her stomach about ten gallons of black sludge.

The elevator dropped a half-story. Metal rattled, grinding together. Flashing red lights warned them about a mistake Kevin couldn't fix, and the only other person who could stop it was dying at his feet.

Holding back tears, Kevin covered Maïmoú with his wings. "What's wrong?"

Maïmoú screamed as if her stomach was spilling out from her belly button. Her wailing was bestial. "STOP!" she screamed. "STOP, STOP, *STOP!*"

The elevator dropped quicker, metal grating against metal, a scream echoing down the pit.

Kevin grabbed Maïmoú's hand, hoping this wasn't the last time he got to see her. He still needed to know what she was about. He wanted to know her last name, if such a girl had been born—created—with one.

Shoving her arm through the door, Maïmoú stopped the elevator by herself and grounded them.

Kevin's head cracked on the wall as his body went skybound. The elevator landed hard at an odd angle. He smelled iron and smoke, the start of a fire that'd been doused out before erupting. The alarm was a broken cry before dying out on the intercom.

Maïmoú ripped her arm free and groaned.

"Maïmoú."

She rolled over and held her stomach.

Unforeseen tears welled up in his eyes. He walked over the broken floor to meet her. "Maïmoú, please. Stop doing this to yourself. I'll be okay. I'll serve out the time I have, whether that's forever or not. I'm sure my mom and dad will work something out for me. Just stop pushing yourself, *please.*"

She gurgled something into his chest.

"Huh?"

The elevator doors opened.

"Don't...tell me...what to do," she whispered, and disappeared, taking her darkness with her.

Alone, Kevin held himself until his head cleared. The adrenaline was mixing with the sedatives, leaving him feeling sick and stationary. He needed to crawl out of the broken elevator to escape, but he didn't know how.

But he had to, despite it all.

He followed the hall's dim lights. This floor was the exact opposite of his floor. It didn't pretend to look nice. It was moldy, the scent of rust clinging to the machinery chugging in the walls. There was green growing in the cracks and rusted pipes snaking along the ceiling: a waterlogged hospital left to decay.

There was no way Maïmoú was holding up the whole Muralha, right? It was hundreds of stories tall, stretching around the whole city. She said she was a Deity, whatever that meant, but she was just one little girl.

How strong was she, if she could do such a thing for days, *years*?

What were her true powers, if she were at her full potential?

He came across a few rooms. They looked recently abandoned, filled with IVs that dangled to the cracked tiles. The operating tables looked normal, but some of them had handcuffs fastened to the frames.

Directions were etched into the wall. Some of them made sense, like the ones that pointed him to the elevators and laundry rooms. Some wanted to send him to *WHALES*, *SHARKS*, and *FISH*. He didn't know what those words meant. He only needed the ground level. The way home. He couldn't dawdle or ask questions. For Maïmoú's sake, to keep her away.

One hall led him down the deepest and farthest, and when he thought about backtracking to find another way out, he came across a heavy metal door with a crank-like handle. It was the largest, most accessible door that he'd passed, hiding the most important room. Or the way out.

It was cracked ajar. Kevin struggled through the fissure.

The room was circular. And blue. Bluer than the juiciest blueberry in summer. In the center was a tank full of water stretching from floor to ceiling, about twenty feet in circumference. In the corners of the room were machines and filters bubbling with liquid. The water sparkled in the limited light, casting shadows across the floor.

He walked up to the tank. It continued through the floor and branched out like tree roots. He pressed his cheek against the glass to see more.

Something floated past him, and he looked up into the blurred lights, blinded.

It was a person. A girl his age, swimming with her clothes on. She stayed as still as the water, staring at him like she'd caught him where he shouldn't be.

Kevin's wings dropped. The water made her dark skin appear cobalt and freckles shine turquoise. Her long, black hair floated around her round face like it was intentionally framing it. She was beautiful.

And dying. She was underwater. She was in the water and she was drowning and he *had* to save her. Bubbles weren't leaving her lips.

He pressed his hands to the tank. A coolness froze his fingers to the glass. "Are you okay?"

The girl rippled the water with her thick, finned tail, keeping her centered. He'd never seen someone like this before. Her freckles didn't *look* blue, they *were* blue. She had cuts on the sides of her neck. An injury?

Another figure swam up to her in the tank. A big girl, with hair and skin as white as ice. Cupping her hand so Kevin wouldn't hear, she whispered secrets to her friend. Her eyes never left Kevin's.

Kevin, amazed, stepped back to see these girls more properly. They didn't *need* to breathe. No, they did, but they were breathing in the water. He watched their chests fill and collapse.

The dark-haired girl swam up to Kevin. She brought her hands up to the glass, meeting his. Her fingers were webbed, with thin pieces of skin connecting them together.

Even though a few inches of glass separated them, it was as if this girl was living in a completely other world to him. Maybe she was like Maïmoú in that way, a fantasy God talked about in fairy tales and nursery rhymes, with powers nobody in Raeleen could understand.

"Who are you?" he asked her.

Her mouth moved. He didn't expect to hear anything, but through the water and glass, he heard the word, *"Viper."*

"Viper?"

She nodded, then pointed at him. "Who are you?"

"Oh. Kevin," he said.

"*See*?" the white-haired girl asked. Her breed was also a mystery. She didn't have a finned tail like Viper had, but a scaly, pointed one as white as her. Her eyes were this pale pink, too. She was albino. "Keep an eye on him," she warned Viper. "I've heard all about him from Pippa. Awfully strange things have been happening to him topside."

Viper looked away from her friend, clearly ignoring her but not being rude about it. "This's Tokala, my friend."

"It's nice to meet you," he said. "I'm sorry for staring. I've never met anyone like you before."

"Me neither." Viper looked him over, making him feel hot, and turned to show him a fin on her back. It looked like a palm leaf. She wiggled it. "Those are called wings, right?"

He touched behind him, to his wings. "Oh, yeah. I'm an osprey, a bird," he clarified. "What're you?"

"Tokala's an alligator. I'm..." She frowned. "They don't know. They're still trying to understand it."

"Can I ask you why you're here? Do you need help?"

"I don't think so. We're swimming."

"And you breathe underwater?"

She nodded, like it was that easy to explain. Some breeds *did* have stronger lungs than others, and he flew. Why not open doors to newer, cooler, prettier breeds?

He nixed that last part, as it embarrassed him too much. "Why're you down here? I've never heard of your breeds before."

"That's because we're not allowed to leave."

A door clicked open.

Kevin's wings puffed out. Right. His escape. The whole reason he was down here.

He bowed to Viper and Tokala and ran behind a tank for safety, pushing down his wings so he wouldn't be seen. They seemed to understand—as soon as the door clicked closed, they swam away.

Two pairs of boots walked into the dark room. Kevin held his breath as if he'd gone underwater with Viper to hide.

"I still don't understand why you care for a baby who doesn't even know who you are. It's not like it cares for you."

Zantl.

"I try to be kind to every child who lives down here."

Marcos. Kevin was tempted to go to him for help, but he stayed hidden. His programming would've turned him in the second he got caught.

"I don't see why. It's not like any of them down here *like* you." Zantl rounded the tank. Marcos was holding a baby that looked like Viper, with the same slits in its neck and tail. He climbed up a ladder attached to the tank and carefully dropped her in.

Kevin watched, stunned, as the baby gulped in mouthfuls of water to acclimate itself. Kicking its little feet, it swam a bit before diving deep into the tank.

"I try my best to be approachable," Marcos said. "I don't know what I'm doing wrong."

Zantl held the back of their head and started pacing in circles. "You're different, so that automatically means people hate you. You should stop caring about what they say. Become indifferent. Soon, you'll find out how little people actually care about you, and you'll be ready to live only for yourself."

"That's a really negative way of living, Zantl. Is that how you feel about the world?"

"It's the most practical."

"Zantl—" Marcos touched something in his ear. "What is that?"

"Huh?"

"Is there an alarm going out right now?"

"I dunno." Zantl, moving quicker than Kevin had anticipated, jumped onto a railing in the room and started walking atop it. Without any time to hide, Kevin backed up and clipped a piece of metal that echoed his movements.

Their eyes met. Zantl lowered their lax arms. "Oh, fuck," they whispered, and touched something on their wrist. They held it up to their mouth. "Mom!" they screamed. "Mom, the Harrow kid's in the fallout shelter! W4, west wing!"

"No!" Kevin got up using his wings. He met eyes with Marcos in pleading desperation. "Don't do this!"

"Yes, he's here. Why the *fuck*"—Zantl opened a hidden panel connected to the wall and pressed its button—"would I lie about this?"

Sirens from upstairs rang out just as loudly down here. Red lights flashed. Shadows danced across the tanks and filters.

The door Kevin had come in from creaked open, and three armed guards tackled him to the ground.

"No!"

"No, you idiots, don't hurt—!"

It felt like being hit by a truck. An "all-over sensation" that numbed his torso and arms. They tackled him. Something cracked in his jaw and his wing bent due to someone sitting on it. His head was thrumming like a lute.

"Get off of him!" Marcos commanded. "Get off—you're on his wings! Get off!"

Kevin struggled to breathe. A guard's knee was digging between his shoulder blades.

Zantl squeezed Marcos' shoulder for protection. Their yellow eyes wavered over Kevin's body. "What the *fuck* was he doing down here? I thought you were supposed to watch him."

"Zantl, please," Marcos begged. "They won't listen to me. Tell them to stop."

Zantl grabbed the nearest guard and punched them in the head. "Off! Now!" They kicked another in the rear. "God, do you have any idea what she'll do to us if she finds out you hurt him?"

Kevin sat up and checked himself for injury. He was hurt but mostly confused.

He looked up at Zantl. The dim lights were flickering with feelings. He waited for Maïmoú's return.

But this was from Zantl. Things like this happened around them, things even Morgan couldn't understand. The public knew about it but didn't know why, because how could they? Only a handful of people, according to Maïmoú, had ever witnessed entities like this.

"Kevin."

He held his heart. That voice, echoing through his mind...

The door behind them opened. "What the *fuck* is going on?"

Nadia and Mikhail entered with an entourage of guards at their side. Nadia started ordering those around her to move, separate. Mikhail went for their only child.

"What the *fuck* happened?" Zantl asked them. "He was sup- posed to be *contained*."

"We just received word that the door...exploded? Zantl—"

"I told you to keep him away from—*no*!" Their mother was trying to touch them. They shook both of them off. "I told you, he can't be touched. Why is he still here? Get him away from us."

"Because you said he was special like you," their mother said. "We wanted to test him as we do you."

"He doesn't *need* to be tested, he *needs* to get away from me!" Zantl started for the door. "I can't be near him. She'll kill all of us when she finds out—nope. Not doing this. Not in- volved."

But they were. If they and Kevin were the same, that meant that all their special powers, all the strange occurrences that happened around them, they weren't from magic. Well, maybe they were, but it went by a different name, and came from a dif- ferent source.

Kevin pushed himself up with his wings. "You're just like me," he asked Zantl, "aren't you?"

Zantl looked back at Kevin, fear freezing them at the thought of being related to such a power.

Someone picked him up by the scruff of his collar. Mikhail, who needed a cane to walk, was strong. "Okay," he said, "come now. Let's get you back in a cell so we can find out just what's going on with you."

"What's happening to you?" Nadia asked Zantl. "Tell us. We've kept on your side for years, we've never pressed you because you told us not to."

"Mom, now is *not* the time."

"*Why*? Why is it never the time? What's happening to you and our world?"

"You wouldn't understand. This isn't about you. Life revolves around Deities and their messy, fucked up lives that we're forced to witness."

"I know, so let us help you," their mother said. "Please, honey, that's all we want to do. Let us find a way to help. This connection you share hurts you, doesn't it?"

"Stop it!" Zantl covered their furry ears. "I don't want your help! You're gonna get killed, all of you!"

Mikhail held up his wrist to the door.

It didn't open.

He tried again and again. "Uh, hello?" he asked.

"But we want to see you protected!" Nadia said. "How can we do that as your parents if you don't talk to us?"

"Because I don't *want* to be your kid!" Zantl screamed. "I just want to be left *alone!*"

A bulb exploded above Kevin's head. He felt glass land on him and instincts took hold. He ripped his hand away from Mikhail and shook out his body of danger.

His foot slipped. Dripping water from the pipes above had made a sizable puddle on the ground, and he flipped and landed hard on his head.

He tasted iron, head pounding. He touched the back of his skull. His fingers came back red.

Zantl stopped arguing with their mother. Marcos gasped at the sight of pain. Nadia, Mikhail, and their guards didn't even notice the fall until they followed Zantl's paralyzed gaze.

"Ow," Kevin moaned. With the drugs still in his system, the sight of losing a little bit of blood had made him lightheaded. He closed his eyes and covered most of his face to control himself in front of strangers.

A droplet hit his face. Touching it, he pulled back to see that darkness Maïmoú puked up. It shimmered with distant sky dots.

Above him, crouched on a water heater, appeared his alleged daughter. She was seizing like an animal in need to tear everything apart. Her teeth were bared. A dribble of darkness was leaking out of her mouth as she hunted those before her.

Zantl backed up into Viper's tank. Unathi," they whispered to themselves. "U-Unathi, save me."

"What's happening?" Nadia asked her child. "What do you see?"

Marcos looked between all of them. "Who is that?" he asked them. "Who's that girl?"

"What girl?"

"Maïmoú." Kevin grabbed the closest part of her he could, which was her ankle. "M-Maïmoú, calm down. I'm okay."

She didn't even look at him. She moved her head like a dog ready to bite whoever dared to move first.

He got up, got in her line of sight. "Maïmoú, look. I'm fine. It was an accident. Everything's okay."

Zantl ran to the nearest door. They banged their wrist into the crack to get it to open. "Let me out!" they screamed. "Unathi, save me! She's here! She—*Unathi!*"

Something, or someone, came to heed their desperate call. They appeared how Maïmoú did, glitching out of thin air. They kept their back to Kevin, obscuring their face, as they scooped Zantl up like they were a child. They were impossibly tall and beautifully poised, with jet-black hair cascading down their back, wearing a white dress that hugged their curvy body.

Maïmoú screamed. Rage and anger Kevin could *feel* concentrated in the room. The walls bent inwards. A pipe burst. Growling through pure animalistic synapses, she jumped over Kevin and ran towards the mysterious person.

Without looking back, the person teleported away, taking Zantl with them.

Maïmoú missed them by a hair. She skidded into the wall and screeched with frustration at a lost kill. She hammered her head against the floor, screaming incoherently. Those who couldn't see her listened for her movements. Kevin and Marcos watched her as one watched a car accident.

Kevin tried to move. He tried to speak out, defend, calm things down, but he couldn't breathe. Or he was breathing too much, hyperventilating to the point of passing out. What'd just happened? What was wrong with her?

Mikhail was the first to move. Whether to find out where his child went or locate the source of the noise, he made a move too close to Maïmoú.

She moved too fast, blinking in and out of existence. One arm struck Mikhail in the chest, and his body was thrown into the wall.

His neck snapped. Eyes rolled back. His body fell and crumpled to the floor. He didn't move again.

Nadia covered her mouth. Marcos tried for Zantl, but they were still gone, taken away by some unforeseen entity.

Deity.

Kevin, again, awaited for Maïmoú to explain herself and what'd just happened.

But she, again, disappeared.

13
Nikki

The fire escape saved Nikki's life. Right before falling off the roof, she grabbed hold of the railing and righted herself only to inhale smoke.

Black smoke rolled out of the doors and windows of the coffeehouse. The initial blast had left the place intact, but it'd been strong enough to bounce Nikki into midair. Who knew if more were on the way, or what'd caused it in the first place.

Nikki coughed as she hauled herself back through the hallway window. The smoke didn't smell like a wood fire, it was more mechanical. She rubbed her watering eyes. "Vanna!" she called out.

She bumped into a body. Vanna was halfway out of bed, breathing like he'd just run the mile.

"Vanna, come on, we need to get outside."

"I-I—I—" He held his head and rocked. His fingernails dug into his orange hair.

"Vanna." She took a knee. "Hey—"

She pulled back, blinked. The hand reaching out to him wasn't hers. This one was lighter, with thicker hair on her forearms.

Lí. Her dream. That boy she'd become and the boy she'd met. That blond-haired girl. The explosion.

She rubbed her hands until they went back to normal. No way was this happening right now. She was awake, this was real. Dreams needed to stay oceans away from her reality, whatever "oceans" were.

Vanna looked up at her with bloodshot eyes. "Nikki?"

She grounded herself by breathing in the heavy air. "You're okay, you're fine," she told both herself and Vanna. "You're not hurt, yeah?"

"They're gonna—Mom and Momma, they're gonna get found out—they—" He sucked in air he couldn't keep in. "I can't do this."

She shook the nonsense out of him. "Yes, you can. Look at me. You're not hurt. You can walk. You wanna find them, yeah?"

"But we're gonna get in trouble. That explosion was the loudest they've had."

She wrapped a supportive arm around her cousin, and through determined optimism she herself didn't believe in, she got Vanna into the hall and down the stairs.

She couldn't breathe. Black smoke was trailing around the tables and into the living room, ballooning on the ceiling and around the lights. It originated from the kitchen.

Del stood in the middle of the floor. Thick soot clung to her emotionless face as she readied a new fire extinguisher against the flames.

"Mom!" Vanna ran into her for a hug. She gave him a sloppy, one-armed hug in return.

"Del, what's going on?" Nikki said.

"Stove broke," she told them.

"The *stove*? But the entire house shook. It was like—"

"*Maïmoú had attacked the house,*" she thought but stopped herself because that sounded crazy. What kind of name was Maïmoú?

Del started opening windows for the smoke to escape. "Outside. Vanna, go."

Trained to abide by his mother's word, Vanna did as told and ran.

"Del, what's going on?" Nikki asked. "Let me help."

"We have it under control." She shooed her out like a stray cat.

"Del!"

But she ran back inside.

The Guard arrived thirty minutes later and tried to find the source of the smoke for another fifty. They walked the perimeter, flipped over the basement, and checked the alleys, but they ended up scratching their heads and searching other houses for the cause.

Nikki and Vanna were waiting across the street underneath a tram stop awning. Vanna was rocking back and forth for some amount of comfort. He hadn't blinked in minutes. He got like this sometimes when life became too much. Uncontrolled variables left him mute and catatonic, and Nikki understood. People handled stress differently, and all she could do was be there for him when he was ready to talk.

Though right now, she didn't think she was in the right mindset to help anyone.

She rubbed her hands together. She always, *always* knew when she dreamed. Sleeping without locks had hardened her into becoming more aware. She had to be ready to flee or fight at a moment's notice.

But she'd *felt* Shào's touch. His tiny hand and birthmark under the eye, his undercut, his smile, she knew it all, and she knew the boy she had turned into, too. She didn't know him well due to how quickly she was in and out of his mind, but she had the basics memorized:

His name was Lí, with an accent over the "i." He liked spending his free time watching baseball games and cooking something called *tsuivan*. He hated public speaking. He loved a man named Tai. The dream which had taken seconds to create expanded into a blurry life of some "human" who spent his time with...

Shào didn't look like any crossbreed she knew, more like a distant cousin of something that once was, a dream-like version of an original.

Casting off their encounter as a dream felt foolish. Even though Nikki couldn't presently see them, Lí and Shào had either existed once before or were currently somewhere over the Muralha.

Same with Maïmoú. She rubbed her neck, remembering how that little girl had tried ending her life for just being near Shào.

An hour and a half after the explosion, Morgan waved off the Guard with a grinning face charred black. Her hair was sticking out unevenly around her white ears. She smelled like an evening barbecue.

Upon seeing her, Vanna sighed in relief and ran across the street to hug her. She returned the affection with a fake smile.

"So, what do you say?" one guard asked Morgan. "What happened here?"

"Well, this's a shop, yeah? Shops burn down all the time."

"It's the middle of the night."

"And we start brewing early. We're known for that, you know, not for fiery explosions. See, we were trying out a new batch of cupcakes and it backfired terribly. Anyway, I think we should get everyone inside. Del, dear, help bring the little ones inside."

The guards took to their earpieces for guidance, but most of them departed the crazed city block, too tired to deal with Morgan. Some loitered behind, keeping watch on the coffeehouse. Morgan grinned at them as she hustled her family inside.

When the door shut, she pointed Del and Vanna to the windows, and the three of them began detangling the shutters.

Nikki hid her hands in her hoodie. "This wasn't from a stove fire."

She'd said it at the adults, but Vanna took the blame. He moved around the tables, avoiding her and his quiet parents, and disappeared upstairs, his scarf covering his mouth.

"Boy, I hope he's alright," Morgan said. "Poor kid. We should bake him something."

"This wasn't from a stove fire," Nikki repeated, now directly at Morgan, "so what happened?"

Morgan gave her a fake smile and wiped away the bad air. "I think it's time everyone went to bed. We've had a long day and it's time for—"

Nikki started for the kitchen. Morgan placed a hand on her. "It's time for bed," she repeated.

Nikki shoved her back and eyed the people she thought she trusted. She'd been trying so hard with them for years. It'd been easy with Shào. For an anxiety-ridden moment, she wished Shào was here instead of her family.

"Upstairs. Now," Morgan said, and barred Nikki from continuing her investigations.

Glaring each of them down, Nikki forwent another fight and stormed into the living room. Vanna was going to tell her jack all about this, the adults in her life sucked. The government hated her, her parents were unavailable. Some floating kid wanted to know everything about her but currently only lived in her dreams. It felt fitting for someone as unlucky as her—her last saving grace was likely imaginary.

Ignoring all of them, Nikki flopped onto the sofa and buried herself in throw pillows. She fell asleep holding her wrists, wondering if another dream scenario would end up killing her.

Back before her world imploded, back when her family was still together, she, Derek, Kevin, and Vanna would have sleepovers in the same bedroom. Tangled up in each other's arms and legs and wings and tails, falling off the bed and drooling on the floor. Drinks would be involved, usually supplied by Derek, and everyone but Nikki would wake up drunk and groggy, eager for a free breakfast at Morgan's.

When Nikki awoke that morning, she was alone, but those memories flooded her mind. She smelled the bubbling scent of cooked bacon and coffee brewing. She must've been totally out of it. The coffeehouse had just opened for business, and she was halfway on the floor.

She checked the clock ticking above the radio. Mornings were always busy at Morgan's. She needed every family member on call for the morning elderly rush.

Caving with a growling stomach, Nikki fixed her bedhead the best she could and faced the world.

Morgan's Delicate Sweets and Drinks was filled to bursting with hungry patrons. Older couples shared baskets of cookies and flirtatious one-liners. Students chatted with their friends over coffee. Two cats made jokes as they waited for their orders to be placed, and Morgan was working the cash register alone. Vanna and her mother were the servers for the morning while someone—Del and most likely her father—worked in the kitchen that'd been mysteriously fixed.

Nikki inched out, watching her family act like nothing was wrong. Not only were they pretending like Derek and Kevin weren't gone, now their last child hadn't almost fallen to their death. Like their workplace and family store hadn't almost exploded. It had *exploded*, just with no fire she could originate.

She looked into the back. Maybe she should've helped with the morning rush. Don on an apron and aid in the family business. Kevin sometimes picked up shifts during the busy season. Even Derek had closed once or twice. They were good at it, they were people-pleasers. Nikki wasn't. Nikki hadn't been born with the innate understanding of people, despite her best efforts.

They all had trouble expressing love, but Nikki should've known better when she'd lashed out at Vanna. She should've *been* better, acting as the sister who kept the family together.

She ducked into a booth close to the windows and people-watched. Her mother faked a customer service voice with every table she waited. Vanna barely made conversation with anyone. Her father called out orders from the serving hatch as Del sweated away over everyone's order. Nikki wanted to order but knew she didn't deserve food yet. She tortured herself with eyeing the best platters that came out.

The front bell chimed. A guard came in. She was a poodle, with curly, strawberry blond hair that made her look young. She looked new—right out of the academy—but proudly entered an establishment that'd discriminate against her. Everyone knew Morgan's hatred of the Guard was deep and personal.

Nikki doubletook her. Her nose, freckled and small, had been recently broken.

She gasped. She was the guard Derek had kicked a rock at.

Vanna, who was coming out to deliver an order, caught sight of the girl from across the coffeehouse.

The girl, once she found him, smiled and waved.

Blushing a deep, noticeable red, Vanna shuffled his menus and took off into the kitchen. This caused the girl to lower her hand, ears and tail down.

Since when did he get embarrassed by kids their age? Did he know her? It seemed that way. If a normal girl or boy looked at him that way, he would've scoffed. He didn't entertain the idea of people.

Morgan, after finishing taking an order, doubletook the guard standing daftly in her bakery and stormed over to her. Nikki tensed, ready to break up a fight.

Taking her by the tie, Morgan dragged the girl down to eye level and whispered something into her ear. Nikki strained to read their lips.

The girl shook her head. "No," she whispered. "Well, uh, not really. It's kinda all fallen to shit."

"I have a limited time for vagueness, Pippa," Morgan said. "Do we need to go outside?"

"No. I'm saying that everything's okay. He got put down to W4 for the time being. Did you hear about the Líder?"

"Of course I did, I heard about it the hour it happened. So he's good?"

"He's good."

Catching the attention of a nosy table, Morgan dragged the guard back to the door. "Can't you read the atmosphere of my dear bakery?" she said for all to hear. "I'll have to ask you to take your business elsewhere!"

"Morg—"

"And stay out!" She pushed her out of the door and let it close with the softest of bell jingles.

Nikki watched Morgan stare the girl down until she crossed the road, then sighed and ran back into the kitchens to continue on with the day.

Something in Nikki's stomach churned. Dubious talk. Secrets and hiding. She hated when they acted like this, and when their hatred for a breed permeated through their kindness. It was difficult, calling out a family member for actions that hurt you. If she did say something, she imagined the entire family coming apart or worse, her being thrown out. It was a stretch, but it was something that haunted her mind, her being unwanted.

Vanna crossed the serving hatch. His ears were pulled back as he looked between the kitchen back door and Morgan at the register.

He slyly took off his apron, hung it up, and disappeared outside by the dumpsters.

Nikki, giving it a beat of thought, slipped out the front door just as quickly and rounded the coffeehouse on tiptoes.

It was drizzling, enhancing that putrid dumpster smell. Puddles became land mines to blow her cover. For what, and whom, she didn't know. With all this secret-keeping, she didn't know what to expect.

"You could've called."

Nikki stopped creeping. She hid behind the dumpster right outside the back steps. The kitchen door closed slowly so it wouldn't make a sound.

"I didn't want one of your moms picking up," said that guard, Pippa. "They don't want me calling, anyway. They don't want my calls getting traced."

"We wouldn't have to talk about work. I just like hearing your voice."

"Aw, did you miss me that much?"

"You know I do."

Nikki dared a peep.

Pippa was standing on the ground, Vanna on the steps. From her low vantage point, she booped his nose. "Your family's so serious. It's cute."

Vanna turned away but didn't push her back.

"Hey." She waited until he looked back at her. "You okay? You didn't sound good on the phone last night."

"I still can't believe what Nikki said to me. She said I didn't love Derek and Kev as much as she did."

Nikki shut her eyes. Had she really said that?

"I'm sorry," Pippa said. "I'm sure she didn't mean it. She must be dealing with a lot right now. I can't imagine her not knowing what happened."

"He's okay, right?" Vanna asked.

"Yeah, yeah, all good. They put him on sedatives and he's been asleep for a few days, but he's good." She got closer to him. She touched the top of his hand, his wrist. She caressed his skin. "You good?"

"I did it again last night. I couldn't stop myself." His hand met hers. "I wish you could've been there. Sleeping's easier when you're next to me."

"I wish I was *always* there." She wrapped her arms around him for a warm embrace.

And Vanna reciprocated, melting into her touch.

Nikki's face went hot with second-hand embarrassment. This was *not* what she'd been expecting. What kind of relationship was this, and what were they alluding to? Him? Sedatives? The Líders? Her mind wandered.

"You're doing so well," Pippa whispered, petting him. "You're dealing with so much right now, and I'm so proud of you for sticking through it, no matter the challenge."

Vanna's tiny tail began wagging.

Pippa caught it and giggled. "Aw, are you excited?"

"I'm not," he so clearly lied.

"Oh, you're not?" Pippa leaned her face towards his. It took a second for Nikki to notice that Pippa had her lips on Vanna's cheek. She was *kissing* him.

Vanna closed his eyes, only opening them when Pippa pulled back. Their hands were on each other's petting one another to make the moment last.

Pippa booped her nose with his. "I love you," she said, quiet as night.

His response, just as quiet, washed away with the rain.

—————◇◇◇—————

Nikki wasn't unfamiliar with hiding in a dumpster, but it still sucked every time she found herself in one.

Her foot sank into something rotten. Around her, expired eggs and warm milk melted with the rain, creating a biohazard of trash. The coffeehouse had closed ten minutes ago, and she'd been waiting around this smelling garbage can for hours.

She'd spied on Vanna's and Pippa's conversation until they parted with a kiss and went back to their separate lives, Vanna to work, Pippa off doing whatever Guard task she was neglecting in favor of their date.

Nikki still couldn't wrap her head around it. Vanna was her best friend *and* cousin, how hadn't he told her that he had a secret lover? Surely he couldn't have told his parents, otherwise they would've prohibited him from speaking with her. But they seemed close.

And their conversations had been so cryptic. Who'd they been talking about, and what was so important about the Líder that Morgan would've known the hour it happened?

She racked her brain for clues as she hid in the smelliest place imaginable. Derek and Kevin? No, that would've been too cruel. The person they'd been talking about was in present tense.

Shào?

Lí?

Someone opened the kitchen door.

"I just don't understand why she isn't picking up," her mother said.

Nikki sucked in her lips, turning off her brain.

Her mother opened the other dumpster in the alleyway and took out the trash. "Do you think she's mad at us?"

"Likely," her father said from the kitchen. "*I* would be. She's smarter than us, Iysra. She's smart enough to pick up hints."

Nikki's ears were flicking every which way. Had her parents picked up a late-night shift? She hadn't heard them leave.

"Vanna said that the explosion nearly knocked her off the roof. I wanted to make sure she was okay, but she was giving death glares at everyone in the coffeehouse."

Nikki rubbed the creases in her brow.

Her mother sighed. "That explosion really got ahead of Morg. She's nervous. You don't see that often. Back in school, maybe."

"When she didn't know what the fuck she was doing."

"You think she's okay?" her mother asked, heading back up.

Her father closed the door behind them. "Are any of us?"

Nikki's heart was pounding so hard, she wondered if her parents had heard it. After ten minutes of silence, she crawled out of hiding, snuck up the concrete steps, and pressed her ear against the kitchen door. Machinery whirled into the night: a dishwasher, a coffee machine, but no voices.

She unlocked the door with her spare key and slipped inside.

In the kitchen, she found stoves, refrigerators, storage cabinets above and below her, and large sinks. Nothing about faulty appliances, and no fire damage other than the ceiling being a crispy black. Being that an explosion had almost knocked her off the roof, the kitchen looked too spotless. It had a certain non-biological smell to it, something less conventional than coffee beans and sugar. With her sensitive nose, she found salt-shakers and rusted pans, but nothing to raise suspicion.

She closed the fridge. What was she doing? This paranoia was eating her alive. She had to walk it off, concern herself with reality.

She walked over a change in the flooring. It went from tile to cement, her sole connecting with solid earth. Feeling particularly snoopy, Nikki flipped up the padding to reveal a block of concrete recessed into the floor. Someone had carved a handle into the block and drilled two hinges on the opposite side: a basement door.

Nikki bent down and lifted. The door weighed more than her punching bag at home, but she followed through with the motion and opened it. It jumped her tail when it crashed down on the other side.

Cold air huffed at her like an opened freezer. A metal ladder extended into darkness. Even with her enhanced eyesight, she couldn't see the bottom.

Her aunts, she wouldn't have put it past them to keep secrets from her.

Vanna, it made sense, given their tumultuous relationship.

Her *parents*, the ones who'd chosen and provided for her, *that* stung more than any wound she could give herself.

"Fuck all of you for whatever I find down here," she whispered to herself, and started her descent into Earth.

A whole half-minute passed as she climbed farther down. Her ears popped. The moonlight faded and the ladder turned cold in her hands. She cursed herself with each new rung.

When she hit the floor, she flipped on a dusty light switch and discovered her family's secret.

Their secret of dull cleaning supplies and decommissioned bagel carts. It was a ten-by-ten storage basement of food supplies and utensils—they didn't even have butter knives down here.

Nikki opened cardboard boxes to folded napkins and cans of coffee. She dragged around shelves and found nothing but rat droppings. And dirt. Thick, dark dirt that looked recently scrubbed down.

She knelt down and wiped a line of dirt off the wall. It was the soot that blackened the kitchen upstairs. Someone had missed cleaning it.

She yelped. A sharp, intense pain buried into the back of her knee. She immediately swatted it, fearing it to be a spider, but her leg buckled as if someone had kicked her from behind.

A small dart clattered to the floor. Mysterious, clear liquid dripped from the tip down her leg.

Her knees gave out, numbing from a quick-working sedative. She fought against it, but it worked into her brain like a scurrying bug in need to lay eggs. Her mouth felt stuffed with cotton balls. She couldn't keep her eyes open.

She caught sight of a thin line in the wall she'd mistaken for a tension crack. It parted like two sliding doors to the Asilo buildings.

Using her remaining strength, Nikki grasped for the ladder rung.

Her drugged hand slipped away along with her consciousness.

14

Derek

Being an angel had its perks. Glue some feathers to his ass and suddenly room and board were free. He was delivered three-course meals without lifting a wing and could drink as much alcohol as he could stomach.

The maids made him clothes, which he hated. They were so excited to show off their tailor-made, wing- and tail-accessible outfits, but they had so many frills. Ugly designs, luxury seams. When they offered to cut and style his hair, Derek was beginning to feel more like a doll and started declining their services. He couldn't knock them, the maids. It wasn't like they were acting of their own free will.

The royals didn't want Derek "wandering." He didn't think he was one to "wander," but when they'd found him lost in the dungeons, digging in closets he'd picked the locks to, Nero had scolded him.

"What's wrong?" Derek had asked. "I looked. There're no prisoners down here. Do you really keep people down here? Isn't that kind of ghoulish?"

"Not usually." He glanced around the darkness before escorting him back up. "The royals don't want you underground."

"How come?"

"We don't normally—how can I put this—stay underground too often."

"What, because of the literal Underground?" He'd remembered that from the king and queen. It was the place demons came from. "You know it's just a basement, right? And I thought that was a made-up, theoretical place. You mean it actually exists?"

"Of course it does. You're from the Heavens. Don't you believe in the opposite?"

To have an opposite opinion, Derek would've had to understand what it meant to *live* in the Heavens. To him, it sounded like a fantasy too good to be true. All the bad people go to one place, all the good go to the other, and never the two shall meet? That meant he should've been the pinnacle of good faith, but what did having faith mean? He was still lost on the concept of their God. Cellena had said you saw Him during pretty sunrises and happy moments. Derek had looked everywhere and couldn't find shit.

He didn't tell Nero this and only shrugged. "I guess," he'd said. "Hey, when you go to the Heavens, how do you walk on clouds?"

Nero hadn't a solid answer for him.

The "townspeople" supposedly wanted to meet Derek. Like, real bad. Like, some had tried breaking into the castle to see him. He hadn't heard about it until Nero told him. It was wild. These people hadn't even met him, yet they were risking their lives to see a feather.

They wanted to throw a party for him. The royals called it a "festival," but at this point, he'd take anything. He was itching to let loose and drop these expectations into the ocean. As long as he could drink, though that was called a "sin" if you drank it in large quantities. He forgot that every time he took a swig.

What he had with Oliver was definitely considered a "sin." Not only a demon, not only a boy. They'd *mated*, or Oliver had, and that was serious to him. He was shy and ticklish and easy to talk to. Derek *thought* he liked him, but if the king or queen found out, he'd be thrown into that dungeon. Or murdered. Or tossed into the sky to become a sky dot. Whatever they did for angelic punishment, he'd receive. Oliver had come back a few more times since that night Derek almost died by Shào's hands. It was the only time he could relax, and now his relaxation had to be done in secret.

He supposed church was important to the humans, so he kept his opinions about it to himself. He didn't understand why the book on how to be a good person had super thin pages, and he didn't like how loud the "church organ" was, but he liked the songs. Or hymns. But it was all negated by the fact that the "sermons" were three hours long and made him want to kill himself. He always drank before coming in.

He was able to empty out the church just by asking, so it was only him and the royal family inside with the pastor on Sundays. He sat next to Cellena for the most part, but he usually got bored and walked around, familiarizing himself with this tight space and making it feel less chest-tightening.

The art was pretty, and the windows with tiny people told stories that were probably in that book he wouldn't read. He noticed the people—mostly girls with big boobs—were like him, winged. He spotted a handful of demons being tortured beneath the angels' feet. The angels wore serene smiles as they ended their lives.

"Is it true you can't get tattoos?" he whispered to Cellena during a boring part of the sermon. "At all?"

"That's right."

"But the men in the royal line can?"

"Yes."

"And you can't..." He checked his hand. He'd written all the sins that affected him. "This marriage thing. Once you find someone you love and get "married" to, you can't get unmarried?"

"You can't get divorced, no."

"No jealousy?"

"No."

"No cursing?"

"No."

"No sex before marriage? No girls kissing girls? But *slaves* are okay?"

She winced at the truth. "We don't really follow those guidelines anymore, and gendered marriages really only apply to royal families to preserve the bloodlines."

"But that's not fair to *you*."

"Shh," Jabel said. He was sitting beside Cellena, pretending to ignore them but finding it hard not to butt his nose in. "You mustn't talk in church. It's rude."

"I'm trying to learn. You don't like these rules either, right?"

"I do what's expected of me. I am soon to be king, and as such, I need to hold myself to a higher standard. If you can't find yourself abiding by these rules, then...hide it. Mask the indulgences. Or. I don't know." He pressed his nosy nose into the book. "Listen to the sermon, Your Grace."

While Derek couldn't nail Jabel as any kind of rule breaker, he hadn't expected him to give such an understanding second option for those who couldn't fit into their societal boxes. He got behind that part of Jabel he likely hated about himself.

But that name still ticked him off. Call him anything you wanted, but that one, with unreasonably high expectations chained to it, was off limits. "I told you, that's not my name."

"And I told you to be quiet. You aren't allowed to talk in church."

"What, is *that* another sin? I don't have enough room on my hand."

The pastor, who'd been going on and on about a tree, stopped his sermon, making everyone look at him. "Is everything alright, Your Grace?"

Derek, getting heated, got up and started for the door. "I need more ink for my pen, or quill, or—" He tossed the pen/quill into a fountain. "I need some air."

Fresh air was nice.

Fresh air for six hours was even nicer.

He found a library balcony too small for an actual person to stand on and perfect for him to perch on. He'd burgled a bottle of vodka from one of the kitchens and nestled into the view stretching out before him. He saw over the forest trees and the tips of the "snow-covered" mountains. Some of the trees were turning orange and yellow for some reason. He didn't know why, but he liked how it made the world smell like wet leaves and frosty air. Autumn here smelled like Oliver.

He bit his lower lip, playing with the ends of his hair. According to the humans, the demons were lustful, hateful, evil creatures who wanted humanity to perish, but he didn't agree. Call him stupid, but he didn't think a group of special people should've been murdered en masse for existing near other people.

He took another swig of the stuff that burned and kept him warm. He wanted to masturbate, to think of Oliver and lose himself in his own feelings, something no one seemed to care about other than Cellena and Oliver.

And Maïmoú. He kept that secret to himself. He didn't even know what that was, hearing a little girl in his head. If he started telling people that he was hearing voices, they'd think he'd been possessed.

He kicked his feet over the ledge, looking up into the sky. The deep blue was dying itself red. The sky dots were coming out, lighting up the Moon that was still with the Sun. He could taste the cold slowly freezing the world. He wondered how cold it got here. Earlier that morning, he could see his breath.

He could've just left, right? Fly into that cold sky and find a new world to live in. He wasn't tethered to humanity. He didn't have to be their angel. Maybe he'd fly until he got bored and plant roots wherever he landed. Maybe with Oliver, really fuck things over for everyone.

Someone came up to the window and unlocked it.

He turned and found Runa with a handful of books under her arm. "Oh, hey," he said.

"Good evening. I heard you disappeared from church. The royals have been looking for you."

"I should be able to go wherever I like, right? I'm their 'angel'." He air-quoted himself and took another sip. "Do you go to church?"

She smiled. "I don't."

"Do you hate small spaces, too? I mean, if it's so important to them, why make the building so small?"

"I don't wish to offend you with my beliefs."

"Do it. You won't, by the way, unless you force me to do things I don't wanna do."

She smiled. "My reasons are a little...uncouth to share publicly."

"What, do you not believe it or something, because..."

He stopped talking. Runa looked genuinely afraid that she'd been caught in some type of word trickery.

"Because I don't care," Derek responded quickly, "at all. Honestly."

"That's good to hear." She cleared her throat. "Maybe another time. Since I have you here, I actually wanted to ask you something."

"Shoot."

"I wanted to ask you if the royal family has gone into detail about the origins of our world."

He thought about it. "Like, a little, I guess. Something about dragons carving up the world, humans coming from the Heavens, demons coming from the Underground."

"Is that all?"

He gave her his full attention. "Is there more?"

She leaned her hip on the windowsill. "Our modern history starts 275 years ago, however, some of our pottery and ancient scrolls go beyond 500 years. We have theories about the dragons carving out the world, but—" She rolled her eyes. "We don't have any evidence of draconian activity, only stories and paintings done by famous men. I believe there's something *more* out there and want so dearly to look into it, but the royal family don't like their ideals being contested."

"I noticed."

"If—since—you're from the Heavens, I wanted to know if you knew anything about this." From one of her books, she pulled out a photo that looked thousands of years old. It was preserved in some type of lamination and secured onto a piece of wood. Runa was very careful while touching it.

She looked behind her before offering it to Derek. "This is one of the oldest documents we own. We haven't been able to identify the type of paper nor how to replicate it. The king asks that we don't look into such matters. They want to believe in our God, that He has all the answers we'll ever need, but I'm not satisfied by that."

Derek looked closer at the photo. It was smudged and curling like it'd been damaged by water, but he could make out a person on it. It looked like they were behind a golden sunrise wearing a white dress.

He leaned in, idolizing it like a true sunrise. "Looks like a person."

"A person?" Runa looked over his shoulder. "I don't see it, but I trust your judgement." She took in a big inhale. "Derek, may I invite you to a gathering?"

"A gathering?"

"It's an event I host the first Sunday of every month for those who want to learn more about the world."

"Like a party?" Derek tossed his empty bottle over his shoulder. "*Yes*. I've been *dying* for a party. What're we celebrating?"

"A comet is to fly over our skies tonight. It happens once a year, but I find it quite exciting to watch it with Nero and a few of our friends. If you'd like to come, you're more than welcome to."

"What's a comet?"

Her face brightened with the chance to teach. "It's an enormous piece of fiery rock that flies through the sky. Many people call them a falling star, and some of them are really meteors, but if it lands on Earth, it's called a meteoroid. I study the sky in my free time. I love it. If you'd like to learn more, I can teach you. Forgive me, I'm a bit of a chatterbox when it comes to things I enjoy."

"I can tell." He leaned backwards, looking upside down at this mysterious sky. "Yeah, I'll go," he said. "Should be fun."

Sneaking out of the castle was easier when his own knight was the one breaking him out. It didn't take much convincing when Derek had told him about his conversation with Runa.

Nero licked his lips. "What else did she tell you?" he asked.

"That she didn't like the church. Don't freak, I won't tell our God or whatever. I'm pretty sure they wouldn't care, either."

It looked like a comet was lodged in Nero's throat. "Okay. Let us go, then. I don't want His Majesty seeing us out so late."

"Trouble maker," Derek teased.

He didn't disagree.

Using a chamberstick as their light, Derek and Nero traversed down the halls and climbed down staircases to reach the bottom floors. It got super cold at night now—Derek needed to wear a jacket his maids had made for him. Nero advised him to wear a hat. Derek would've rather died.

They snuck out through the kitchen doors and made their way into the field Derek had first met Oliver. He liked how bright the stars were near the ocean, massive clusters of rainbow bulbs in the sky.

"What is it about the church that Runa hates?" Derek asked, because he was getting too curious not to know. "Is it her comet stuff?"

Nero walked slower. His hands were in fists by his side. "Do you know about us?"

"Huh? What, just because I'm a magical angel person, suddenly I have all the answers?"

"No, I...our relationship could be considered frowned upon, given how she grew up."

Derek made a face. Nero had been so strong, mentally and physically. This was the first time he saw him crack.

"She'd asked me to ask you if you knew, and that if you did, that you keep it between us. She doesn't want it coming out and risking either of our lives."

"What do you mean?"

Nero fiddled with the ring on his ring finger. "When Runa was born," he said, "she was born a man. Is all."

Derek cocked his head.

"A-and if you already knew that, I ask that you refrain from judging her too harshly. She's a very kind and smart woman, and I know she doesn't go to church because of this, but I cannot live in good conscience knowing you're casting judgements on us."

Derek was still trying to understand half of what Nero was spewing out, but the part Nero concerned himself with was obvious. "Nero, I don't care."

"Excuse me?"

"I. Don't. Care. Stuff like gender and love don't bother me nearly as much as it does you humans. I'm in the same boat she is. Well, sort of." This was so much easier with Oliver. He rushed through it. "Things like this used to be so simple to get my head around, but humankind makes it so complicated. I feel like, back where I'm from, love was just love. If this coming out will get you in hot water, my lips are sealed, but it literally does not matter to me who you choose to love."

An invisible weight lifted off of Nero's shoulders. "Okay. Thank you. We were so uneasy, we'd started plotting out ways of leaving the county and joining up with the demons if you didn't approve of us."

"Ugh," Derek groaned. Yet another responsibility to the growing list: people's relationships. "That's another thing. You seem to care about demonkind."

"I do."

"Then why'd you become a knight? Aren't knights supposed to support the king and all of his decisions? He's been murdering demons for generations and you decided that this was the best job to apply for?"

He defended, "I wanted to see change in the royal family. I see it in Jabel and Cellena."

"It's still shitty. You could've become a historian or horse herder or something. Have you ever killed—?"

"Of course not. There weren't..." He grew somber. "There weren't any left to kill. Look, this isn't where I wanted the conversation to go. I've tried teaching their Highnesses all that I can about fairness and justice. I take pride in that, but I know my work is rooted in unfair acts."

"Killings," Derek reworded.

"I was going to say murders, but I didn't want to sound so hurtful."

"It's the truth."

They walked over a short hill. In the distance was a small cluster of lights illuminating the valley.

"I want to see change in the world," Nero said. "I try to live by my truths and not change for the king. I've done many things for demonkind."

"It's fine," Derek said. "You know, I'm sort of a hypocrite, being that I haven't left yet. I like Cellena too much. Hopefully, with your help, we can change some shit in this backwards country and make Cellena king."

"Jabel will become king," Nero reminded him. "He's the male heir."

"Then we'll change that next. She deserves it."

"She's ten."

"Not for long."

Out in the valley was a group of maids huddled around a strange contraption. It stood on three legs and lifted a three-foot-long cylinder to the sky, a rocket ready to explore the sky dots.

Upon seeing them, Runa ran over. "Good evening! Hello! I'm so glad you made it. Are you warm enough? Did anyone see you?"

"Yeah," Derek said, "and no."

"We're okay," Nero said, and nodded to Runa in a way that meant more.

Runa exhaled, and a little smile tickled her lips. "Oh, good. Thank you for understanding, Derek. That relieves most of my anxieties."

"No problem," he said. He knew his acceptance meant more to this couple than he could've imagined, but it felt gross. It was like pardoning someone who was afraid of breathing.

"Well then!" Runa clapped her hands. "Come, come. The telescope should be ready. You can be the first one to use it, okay? Do you know how to use it? Do you need help?"

"You're being overbearing," Nero reminded her, and the crowd of maids giggled.

One person didn't laugh. She was sitting on the grass, squatting in a heavy skirt and wearing a knitted hat that couldn't cover her ears.

"Ah!" Derek said, and pointed at Holly. "You."

Runa and Nero acknowledged Holly with a bow. "Derek, this's Holly. She's one of the breeds that live with demonkind. I hope it's alright that she's here."

"Yeah, I know her," Derek said, but didn't rat her out for saving him from Shào. "We've met once."

Holly flicked one of her ears, then fell back on her butt and hid her chin in her knees, watching Derek intently.

"She's a very timid girl, but she loves being with us when we stargaze," Runa explained. "She's a very active listener, even though she has trouble speaking. Now! If the clouds part a *bit* more, we'll be able to see the Moon very soon. The comet will pass right behind it."

One maid at the telescope raised her hand. "I think I found it."

Runa helped position Derek behind the telescope. "Now, don't touch it. Crouch down and peer—Yes, just like that."

The eyepiece showed him nothing but darkness. Guessing he was doing something wrong, he pulled away to find the magic.

Holly was staring down the scope and blurring his vision.

"Holly, dear," Runa said. "I know you're excited, but it's Derek's turn right now."

"It's cool," Derek said, and tried again.

Darkness.

Darkness.

A blur of stars.

Then, bright white.

It wasn't the Moon. It looked like a painting, with holes here and there and blotches of grey marking the shadowy parts. Surely, it wasn't the Moon. The Moon didn't have this much detail to it.

"You see it, don't you?" Runa asked.

"What is it?"

"The Moon."

Derek looked through the telescope, then at the Moon, then at Holly, then back at the Moon. "You're kidding."

"I know, isn't it amazing? Why they don't teach this in schools is beyond me. I nearly cried when I first saw it."

"You *did* cry," Nero reminded her, "for several minutes, in my arms."

"Wait until I tell you my theory about the people living there."

The crowd laughed.

"No, I swear I've seen them! They're not only outcrops of rock, they're houses! There've been people living on the Moon for years and we don't even know about it! Here, Derek, let me show you, it's fascinating!"

Derek backed up around Holly's tail. "Uh, give me a second."

"Are you alright?"

Feeling out of sorts, Derek took one more look at the iffy Moon before going back to the castle.

"Where are you going?"

"Gotta clear my head," he said, and walked all the way around the other side of the castle.

What else floated above them? Where were the Heavens in all this, and the Underground, did that even exist? How many twinkling sky dots were actually moons and planets and "stars" in disguise? What types of people lived on the Moon? They said angels came from the clouds, but why stop there? So much more supposedly existed beyond.

He honestly should've ignored the humans and put caution tape around the thickest evergreen bases that read: *STOP FIGHTING, STOP LOOKING UP AT THE SKY, AND INVENT ELECTRICITY ALREADY.*

"What a good plan," they'd say.

"I know," Derek would reply, and with demons and humans carousing together, they'd find a way to bring him back home where life made sense.

He walked himself into the garden area built up against the castle. He easily flew over the iron-wrought gate keeping out trespassers. The hedges were tall, creating winding paths for people to wander. Flowers bloomed around water fountains. Statues of angels had their wings spread, but they were built into the ground.

He glanced over to the forest not far away. He wasn't bound to the humans, so why was he so hesitant on leaving?

One of the gates opened, and Holly, being as graceful as a blind cat, tripped over the iron gating and fell into a bush.

"Above," Derek cursed, and helped her upright. "Why do you keep following me around? You're gonna get yourself killed."

She shook out her hair of leaves and spat one out of her mouth. She then looked at him with those wide eyes of hers, as if she was waiting for Derek to tell her something important.

"Holly."

For the first time that week, Derek grinned at the chance to be himself.

Two feet from his right burst a plume of darkness, and Oliver, floating in midair, arrived.

"There you are," Derek said.

"Good evening," Oliver said.

"Wow, no stutter? You're getting better at this."

"I'm trying. Are you okay? Is she alright?"

"Yeah. She can't seem to let go of me." He said this as Holly was currently wrapping her arms around him. When Oliver fell to Earth, she let go in exchange for him.

Oliver petted her head. "Uh, Holly, would you be able to leave us alone for a few minutes? I need to speak with him privately."

Holly wagged her tail, waiting for her brain to process that request, before she let go and jogged behind one of the hedges she'd fallen into. Her tall ears poked out from above the leaves as she hid.

"She's so silly," Derek said.

"Very." Oliver crossed his ankles. "So," he said, "you're okay?"

"Yeah, but you should know that already, being all in-tune with my emotions. Here to see me?"

"Mm."

"*Mm*? Hey, are you supposed to be here? You know the humans are down that way."

"I know. I just wanted to see you."

Derek's feathers puffed out. He tried calming them down by brushing them. "Really? Just me?"

He nodded, and one of the black blobs that appeared when he travelled bubbled around his head. He flicked it away.

"How do you do that?" Derek asked. "The jumping and dis-appearing thing. I don't think I've ever asked. Seems cool."

"It's a power we can do with our dark matter."

"Dark matter?"

He created a liquidy mass of that dark stuff into his hand. He played with it like balls before making it disappear. "It's a power we can use."

"That's cool. Hey."

"Yes?"

"Do you ever wake up one day and realize that you might not know anything about the world or where you are in it, but you want to hang out with your special person and forget about life's problems?"

Like always, Oliver took his time before answering. His pointed ears fell as he worked it out in his head. "Sometimes. I try to do better than I did yesterday, improving little by little until I feel good about being alive."

"I don't think I've ever done that before."

Oliver's fingers found his tail. "Derek, if this becomes too much for you, or if you need some place to go, you can find us in the forest. I mean, if you want to. You don't have to, come with us, I mean. I know how protective the humans are of you, and I know you're friends with the princess, but we live north of the castle. Uhm, this way." He used his dark arms to lead Derek's way. They blended in with the forest backdrop.

"I don't think the royals would like that," Derek said. "They hate you."

"I know. I shouldn't even be here, but one of my friends heard they're bringing you to Devnya Town."

"Devnya Town?"

"It's a port town a few miles north. We've been taking notes on how the people have been acting there. I wanted to warn you to be careful. Humankind is desperate to see you."

"I can probably handle it," Derek guessed.

Holly sneezed a leaf off her nose.

"So, is she like a cat?" Derek asked.

"I believe so, yes. A wild cat." Oliver went to say more, but a human's boisterous laughter startled him. He jumped back into the air.

"You should get going before one of them notices I've been gone for too long," Derek said.

"You're right. It was nice seeing you again. I've really been enjoying our nightly meetings."

Derek felt himself on the edge of a cliff. His feet were teetering, tempting him to take the dive. "Well, if you want to do more than meet up during the night, I'm down."

Oliver covered his heart, then mouth, but he couldn't cover the emotions in his face. His tail couldn't curl any more around his leg, but he tried. Good for him for trying to act like he hadn't wanted to hear that all week.

"I don't give a damn about what the humans think," Derek stated outright, "I want to be closer to you. I want to get to know you. I want you."

"I..." Oliver swallowed loudly. "I don't know what to say."

"Are you into it, first off? I know that you're mated with me and it's a sin or whatever to be like this, but I don't care."

Oliver looked off to the side, considering the offer, the consequences of a kiss.

It's what *Derek* wanted. Screw the king and everything he wanted. Oliver said he had no control over what ailment the humans were dealing with. Why bother with something that wasn't his business?

This business, however...

"C'mere." Derek beckoned for him.

He stepped up closer. "A-are you sure?"

"Are you?" Derek readied his lips. Not only a nervous wreck, but a boy his type with an actual stutter he couldn't control. He'd put that to the test.

Taking him by the horns, Derek pulled him in and claimed his lips as his.

They were soft. Big and grey and cool and wet, like he'd just licked them beforehand. He was so nervous, barely putting any pressure on Derek's face. Derek made up for it. He trailed his tongue over Oliver's lower lip until he opened his mouth for him. Then Derek couldn't think. He was an animal indulging in primal desire. Oliver's hands, touching him in ways he'd been craving for weeks. It warmed him up by scent and touch. He needed this connection with a person. He needed to feel loved and be held and touched because his brain, finally switching off, was telling him that these feelings were good.

Humankind called what he loved a sin.

Derek called it being alive.

Oliver pulled back. His pointed ears went up.

Derek heard it too late, or Oliver's hearing was just that in-tune at sensing trouble.

The castle had many balconies. Some small enough for birds like him to perch, some large enough to hold gatherings. The one overlooking the gardens was open, the curtains fluttering in the breeze.

The queen, holding up her dress, was leaning over the railing, watching her angel and her most hated rival share an intimate moment.

Before any of them could defend themselves, the queen clutched her cross and ran back into the castle.

15

Kevin

He'd been walking for a while, though he couldn't tell for how long. Time affected you differently in dreams like this.

At least he was himself this time, and more aware of said self than the previous dream. He hadn't switched bodies or was living a new life. He was, for now, Kevin Harrow.

He hadn't dreamt up a warm, cozy cottage he'd once shared with Maïmoú. This place was a void, darkness in every direction, including the sky. There were no roads, no grass. Just darkness and ruins jutting out from the ground, like this world was half-finished. Columns were cracked and tilted, holding up nothing. Arches crumbled above his head. It had an empty, confined feeling to it. Derek would've hated it here. He hated feeling trapped.

He couldn't remember what'd happened before he'd passed out. He remembered Maïmoú trying to break him out, the Líder's death, that girl. She'd said her name was Viper. Kevin didn't know why, but out of everything that'd happened to him that day, she came through the clearest.

How foolish a lovesick heart was. One look from the prettiest girl he'd seen and all his thoughts drew back to her. Had he introduced himself? Had he been kind enough to ask her about her own internment? Had he been smart enough not to? She lived underwater. He hadn't known that was possible.

He turned the corner to one of the ruins. He'd been snaking through them, trying to find a clue to jumpstart a new dream, though this didn't feel like an ordinary dream. It felt like a vision, something implanted.

A yellow and white figure emerged between two pillars, Kevin's only reference point.

Maïmoú had her head down, her long hair cascading over her shoulders. She had her arms out like she was holding something back. Her nails were digging into nothing.

"Maïmoú, can you hear me?" Kevin called out.

She grunted. The world thumped like a heartbeat. Her eyes, once light and blue, were darker in color, dilated to fit the scenery.

He knelt beside her. "Can you hear me?"

Maïmoú looked up through her bangs.

"What're you doing?"

"...Keeping up the Muralha."

He looked around them. "With your mind?"

She said nothing.

"But you're bleeding again, or breaking. Whatever this is." He wiped some of the darkness from her nose. "You have to stop."

"Can't. Every minute I stop"—her foot slipped—"the more it breaks."

"But it's killing you."

"Nothing can kill me." Her eyes unfocused as her head sagged. Somewhere off in this void, Kevin heard the sound of underwater cracking.

He couldn't do this. He couldn't let her kill herself trying to do the impossible. "Maïmoú, stop it."

She coughed up blackness.

"Don't ignore me."

She wiped her lips as she kept giving him, a person she liked, a person who liked her, the cold shoulder.

"*Maïmoú.*"

"I can't let you die again—"

"Oh, knock it off!" He raised his voice and kept it strong. "Please! You have to talk to me. You have to tell me what's going on. Don't leave me in the dark. What can I do to help?"

"You can't."

"Stop *talking* to me like that. You're getting hurt and hurting others and I don't know what to do. I'm important to you, aren't I? Important people talk to their people. Am I wrong?"

After thinking about it for a heartbeat, the tenseness in Maïmoú's arms relaxed. She dropped her arms and fell into his.

Her body was so limp, like she'd fallen asleep. He checked to make sure, but she was just collecting herself. She painfully sat back against a pillar. Kevin did the same.

She refused to look at him.

"You killed Mikhail," he said. "You killed one of the Líders."

"He hurt you."

"No, he didn't. I tripped."

"But they chose to keep you there, and then you got hurt. People who hurt me deserve to get hurt."

Kevin felt something die inside of him. "Maïmoú."

"I need to save you," she reiterated.

"From the Muralha breaking, I know, but don't you know how badly I feel, knowing you're hurting yourself for my sake?"

She nodded. "I messed up."

"How?"

"I can't tell you."

"Why not?"

"Because you'll think I'm a monster."

"That's impossible. You're a kid." He touched her knee. "Tell me how you messed up."

Maïmoú looked off to the side again. He went to bring her back when the scene around them shifted. The ruins dissolved into sand. A wind he couldn't feel took them away. Through the darkness, that day came back to them like a developing photograph.

It'd been gloomy. The sky had been this shade of grey that dyed the town colorless. He remembered it well. It was going to rain soon.

Kevin looked down. He was on a telephone wire with Maïmoú, watching a street corner like ghostly crows. Kevin recognized the street as the one they took to pick Nikki up from school. It was the quickest way to Morgan's.

Beneath him, Past Derek, arms and wings spread, danced over a canal's steep ledge. His shirt caught on the waves of summer heat as he moved closer to the edge. Every time his foot crossed over the chasm or he tried taking flight, Kevin's heart—back then and now—thumped a little louder.

"Careful," Past Nikki had said. They'd all been together, that day. They'd always been. "You're going to fall."

"I won't fall."

"Derek, listen to her," Past Kevin had begged.

"Why?" Past Derek asked. "Let me live."

Kevin's heart hurt again. Every move his past self was making was only a reminder of how the day would turn out. He should've been nicer to him. He should've been walking with him, together.

Maïmoú reached her hand around Derek, like she could keep him from doing what he did next.

At the end of the street loitered three guards of varying ages and ranks. They had their hands latched on to their belts, watching Derek.

Kevin's stomach twisted with guilt. He couldn't watch.

Past Derek sized each of them up. "Look at them. Busy protecting us like the good pups they are. They're such pieces of shit. Hey!" he called out to them. "Why you on the street corner? Y'all look mighty suspicious doing nothing. I see you staring at us, you're not slick."

"He was always so confrontational with the Guard," he told Maïmoú.

"I was there," Maïmoú said, "right there next to you. I *never* left your sides. I was too weak to make myself visible, but I was trying so *hard*." She reached out again. "I could've saved you."

"Derek, no." Past Nikki grabbed Past Derek's shirt. "Why've you been acting like this? We're not doing this again. Come on."

Kevin knew why. It was all because of Morgan, all of her secrets about the Guard and Asilo that Derek and Kevin had just learned about from her. It made Derek think he was above the law, that they were somehow special. If only Nikki had known.

"But look at them," Past Derek said. "They're *dying* to be fucked with. They'd probably like it. I heard guards are into some freaky stuff."

Past Kevin placed himself between them. "Derek, please. Let's go home."

Beaten by Kevin's urgency, Past Derek withdrew. He kicked asphalt down the road with a childish pout, the guards returned to their own alley, and Nikki held Kevin's hand for safety. Everything returned to normal.

Then a piece of asphalt cracked off Derek's shoe and rocketed to his left.

The guard buckled into her comrades. A steady flow of blood was dripping down her nose as the rock ricocheted through the alley.

Past Derek, as a defense mechanism, started chuckling, undermining the severity of his criminal offense. Nikki's grip whitened Kevin's fingertips. Kevin's heart stopped beating.

Kevin, the real Kevin, almost closed his eyes so he didn't have to see what happened next.

"Derek, say you're sorry," Past Nikki whispered.

Past Derek didn't move.

"Derek, say sorry," Past Kevin begged. "Please!"

"He didn't mean it!" Past Nikki shouted, trying to save them all. "It was an accident! Derek, *say* something, For All That's Above."

Past Derek took a step back, waiting for gunshots or batons or worse. Then, without taking his eyes off the alley, he took Past Kevin's hand and escaped with him down the street, leaving Nikki to fend off the agitated guards by herself.

Kevin and Maïmoú glitched and followed his past self.

"You were talking to me now," Kevin said, remembering how confused he'd been. She'd been a little voice calling to him, distorted and broken. It must've taken so much of her energy back then.

"I was trying to lead you to safety," Maïmoú said. "I knew you were gonna get shot and I needed...I *needed* to..."

"But I hadn't heard you up until that point. Were you always there?"

Her fingernails dug into her forearms as she watched. "Always."

One guard, following their military training, fired at two escaping criminals. It hadn't been their fault—they were just doing their jobs.

What their jobs hadn't prepared them for was Maïmoú. When they fired at Derek's and Kevin's backs, Maïmoú, using her building strength, took their bullet and backfired it straight into their own head.

Kevin turned away before their body hit the ground. When it'd happened in real time, he'd been too stunned to process it. It'd all come out when he'd entered the Asilo. Honestly, he didn't know if he'd yet processed it. It felt like something that'd always stay with him, a scar in his brain. "That was you, wasn't it? You took their own bullet and killed them."

"Better them than you."

He couldn't disagree. "You told us to go to the Muralha at that point."

"And you did."

And they did. Flying wasn't new to them, but flying over the tops of houses and then meadows while being hunted down, not knowing if Nikki was safe or not, *that* feeling had been new. The adrenaline of knowing you were doing something wrong and continuing on with it, becoming more of a criminal when that wasn't your intention. He hadn't stopped shivering.

"We're screwed," Past Derek had said, breaking their flight of silence.

"But you hear her, too, right?" Past Kevin asked. "This voice."

"Yeah. Unfortunately." He laughed. "I think we're going crazy."

"Why did you run?" Past Kevin asked. It was a question he still had to this day. "Why didn't you stay back and explain yourself?"

"The voice said to run," was all Past Derek said.

Kevin tried not looking at Maïmoú when he said that.

The forest beneath them faded into mist. Their world expanded into lengths Kevin never knew it could reach. The rain was heavier up here, drenching Raeleen in a grey paste.

Continual thunder and mist roared behind the Barreira. Here, connected to the Muralha, it had mass. The material Kevin had once thought was solid shifted like sparkling sludge through an unbreakable glass. He hadn't learned about this in school. In hindsight, Kevin wondered if only he and Derek could see it for what it truly was.

Past Derek jumped over a large crack in the wall. Small pieces of it crumbled off the edge into the forest.

"Careful," Past Kevin said. "Oh, Derek, we shouldn't have come here. We're not allowed to be here."

Derek leaned back as he traced the curve of the Barreira. "The voice said to come here, and *you* followed me."

"The voice is probably our conscience telling us this's a bad idea. We shouldn't have left Nikki. We shouldn't have done this."

"You don't have to tell me that."

They paused. Maïmoú had been speaking to them.

"I was trying so hard to talk to you," Maïmoú said as she watched. "You were so close, *so close* to being free. I needed to put everything I had into getting to you."

"Your voice had sounded so broken," Kevin said.

"Their voice's broken," Past Derek commented on. "Do you need help, Little Voice?"

"Don't talk to it like that," Past Kevin warned.

"Why not? We should know who this person is. Can you speak up, Little Voice? Oh. Listen to that. It knows our names." The color drained from his face. "How does it know our names?"

A blasting air raid siren punctured through the fog. The alarm extended hundreds of miles out. It sounded like a dying elk.

Past Kevin covered his ears. "Is this because of us? Is this because we ran?"

"I don't know! Voice, talk to us! What's going on?"

Maïmoú hit her thigh. "Get over the Barreira!" Watching her failures must've been torturous for her.

The invisible voice took Past Kevin's hand and pulled him towards the start of the Barreira. Towards the end of the world.

"Wait," Past Kevin said. "We can't go that way. We'll die."

"You *won't*," Maïmoú said to their past selves. She was talking through gritted teeth. "Just trust me."

The invisible Maïmoú kept pulling. He'd felt her strength gaining in power.

He tried prying her off. "No! Derek, help me!"

"Help with what?" He kicked at where he thought the invisible person stood, but when nothing hit, he wrapped his arms around Kevin and pulled the other way. "Fuck off!"

Derek's wing hit something—her—and freed Kevin, but only for a moment. She'd grabbed his heel and threw him to the ground.

Past Kevin pulled down his skirt. "Why're you doing this!?"

"Because I'm trying to save you!" Maïmoú shouted at them. "Why didn't you listen to me? I could've saved you! I could've saved both of you!"

"Fuck!" Derek tried repositioning his arms around Kevin and pulled.

"Please, I don't want to become a sky dot!" Past Kevin yelled.

"You won't!" Maïmoú began getting up, and Kevin took her hand to calm her down. He could feel every tendon in her wrist tightening.

Derek kept kicking and screaming at nothing while Kevin's foot phased through the Barreira. The air outside either burned or froze. He couldn't remember. "I thought you were on our side! If you wanted us dead, you should've let the Guard shoot us!"

Freeing one of his legs, Derek kicked something physical, and the person—Maïmoú—had screamed so loud in their ears, it muted the sirens.

Past Kevin's hand fell into a crevasse. The rock scratched his palm, but he held on. He had to. He hadn't wanted to die so young.

The grip on his ankle dropped.

Momentarily free, he scrambled to his hands and knees and went to grab Derek.

Derek, starstruck, was thrown into the Barreira. He dropped for only a moment before his body disappeared through the haze, never to be seen again.

The memory of that night hardened from seeing it from a different angle. Kevin's head had iced over. Two seconds. Three seconds. Four. His words failed him. His feet were locked.

He'd screamed through the siren. It hadn't happened. It couldn't have. He'd tried convincing himself that this was all a nightmare and that Derek was still with him. Back at the house. With Mom and Dad and Nikki. Back to normal in their normal lives. It was just as likely.

Nobody could survive through the Barreira.

The scene glitched. They were back in the ruins. Maïmoú's leg was hopping against the column, her arms crossed.

"Why'd you do it?" Kevin asked. "Why'd you throw him off?"

"I didn't *throw* him," she said. "Look, the Muralha's going to fall any day now. I don't know when or where—I think it'll be the north, that's where the most cracks are—but it'll happen soon and I'm doing my best to keep it up but I—I needed you two out. That's always been my mission since the two of you were born. You can't stay here."

"But why—"

"I talked to Derek, by the way," she added, "on the other side. He's okay."

His jaw slipped. He'd been replaying everything Maïmoú had been telling him, but that last minor tidbit scrambled everything from his mind into his own empty Void.

"You don't look too surprised," Maïmoú said. "I expected tears."

He shook his head, his empty, empty head. "You know it? For sure?"

"Yes."

"Where is he?"

"I have no idea, but he's safe." She smiled. "You put too much faith in me. What if I was lying to you?"

He didn't know what to say to that. "I hope you wouldn't."

"Then you don't know me at all." She smiled, but he knew it wasn't as heartfelt as he wished it to be.

He touched her hopping knee. "Then tell me who you are so I can put proper faith in you."

She closed her eyes, coming to terms with herself. "I'm a Deity."

"And what is that, exactly?"

"We're creatures of the Earth, dominant, nearly-immortal beings connected to a Domain."

"What's a Domain?"

She got better comfortable sitting on nothing. "It's what we're in control of, what we've been assigned to. Mine was a group of beings called humans, which I thought had died out up until a few years ago. That's why I look the way that I do. If a Deity's Domain is strong and thriving, then so are we. If they're dying or become extinct, we're done, erased."

"You die?"

"Worse. Their numbers used to be in the billions, my humans. Billions of intelligent, creative beings discovering new ways to live longer. Sure, a lot of them were warmongers and sexist and specist, but I tried keeping them in line. I was there through it all. But now, I don't think there's even a million of them left. It's like here with you crossbreeds. It's pathetic, and makes me pathetic as a result."

"But there're so many people that live in Raeleen," Kevin said. How could anything more than Raeleen exist? He couldn't fathom a million people, let alone billions.

She sighed. "There were pockets of centuries where it was *so* good. Hardly any famine and war, progress was limitless. Then, well..." She trailed away, and Kevin waited until she was ready.

"There was a boy," she said, "born around the same time I was. He was in charge of you crossbreeds, and I can't say he was weak because he wasn't, but he was...different from me. He was smarter, and more emotional. We didn't see eye-to-eye on anything and fought a ton. He took a backseat when it came to how he controlled his Domain that I never understood."

"Was it only you and him?" Kevin asked. "Was there a Deity for, say, bird crossbreeds, or was it just Shào in control of all of us?"

"Shào was in control of all of you. He's a crossbreed, too. But there're other Deities."

"Like the one I saw today," he said. "The one you tried attacking. Was their name Unathi?"

At the mention of their name, Maïmoú tightened her core.

"What do they control?" Kevin reworded.

"Death. Rebirth. The cycle of taking things away from us." She moved on. "There's a...water Deity, too. She's in charge of the weather, rivers, glaciers, stuff like that. *Sabah.*" She spat out her name like venom. "Then there's Tsvetan. He's this old guy who governs the soil. Any earthquake or volcano eruption you feel is his deal, though you don't get many where you're from. He's the weakest outta the bunch, no spine at all, easily manipulable."

Kevin didn't like how she knew that word. She was also so hung up on the idea of being "weak." It wasn't healthy.

She gave pause before speaking again. "There *are* two Others, technically, two who Sabah, Unathi, and Tsvetan had been friends with, but I never really met them."

"What do they govern?"

"Ataleah was in charge of animals, but she's been out of commission for two billion years. According to the Others, the animal population was so exhausted from mass extinctions one after the other, she keeled over like a motherless fawn. This was before my humans, by the way, so none of it was my fault."

Kevin hadn't said it was.

"So I never knew her. She's trapped in her own mind like this, waiting to wake up when her animals return to their former glory. Like that's ever gonna happen."

"And the other one?" Kevin asked, trying to keep up in her world. "Who's the last Deity?"

Maïmoú looked up to her sky. "Fate," she said. "That's his name, too. Nothing else. Never met him, either. Don't even know what he looks like. The Others don't talk about him, aside from cursing his name and his literal Domain. I don't even know if he actually exists."

"Are they like you?" he asked. "Are they...strong?"

"*I* was the strongest," she clarified, "but when I'm like this, we're probably...evenly matched."

"Were you friends? It sounds like you were close at one point, and you're all Deities. Did you talk?"

"We were...fine, I guess. We were like a family, but you know how families can be. We fought a lot."

The ground—darkness—simmered as she spoke. Grassy fields and animals he couldn't name were birthed from nothing and spread beneath them like a tapestry woven in time with her words.

Kevin backed up on his butt, feeling the grass curl around his fingers. Giant trees grew up and over them, the sky turning these brilliant shades of colors. Little animals swarmed the fields in packs like aimless chickens, but then he saw larger ones. *Massive* ones, ones that didn't even look like any animals he knew. He arched his neck as one slowly stomped his way. It shook the ground with every step. It had such a long neck. He couldn't understand why Maïmoú wasn't staring with him. She seemed bored with her history, or ashamed.

"Back before humans and crossbreeds," she explained, "those five other Deities—we called them the Others, Shào and me—lived together for billions of years. I don't know how to describe this, since your history only dates back 500 years, but during this time, animals evolved from little specks of dust in the water to massive, house-sized creatures. The grounds grew into new mountains, oceans, canyons."

Kevin watched the scenes develop around him. The ground, soft as sand, morphed into mountains. Grassy fields became vast deserts and rainforests. The animals changed, starting off small and evolving into newer, better, *stronger* creatures.

"Then Shào and I were born, and in a couple thousand years, we altered the course the Others had started for us."

A jumble of houses, once built from sand, quickly developed into wood, then concrete, then metal towns. Cities, *metropolises*, growing high into the skies with new technological advancements. Time flew by so fast, he couldn't take it all in.

"My," he awed. "And this happened because of you?"

"It happened because of *us*, of what my humans were able to achieve. Everything grew faster than the Others could process. They weren't prepared for us. Time works differently for us, you know."

He didn't but let her continue.

"A year to you could sometimes be a month for us, a *day*, if we're really spaced out. As we changed the world, the Others couldn't keep up with it. They hadn't experienced immense growth in such a short time before us.

"It wasn't like we could control it. Unlike with water or fate or animals, humans and crossbreeds were born to *make*, to create things with their own two hands. They learned how to make waterborne breathe outside of water. We created bombs and robots. We made Earth *ours*." She ran a hand through her long hair. A smile was creeping onto her face.

It was killed off by her next words. "The Others didn't see it like I did."

The cities she'd created crumbled away into darkness, leaving behind that hollow feeling. "They saw us as parasites. They didn't like us and always wanted us dead."

"*Were* we parasites?"

"*No*! That's the thing—that's the freaking thing! Beings *aren't* parasites. We're monkeys with above-average brain capability that Ataleah futzed around with to make cooler. We're *allowed* to be alive." She huffed. "I hate them. I wasn't born wrong. I was perfect the way I was."

If Kevin had been told all his life that his accomplishments were parasitic, he, too, would've been miffed. "So why're you hurting right now? Why're you in so much pain?"

"If anything in our Domains were to get hurt, we'd receive the damage. It's also a double-edged sword. If I were, say, happy, my humans would prosper for a few years. If I'm angry..." She shrugged. "Plague, war, anything that hurts the population. It's all tied back to us. They tried killing me and Shào and couldn't finish the job, so now we and our Domains are hanging on by a thread."

"Above, Maïmoú," Kevin said. "I'm sorry."

Maïmoú just shrugged, like these hundreds of years in captivity were only memories she could reminisce about and not the history of everything. Not just Raeleen, but, if he was to believe her, a world that embodied more. Bodies of water and cities and continents. That cottage Hassan had once lived in, it must've been beyond the Muralha. "I'm okay."

"But you're not. I know you're not."

Her eye twitched again. "You don't have to worry about me. I'll fix everything."

"But—"

"*Don't*, okay? Don't say I can't do what I know I can. I *will* fix this. I promise."

He looked up to the black sky. "Where are we exactly?"

"The inside of my head. We call it the Void. It's the place Deities go to heal. When I'm in here, I don't exist. I'm probably floating around the city like an aimless corpse right now, invisible. It takes a lot of energy to become visible since so much of my Domain has been destroyed. I don't like spending too much time here, though. It makes me feel powerless."

At least Kevin understood the feeling of being confined against your will. "Who's Shào?" he asked.

Maïmoú mentally prepared herself with a long inhale. "He was my best friend. We were the babies of the group, so we stuck together. We did everything together. We travelled the world, found hidden treasures only the two of us would ever know about. It was...nice...while it lasted."

"What happened to change that?"

She looked away again. She had a lot of trouble looking him in the eye when explaining her life. "I did something I don't necessarily *regret*, but it was something that messed the world over so hard, a meteorite would've been better for it."

She hung her head. Her bangs fell into her lap. "Shào was dying, and I was trying to save him. When I did, I made a mistake and hurt the world, and then he didn't want anything to do with me. He called me a monster for saving him. He said he'd wanted to die all because of what I did. After that, he got messed up in the head. He fought with me. He ruined cities. *Countries*. He was insane. Then he did something that was...unforgivable."

The look in her eyes turned savage. "Unlike *him*, I didn't kill the innocent, I killed people who *deserved* to die. I wasn't a murderer who killed without reason. I never declared war on the only friend I had! I'm not the insane one here!"

Kevin touched her knee as one touched a rabid dog in need of compassion. "It's okay," he lied, because everything she was saying was definitely *not* okay. She'd saved one of her friends and the Others hated her for it? *Shào* was the murderer, she, an innocent bystander? He felt like he was missing key details that would've painted a better picture of her past.

She exhaled. It hit his cheek. "*He* messed everything up, not me. I know I'm not the most perfect soul in the timeline, but at least I tried to keep this world alive. I didn't give up like a coward and wanted to kill off my Domain because I was depressed.

I am, too, Shào!" she shouted above her. "We all are, you're not the only one dealing with the pain of being alive!"

Kevin cringed. However many years she'd been alive, no child deserved the pain she'd been harboring. It was too existential for her. "I-I believe you," he repeated, not necessarily agreeing with her but trying to get her to relax, "but who are you to me? That's the part I'm having trouble understanding. Why're you doing all of this for me, for Derek? You said we were your...parents?"

She nodded. He could feel her body calming down more. "Nearly each one of us has had a soulmate at one point. I think Fate gave us one to mellow us out. It's a being that will always love us, and who we'll always love. They're the only ones who can see us. They're our love."

"So I'm one," he said. "Derek's one. You have two?"

"Yeah. Lucky me."

"Is Zantl one?"

"Yeah. And Marcos, and a few others." Her face soured. "*Shào's* got one, and I should've killed them when I had the chance."

"What?"

"*Some* soulmates are good, Kevin. You and Derek are good. You've always been the good ones. The rest totally mess up their Deity. They change the opinions they've had for *centuries* and make them soft. Shào's soulmate..." She wrangled an invisible neck in front of her. "They warp their minds and make him...*stupid*. He gets so, *so* stupid around Lí, it's sick. He used to be smart, he used to know everything, from every single language to every single landmark, but then Lí came into his life and suddenly, Shào's a fool who'd do anything for him."

Kevin had trouble seeing that in a bad light. "But you said that a soulmate makes a Deity happy. Wouldn't it make you happy if Shào was—"

"No! I *hate* Shào now, and I hate what he's become. I hate all of the Others and none of them deserve a soulmate like I do."

She hugged her knees. "I do my best every day to be a stronger person than I was yesterday, and now a wall those *jerks* constructed to keep me in is falling apart, Derek's gone, Shào's gallivanting around with his soulmate that's been reincarnated as a thorn in my side, and you're in a 1950's asylum. Literally nothing about my life is going right."

"Who's Shào's soulmate—"

"And when I try to keep the wall up, something bad happens to you. Every time I try to save you, a little more of it chips away, and the leaders of this world won't do a damn thing about any of it. *Leader*," she corrected, remembering how she'd murdered the other.

Kevin pulled back his hair, trying to air out his brain. "The Muralha's here to keep you in?"

"Yes! It's so *stupid*! The Others must've been so scared about me saving the world that they murdered almost all my humans, then trapped me and you crossbreeds here 500 years ago, separating me from Shào *and* my humans. They took away everything that made me strong, everything I ever loved! It's all *gone!*"

The world splintered. A night sky opened above them, sprayed with sky dots, moons, and strange circles.

Like a scab spreading over a wound, the darkness healed itself and shrouded Kevin and Maïmoú back in their temporary bubble of nothingness.

Maïmoú held her eye socket as the world stitched itself back together. "I'm breaking," she conceded, "but I need to save you. You're all I have left, all that I can touch. Do you know how lonely it is not to be touched for years?"

"I'm sorry. Where're the other Deities? These 'Others'? Maybe we can ask them to let you out. Maybe they can help you."

She choked on a laugh. "Don't bother. I haven't seen those jerks in 500-some-odd years. They left me here to die. Unathi came only to save their soulmate from me, and they didn't even say hi."

"But they must've kept you alive for a reason."

"If a parent beat you your whole life and told you how much of a horrible monster you were, but didn't have the guts to kill you off, would you see them as a loving parent, that they secretly loved you this whole time?"

Kevin said nothing.

"They've wanted me dead from the moment I was bestowed these powers. They thought humans and crossbreeds were a plague. But they failed to kill me. They failed with Shào. You *cannot* kill something so desperate to live. Now, I need to push myself to get you out of this world they've imprisoned us in."

"How was Derek able to pass through the Barreira?"

"I don't know. Back in the day, we found out that soulmates react differently to our powers, so I thought you two wouldn't be affected by Barriers. Since I can't get out right now, I figured I could push you and Derek out so you could fly out of here. I tried talking to him—"

"Wait, so you threw him off without knowing if the Barreira would hurt him?"

Maïmoú's eye twitched. "I said—"

"You didn't know if he'd survive or not?"

"I—"

"What were you thinking?"

"I tried my best!"

Her shout hit Kevin's face in black splatters and heated breath. Once she realized who she'd yelled at, she sat back down and wiped off her lips.

"I'm sorry," Kevin said, knowing deep down that Maïmoú would never apologize first, if at all. "I appreciate you trying. But you know he's alive now, right?"

"Currently, yes."

"Okay."

"I'm trying my best," she said in a softer voice. "I hate you seeing me like this. I used to be so much stronger, so much better."

"Maïmoú, I believe you. You don't have to keep telling me that."

She gave him a look telling him that she had to. "If I don't see my humans again, I'm gonna go crazy. I wanna feel strong again. I wanna feel *whole* again."

Sitting up in the darkness, Kevin stretched out his arms and hugged her. That familial feeling of warmth rose in his chest.

"That dream I had, was it real?" he whispered. "Was that man really me?"

"Yeah. Hassan Kariam. That was, what, in the 1100s, so more than 1,500 years ago." She sighed blissfully. "The 1,100s were so nice, Kevin. You and Derek had found each other and took me in without a second thought, this strange girl with no place in the world. Eating meals around the dinner table, helping you with the harvest, napping on the floor mats..."

He nodded along with the memories. Even though it wasn't his life currently, he envisioned it perfectly. "He didn't really look like me, though."

"Believe me, as someone who will love you the most, your souls are indistinguishable." She touched his back. "I've missed this," she said, "a being's touch."

"500 years is a long time not to be hugged."

She held him tighter, almost hurting him, but he didn't mind it. He liked her hugs. It was like hugging a bear.

"You need to stay here, wherever 'here' is, alright?" he said. "You need to heal."

"I don't like being ordered around."

"Well, deal with it. I care about your wellbeing, so make me happy and focus on you, okay?"

197

Maïmoú's laughter sent him out of her Void. Whether she was laughing at him or at the prospect of finally, finally being saved from this mind prison, he didn't know.

But he'd make sure he'd do his best to help her, however he could.

16

Nikki

Nikki's brain lagged as she slowly willed herself awake. Spit glued her cheek to her pillow. Her headache was the worst she'd faced to date, like she'd gone to bed trying to drink Derek under the table. It took several long minutes before she gained back control over her own body.

She blinked tiredly, encouraging her senses to focus. The scent of this room, oil and metal. The sound, an engine room. The bed sheets, starchy.

It was an incredibly small room—she could probably lay flat on the metal floorboards and reach every concrete corner. There were two bunk beds built within the wall with little knick-knacks sitting on the shelves. Old books and baseballs, things from hers and Vanna's childhood.

Vanna sat on a bunk bed across from hers, beside that guard he'd been snogging behind the coffeehouse. They were both wearing matching pairs of olive-green coveralls, something Nikki had never seen in Vanna's closet. His homework surrounded them on the sheets as he studied them with his "friend."

"I don't see why you put so much care into schoolwork," Pippa said, twirling the ends of his hair between her fingers.

"It's my one thing, Pip. Let me do what I can."

"Oh, you can do *much* more than that, love," she teased, and his pointed nose burned red.

Pippa's floppy poodle ears sat upright in her curly hair, and she turned to Nikki.

Vanna, following her instincts, looked up and closed his math text. "Nikki."

Before he said another word, Nikki jumped him. She kicked out his textbooks to get a better grip on his uniform. These clothes, this girl, this place, none of this was her world. "What'd you do to me? What happened back in the basement? Where am I?"

"You—We—"

Not getting answers quick enough, Nikki grabbed his math compass and stuck it close to his neck.

"Nikki, stop it!"

"Hey, it's okay," Pippa said, resting her hand over Nikki. "Please, this can all be explained if—"

Nikki dropped him. She'd get nothing from him, and she sure wasn't going to entertain this girl she didn't know. Attempting an escape, she jumped for the door and lifted its heavy latch. Her shoulder hooked the doorway as she left, her eyesight dragging along the floor. She'd been *drugged*.

"*Nikki!*"

They'd locked her in a room at the end of a long hall. It looked like the Asilo: sterile, industrial walls, no windows. She must've been underground, deeper in that heinous basement Morgan was so keen on keeping hidden.

She ran. The moment she found a turn, she'd use her immaculate yet drugged senses to get back to the ladder. Then she'd go to the Guard, or run away. Anywhere other than underground in this...

This...

Upon the final turn, Nikki found herself in a foyer three times the size of her own apartment complex. It rose four stories high into a myriad of pathways that led down numerous halls. One wall had signs pointing where to go while another hung up a blown-up version of the Raeleenian flag—a red flag with a yellow crescent moon in its center. Someone had besmirched it with a rebellious *X*.

The foyer opened up to another equally large room. Strange machines were connected to each other via hanging wires. A grey tarp covered a giant thing near a floor-to-ceiling door. Doors upon doors, hallways leading this way and next. She wasn't in a basement. She was in some type of shopping center, or major hospital.

Something from Li's time. Within her—his—memory, she remembered a place just like this, though what it was for and why she was here was a mystery.

Her mother, father, and Aunt Del were all sitting in the foyer, whispering with cups of coffee in one hand and wrenches in the other.

Nikki pushed off the wall and tried for a door. What felt like solid concrete stopped her.

"Oh, Nikki," she heard her mother say, "you're awake."

Nikki refused to acknowledge them. They sounded upbeat, as if they hadn't done something evil to her body. She expected anything from the coffeehouse's basement, but this was over the line of redemption. To her, they'd become strangers all over again, and just like when they'd introduced her to their home, she immediately searched for a way out.

Down the hall, Morgan exited one of the locked rooms holding a giant pipe. "Hey, there she is!" she said excitedly. "Oh, you're angry. Okay, you're pissed, and that's completely understanda—"

Nikki disarmed her aunt, threw her to the floor, and picked up the pipe. She lifted it as if to swing it like a bat. "What did you do to me?"

"Nikki!" her mother shouted. "Get off her! What're you doing?"

"No! Tell me where I am!"

"*Wait!*"

Behind her parents, Vanna watched as his mother was about to be beaten. "Please, don't hurt her!"

Nikki looked each of them in the eyes, then lowered the pipe until it clunked to the floor. The adrenaline leaked out of her limbs.

Pippa ran up behind Vanna. "You can't blame her, can you?" she asked the room. "For this reaction, I mean. Any one of you would've done the same."

"I would've gone for the eyes, myself." Morgan fiddled with something in her ear: her hearing aid, messed up by Nikki's doing. "It's fine. Vanna, it's fine! You just woke up, yeah? You're probably lightheaded. And angry. Come, sit in the lounge. We'll explain everything there over a cup of coffee."

They brought her back into the foyer where she'd first seen her traitorous parents scheming. And they knew where to go. The wall signs were in a language she couldn't read but had symbols on it for easy reference. Behind her led to a fork and knife, a potted plant, washing machine, a radio-looking contraption, flames, and an opened cardboard box. To her left pointed a needle, a pencil writing on paper, a water droplet, and a bed, likely leading to the bedroom she'd woken up in.

She looked up at the levels to this place, down the halls that spider-webbed from this center. The lights hummed. The walls creaked with overused machinery. It was like she'd been taken into an underground world nobody had known about. Nobody other than her family.

The coffee table between them provided them sugar packets and fresh coffee to drink, but only Morgan and Vanna drank. Vanna finished about three cups in two minutes. Pippa kept trying to touch him but put a leash on her roaming hands.

"Pippa, dear," Morgan said. "Go be anywhere other than here, will you? I have some documents in my study that need to be reorganized for the Asilo. Take care of those for me, yeah?"

"Sure," Pippa said. "I need to get ready for work, anyway." She shared a parting glance with Vanna as she left, wanting to reassure him but being unable to speak around his family. Vanna watched her go before returning to his cup.

Morgan turned her cup in her hands. "Well, this's always the tricky part."

"Where am I?" Nikki asked.

"Would you believe that's the hardest question to answer?" She faked a smile. "The documents here call this place a fallout shelter. We don't have the exact dates, but we believe it's fairly old—we're guessing around the beginning of time. We think it was used for wartime—"

Nikki crossed her arms and fell back into the couch.

"Hey, don't be mad at us! *You* were the one sneaking around, listening in on our conversations. We didn't have a choice."

"How can you blame me?" Nikki demanded. "This place was ripped out of a nightmare. I'm still under the impression you kidnapped me and are holding me hostage for some weird bounty, so fess up quicker, otherwise I'll bring all your names to the Líders."

Hearing that clouded Morgan's sunny disposition. "First of all, no, we haven't kidnapped you. Second, I'm not blaming anyone. This was fate's fault. Sorry, Nikki. Usually in this situation, people already have a grasp on what we do. It's not always this topsy-turvy."

She downed the rest of her cup. "Back when Del and I bought the coffeehouse—we're underneath it, by the way, underground—we made sure the previous owners hadn't sold us anything faulty. They hadn't, but strangely enough, we found a hole in that basement we'd sedated you in. It wasn't mentioned in our lease and was blocked off by concrete, but with power tools and determination, we managed to *drill* our way through, so to speak.

"Right now, we're about 250 feet underground in a bunker meant for some type of underground living. These walls are reinforced with twenty feet of concrete with a foot of steel behind it. You see that crack in the wall behind you?"

Nikki didn't move. Who knew if they were planning on gutting her the second she turned around?

"Right," Morgan said. "Sorry about the tranquilizer, by the way. We use it for precautions to make sure the Guard don't sniff us out. We'll give you some of our generously donated painkillers for it. And that explosion you lived through, back when you got shaken off the roof? That was from down here. One of our idiot members had lit a cigarette in a very flammable room. Nearly lost all our work down here."

"Tell me what you did to me."

"We didn't do anything! You just learned too much, so we sedated you and put you in one of our bunker rooms until we found a way to tell you."

"Tell me *what*?" Nikki was on her feet now. She had to lock her knees to keep from falling. Her parents held out their hands to catch her.

"You know," Nikki said, "I always thought you were all funny, but especially you."

Morgan grinned nervously. "I'm a natural comedian?"

"Stop it. You smile even when you're upset, you dodge questions about your true intentions. So tell me what's really going on, right now, or so help me, Morg, I'm going straight to the Asilo and telling them everything."

"O-okay, let me get my notes altogether. Above, you're taking this much harder than Derek and Kev did."

Nikki's eyes widened. "Derek and Kev knew about this?" she asked. "They knew and I didn't?"

Morgan's smile fell. "Oh."

"Is this why they're gone? Is this why you never told me, because you lost them to *this*?"

"No," her mother said. "We didn't think..."

Nikki's body stiffened, headache pounding. Weeks without her siblings, weeks of living with every person in this room who'd been keeping it a secret from her. She held on for anyone to prove her wrong, to tell her she didn't have to disown five family members for the memory of two.

The adults lowered their heads. Del rubbed the top of Vanna's hand, but Vanna got up and ran down one of the halls.

Morgan sighed and cleaned her glasses on her coveralls. "We didn't intend on losing them."

"Screw you," Nikki said. "You're monsters."

"We're not," Del said. "We loved them. We just mishandled the situation."

"Don't you think we feel awful about it?" her mother asked. "We didn't know."

"Know *what*?" Nikki yelled. "What did you do to get both of them killed?"

"Okay, don't chew our heads off," Morgan said, which only made her want to chew them off more, "but you're not going to like the answer. You see, Del and I rebuilt this underground bunker to house a coup."

"A what?"

"An uprising. Ever since we were your age, we've always wanted to get back at the Líders for treating us so poorly. We were sick of them using their guards to keep us caged like animals. We wanted to rise up, but how are you to do such a thing with packs of lawless officers patrolling the streets? Then we found the secrets of this place.

"I invited your parents in as soon as I found it. Del here can keep a secret like her life depended on it, and Vanna, well..." She laughed at nothing funny. "We weren't ready to adopt a child during all of this, but Del couldn't say no to little Vanna when he'd sniffed his way down here, looking for food. N-not that I'm upset about it!" she called out for Vanna to hear. "Now he's part of the family business! It's fine!"

"So you started an underground revolution," Nikki said, "and you *built* all of this?"

"Oh, no, no. Above, Nikki, I'm a pastry artist and revolutionist, not an architect. Most of this was here when we found it, albeit covered with much more dust. We've been renovating it, bringing back its electricity, trying to get the blasted machines to start back up. I mean, have you ever seen anything like this before in your life? Some of these rooms had ingenious pieces of tech in it laying to waste."

"So what's this got to do with Derek and Kev?"

"We invited them to be part of the revolution when we thought they were old enough to understand. I have nearly a hundred people in on this, so I figured they'd be ready to get involved when they were twenty."

Nikki flared out her nostrils. "So everyone in the family knew about this but me? Is this why you didn't want me asking about Derek and Kev, because you wanted to keep your petty little revolution alive?"

"No," her mother argued. "When Derek had kicked that rock at Pippa—"

"What on Earth is *wrong* with you?" Nikki asked. "You're messed in the heads."

"Okay, calm down," Morgan said. "Nikki, no. We didn't value their lives beneath our rebellion. Derek acted recklessly and ran away."

"Probably because he didn't want all of you to go to jail for starting an uprising! He saved you lot and lost his life because of it!"

Morgan glared her down. Nikki returned it with vengeance, planning how she was going to live the rest of her life without a family again.

Morgan nodded to Del, and she left and came back a few seconds later with a handful of documents.

"What're these?" Nikki asked.

"Documents we found down here. Most of them fall apart in your hands, but these were protected with lamented paper."

Nikki looked over one of the pages.

"These documents tell of another world," Morgan explained. "We know the world only as Raeleen, yeah? This one place surrounded by the Muralha we can't ever leave? These tell a different story."

She gave the papers a chance. There were walls of text written on them with things crossed out and circled in red ink, photos of landscapes taped to the edges.

"You see them, yeah? Those towns, those rivers? Nothing you've ever seen in Raeleen, yeah?"

She saw them. Buildings as tall as the Muralha, expanses of water. She'd seen such sights once before, this world...

"Look. Look really hard. Buildings that defy gravity and technology that glows in the streets. Some cities are bustling and strong, while others look decimated by bombs."

Nikki read it for herself. Names she couldn't pronounce. Pictures of cities she didn't know, some futuristic, others war-torn and desolate.

Bombs caught mid-explosion.

Hundreds of people walking for safety.

And two words that kept repeating in every paragraph. Maïmoú. And Shào.

The papers fluttered from Nikki's hands. She shivered. That's how their names were spelled in Lí's memories.

It'd all been real. Shào was *real*, and Maïmoú, too, or had been. Her dream hadn't been a psychotic break that would've sent her to a hospital. She didn't know what would've scared her more, but seeing the proof made her question things more.

"Nikki?" her mother asked. "You okay?"

"It's groundbreaking news, Iysra," Morgan said, "and our girl here's quite the skeptic. It'll take much more time for her to believe us."

Ignoring them, Nikki picked up the papers and read the documents more carefully, but it was impossible. The rest of the pages were either stained or faded, and the language, while somewhat readable, was like reading in a different dialect. She saw letters in neither Raeleenian nor whatever language Lí spoke in his head.

"Don't give yourself more of a headache, Nikki," Morgan said. "I've run these babies through people much smarter than all of us combined, and we can't grasp much of anything from it. It talks a lot about Deities, did you notice? That word there. Can't translate it for the life of us, but it's written on every page. We thought it a name, but it looks pluralized."

A wave of guilt washed over Nikki. She knew it. She knew all of it. What that word meant and the powers it carried. How she'd once existed as a man from beyond the walls, who knew Shào, knew Maïmoú. This was part of her, and she'd had a hand in it.

But how could she tell them? Confidently? With a leveled head? They'd think her mad, talking about such things.

She lowered her shoulders. She needed to meet with Shào again and learn more about what these papers entailed. If her parents found Maïmoú, or if Maïmoú came looking for her...

"We're trapped, Nikki," Morgan said, "like rats. Excuse the pun. The Líders must've been keeping this from the public for generations, but we've uncovered it. On the other side of the Muralha could be millions of people we haven't seen in centuries. And that doesn't even begin to cover what's happening inside the Asilo. Mikhail's MIA, and there're people being kept in tanks...Nikki?"

She blinked hard and came back to the present. She needed to be a rock that would not erode. "D-Derek and Kev," she said. "Derek fell off the wall. Does that mean he's with these people?"

"...Yes," Morgan said. "If we take these papers at face value, then yes, we believe so."

"And Kev?"

Her mother shook her head. Her father took off his glasses to wipe his eyes.

"What happened to Kevin?" Nikki asked again.

"We don't know whether or not he pushed Derek off," Morgan said. "He told the Líders that he hadn't, but he was taken away before he told us the truth. He ran to the Muralha, then..." She held her tongue, but something other than Derek's disappearance pulsated underneath her eye.

"She has to know," Del said.

"I don't think it's the right time."

"What's not the right time?" Nikki asked.

"She just woke up," her father argued. "Give it time."

"I think she should know," her mother said.

"Know what?" Nikki asked. "Morgan, look at me. You know I can handle it."

She did, though the two things Morgan hid best—sadness and age—cracked through. In an exhausted sigh, she announced drearily, "Kevin's being held captive in the Asilo."

The fogginess in Nikki's head, from this new information to information she must've known all this time, cleared. "He's alive?"

"As of a few hours ago, yes. That guard you just saw, Pippa? She sends us intel about his situation. She's been working with me for years, updating me on everything the Líders do. Ever wonder why there're always guards around us? Most of them work weekends down here."

To a normal person, that sounded rejoiceful. Not one, but perhaps *two* of her best friends were alive, and they were being kept updated on one of them.

Her parents kept their sullen faces down. Not even Morgan looked happy about the news.

"What?" Nikki asked. "What's wrong? He's alive, yeah? He's okay."

"Not entirely," Morgan dropped. "You see this fallout shelter, yeah? Meant to keep people safe, hidden? If we wanted to, we could hold up to a thousand people down here. The people who'd built this place made working kitchens and septic tanks. We even have a workout center. If we wanted to, we could imprison a whole city down here, and nobody would ever hear them scream."

Nikki took another look around. No windows, with walls thicker than concrete. If Morgan *had* wanted to, she could've converted this place into a prison.

"There's at least one more fallout shelter in Raeleen that I've found," Morgan said. "It's under the Asilo, and it's been converted to house...waterborne crossbreeds."

Before Nikki could question that, Morgan took a page from Del and showed Nikki. It was of a naked crossbreed with a strange fin and tail submerged in water. Across their neck were thick slashes that should've been dying the water red, but they seemed content living in the water, or drugged, moments away from drowning.

"What is this?" she asked.

"They're a rare group of crossbreeds that the government has been hiding from us. They come from something called a fish, a type of animal that lives in the water. We don't know much about them because the Líder's themselves don't know much, but apparently, from what we can gather, Líders from hundreds of years ago kept these people contained underneath the Asilo. They're being experimented on."

"It's torture," Del said. "I can't—" She pinched the bridge of her nose. "There're *children* down there."

"I know." Morgan rubbed her other half's knee. "We never told Derek or Kev about this part. Didn't think they could stomach it. What a turn, knowing Kevin is with them now."

"So this...fallout shelter, you call it, is that...where Kevin is?" Nikki asked. "Is he being experimented on, too?

"Not to the extent of the others, but yes," Morgan said. "Pippa has told us that the Líders have taken a particular interest in Kevin based on what happened on the Muralha. He'd said that he and Derek had heard a voice guiding them to the wall, said the voice had taken Derek and thrown him over.

"You know Zantl, don't you?" she asked Nikki. "The hidden heir kept in the Asilo?"

"Course I do. What do they have to do with this?"

"You've heard the rumors about their powers?"

"Yeah, they're rumors."

"Not exactly. Zantl, by themselves, is not special in any regard, but they are connected by a special power. It's why the Líders took them in as a child. It's why Kevin hasn't been murdered for breaking the laws he and Derek broke that day. Hearing voices, being touched by an invisible hand, these were all experiences felt by Zantl as a child."

Nikki held her heart through her sweatshirt. She, too, had heard voices, and while she hadn't been touched by an invisible hand, Maïmoú had tried killing her through strangulation. She'd felt Shào's touch through a dream.

"Kev's the same as Zantl," Nikki said, then, internally, *the same as me.*

She swallowed thickly, trying to get herself to calm down, but she couldn't. Kevin was connected to a Deity like she was. Did he know Shào? Maïmoú? For how long?

She needed to save him. How scared he must've been, being thrown into this world without the means to defend himself. She'd grown up fighting. Kevin hadn't.

"We don't know too much about it," Morgan summarized. "We don't know how Zantl's powers work, we just know that there're secrets Nadia and Mikhail didn't want us knowing about, and Kevin is displaying similar attributes that Zantl had."

Nikki grasped onto whatever line they threw at her. "S-so what're we doing here? We have to save him, all of them."

"There it is. Here we go," Morgan said. "This's *exactly* what I was telling you all, but does anybody listen to me?"

"We have to save him," Nikki repeated. "Why's that crazy to think?"

"Because I've run through every possible plan to get him out, and there's no way we can do it. I think we can all say that yes, saving these people is the most morally just action to take."

"Kev's my brother."

"And I'm his aunt, Nikki. I was there when he was born, but reality pops her little head in and says, *'Hey, little tidbit: The Líders have control over the most authoritative hands in the world'*. And those children—and let's be sensible, *adults*—are in the hundreds of thousands. Saving Kev and all those people who haven't seen the light of day, who need to be in water to stay alive, *plus* evading the Guard not under my control, is a suicide mission."

"But we have to try!"

"If we don't want them or us murdered, we can't."

"We *have* to."

"Nikki."

"No. Kev's in there right now. You owe it to him."

212

"Okay, then do that," Morgan said. "Find the maps and the layouts to get there, round up the army, steal the guns, avoid Nadia and the Guard, and don't get killed. There're just too many variables. And the people who're living there won't be able to leave so abruptly."

"Oh, that's bull."

"Most of them need to be in water to breathe, Nicole. Think about it. The underground is all they've ever known. Can you imagine how jarring it would be for a stranger to force you out of your home with promises of a better life somewhere you've never been?"

Nikki stopped rummaging and touched her throat.

"We need more time to work out that rescue mission," Morgan said, "but in the meantime, we have plans for something else, something that's been in the works since we were your age."

"What can be bigger than saving those people?" Nikki asked.

"Follow me."

Defying her instincts, Nikki followed Morgan into that open room with wires and strange machinery.

"Have you ever wondered what's on the other side?" Morgan asked.

"Of the Muralha? Everyone has."

That cheeky Morgan Grin bloomed back on her pudgy cheeks. She entered a code on a hanging remote connected to the ceiling. The tarp around the thing lifted like a curtain at a school play.

First, Nikki saw wheels, or what looked like wheels. Eight tires, each about eight inches thick, with metal plates shielding them like armor. Teeth-like spikes pointed down at her, ready to skewer her on Morgan's order.

Morgan patted Nikki's back. "The Líders think they can keep us underground, but they're wrong. We know their secrets. We have the tech to find out the truth. With this baby, we're going to drill a hole straight through the Muralha and find out what really lies beyond the walls."

Nikki stared at the automobile before her. Something about its construction was familiar to her, something from Lí's world. It was like remembering a nightmare. "What is it?"

"A drill. Well, technically, it's something called a tank. We found blueprints for it in this very shelter. The files had almost disintegrated and were written in a different language, but we guessed here and there and made a few alterations to its natural beauty."

Nikki knelt down to study its undercarriage. "How do you know the sky isn't going to spill into Raeleen once you drill through the Muralha?"

"The documents say otherwise. It's hard to believe, but we think there'll be land awaiting us on the other side. We'll be free to explore, free to find Derek."

"If you get caught," Nikki said, "you'll be executed."

"We would be."

"And you're risking your life to find out something that might kill you regardless."

"That's true."

"You're insane."

"You're realizing that now?"

Nikki's nails cut into her palm as she made a tight fist. She didn't want to follow along with anything Morgan said, but she knew it'd be even crazier to take on the government by herself, and it was absolutely out of the question to tell them that she was as powerful, or dangerous, as Zantl was.

And she needed her twins back. She'd do anything, *anything*, to get them back, including joining a batshit revolution.

With variabilities swimming around her head, Nikki held out her fist to Morgan. "I'm only doing this because you're one of my only tickets to saving Kev, and if this plan of yours falls apart, I'm planning my own rescue mission to save him, and none of you are going to stop me."

"That's the type of compliant personality we need down here." Morgan returned her niece's fist bump. "Welcome to the rebellion, Nikki."

17

Marcos

"Fuck!"

Marcos winced as Nadia threw another emptied bottle against the wall. It'd meant to be for him, but she'd been intoxicated for forty-eight hours and her aim was worsening.

Forty-eight hours after the death of her partner, murdered by, what she'd assumed, was an invisible threat.

Forty-eight hours after Zantl's disappearance, taken by someone only Marcos and Kevin could see.

And forty-eight hours since Marcos' brain had been spinning in circles for answers.

He'd asked Nadia questions about what he'd seen in W4. Simple questions about the blond-haired girl, more complex questions like what Nadia had been insinuating to Zantl before they disappeared.

"Let us help you."

"We've never pressed you because you told us not to."

"This connection you share hurts you, doesn't it?"

Each question Marcos had resulted in something being thrown at him.

"What do *you* need to know?" Nadia demanded from him. "You're not sentient, you don't deserve to know anything about our lives. This's about my child and their contribution to the world. You needn't know anything other than the directions you're given!"

Marcos steeled himself, hands folded behind his back. "What are my current directions?"

Nadia crumpled at her desk, legs splayed out like a broken doll. "Find my *child*," she wept. "Find our purpose."

So he had. Turning himself on low power mode, Marcos spent those forty-eight hours combing through every level of the Asilo, every room, every street of Raeleen, for a child who didn't want to be found.

He assumed. He assumed Zantl had called for that mysterious, beautiful person—Unathi—to come save them from that girl—Maïmoú. He assumed they were on the run.

He assumed, because Nadia was keen on keeping Marcos in the dark about what'd happened that day.

The government kept secrets. Easy secrets, like how canine breeds earned more than other breeds simply because of specism. Dark secrets, like the fallout shelter housing hundreds of waterborne crossbreeds for study and experimentation. Secrets like those, he knew.

He'd worked so intimately with the Líders, from serving them breakfast to bathing Zantl when their depressive episodes went too far.

And still, when it was business related to Zantl's mind, Marcos was pushed away. He was kept out of meeting rooms, he was forbidden from asking more into Zantl's near-divinity. It was like part of his own head was locked away from him, protected by a passcode he wasn't privy to know.

After an unsuccessful night of searching the city, Marcos went back into the Asilo and took an elevator down to W4. There were five main sections to the underground facility. One for administrative work, one for freshwater-borne, one for saltwater, one for animals, and one for those in need of special care, those who needed monitored salinity levels to breathe or extra care for their disabilities. Unknown breeds they couldn't fit into boxes, they all lived at the bottom of the Earth.

He needed some time with Alexi. After fighting through Nadia's grief and coming up to dead ends about those mysterious, invisible people, he needed her. Burp her, feed her, let her swim around so he could watch and make funny faces at her. Something to give his life meaning.

Three guards rounded the corner, laughing at a joke one of them had told. Once they saw Marcos, they looked around to make sure Nadia wasn't with him, tucked their tails between their legs, and ran, whispering about how scary he looked alone.

Unlocking a heavy door, Marcos entered the hall quickest to Alexi. She was in enrichment today where she could swim about with others like her, other shark pups.

There was only one guard supervising today, Pippa, sitting on a stool and watching the twelve little ones swim about in a pool. Their back fins cut the water like knives.

The only good thing about being a robot was that Marcos could be incredibly anal about his programming. Technically, Nadia had said to search for Zantl, and *technically*, he hadn't searched here yet. Maybe people hated him for that, but it was the one thing he could call his own: his pettiness.

When Alexi saw him, she let go of the child she was biting and reached up for him.

"Oh." The guard, almost woken from her daze, sat upright. "Hiya, Marcos."

Marcos gave her a nod. Pippa was a strange guard. Newly recruited from a top-ranking academy, she was getting far into the Asilo secrets at an alarming rate. Only a few trusted guards could come down here, and she, somehow, had found herself in the midst of Raeleen's most coveted secret. She was even dating Nicole Lenore's cousin, Vanna Acres. Marcos had wiretapped their explicit phone calls.

Upsetting himself with thoughts of romance, Marcos let himself in and kept Alexi away from permanently injuring her friend.

As he tried enjoying himself with her, the guard tried her hardest to make small talk with him. Everything from his day to his week to where Mikhail was, nothing that Marcos could tell her because it was confidential to everyone other than the guards who'd witnessed it. To this hour, no one else in Raeleen should've known that Mikhail had been murdered.

"It's odd, because I haven't seen Mikhail in days," Pippa went on. "Usually he's down here working or testing or the like. And Zantl, too. Do you know—?"

It wasn't that he was annoyed by her, it was annoying that he couldn't tell her all that he knew. He couldn't even have a friend if he wanted to, or at least a person to talk to.

"Are you alright?"

Kissing the top of Alexi's wet head, Marcos excused himself and walked into a better headspace. He was becoming unnaturally angry and needed to calm down away from the living.

So he went to Kevin. Because he couldn't help himself.

Currently, he was being kept in W4. His room, a utility closet, had been cleared out in a frenzy to house him in a room not blown apart from his escape. They'd found that he'd killed three guards and injured two more before landing in W4. Their bodies had indented the wall, just like Mikhail, just like how that girl had done.

"Maïmoú," Kevin had called her. Marcos didn't know why he had trouble saying that name aloud.

He opened the door with his wrist. Kevin was asleep in bed, wings wilted over the mattress. He'd been in a deep sleep like this since Marcos had last checked up on him. Marcos knew he wasn't a deep sleeper from his records, but if he hadn't woken up yet, that meant he'd been asleep for sixteen hours.

That, or he was faking it.

Marcos watched him from the crack of the door, timing his breathing, the way his toes curled slightly on the starchy sheets. His skirt was pulled up from tossing and turning. Due to being an avian, his legs were exceptionally smooth and toned.

Marcos forced the door shut and stormed off. Curse his brain, and curse himself for being such a fool bent on trying to be normal. Not in this life nor the next, if such an option was possible. He didn't know why he thought this, as he'd never met another person who shared it, but there was a comfort in knowing that "you" could be a different "you" a hundred years in the future.

Marcos took the stairs to buy his "free" time. Zantl had *disappeared* with that Unathi person. For all he knew, they were up in the sky, never planning on coming back down.

As a child, Zantl would often play hide and seek with Marcos. They were quite good at it, even as a young child, and would keep the game going for hours before Marcos eventually caught them. While they'd grown out of childish games, Marcos remembered their go-to hiding spots: deep, dark corners of the Asilo, where not even spiders would cast their webs.

He tried every door with dust in the cracks, ones padlocked for years. He found new brooms in supply closets and chairs that were still in their boxes. How wasteful—Nadia had just ordered new ones.

One door, a door that was labeled "janitorial closet," caught his attention. It was at a dead end with lights that hadn't turned on because they were motion-operated.

He checked his interior maps of the Asilo. He had them perfectly memorized and hadn't needed to mentally bring them up in decades. The hall existed.

But the door, it wasn't labeled. To him, the room didn't exist.

With the need to continue moving his body, Marcos tried unlocking the door. His wrist chip wouldn't open it, but he had orders, didn't he? He was told to check every corner of Raeleen to find Zantl. It wouldn't have been right to disobey.

Using downward momentum, Marcos rammed his body into the corner of the door, snapping it off its hinges. With a quick glance down the deserted hall, he shoved his shoulder into the gap and easily broke his way through.

He stilled in the doorway. The smell caught him off guard first, aged technology, the smell of iron.

Instead of unused mops and cleaning supplies, this room was cluttered with ageless technology. Boxy tech with wires crossed the floor and ceiling. They had so much dust on them, a living person would find themselves in a sneezing fit upon entering.

Marcos scanned the space for any signs of life, then flipped on the nearest light switch.

The screens flickered like firecrackers. Machinery chugged and whirled into life. Some of them were so loud that Marcos was sure they'd explode. It wasn't like anything he'd seen before in the Asilo, one of the most technologically advanced places in Raeleen. This was...

Somewhere he shouldn't have been. He should've left, continued his search for Zantl elsewhere, but the whirring, the sounds of technology coming to life in a world not meant for them, something about their existence spoke to Marcos. He related to them.

He walked up to the largest screen. It had one line of text in its center.

Press Any Key

Marcos looked down at its keypad. It had every letter and number on it as well as a few other ones. After searching for the "Any Key," Marcos gave up and pressed a key at random.

The screen went black. Something behind the machine powered down and a blinking light turned off.

Marcos searched around the machine. It looked like a standing radio with a screen instead of a speaker. It had more whirling fans behind it, nothing of which Marcos knew how to fix.

A machine next to his foot powered up. It chugged through layers of dust. He knew how terrible it felt to be used against one's will. He knew sentience played a big factor in this sentiment, but he still felt bad. The machine's tower was smoking.

00:00:01
00:00:02

Bright colors flashed on screen. It looked like an image, with blots of color moving in sync, but pictures didn't move.

He placed his hands on the table as he willed a cleaner picture to form. Brightness mixing with darkness, shapes coming into form.

Biting his lower lip, Marcos did what he hated and gently hit the side of the moving-picture box. With each hit, the picture focused into a scene.

A pair of eyes opened to a white ceiling. Blond hair covered part of the sight. Code welcomed him awake.

Good Morning, Marcos

Today is **Wednesday**, **July 1**
The temperature is **38°C**
07:00

Marcos leaned forwards. That wasn't Raeleenian, but he could read it. He was reading his name through someone else's eyesight.

He stepped back on a thick wire. The camera belonged to *him*. He was seeing through *his* eyes.

Past Marcos sat up in a bed. He'd been resting on a fresh white pillow. His room, more furnished than any room in the Asilo, had bookshelves full of novels and succulents. There was a walk-in closet filled with stylish clothes and signed posters up on the walls. Plants hung in his open windows, taking in the warm Sun.

Marcos inspected every piece of furniture and knickknack he saw. He didn't own anything in Raeleen. He didn't even own a bed. He slept in a corner of Nadia's and Mikhail's office.

Past Marcos started his day by making his bed. There was a stuffed animal on his end table, a bird, and a desk where he likely worked. What had he been working on? Was it just for show?

Was this even him? Was he able to record what he saw for future viewings? If he could've, the Líders hadn't told him.

Past Marcos walked by a full-length mirror. Shove that doubt aside: This was most certainly Marcos. Same face and height, same hair, although this version's was unkempt. He undressed quickly from his pajamas to a set of black clothes of belts and zippers.

Marcos had two outfits in the Asilo, one to wear upon all hours of the day, another if the first one got stained. This Past Marcos, one without any duties, wasted time by posing in the mirror, checking himself out to make sure he looked good at every angle. He was *vain*.

After sprucing up his already clean room, Past Marcos looked down to a blue, blinking light in his right wrist. Real Marcos had the same chip there, but instead of connecting him to Zantl and the operations of the Asilo, his was something different.

Someone opened up his bedroom door, and a teenage girl answered his call.

She was a short, dark-skinned girl with short, brown hair curled around her eyes. Splatters of white painted her skin and hair like spots. She wore a beautiful flower necklace and many colorful rainbow bracelets as charming accessories. She had no animal ears or tails like him.

She looked like him.

She looked like him.

And her name...

Marcos' knees buckled from shock. A vision, a spark. It came and went, but a flashing memory of this girl smiled her way into his core processors. She was...

"Alliroue," Past Marcos said.

Alliroue. Her name was Alliroue. In that millisecond of memory, Marcos knew her as a twenty-year-old "human" girl who enjoyed nature and life, a beautiful...

Marcos palmed the screen like a dog. She was bright and smiling and evoked something deep inside of him. Her precious laugh melted his exterior into something warm, real, and alive.

The video skipped to them on a balcony. It stretched across the whole side of whatever building they lived on, expensive and grand with every type of fern and flower he could possibly name potted around it.

Approximately sixty stories high, Marcos was introduced to a world he didn't recognize: green parks, giant windmills, apartment buildings as tall as theirs. Hundreds upon hundreds of buildings spread across the land, none as tall as the one Past Marcos and Alliroue lived in. The Sun shone upon the glass windows and beyond, where blurry sand dunes miles away encapsulated the futuristic city he'd once called home.

Alliroue lit something like a cigarette and put it in her mouth. Music must've been playing, because she suddenly began to sing. Marcos heard her staticky voice tear through the recording as she danced to a beat.

Past Marcos joined in. His hair swayed in front of his eyes, his feet moved in the same way hers did, a dance only the two of them knew.

Alliroue grabbed Marcos and brought him in close. A floating, transparent screen came up in front of them and mirrored their smiles. Alliroue threw up a peace sign. Marcos pulled a funny face.

The video quality cut in half. Frames decreased. Audio skipped. The last thing he saw was Alliroue's smile. She had dimples.

00:15:10

"No." Marcos tried rewinding the recording. He tapped the sides of the monitor, unplugged and replugged the machine back in.

He backed up. He'd always been told he'd been found in Raeleen. He was meant to serve and be ordered by the Líders of the world, to be of use, to be a machine.

He didn't have a past beyond waking up in front of Zantl. He didn't deserve a life beyond servitude.

How *dare* they? How dare they hide this from him and take away the one good thing, the *one good* person, in his life, who liked him not for his services but for his love? He'd been born with nothing and had been enslaved for decades, and for what? Why take away his memories? Why hide this girl from him?

Something clicked and ejected itself out of the machine. The "computer," though he didn't know how he knew that.

It was a little drive the size of his thumb. Marcos waited for it to do anything more, then gently extracted and pocketed it for later. It was his—it held *his* memories. He had a right to keep it.

He shut down the room just like he'd found it and fixed the door he'd broken. If the Líders were allowed to keep secrets, then let him have a few. Let him own something in this backwards world that he didn't belong in. He belonged back *there*, with Alliroue, wherever she resided.

Something in his mind beeped, alerting him to what Nadia had once told him mattered.

"Zantl," he whispered. They were close.

He travelled up west, down this floor's laundry room and breakroom for guards. Marcos made sure to use the stairs so he didn't pass by any other guards who hated his existence.

Alliroue hadn't hated him. He knew that for a fact. The way she'd held him and smiled at him, that's how friends acted. Family, lovers, people who were bound by their hearts. He ached for a feeling he couldn't remember experiencing.

He came up to a storage room that smelled of soaps. Its door was ajar, broken. Someone had disabled the locking feature.

Marcos reached for it when his whole body froze. He heard it again, that hateful noise that came out muffled in Zantl's room. The sound beings made when they were being intimate with one another. The sound of sex.

Marcos' hand wavered at the slit of the door. He didn't want to go in and disturb whatever was occurring, but he had a code to follow: Find Zantl, even if it meant interrupting their closeted affairs.

There was a hidden bed in this closet, large enough for one person but able to fit two. There were snacks laid out half-eaten on the sheets with bottles of water lining the frame. A bag of clothes was tucked away underneath the mattress.

The person Zantl had found themselves with, the one they were entangled with in sweat...

Unathi saw Marcos first, their golden eyes piercing him. They were embracing Zantl in the bed. Zantl lay limp against them, panting and trying to gain back their senses.

Before Zantl had time to notice Marcos, Unathi disappeared, just like before but without Zantl. When Zantl found themselves alone, when they saw Marcos watching them, they shrieked and covered up their body. "W-what're you—get out! How'd you...Unathi—"

That unnatural anger heated up Marcos' processors again, and he grabbed Zantl by the wrist.

"Let me go!" they said. "Marcos, that hurts!"

"No," Marcos said. "You need to tell me what's going on, right now. Who was that?"

"I don't need to tell you anything."

Marcos squeezed harder, making Zantl yelp. With his free hand, he took out the chip—the thumb drive—from his pocket.

Zantl stopped struggling. Their ears folded back.

"Tell me what's going on," Marcos demanded, "and tell me what your family's been hiding from me."

18
Derek

Derek thought he was in the clear.

When the queen didn't come searching for him after his kiss with Oliver, he thought they were chill. It wasn't that big a deal if he wasn't in trouble. Nero wasn't particularly thrilled about finding out—he didn't speak to Derek until they got to his bedroom.

"Just go to sleep," he said. "We'll deal with this in the morning."

"Are we good?"

He locked his bedroom door without an answer.

Normally, the royals got vertical at around seven, ate, went to church, and attended their royal duties until lunch. They were pretty lax—nothing happened at a fast pace.

Today, Nero stood over his bed before the Sun rose, a hand on the hilt of his sword. "Come with me," he said grimly. "The king wants to have a word with you."

The walk to the king's room was one of the most humiliating walks Derek had endured. All this time, he'd been treated like a person who could do no wrong. They forgave him because of his missing memories. He'd become invincible to sin, like the glass ceiling would never break.

Now, he was being forced to walk over a sea of shattered glass, barefoot and blindfolded.

The king, queen, Cellena, Jabel, and six others were waiting in the room. The king, who was sitting at a very important chair, got up before Nero closed the door.

Derek winced. This was looking bad. "Sorry," he said, "for—"

"Is it true, then?" the king asked. "You don't deny what my wife saw?"

"Uh..." He checked in with the queen, but her face was as still as stone, silently judging him with the rest of her family.

Aside from Cellena. She looked confused, trying to get a read on the situation. Jabel wouldn't meet her nor Derek's eyes.

"I..." Derek hid in his wings. "I don't know."

"You understand the severity of these actions, do you not? Have we not made them evident to you?"

"You have," he admitted, "I just didn't think it was a big deal."

"You were with a demon," he stated outright, "at night, in a highly provocative state. We have taught you our ways. We thought you understood us."

"I did. I do."

"And we were planning on bringing you into town this month. How can we do that now?"

Derek knew that saying sorry would've made everything better, and he could've blamed it on a number of things: how dark it was, how late it'd been. The demons had something to do with love. He could've blamed Oliver for tempting him.

But that wasn't the truth. He didn't feel like apologizing because, in his eyes, he hadn't done anything wrong. And it'd been *one* kiss. It wasn't like he was caught fucking him, though he wouldn't have said no if Oliver had asked.

He finally looked the king in his dark eyes. "Yeah, I kissed Oliver because I wanted to. So what? Why're you so threatened by that?"

The queen went for her cross, physically disgusted by his statement. Jabel and Cellena flinched as if they'd been struck and hid behind their mother.

The king took a step around his desk.

"What?" Derek fluffed up his feathers to look bigger. He was getting way too close. "I'm an angel, yeah? I can do no wrong, can't I?"

The strike hit him before his brain could register the attack. It was acute and prickly, stinging his whole face into a numbing rash.

Derek held his panging cheek. He tasted blood, felt like a tooth had come loose. His mind went cold as his heart poured into his mouth.

The king lowered his hand. "You are in *my* castle," he said, "under *my* roof and under *my* rule. I have the final say who can do no wrong, and you, Your Grace, have cursed my home with your sinful lust. You are meant to rid our world of demonkind, and you have shown a tremendous lack of care for the safety of our humanity."

Their humanity. Their castle. Their world and their rules. Everything came down to greed and power with these people, it made Derek sick.

Humanity made him sick.

He flapped his wings to cover up the tears in his eyes. "Fuck this!" he yelled. "Fuck all this. I don't have to abide by your stupid laws. I'm my own person."

"You are in *my* castle—"

"And I never asked to stay!" he screamed. "Fuck me, you're acting like I had a choice to be here. I had nowhere else to go and you took me in because I thought you cared about me, but all you want me to do is fix *your* problems. Have you even cared to learn about the real me, what *I* wanted?"

"How dare you."

"Fuck off!" He stormed off, kicking open the door with his foot. "I hate this place! I'm gonna—gonna tell your God about this! You're all gonna get spited and sent to the Underground for this."

The king, who was calling for Nero to stop him, withdrew his hand. "Your Grace, wait."

"No!" He laughed through the hurt. "You're going to hear it from your God. Oh, yeah. You thought the Barrier was hard to live with? You think the demons are the least of your worries? Wait until you meet, uh, Shào. Yeah, then you'll be sorry. Y'all're gonna be so fucked when he hears about this. Except for Cellena," he added. "Everyone else can suck my cock!"

"Derek—"

Opening up the nearest window he could fit through, Derek flared out his feathers and dove straight out of it.

The Drail Kingdom had changed outfits overnight. The pine trees he once loved were now covered in a blanket of white. He saw no grass or flowers. White flecks were floating from the sky like rain, but slower and softer like ash, coating everything. His breath came out like cigarette smoke. He needed a smoke after today.

He flew, letting the icy wind mess up his hair and face. It stung so good, he almost dared himself to plunge straight into the ocean. Scramble his brains in the waves, tear off his wings at the bone. He clawed at his arms to feel something stronger than the hurt, but it wasn't enough. All of their staring, the hatred...

His nails dug too deep, and he realized what he was doing and came back to reality. He was half a mile away from the castle, over the trees and passing-by clouds. His cheeks were beginning to hurt by how wet they were.

He landed on top of the church, on the belfry. It was where the bell rang. There was enough space here for him to sit and have a good, long think with the forest trees.

He pressed his cheek into the cold, white wood. Nothing was stopping him from flying in and meeting up with the demons now. They obviously knew about him and were curious to get to know him. It was more than what the king and queen had managed. He deserved to be with them rather than these clowns.

But he couldn't say that. Cellena was the good egg. Nero and Runa were nice and treated him like a human being or whatever the fuck he was. And the food and security were nice, not everything was terrible. He probably shouldn't have cussed out the king like that, at least not in front of everyone.

Beneath him, a courtyard was filling up with "snow," creating hills. Tiny birds flittered near cages built up against the arches, stacked like building blocks underneath snowy hay. Stupid idiots didn't know there was nothing in the castle for them.

A door opened near them, scaring them into the forest.

Jabel stomped out in circles, creating figure eights in the snow. Cellena followed out behind him, lifting up her dress so it didn't get dirty by pure white.

"What the fuck were we thinking?" Jabel asked. The wind carried his voice to Derek's sensitive ears. He eyed them from his hiding spot. "We should've spoken out. We should've defended him."

"I'm sorry," Cellena said. "I was too afraid. You're the older one."

"You know I can't." Jabel's voice broke in a cry. He covered it with a balled fist and turned away from his little sister.

"It'll be okay," she said.

"No, it won't. Now Father will come to me asking about...who I am again. He's going to blame me for making

Derek like this, that I somehow corrupted him. I can't take another beating."

Cellena looked around the empty courtyard. "You came here," she said. "Are you going to call for Maxwell?"

"No, I can't. I—" He took a deep breath. "I shouldn't."

Derek whispered that name under his breath. If he wasn't mistaken, that was the name of the water demon that'd saved Jabel from a heart attack. He'd brought him back to the castle and saved him.

"Has he returned your letter?" Cellena asked. "You sent one last night, right?"

"It's not safe for carrier hawks to fly in this weather, and Oliver must be in a wreck with what happened. God, why'd they meet up in public? They should know better."

"He doesn't know any better."

"Oliver does. Boys can't go around kissing boys."

"Perhaps it's different in the Heavens."

Jabel laughed. "What, now *I'm* a saint? Fantastic." He wiped the corner of his eye before walking Cellena back into their home. Their hands only touched once the double doors began to close.

Derek let go a draconic breath of white. He replayed that conversation over in his head, wondering what they'd been talking about, what hidden meanings they were keeping from their family, church.

Jabel was in cahoots with one of the demons, and they seemed to be on good terms, good enough to expect letters from the other when things in the castle got bad.

He shivered, and felt a sneeze come up from his lungs. Jabel was right. This weather was not good for hawks.

Someone behind him finished the sneeze.

Holly was once again spying on him. She was hiding inside the large bell, holding her scarf to her lips like she had a secret

233

to keep. Up this close, Derek saw that she had thick freckles across her nose like he did.

"Hey, Holly." He wiped away stray tears. "Did you just materialize yourself here, or have you been spying on me like everyone else?"

Holly stepped away from her obvious hiding space and ducked her head into the bell. She hit her head on its curved metal.

"You good?" He went to steady her, but she didn't want to be touched and he backed off. "Can you understand me?"

She shook out her long hair from her scarf. It was such a tattered thing. She must've had it for years, being immortal.

"Is Oliver coming to save you?" Derek then asked. "I hope so. He probably hates me for getting him in trouble. If you can, tell him I'm sorry. It was a nice kiss."

Holly cocked her head at him, then her sharp eyes turned to slits and she looked up like she'd seen a squirrel.

Humoring her, Derek looked up. "What do you..."

Shào, in his lifeless state, was hovering across the snowy grounds. He floated in a straight line like a wayward balloon, his tail acting as his limp string.

"Woah," Derek said, "you can see him, too?"

Holly crawled underneath his wings and over his lap and legs. With her hair flared and ears down, she put herself right in front of Derek to protect him until Shào came and went, floating somewhere into the forest.

She stayed over him for several seconds until they lost sight of him. When they were in the clear, she fell back on her butt.

Repaying her kindness, Derek wrapped a wing around her to protect her from the cold. "Is this a non-human thing, to see Deities?" he asked. "You know, that Shào guy told me something. He attacked me. I think he wanted to kill me. I forgot a lot of what he said, but he said something about me being a soulmate? With some type of connection to something called a Deity? Do you know what that's about?"

Holly rolled on her butt, tail flicking.

"Whatever. Doesn't matter. This sucks, Holly. I mean, you have cat ears and demons can float or breathe fire or whatever, but for some reason, that's easier to understand than *this*." He motioned to the church underneath them. "I'm glad that you're here. You're really easy to talk to. Maybe it's a soulmate thing."

He twiddled with his fingers, looking down at Holly's hand. She was wearing fingerless gloves. The ends had been torn from being picked at.

"Hey," he said, "was I in the wrong? For kissing Oliver? I don't know much about him, but I want to. He's nice and genuinely cares about me. Am I bad for liking someone like that?"

Holly, who was playing with her hair, finally looked at him, knees hiding her mouth.

"I am, aren't I? I'm the most sinful angel in the world. It must've been hilarious watching me act like a good person. I'm not even an angel, I'm—"

"Mm."

He looked up. Holly was pulling something out of her sweater.

It was a doll. A little girl with brown hair made of yarn with two button eyes. Her clothes had teeth marks in it and a little slobber. Holly presented it to Derek with both hands. Its little head bobbled from being overstuffed.

"Oh." He took it, looked it over. He didn't get it, but it must've meant a lot to her. "This your baby?"

She nodded excitedly and placed the doll on his head.

"Oh, okay."

Then, feeling like it was the wrong place, she put the doll against his cheek, then underneath his chin.

"Holly, stop." He laughed. "That tickles."

But that only made her find more places to put the doll. She danced her little friend around his face and pits and wings, forcing a needed smile out of him, until the tears dried up.

19

Kevin

Kevin almost didn't want to wake up. Maïmoú's dream-scape—her Void—was strangely comforting, like a long hug you needed at the right time. If she'd let him, he would've stayed there for hours to keep her company.

But he couldn't dream any longer.

He woke up in that room Nadia had escorted him to. It was a small, metal box that had an industrial feel to it, like the inside of a robot's body. There were more pipes along the ceiling and missing tiles that revealed metal plating. With no windows or vents to keep the air clean, it reminded him of Morgan's secret basement, her fallout shelter. She'd said there was a possibility of more fallout shelters being built around Raeleen. She'd never told him there was one underneath the Asilo. He guessed this wasn't news to her.

He threw his legs over the side of his bed. All the revelations Maïmoú had dropped on him came back one by one. Those scenes from the past. Her history, or the most she was willing to tell him. All the Deities who hated her, a *child*.

He needed to get back home. There had to have been a way to leave the Asilo peacefully without Maïmoú's help. Maybe if he persuaded Marcos. They were friends, he should've

237

understood. Maybe not the whole Deity situation, but still. He needed to get back home. He needed to tell them everything.

Derek was alive. One of the Líders was dead. Zantl was connected to a Deity like him. There were people living underwater. Maïmoú existed.

He examined his new room. He couldn't tell if this was an upgrade or not. It was quite dirty with spiderwebs and starchy blankets. After trying to listen through the five-inch-thick door, Kevin gave the door a push.

It didn't open.

He remembered how everyone in the Asilo opened doors with their wrists. Morgan had once told him about Asilo workers being equipped with a special chip to get them places. Daftly, he pressed his own wrist against the door.

It didn't open.

"Figured," he said, though he wouldn't have put it past the Asilo to implant things under his skin while he slept.

With no other options, Kevin tried for the handle. It was an average-looking handle like the ones back home. None of the doors here opened normally, but having no other options, he tested his poor luck.

It opened effortlessly.

He kept himself from picking at his finger beds. A plan of action, that's what he needed now. He had to find an elevator that hadn't been broken by Maïmoú, or a stairwell. He couldn't fly in these tight halls, but he could run. Run as fast as he could to save Maïmoú the trouble of becoming visible again. She still needed to heal.

He looked left, then right. The hall was abandoned. He heard water sloshing through the walls. Someone's footsteps, a growl.

He chose left and jogged towards the corner. Thank the Above he hadn't been given any sedatives down here, none that he could feel, anyway. His mind was sharper with the knowledge that Maïmoú had given him. He felt like he could do this.

The next turn introduced him to two guards enjoying a cup of coffee together.

He flapped his wings to bring him back, but it was too late. They'd seen him. He gaped at them.

He booked it back around the corner. He couldn't let them die, too, and he *so* wasn't prepared for another fight for his life. He wasn't a fast runner when it came to staying alive.

Yet as he ran back to his room, thinking of a new strategy now that the element of surprise was gone, he didn't hear boot-steps. No yelling, no threats of gun violence.

They weren't chasing him. There weren't even any sirens.

"What?" he asked himself. Was he still dreaming?

Two new people walked down the hall, one curly-haired poodle guard leading a petite girl through the shelter.

"Viper," he breathed out.

She looked up, those bright blue eyes sparkling the blue freckles across her nose.

"Oh, look, you're up!" The guard waved him over. "Good morning. Or afternoon. You were out for quite a while there. Some of us were thinking you kicked the bucket."

Kevin didn't know what to say. He *knew* this guard. She was the girl Derek had kicked the rock at, the one that'd pivoted their lives. He almost recognized her from other places. Around the Asilo?

"*Hello?*" the guard said. She was exceptionally loud for being in the Guard, getting right in Kevin's face. "You good?"

"I...suppose so," he said. "Um, what's going on?"

"Nothing much. I was just walking Viper here around for a little out-of-tank exercise before I brought her to her doctor visit."

Viper shrunk away.

239

"My name's Pippa," the guard said. "Do you remember me? Your twin nearly knocked a tooth outta me."

"Yeah. Sorry about that."

"Eh, no worries. Glad to see you're okay."

"Am...I not going to get in trouble? My door was unlocked."

"And that's how it'll stay. That blast upstairs told us very loudly that doors don't work for you. They're not telling us how you did it, so I can only imagine it was from those huge muscles you got!"

Kevin squeezed his incredibly scrawny arm.

Pippa laughed. "Okay, that was mean. My bad. After some consideration, Nadia decided to take away almost all your restrictions so the Asilo doesn't get more destroyed. In fact, I think you're now one of the freest inmates here."

The memory brought up bile from his throat. Nobody deserved to die, even someone like Mikhail. His body, being thrown against the wall like that, was animalistic.

"Wait, are you hungry?" Pippa asked. "Can't imagine anyone came to check on you while you were zonked out. I guess we can stop by the cafeteria before the exam. Follow me."

The hall he was in now had the same layout as the upper floors. Nothing but empty halls and doors that might've led nowhere, might've led to another detention hall of caged innocence. Did more people like Viper and Tokala live down here?

They passed by guards wasting time by talking or joking around with each other. They passed by scientists or doctors wearing surgical masks and gloves to their elbows, carrying medical equipment with stern faces. They each gave Kevin a once-over that made him feel dirty.

When they passed by the medical rooms, Viper shut her eyes and let her guard lead her down the hall. Inside the open rooms were people getting blood drawn, in tanks with guards monitoring something around their neck. Some infants were being prepped naked on a table while older people breathed into tubes before coughing up phlegm.

Each one of them, in essence, looked like Viper. The markings, the fins, the cuts in their necks. There was a whole other world down here.

"What's going on?" Kevin asked.

Pippa bobbed her head between good and evil. She looked so familiar, it was right on the tip of his tongue. "It's...necessary, according to the Líders. We try to see how these people live without being able to breathe like you and me."

"What's the difference between them breathing underwater and me flying?" he asked earnestly. "It's just something that makes us different."

"Your flying doesn't impact your survival. These people need water to breathe, it's not something they choose to do. Líders in the past have tried to help them breathe on their own, but it's been an uphill battle. Some of the water they need is really hard to come by. We've lost a good number of waterborne from this, and unclean tanks and filtration systems have led to some...unfortunate deaths."

Viper curled more inwards towards Pippa.

Kevin fell back to watch her body language. She'd looked so free in the tank. Now, walking, she looked trapped in her own skin. She held her elbows tight and kept her gait short like a true prisoner.

As Kevin thought of a way to bridge a new topic, Viper caught him staring. He went to look away when she pointed in front of them. Two double doors were coming up, somewhere she didn't want to go.

And then, just then, Kevin understood a little more about Maïmoú's psyche. How she dedicated her efforts to saving someone precious—a conditioned selflessness. He had to do something, say something. He had to help.

"Uh, Pippa?"

"Yeah?"

"I'm actually not feeling too good to eat. Can I go back to my room?"

"Do you need some medication?" Pippa asked. "Let's head to the hospital wing and pick up some tablets for you."

Viper panicked, and Kevin cringed at himself. He might've been a decent liar, but he didn't know this world. These guards and doctors, they weren't good people to Viper, and she needed to get away from them before something terrible happened.

As Pippa turned down a darker hall, Kevin took a page out of Maïmoú's and Derek's handbook. Grabbing Viper's wrist, he turned on his heel and bolted.

He knew he'd done well when Viper didn't hesitate. She kept up with his sporadic pace as they dodged guards who didn't try to nab them. They looked at them like two rambunctious teenagers having a night out on the town.

"Sorry, I couldn't think," Kevin panted.

"What're we doing?" Viper asked.

"Running. This's what you wanted, right?"

She looked behind them. "Is this allowed?"

"Probably not, but she'd said something about me having restrictions lifted. I assumed you didn't want to go to the doctors, so I...ran. Where should we go?"

She bit her soft lip, then pointed to an upcoming turn.

It was like she'd been born down here. She led him down steps into vacant halls, through an unmarked closet that had a secret door behind dirty mops. They even crossed through a room made entirely of water valves and heavy tanks. Thick pipes dug through the ground and transported water to needed tanks.

"What is this?" he asked.

"The filtration system," she said. "This floor's for the brackish-borne, so our water has to be filtered in a special way. The water comes from underground, or so the guards say."

"What does brackish mean?"

"It's a term they call people like me. It's one who needs both drinking water and saltwater to breathe."

"So, if you swam in a river, would you be able to breathe?"

She thought about it. "I don't know. I've never been in one to find out."

They ran down a stairwell that spiraled tight like a corkscrew. Kevin's ears popped from the pressure as they descended deeper underground.

Even as a child, Kevin had splashed in riverbeds with Derek and Nikki. They'd explored underneath bridges and scavenged for the prettiest rocks. He'd share a beer with Derek on bridges, stargaze with Nikki on embankments. It was a rite of passage, to taste freedom in the form of a river.

And Viper had never been in one before. Did she even know what one was? Surely, right? But Kevin had never seen someone like her before. He didn't know such breeds existed, or such girls could be so beautiful.

He skidded to a stop. At the end of the hall was a circular atrium surrounded by railings. Down the drop were elevators and staircases that went even deeper down. The top sealed them in with a moldy ceiling, the bottom disappeared into darkness.

Viper gaped at the elevator she'd been beelining for. A *DO NOT USE* sign signalled their dead end.

Kevin peered down the drop. While the railing was a little high, the empty space gave him more than enough room to take flight.

He held out his hand to Viper. Viper, in turn, looked over the railing, rubbing the webbing in-between her fingers. "It's impossible."

"I can fly," he told her. "I used to fly with Derek, my twin."

Viper reassessed the drop and blew out her cheeks. The gill flaps around her neck opened and closed more rapidly than when she'd been running.

Kevin stepped up to the railing. He kept one foot on the ground as he stretched out his wings for what felt like the first time in months. He wasn't a bird to fly for the fun of it. It was too tiring for him. Derek was, but he wasn't as free as his other half.

In the distance, he heard the footsteps of guards running.

Viper unfurled her webbed fingers and laced them carefully with his. "I trust you."

He let her climb onto his back. Even with her long tail and extra fins, she wasn't as heavy as he imagined. Her arms and thighs were thinner than his and made herself born for the air.

He was glad she couldn't see his blushing face. He'd never held a girl so intimately before. Her skin was ice-cold. He wanted to warm her up.

A door opened and someone ran down the staircase they'd just come from.

"You ready?" Kevin asked, and he felt her nod against him.

"Mhm," she said, and with her permission, Kevin pushed himself up and over the ledge.

He curved in with the wind, feeling all the blood rush to his head. How he missed this. What a joy it was to finally spread your wings when you'd been caged for so long. He almost wanted to curve upwards to gain speed, but that was risky with a person on your back. He couldn't show off now.

He sensed he'd hit ground soon, but no, it kept going. He made sure to keep a firm grip on Viper's legs, but she had no problem doing that on her own. Her arms tightened around his neck as if she'd die. Despite her nature, she was very trusting of him and his wings.

"You okay?" he asked again.

"Is this how you always are?" she nearly screamed. "This fast? This free?"

"Sometimes." Flapping his wings, he veered them up and over a railing and hit the new level.

There must've still been sedatives in his system. As he landed, his feet couldn't find the will to stand. He took the fall first, crashing into the tile and keeping Viper from sustaining any injury. "Woah—!"

Her hair tickled the tip of his nose. She balanced atop him so she didn't crush him, but the way she'd saved herself pinned him underneath her. Her hands so close to his face, her knees...

She looked up, face red with tears from flying so fast. She rolled off of him, letting her tail slip over his thighs. "Sorry."

"No, you're okay." He got up, trying to calm down his rapidly beating heart. She'd definitely felt his thing. A skirt could only hide so much.

Viper gave him her hand, and the two of them continued their escape. "That was incredible," she said. "I've never flown before. Is it natural for you? Was it scary?"

"As scary as it is to swim for you. I don't think I've ever gone that deep into water."

"Really?" It honestly sounded like that shocked her. "I like swimming. I like floating, really. But that was fun. Real fun."

"I'm glad I was your first. At flying," he corrected. "I'll try to fly you to more places."

"I'd like that." She led him down new rooms of filtration tanks and brought them to a heavy door locked with a crank. Both he and her helped crank it open together.

Tanks like the one Viper lived in lined both walls. There was more room here for Kevin's wings, but he pushed them down to better see these tanks, these...

They had to be animals, for they had eyes and mouths. They looked like little birds, but instead of wings, they had fins and gills, and varied in sizes, shapes, and colors.

"Those are fish," Viper explained, and she pointed his eyes to a bigger fish. It was grey and sharper than the others. "And that's a shark. It's a predator, but it doesn't eat the fish it's compatible with."

He watched the animals swim through the water. The deeper they were in the tank, the better camouflaged they became, until they were nothing but shadows. "So these are your animal equivalents?"

"Yes."

"You're a shark?"

"Oh, no. They still have trouble with my breed, but they think I'm more or less one of these little ones." Walking up to the edge of the tank, she pointed at one of the smallest fish treading along the sand. It had beady eyes and the same blue freckles as her. "They clean the bottom of the tanks. Have you ever seen one before?"

"Never."

Her eyes lightened, catching the blue of the tank. She brought him down to the end of the room to a hidden stairwell that led underneath the floor tiles. Kevin folded in his wings to fit.

"This's a safe space," she explained. "At least, a place I know about from Tokala. She likes finding hidden spots to give the guards grief."

"She sounds a bit like a troublemaker. You said she's your friend, right?"

"Yeah. We grew up in the same tank."

Kevin marvelled at this hidden world. It was an empty space between two tanks underneath a walkway. The grate above them dotted the floor with blue light. The tanks sparkled rainbows across their feet.

Viper fell back against one of the tanks in a huff. Tiny fish swam around her head, wondering why she wasn't with them.

Kevin sat beside her. "So, that was exciting."

"It was. I've never done anything like that before."

"What, go for a run?" he asked, attempting to make her smile.

She did. "Yeah, and they didn't get mad at us or hit us. That doesn't happen. Tokala was right, you *are* special."

"I-I wouldn't say that. A lot of things just happen around me. Sorry about that scene back there."

"It's okay. I didn't see much of it happen."

"Huh?"

"From before," she said, "with Mikhail?"

His skin went colder than hers. "Oh. Above, right. I'm so sorry. I didn't know you saw any of it."

"It's okay. You didn't do anything wrong. That was Zantl's powers, wasn't it? The way they..." She silenced herself. "It must've been scary, being in the room when it happened. I'm sorry."

"You shouldn't have seen that."

"You shouldn't have, either. Do you know exactly what happened? I saw you talking with someone, I think?"

"I..." He couldn't stop himself. If only one other person could understand his situation, he wanted it to be someone who trusted him, who he could, in time, put his trust into. "The same thing that happens to Zantl happens to me," he explained. "All the violent bursts and special powers. I can't control it. It just...happens."

"Oh," she said. "Are you okay?"

He went to say, *"Yeah, of course I am."*

But he didn't, and he closed his mouth to think harder about his feelings. Not his family's, not the Líders, not even Maïmoú, but him.

And he felt shitty. Stuck in mud from which he couldn't escape. He was tired, and frightened. He wanted to cry again, it was so bad, but he'd had a thousand and one things to worry about, he hadn't any time for himself.

But his feelings mattered, at least to Viper, this stranger who only knew him through brief encounters separating them by glass walls and violence.

"I'm sorry," Viper said. "I shouldn't have brought it up."

"It's okay. It's nice to talk about it with someone."

She filled her mouth with air again. "Who are you?" she then asked. "Where'd you come from? I heard the Guard making up different stories about you. You lived on the upper floors before an accident sent you down here."

The news must've not travelled as far as he'd thought. "My twin fell off the Muralha. He was able to pass through the Barreira and I was framed for pushing him off. I suppose the Líders wanted to question me more, so I've been here for, Above, I don't even know how long. A month? Maybe two? How long have you been here?"

"Forever."

"Does it really feel that way? What did you do? Sorry," he said instantly. "That was rude. You don't have to answer."

"I don't think I did anything. None of us did. We were born here."

"What?"

"All of us. We were born here." She wiggled her bare feet over each other. "Our mothers and fathers, our grandparents, their grandparents before them. Each one of us has lived here forever."

Morgan hadn't clued him in about this underground fallout shelter. She'd never told him that it'd been converted to a prison for rare species who could breathe water and lived in tanks. Had she'd known, and if so, to what extent? Did anyone know about this besides the Líders and their guards, who acted like it was perfectly alright to seal people away from the world? And he'd trusted Marcos.

"How?" he asked. "I mean, I've never seen someone like you before. Someone so—"

She glanced up at him, those blue eyes capturing him like a net.

"Unique," he landed on. "I-I mean, I hardly know you—I only know your name—but your tail and scales and eyes. How you breathe underwater, that's unheard of outside of the Asilo. You're so special."

"S-says you," she said, adding a little more energy to her words. "Your wings are so pretty. I mean, they're cool. I've heard guards describe birds to me before, both bird crossbreeds and regular birds. I hadn't imagined them to be so big. Your wings, I mean. They're beautiful."

"Y-you are, too!" It felt like he'd broken through his own Barreira. He didn't know how far one went with complimenting girls. He'd never had a lover before, Derek had had several, Vanna had tried. Even Nikki had gone on a date with a girl in her class before ghosting her out of fear of her own rejection. Kevin had ultimately agreed he'd never find a love like that because he was awkward, shy. Quiet, nervous, had low self-esteem.

But here was Viper, someone way out of his league, calling him beautiful. He felt his heart unlock with newfound confidence. "You're...really pretty," he continued. "I keep staring at your eyes. They're almost glowing."

"Sometimes they do that. Waterborne perks." She played with the thin hair surrounding those pretty eyes, and Kevin wanted to keep feeding her compliments until it wrecked him with embarrassment.

"Raeleen," she then said. "That's the place you live right, outside of the Asilo? That's where the guards come from."

"Yeah. I live there. A bunch of people do. There're schools and grocery stores and better hospitals that aren't scary. It's all up there. Have you *ever* left the Asilo before?"

"Never. The Líders say that the world isn't designed for us. And many of us can't stay out of the water as long as I can, so it can be unsafe."

"I noticed that. So you can breathe in the air?"

She nodded. "Tokala and I can breathe both air and water. I can stay out of the water for almost six hours without going back in, and my time only increases with every year. I need to rehydrate after that, otherwise my skin gets dry and I get a bad cough, but Tokala's times are better than mine."

"Do you know why you were all placed here? Were you...made?"

"I...don't think so. I think, one day, they collected all of us from the water outside and brought us down here. They test our abilities to stay out of the water."

"Wouldn't that hurt?"

She nodded again. "I don't like the doctors here. Some are nice, but most of them are..." She touched her upper thigh. There was an old bruise there.

"Evil," Kevin guessed.

"Mhm."

"I'm sorry," he said. "I shouldn't have asked."

"No, it's okay. Like you said, it's nice to talk about it with someone. I've never met someone who doesn't know about us. Even new guards already know about our lives, some even know our birth dates and allergies without even calling us by our names, just our medical numbers. It's nice to finally meet someone who's fresh."

"I'm happy that I met someone like you." He chose his next words wisely. "Viper, these tests the Líders have you doing, this way of life, it's scary. You deserve to see the rest of the world, the real world."

"But we get punished if we even think about leaving. Some have tried to and were killed. My parents..." She lowered her head. "I don't want anyone to get in trouble."

He gave her his hand. The rainbows crossed her arm over to his, with fish swimming over to watch this pact being made. "I'll figure out a way to save you. We'll get out of here, together. I promise."

And Kevin's threads, at that moment, were forever tied to hers.

20

Nikki

The fallout shelter reminded Nikki of something she always wanted to live in: a lavish, five-star hotel.

Morgan had yet to assemble a swimming pool or fancy check-in desk, but whatever. This hidden, underground bunker had air conditioning, central heating, and communal bathrooms with thirty-some-odd stalls, including these weird showers she didn't know how to work. They went from floor to ceiling and had transparent walls with many buttons and settings. Morgan had told her not to try them, as the pipes were rusted from not being used in decades. All they spurted out was salty water.

After being introduced to this world, Nikki took it upon herself to scope out each room. She poked her nose into the kitchen and living quarters and found stairways that led up to the main floors. She unlocked hidden rooms with careful hands and found meeting rooms, discussion tables with abandoned chairs. Some looked well lived in, others looked lost to time, old tech collecting dust.

In one room closest to the Drill, Nikki found Morgan's main workroom, evidenced by its organized chaos. Stacks of boxes up against the tables and chalkboards that hadn't been washed in years.

There were framed photographs above the door: Morgan throughout her years, of her parents, her goofing off with her newfound friend and soon-to-be lover Del. Nikki's mother and father were introduced during her school life. They laughed in the same school uniforms Nikki and Vanna wore. Them in front of the Drill, Derek and Kevin as babies, Vanna's first 50/50, and finally, the first day Nikki was adopted.

They'd taken three photographs of her, before Nikki refused to get in front of a camera. The second was of her sitting at her favorite booth upstairs, looking small next to a giant iced mocha. Morgan had wanted to document the first time Nikki had come to the coffeehouse without her parents. The third picture was of her, Kevin, and Derek, smiling with their arms wrapped around each other. It'd been that year, at Nikki's eighteenth birthday party.

She left. She'd asked her parents to burn those photos because the past embarrassed her. This was the only place they could keep them.

Despite the size of the fallout shelter, no more than twenty or so people worked here at a given time. She'd come across strangers she hadn't been introduced to before. She'd nearly jumped out of her skin when she bumped into a guard still in uniform.

"I told you dogs to change when you come down here!" Morgan had called out to them. "Get out of that shit before I strip you naked myself!"

With the help of other revolutionists, Morgan had reconstructed the fallout shelter into a legacy of science, technology, and ingenuity. She'd reprogrammed the intercom, restocked the medicine bay with stolen Asilo sedatives, and restored the cafeteria with canned food. All that plus building the Drill while keeping her coffeehouse and family afloat. She was always moving and, in her words, bettering Raeleenian lives with the chance to live.

Yet even with this new world given to her, Nikki couldn't smile like Morgan could. Whenever she walked into the lobby, Vanna would hide away in the bathrooms. Whenever she washed her hands of grease, he'd run for the bedroom area, waiting until they shut down for the night. Even at school, to which Nikki now went under Vanna's earlier pleas, he refused to work with her, talk with her. He hardly ever looked at her now, islanding himself so nobody could swim to his isolated rock.

One day after school, Nikki found herself reaching deep into the Drill between its side door and caterpillar tracks. Her family and some strangers huddled around her as she dislocated her shoulder.

"I believe in you," Morgan whispered.

Nikki groaned and stretched her arm farther in-between the metal plates. She didn't know how she'd found herself working on the Drill, but she liked being helpful. And it got her closer to her family, weirdly enough. Their hesitancy about Kevin now made sense, and she almost didn't fault them for hiding it from her. If the Líders knew about their plan to drill into the Muralha, they'd be more than screwed.

"Almost there," Morgan said.

Nikki spat on the floor. "Why don't you shake it and let the screw fall?"

"Because this baby's 10,000 pounds, and if we lose that screw, it can fall someplace we don't want it to be."

Nikki's cheek pressed against the warm metal. The Drill ticked and gurgled without even being on, and every piece she touched with her glove felt either incredibly hot or burning cold.

She tapped a loose piece with her finger. Before it dropped, she twisted her wrist and caught it. Applause greeted her as she pulled out the screw.

"Good job," her mother said.

"We've been trying to get at that all week," her father added. "Good work."

Nikki rolled her shoulder inside her own pair of green coveralls. The baggy one-piece was drenched in the scent of oil.

"You should think about spending all your evenings here with us," Morgan said. "Now that the cat's outta the bag, you can quit school and work here full time."

"Don't you dare," her mother warned.

"What? It's what you all did when I told you about this place."

"We were different. Nikki still has a future to work for."

Nikki wanted to question what future her mother saw in her. She wasn't exactly trained in any remarkable skill other than baseball, and you couldn't make a career out of throwing a stitched ball when the Muralha was chipping away.

The adults went back to work on the Drill. Her mother and father worked in the fuel tank together while Morgan addressed a couple of dog crossbreeds on where to go. This left Nikki working with Del. Out of everyone, Del was by far the quietest. She did what was asked of her and worked hard for her family.

She stretched over Nikki to place a piece of tape on the Drill's antenna. As she moved, her coveralls lifted, and Nikki noticed a long scar across her forearm.

When Del caught her looking, Nikki asked, "Did you get that scar from working on the Drill?"

Del fell back with the help of her wings. "Got it the day Derek and Kevin were born."

"What happened to give you a scar that big?"

"Don't know. They were born in the house. Iysra doesn't trust hospitals. Morg and I were there to help. I was holding the two kids, Kev first, then Derek six minutes later."

Derek had always hated the fact that he was the younger twin. "What happened then?"

"When I got to drying them off, I felt this..." She touched her scarred arm. "I felt someone touch me—touch them—and I was thrown against the wall. Morg said I tripped, but I know what I felt."

"You *did* trip!" Morgan said. "I wouldn't have let anything happen to you or those kids. She hit her head when she fell, so her brain got all scattered. You know, I used to believe in ghosts for the longest time, and Del was always, *'No, if you can't see it or feel it, it doesn't exist'*. Now, she goes on saying something invisible touched her. I don't buy it."

Nikki, instead of touching her arm, touched her cheek, the one Shào had touched from her dream. It felt like years since then. Was *he* a ghost? He'd called himself something else in his dream. A God? No, a Deity.

Then she touched her throat.

"Never" was the best time to tell her family about her encounter with Shào and Maïmoú, but she had to soon, didn't she? It was all connected, them and the fallout shelter. There were documents here talking about their existence, yet no one other than Nikki knew the truth. From what they could deal to a city, she figured best to keep the connection from her family for eternity.

"Kids were fine, though," Morgan continued. "Trouble follows them every which way, but that's what happens with twins, yeah? Anyway, Nikki, enough talk of invisible people. Between you and me, you should really start thinking about working for us. I don't pay people who come and go, but if you start coming here more frequently, I can give you money under the table."

Nikki pulled a face. "You don't make money doing this."

"On the contrary! People give me hearty donations for both my cakes and my plan to completely demolish the government's stranglehold on its imperceptive commonwealth." She grinned. "I make enough."

Quiet footsteps ran from the cafeteria into the hall.

"You should think about it!" Morgan continued. "It'll give you a place to truly be yourself, free of the Líders and the Guard."

Nikki turned around. "Where's Vanna?"

Morgan's furry ears twitched. "Not sure. He usually doesn't work on the Drill. He likes making us dinner and cleaning up after us. Sometimes, we forget to eat for hours at a time. I want this Drill running by December, yeah? No time to waste!

"Did he just run down the hall behind me?"

Del looked over the Drill's spiraled point, as did Nikki's mother and father.

"Could you talk to him?" Morgan asked, finally breaking. "Del and I don't know our way around him, he's so hidden. Make sure he's okay for us, yeah?"

Nikki cast a glance down the hall. A door closed. "I'll do what I can."

She followed the foreign signs down the halls, looking back to make sure she didn't get caught down a dead end. Resting on her heels, she entered the kitchen and turned on the lowlights. Morgan had told her they needed to save on electricity so they didn't overwork the generators. Their exhaust came out through pipes scattered across twenty streets. It took her four years to rework the piping without notifying the Guard. "Vanna?"

Not finding him in the kitchen, Nikki tiptoed down the hall and opened up a door underneath a fire icon.

The room looked like a hospital lab. It had a blocky machine in the center with tiny doors locked on the wall like lockers. Nikki herself had never been in such a room before, but from its layout, she knew it to be a crematorium.

Vanna was sitting on the floor, up against the machine meant to prepare the bodies. He had his face buried in his knees and was rocking slightly.

Nikki closed the door so he knew she was there. "Hey," she said.

He sniffled. He tried to hide it—his patchy face, his watering eyes—but with Nikki blocking the door, he had no place else to run. He silently cried into his knees and Nikki had to watch and do nothing about it.

She forced herself in, taking long strides to reach him. When she got there, she didn't know what to do. Lost, she thought about what Kevin would've done and, doing what felt unnatural, she squatted down and held his hand.

He sobbed into her shoulder like he was seconds from drowning in his own tears. His voice pitched, and the *ache*, she felt it inside of her. She'd always known Vanna to be emotional, but it was heartbreaking, seeing a loved one break down in front of you.

"It's so hard," he cried.

"What is?" she asked.

"Everything. I couldn't say anything to you. I had to keep it a secret for so long. My moms said I had to pretend like everything was fine, but it wasn't. Of course I wasn't."

"So why're you crying? I know everything now, and they're probably alive, Derek and Kev."

"'*Probably*', Nikki? Probably's not good enough. Pippa tells me what's being done to Kev. They're taking his blood and drugging him. There's something wrong with him, but they haven't figured out what. And Derek, who knows where he could be. Not even the Líders know."

"I keep telling myself I'm going to see them any day now. That's how I handle it."

"Well, I can't do that. I'm not like you." He leaned on her.

She nodded, taking in his coffeehouse scent. She looked down at his wrist.

"Sorry," he said, covering them up. "I couldn't stop myself this week."

"You're trying."

"I'm not, though. I feel like it's the only thing I have control over. I'm just sad and scared all the time. Some days are good, but most of the time, especially at night, it's so hard."

"I'm sorry if I made it worse," she said. "I didn't mean to yell at you, back before. It wasn't right for me to say that I love Derek and Kev more. We all love them equally." She held him tighter. "I'm sorry I hurt you. I'll do better going forwards. I'll be here for you. Always."

"Thanks." He sniffed. "You know, it's not even because of you anymore, or Derek or Kev. It's *them*, out there. I understand why they're doing this, but it's like seeing Derek taunt the Guard when he's drunk, but all the time. When I wake up and see that they're not in bed, I automatically think they've been killed for knowing too much, or another explosion went off down here. But they expect me to work on this, fix that, go here and there, and I want to help them. I don't want to disappoint anyone."

"No normal person could work like this."

"*You* work like this."

"Well, I'm not normal, am I?"

"How're you not?"

She shifted the conversation away from herself. "Never mind that." She smirked at him. "So, now that we're done keeping secrets, I have a question for you."

"No, you can't live down here forever. The air's too stuffy."

"I mean about you and Pippa."

He jerked back and hit his head on the back of the machine. He groaned. "What about it?"

"'Ey, what's this now? Did I hit a nerve? A love-struck nerve?"

"*Enough.*" That blush returned to his pointed features. He used his scarf to cover it up.

"What's going on between you two? Who is she? Are you official?"

"She's...a guard my mom roped into this. She was climbing the ranks in the Asilo and my mom snatched her up, and when Kev got sent away, she asked her to watch over him. So she, you know, comes down a lot now."

"To talk to you?"

He bit his scarf. "Sometimes."

"And kiss you?"

He gently pushed her.

"You're not denying it. How long have you been dating?"

"...A month," he fessed up. "Our anniversary's this week."

"Oh, God, you celebrate anniversaries now? You're such a romantic. You remind me of Derek celebrating his one-week anniversaries with those shitty exes."

"God?"

"Huh?"

"You said God," he said. "What does that mean?"

She blinked. She didn't know. Well, she did, but she didn't know why she'd used that word instead of Above, just a random word people used to describe things they couldn't control, as if it were above their heads.

Something from Lí's head, then? It sounded like something he'd say, though she didn't know how she knew that.

"I knew you in a past life," Shào had said, *"as a boy named Lí Naranbaatar."*

"Nikki?"

She came back. It was so easy, losing yourself to another world. "Sorry," she said. "Lost my train of thought. Must've, uh, read about that word in those documents."

"Whatever," he said. Thank God he wasn't perceptive when he cried. "And stop listening to my conversations with Pippa. Weirdo."

"*You're* the weirdo," she echoed. "So, do your moms know about Pippa?"

"Above, no. They'd kick me out faster than if I told the Líders about this place."

But that blush was slowly crawling up to his ears, and that little, tiny smile she'd gotten out of him was growing. He was *proud* of what he'd accomplished with Pippa, and he hadn't been able to share it with anybody else in the family.

Nikki sat up, hands in her pockets. "I'll make you some coffee, you silly love bird."

"I don't—"

"Extra milk and sugar, yeah?"

Before he could answer the order Nikki already had memorized, she slammed the door a little too hard and jogged for the Drill's hangar.

Morgan and Del were talking over a large paper of schematics. They held it up in the air, blocking their view of Nikki striding up to meet them. With the slight advantage, she ripped the paper in half and punched Morgan in the jaw. Del went to catch her, but Nikki used her height against her and threw them both into a pile of cardboard boxes.

The workers stopped. A box of screws toppled as Nikki's parents stumbled out from the Drill.

"Listen!" Nikki jumped onto the Drill to make her voice heard. "Vanna's in the crematorium right now sobbing because he's terrified of the Guard coming in and executing all you. Did you ever think that maybe he doesn't want to do this? Have you ever *talked* with him about his feelings? He's been getting worse since Derek and Kev left, and you still let him down here? What is *wrong* with you?"

Morgan pulled a nail out of her glove. "He said he wants to help."

"He can't, and you know that. Seeing him like that and not saying anything is shitty parenting. I know it's hard for you,

Morg, because you're like me—you can't deal with feelings— and you, Del, you do everything Morg tells you to do, but you're his parents! I don't care how hard you've found it to be. Make it work, because you two should be the first people he goes to for help, *not* me!"

Morgan looked up to Del, whose jaw had dropped with nothing to say. She tried to find an excuse for their behavior, but she had none. She sat thunderstruck.

"And fix your prejudices," Nikki added. "It's ugly and damaging to your kid. The Guard works for a corrupt system that needs to be changed. Dogs themselves are *not* the problem. And—and stop with all *this*," she added tiredly, throwing a hand over their work. "All this stuff isn't helping the main issues we're facing. People are dying and the world is ending."

"Don't be so bleak, Nikki."

"It *is* bleak. It's been bleak for hundreds of years. You and Dawood need to stop messing around with us and do your jobs."

"Who's Dawood?"

"Oh, shut it, Madriel. I can't deal with any more of your sass today." Nikki jumped off the Drill, her speech done.

Morgan got up with her tail tucked. "Everyone, uh, let's take a break," she told her workers. "Actually, let's wrap things up. Tonight's plans are cancelled for now."

As the room returned to its uneasy chatter, Nikki left the scene. Talking so loud over a sea of people was exhausting. She just wanted everyone safe and to get along, but Fate was making that extremely hard for her.

She fled into that bedroom she'd first woken up in with Vanna and Pippa. It still had Vanna's homework in it. It smelled the most like him, like home.

She curled up in his bunk with her arms crossed. They *were* family, but they took years off her life. Madriel and Dawood, and Vitaliya. They were all like family to her, but she couldn't...

She couldn't...

She blinked, staring off into nothing.

Who was she thinking about? Morgan and Del, with Vanna, her cousin. That's who they were, but...

She sat up. Her vision was distorting. Her mind, thumping with a sudden headache. She held it, but it didn't help, and she slumped forwards into her knees like she was going to be sick. Dawood. Del. Madriel. Morgan. Vitaliya.

"Tai."

She felt her body sinking through the tiles. A sickening, deadly infection spread over her nerves and heart, as if she'd witnessed a murder. She *knew* those names. She'd known them as if they were her family, but they weren't.

"Tai?" she called out again, both asking for him and questioning why she was saying it at all. Her eyes were watering— she was *crying* from emotions she didn't understand, for a person she didn't know.

Tai was someone Lí had known. From his memories, on the roof. Were those other names people he'd known from his past?

She rubbed her hands of sweat, but the feeling did not pass, this remembrance and *need* for a stranger to comfort her.

"Shào," she whispered, "what's going on with me?"

But no one answered.

21

Derek

Each royal got their own royal carriage for their royally stupid trip into Devnya Town. They were driven by these animals called "horses" and were accompanied by a platoon of knights who'd walk beside the wooden wheels. It looked fun if not for the fact that Derek was ready to throw a massive shit fit about it.

His mood was in the Underground from his fight with the king. He was bitter and ready to fight anyone who came near him, even the maids who'd dressed him up extra stupid today. He now wore more frills than Cellena with tighter boots.

He didn't know why. And he didn't know why he was still going along with it. He'd been planning on sulking in his room all day, but Cellena had stuck her little nose through the door crack, her soft eyes glistening with hope.

"You don't have to come," she'd said, "it's just that my father really wants to show you off to the public, and it's better to do what he says, else..."

So, there he was, crammed inside a rickety carriage heading off to a "village." Whatever the fuck that was. A city made more sense, but when he said that, the royals had given him that stupid fucking look again, like they were talking to an idiot.

Maybe they had been. He was to the king. All for kissing a boy.

He cursed to himself and looked out the window. He wanted to drink himself to death for how he was feeling, but at least he was free from the castle walls. His carriage had windows on either side, letting him take in the Drail Kingdom at a human's-eye view.

The sky was snow-white with pockets of blue towards the Barrier. The grounds were stretching out into fields. They patchworked the Kingdom for miles. Some stalks poked out from the snow, but a majority of the crop had died due to the snow.

Derek pressed his cheek into the frosty pane. They should've been more prepared for bad weather. Either that or they didn't care, which didn't make sense to him. Why waste food? Didn't they know the toils of caring for a farm? Even he knew that.

He lifted his head. No, he didn't. He didn't know the first thing about farm life.

He sprawled out his legs to the other side of his carriage. He hadn't worked a day in his life, but as they passed each plot of land, he found faults with their construction. The soil didn't look healthy, there were boulders growing around the crop. If he had the chance, he'd stop his carriage and give them advice about how to grow harvestable wheat.

Then he saw what'd give them the worst crop imaginable: craters. Sizable craters pocketed the Earth like pores in a sponge. Some took up an entire acre of land, morphing the road into S-like patterns.

He sat on his knees to get a better view beyond the craters. The first structure they came across slumped as a single-story house made of stone and hay. Two field workers in tunics and wool hats scooped up leftover crops submerged in the snow. They waved their shovels, greeting the royals so they wouldn't strain their voices.

Derek's tail feathers wagged. Borrowing dozens of acres from the Earth, cultivating crops to keep a family alive, he knew this life. He knew their hardships and it got him feeling weird inside. Not a bad weird, but not a good one, either. Just weird, and wistful.

His carriage jerked. Someone opened their carriage door behind his.

Through the snow, Cellena, dress lifted, ran alongside Derek's carriage. Without stopping the carriage, Derek opened the door and helped her inside.

She exhaled a long puff of white smoke. "Please excuse me."

"Be excused." He forced his attention away from the passing fields. "What's up?"

"I wished to talk with you about what occurred between you and Oliver this week."

"Shit, you're not gonna grill me about that, too, are you? I thought you were cool."

"I am not." She folded her ankles politely for the conversation. "It wasn't right that my father hit you, and for that, I wanted to apologize." She bowed. "You shouldn't have been hit...for something you do not understand. That I," she added, "do not understand. I don't agree that it's a sin to...be with..."

Another carriage door opened far off, and in seconds, Jabel was jogging alongside Derek's carriage.

"Oh, God," Derek cursed, but let him in. He packed himself into a corner as Jabel sat beside his sister.

"It's freezing out," he said with a shiver. "Why on Earth Father agreed to come out now is beyond me."

"Welcome to the Sinner Carriage," Derek said. "All are welcome here."

Jabel gave him a nasty look. "What were you two talking about?"

"That which needs to be discussed," Cellena said. "I don't agree with what father did, nor with his...political views."

"Uh, is something up?" Derek asked. "You two seem more jumpy than usual."

The two siblings looked at one another. Cellena raised her brows like she was edging him on. Jabel shook his head definitively.

"What?" Derek asked.

"Jabel has something he wishes to tell you."

"Cellena Channity Wueng, how dare you!" Jabel said. "This wasn't what I agreed to discuss."

"Then why are we both here?" she asked. "If we're to change anything, let it be *now*, with him."

"Okay, still lost," Derek said.

Jabel, defeated, slumped down beside his sister. She took his hand in support of whatever he was going through.

"I...don't think it's right to talk about these matters in public," he confessed.

"Well, we're not in public, we're in a slightly too-small carriage heading off to somewhere extremely public." Derek leaned in. "What's wrong?"

"I just...I have differing opinions when it comes to the demons," he said. "My father's forefathers have killed every last demon able to die. We've won a battle they'd been waging for years, yet my father hasn't been able to sleep knowing the last few are 'keeping up the Barriers'." He said that with air quotes. "I'm...I'm *sick* of it," he said, now in a whisper. "I'm *sick* of pretending to hate demonkind. I don't hate them. Neither of us do. Nero and Runa, some of the maids and cooks, none of us hate them. We pity them, we see them as citizens, I..."

Jabel fiddled with the rings on his fingers.

"It's alright," Cellena said encouragingly.

He gulped and continued. "Remember what my father told you, about my attack on the shoreline? A demon had saved me and brought me back home."

Derek remembered what he'd seen after being slapped. "Maxwell, yeah?"

"Y-yes. The week after that occurred, I'd found the same demon tied up near the stables. He's a demonic breed who needs to be in water, otherwise his skin will dry out. Knights had found him and tied him up as a joke. I'd found him and replenished him in my bathtub. He stayed with me that night.

"When...I was helping him," he said, now forcing the words to come out, "he told me his side of the story. How none of the demons are responsible for these mental attacks on human-kind, nor how they're the ones keeping up the Barrier. I got to know so many things my father forbade us from learning about that night."

He sucked in his dry lips. "Y-you're not here on Earth be-cause of me, are you?" he suddenly asked. "For everything I've been doing with him, this isn't because of me, is it?"

"What? No," Derek said. "I don't even know why I'm here in the first place. Why would I care if you hung out with a demon? Why does that matter?"

Jabel looked away, ears red. Cellena hugged his arm for moral support.

Derek looked between the two siblings, and then it clicked. "Oh."

Jabel shut his eyes tight.

"Oh, *fuck*." Derek blushed for his sake. "So you and him—"

"Enough," Jabel said. "Y-you can't let this leave the carriage, okay? I can't have any more rumors spreading about me. If my father were to ever find out, he'd hang me."

"So are you *mated* with him? Did he bag you?"

Jabel sucked in his lips again, then said, "That's a rather crude way of interpreting it."

"Because I'm mated with Oliver."

"Yes, I know. He's told me."

"Good job," Cellena whispered to him, and Jabel suppressed a smile.

Derek sat back in his seat. "Above, Jabel."

"I know."

"I didn't."

"You weren't supposed to. I was going to take this secret to my grave, but I couldn't keep it from Cellena. She's helped me...more than words can express."

Cellena hugged him fully, and Jabel finally opened up and hugged her back.

"You people put so much emphasis into who you like and how you choose to express yourself," Derek told them. "You shouldn't feel ashamed about that type of stuff."

"Acceptance doesn't come to us as naturally as it does for you," Jabel said. "There're rules we can't write away. That's why we're here. We need *you* to change it."

The carriage hit a road bump. They passed a fence, then another house.

"We're close," Jabel warned. He reached for the carriage handle.

"Derek," Cellena said, hurried, "Father thinks that the key to saving our humanity is to eliminate the demons, but I've heard Jabel's side."

"I've been with him," Jabel confessed, "at his place. Maxwell. I've talked with all of them. They're really good people."

"The demons aren't the ones at fault for the world being broken," Cellena said.

"Then who is?" Derek asked. "If it's not you, the demons, or me, I don't think, then it has to be your God's fault, right?"

The idea of their own God hurting them showed on their faces. They clutched their inverted crosses for guidance.

The carriage jumped again, and the sound of a bustling town surrounded them on all fronts.

Derek pictured Devnya Town to be smaller. Going off what they'd passed to get here, he'd imagined fifteen or sixteen wooden houses with a stream passing through it. After being in the castle for so long, he thought the human population only amounted to the knights and maids who waited on him.

As they crossed through a stone arch marking the entrance, Devnya Town opened up to over 600 houses, most of which stood two stories tall. There were water wheels and market-places and churches—*so* many churches, as if religion didn't dominate their lives enough. Every corner had a pointed build-ing with the cross towering over the streets.

The streets themselves had been decorated for their arrival. Pennant flags and confetti, the works. And the *humans*, they were packed in the streets in the billions and trillions, it felt like. They flooded the streets and hung out of windows yelling, chanting, *screaming* like animals. Derek had never seen so many people. He'd never heard a crowd so loud.

They were let out of their carriages one at a time. Jabel and Cellena had tried to slip out back into their carriages, but their father was already waiting for them near his knights. He gave them each a disappointed look as they left Derek's carriage.

Derek's chest was clenched as tightly as his fists. His body was pleading for him to stay in the carriage where it was safe, but now it felt too stifling. They were all around him now, with knights pushing the humans back so they didn't create a stam-pede. He had nowhere to go but up, but he didn't trust his wings. They were shivering with his legs.

Nero appeared in the carriage door and cautiously held out his hand.

"I can't go out there," Derek whispered.

"I'm sorry," Nero said, frowning, "but you don't have a choice."

They all climbed onto horseback and continued their jour-ney into town. Derek had no trouble getting onto his—it was second nature, somehow—but this crowd, the noise, the eyes. There had to be a thousand humans ogling him like a God. He hid in his wings, but that only made the humans cheer louder.

Cellena and Jabel drew their horses shoulder to shoulder and waved, keeping a considerable distance from the corralled herds. The people kept shouting Derek's name and asking him for help. Some asked him to kiss baby heads or bless their grandchildren. How could he talk with these people, and how was he supposed to make their lives better?

"My people!" the king shouted. "Here lies the young man who will offer you salvation and prosperity for the rest of your lives!"

Hands not clasped in prayer reached up for Derek. They cried, belted out their undying love for Derek Harrow, Derek Harrow.

Derek Harrow was currently going stress blind from a panic attack. Why were there so many humans in one place waiting for him? What had he done worthy of this?

Following human traditions, Derek grabbed his cross for help. He needed someone to save him. He needed to be heard.

A house with a sunken-in roof marked the next turn in the street. In its doorless entryway waited a family of three going on four. A woman at least eight months pregnant was watching the parade with hatred in her eyes. The man beside her, the exact opposite in character, had his frail arms over his teenage son's shoulders.

When the mother saw Derek, she stormed into the crowd, disappearing as the man, likely her husband, called out her name. "Keva!"

Keva. That was a nice name. A little average, but it rolled off the tongue good. It stuck with him, that name, or some version of it. Kev—

Normally, his eyes were good, better than most humans, but that name kept ringing one of his bells—Keva, Keva—and threw

271

him off. He was wondering if he knew a Keva when something struck him in the face: a boot, women's size, thrown with vitriol.

His horse bucked him off its back. His wings flapped and hit a knight, keeping him from flying, and he fell into a canal built around the street corner.

The crowd echoed into the chasm like a swirling drain. Shadows meant to be people looked down at him, judging him.

He shielded himself with his wings. "Stop looking at me," he begged. His brain was yelling at him to get out, but he was having trouble standing, let alone saving himself from his claustrophobia.

He climbed out, rock by rock, his *sari* catching on the wet stone. Strands of hair were coming loose from his headscarf.

He gasped, nearly falling back into the canal. He wasn't in Devnya Town anymore. He didn't know where he was. The snow had melted into sand. Goats and pigs replaced their horses. Instead of furry coats, the crowd was now wearing robes and had tanner skin made for the Sun, some human, some not. The houses, the roads, the sky, it was all different, foreign.

Someone grabbed Derek by the sleeve and heaved him out, but Derek was no longer Derek. He had a female body, a human's, with large curves and black hair held back by a headscarf. He was barefoot and adorned with jewels, and his hands were bound.

The crowd now chanted a new name. "Hadiya, Hadiya."

"Hadiya!"

Hadiya was thrown into the main square by the temple priests.

"Move, now! On your feet!"

She'd done her best to escape today's ceremony, but her day to die had come. She hadn't broken her shackles in time. Her mind, warped by the priests, had convinced her that she was meant to sacrifice herself for the community. The most beautiful virgin, the one who'd tempted every man. Even if she had broken her shackles that night, she couldn't have tested her luck. A lone woman, backpacking through the scorching deserts to the north, alone? It was a death sentence much graver than human sacrifice.

The priests dragged her away from her suicide attempt back towards the temple. In front of the building was a stone table of slain animal sacrifices. They were saving her for last, their most important victim to their Gods.

"Derek!"

He tripped on a dirtied snowbank. One quick blink and he was back in the Drail Kingdom. His breath came back in white puffs. The humans were back, looking at him.

He covered his mouth to keep from puking. That scene, with the woman. He felt her heart beat as quickly as his, felt the Sun on her back. He knew what it felt like to be her, dolled up to be someone he wasn't.

More hands touched him, Nero's, he thought. He flapped his wings to get them back. Hadiya didn't have wings. She'd been a human.

In the present, the pregnant woman, Keva, had her other boot above her head. She aimed for Derek's head before the knights tackled her. They cuffed her behind her back. Her round stomach moved with her baby.

"Monster!" she shrieked. "Your Majesty, he's no angel! He's been lying to you! He's a fake!"

"You're a disgrace!" one person from the crowd yelled.

"Hang her!"

Derek tried concentrating on the ground again. It'd been sandy and humid in his dream, or nightmare. Whatever it'd been, it never used to snow there. He—*She*—had always wanted to move north where it was cooler, and build a farm with...

"Settle down!" the king ordered. He motioned his knights off Keva. "What happened here?"

"You need to kill that boy, Your Majesty. He's no angel. I know he isn't. Look at him! He's nothing like the pictures or statues we have. He's too young, too rambunctious. He must be a fraud. Do not be deceived!"

The king settled his horse, then raised his hands. Knights darted out from the crowd to properly apprehend this criminal to the crown.

"No, it's true!" the woman said. "Please, believe me! I know the scripture! He isn't who he says he is!"

Derek raised his head to a sea of angry humans. Was he not Derek Harrow, angel to humankind, meant to save them?

No. He was but a person who'd entered this world blind, a dumb, stupid, sinful person who...

Hadiya dug her heels into the Earth. The executioner was above her, ready with sickle in hand, black mask stained red with splattered blood.

"No!" she screamed. "Don't do this!"

"Don't do this," Derek whispered. The two worlds were switching too quickly now. Each blink and he was back in that desert, then back in Drail.

Nero tried speaking to him.

"I can't do this!" Hadiya screamed. "I've changed my mind! I don't want to die!"

"You were chosen out of one hundred women," said the priest. "You were destined to fulfill your duties to our Gods. Have you no dignity for those who created you?"

How could she, if they desired the very blood they'd gifted her?

Someone screamed and brought Derek back. The crowds had broken into the streets, shouting and crying for something to happen. Near Derek cried the family of Keva. The teenager was reaching for something in front of him as his father held him back.

"Derek, what's happening?" Cellena asked.

"You were walking in circles like you were cursed," Jabel said.

"Are you feeling an internal pain?" Nero asked.

He was, but it wasn't the kind they could feel.

Keva tried breaking free from the knights' grasps. They were kneeing her to the ground, doing irreversible damage to her baby. One blinded her with a black hood and dragged her away.

Derek held his throat. "Wait—"

"Wait!"

Hadiya's face was pressed against the slab. She'd lost so much strength after being held captive for the past two days, being fed pretty lies that this was all for the greater good. All her life, she'd been told that being a sacrifice to the Gods was an honor, that she was the prettiest, most beautiful woman in the village to be given up for the Gods.

If that be the case, then fuck the Gods and all they stood for. How incompetent to be in need of mortal flesh that wasn't even blessed by virginhood in the first place? Unbeknownst to the temple she'd pledged her life to, she'd been with Omar since the beginning. He'd been hers, married underneath the stars, him, her, and their promise for a better future together.

Another body bumped into Derek's. He was staring up at a wooden stage built in the center of town. In the middle was a stool, and above it, a noose.

The knights shoved Keva onto the stool. They attached the noose around her neck and tightened it.

"Derek, don't look!" Cellena yelled. "Look away!"

The king took center stage. He readjusted his pendant and spoke: "Keva Antel, today you are to be hanged for a radical attack on the royal family, as well as trying to strike down our beloved angel sent to us from our God."

Derek looked around. What was happening? Which timeline was this?

"I did not!" Keva shouted through the mask. "He's not who he says he is! He's a fake! He's a demon!"

The king hesitated, looked down at Derek in the crowd. He questioned that through Derek's eyes, as if daring him to agree. Derek didn't know if he could. He wasn't a demon, but he was a liar.

"The Young Angel rejects clemency on your soul," the king finally said.

"No, I don't," Derek said, but his voice was a whisper.

"I don't want this!"

"Farewell, Keva Antel," he said, "and may our God have mercy on you."

Feeling time running out, Derek ran for the stage, calling for the king to stop. He even flapped his wings like a bird to distract the crowds from their chanting. Anything to stop it. Anything to keep his name from being stained with blood.

The king kicked the stool off the stage.

Keva's belly bounced. Her body seized as if she'd been struck by lightning, paralyzing her and her final breaths. She kept struggling through her final moments, and then her body swung, lifeless.

Derek stood no more than ten feet from her with his hand still out. The snow fell and melted over his eyes, but he couldn't move to wipe it away. He'd been seconds, *moments*, from saving her.

His body went ice cold and shattered to the stage floor. He threw up whatever was left in his stomach.

Maybe she could've seen Heaven before being excommunicated as a sinner. It would've been nice to be valued by something other than her body. Her mind, her feelings, things that made a person real.

Omar valued her like that. Omar was her everything, her missing piece that made her story complete. She wanted to see him, one last time, before the end took her.

A shadow passed above her.

Derek looked up. The brightness of the sky made his eyes tear up, but his cheeks were already wet.

The king fell off the stage as a man materialized before Derek. He wore a fur hood that hid his face, but once he landed, it fell, revealing his black, curly hair, his horns.

Oliver buried Derek into a hug, pushing up his flight feathers as he lifted him off his feet. "I have you," he said into his ear. "I'm sorry I'm so late."

Derek wiped his snotty face against his cheek. *He* wasn't the one who'd been late.

The king stumbled back from their embrace. "Your Grace, what're you doing?"

Oliver ignored him. "Do you need me to take you away?"

The crowd screamed from either Oliver's arrival, Derek being hugged, or Keva's death. He no longer cared. Nothing about this world made sense.

Neither his nor Hadiya's world, whoever she was, would ever make sense.

"Save me," he begged, and Oliver teleported them away.

22

Kevin

Holding hands with a girl was one of the most pleasurable highlights of Kevin's existence. Her hand was so small compared to his, and his warmth complemented the natural coolness of her webbed fingers.

His circumstances, however, along with the events of the week, kind of spoiled the mood.

But it was still nice, walking with her. After running from the Guard, Viper had asked him if he wanted to see more of this place she called home. He was a free man, after all, able to go wherever he wanted.

He noticed it now. The Guard was avoiding them. They weren't looking at him. They weren't treating him like a prisoner with murderous intent, he was now a sort of...

Líder. Someone to be feared as well as respected.

He watched their bare feet cross the cement floors. Maïmoú had killed Mikhail without hesitation, all because he'd made Kevin trip. That kind of guilt wouldn't wane no matter how many hands he held.

Viper, who'd yet to release his hand, tightened her fingers around him.

He started. They were in a dark hall that let his mind drift. "Yes?"

"Are you okay?"

He nodded and hoped she could read past the lie.

"Anything I can do to help?"

"It's okay. It's just been...a lot, you know? From finding out this place exists to running away to, you know, being sent here in the first place. My mind hasn't stopped."

She blew out her cheeks in thought. "You're probably going to leave soon, then, aren't you?"

He very well could've. Nothing was stopping him from walking straight out the foyer and saying goodbye to this place forever. Nadia had basically opened the doors for him.

But he'd made a promise to Viper. He was going to see that both of them made it out of here alive.

He just...didn't know how yet. Asking Maïmoú was out of the question, and he didn't know how one got in contact with Nadia. He also didn't want to get Viper anywhere near conflict, and that followed the Guard like flies.

"Hey," Viper said, "you wanna go see the babies?"

"The babies?"

"We have special rooms for them. I like seeing them. They make my mind feel...less spinny."

He grinned at her. "I'd like that."

Viper grinned back and started walking a bit faster. "It's easier to swim there, but I can show you the way like this."

"How often do you stay out of the water?"

"A lot more than the others here. Guards don't usually allow us much freedom, but they take me on walks every day, both to keep my bones strong and to test to see how long I can stay out of the water. The walks get sort of boring when I'm with a guard, but I like walking with you. I get to be freer, I guess."

"I'll gladly be your ticket to freedom."

Viper smiled to the floor, allowing Kevin room to kick himself for delivering such a cheesy line. He hadn't learned anything from Derek, the suave romantic in the family. How did one do this so nonchalantly without making a fool of oneself?

"Have you ever tried to swim?" Viper then asked.

"A few times. Can't say I'm any good at it. My wings are water-resistant, but the featherweight makes it hard to stay afloat."

"I can't believe that. Not that I don't believe you. It's just that everyone I know who lives down here can stay underwater for hours, so it's a shock to know someone who doesn't swim."

"How is that possible?"

She opened an unlocked door. "It's how we live."

A rush of cold air blew out through the door crevasse. Kevin closed his eyes as the sudden temperature change, but when he opened them back up, he nearly let go of Viper's hand.

The walls of this room, this tall, oversized room, were tanks. On his left and right, from floor to ceiling, were unending walls of water extending deep into the room. Dozens of people were swimming about freely. They chased one another or skirted across the tank's bottom, which was made of this coarse material like pavement. There were makeshift rooms built against the glass that allowed waterborne to sleep atop what could be described as the ceiling, perfectly curled around their tails.

Their tails, markings, and fins on their backs and legs, were some of the most striking addendums Kevin had ever seen on a person. Every color from jet black to shimmering gold was painted on their bodies. Green freckles, the reddest of eyes, orange stripes that started at their cheeks and ended at the soles of their feet. Their tails were either the tiniest propellers or these enormous, almost sheet-like fins that made them look like they were wrapped in a silk blanket.

He understood where Viper got it. These people looked and felt important, celebrities so beautiful and daring to be breathing underwater, when this was a part of their lives he'd walked into. "Above," he swore.

"Are you okay?"

He laughed in disbelief. "This's incredible. Is this where you *live*?"

"Not in this pod. This's W5, where half of the brackish-borne live. Me, Tokala, and Alexi live in W4, the other side."

"So there're floors for...brackish waterborne." He said it slowly so he didn't mess up her description. "How many floors are there?"

"Five. There're no lakes or rivers big enough for us. They say that we're...special." She frowned at this, unsure of feeling wanted.

Kevin didn't know how. The more time he spent with her, the more fascinated he became. From her mannerisms and knowledge to her body and face, everything attracted him to her. She could live in normal water *and* salt-and-pepper water, which made her even extra special, to him. If he were her, he'd think of himself quite highly.

"I think it's incredibly special how you're able to do all this," he summarized. "It's amazing."

Viper cleared her throat and led him down the hall between both tanks. As they walked, some of the waterborne noticed them and followed. Then some became most. Fast swimmers swam around the community and brought back others to gawk at them. They spoke about him openly, pointing.

Kevin blushed and kept his head down. He felt like he'd earned that celebrity status for the wrong reasons.

One of the waterborne swam up so fast, she bonked her forehead into the glass. Scrunching up her face, she then swam up to the surface and opened a latched door like the one at Morgan's. She was Tokala, Viper's friend.

"Viper!" Tokala took a ladder down the glass. "Viper, where are you? I am *so* peeved at you right now!"

At the sound of shouting, Viper tensed up. "Kala, be careful."

She wasn't. She missed the last rung of the ladder and slipped in the puddle she was creating. She shook out her white hair like nothing happened. "What happened to you? I just heard from Pippa—she told me *all* about it. How you ran off with that bird boy and disappeared down the East Wing. And *then* I hear from Samuel just now that you're walking hand in hand with him like it's no big deal!"

"I didn't mean to frighten you. I've been learning a lot from Kevin here. It's been fun getting to know him and teaching him about us."

Kevin's face reheated from a new type of pride. He stood up a little taller, both from feeling wanted by her and to show Tokala that he was still there. She hadn't looked at him.

"I don't care!" Tokala said. "I don't want you running off. That's not like you at all."

"Well, *you* just left the tanks," Viper noted, then explained to Kevin, "That's not allowed."

"Oh, please. You heard it from Pippa this morning. None of the Level 1 restrictions apply to us right now. See?" She motioned to empty space. If she moved her hand a foot to the left, she would've been motioning to the guards watching them. "They were told to let us do whatever we please, but that doesn't mean you get to go off smooching the boy you think is—"

Viper let go of Kevin's hand to cover Tokala's mouth. Whatever adjective Tokala was going to say got muffled between Viper's webbing.

Tokala shook her off and started looking around. "Where is he? I'd like to talk to him and make sure he's—" She yelped, noticing Kevin had been so close this whole time. "Fuck me, you're startling. That's not a good thing to find pretty in a person, Viper."

"Sorry to startle you," Kevin said. "Can you...see me?"

"I can only see a few feet in front of me." She pointed to her red eyes. Out of the water, they now looked a rosy pink. I'm blind."

"Oh. I'll be sure to make my presence more known to you, then. I'm Kevin, by the way. I don't think we've formally met."

Tokala puffed out her cheeks the way Viper did, just not as cutely. "Tokala," she said, and walked up closer to see Kevin's wings. "They *are* cool," she muttered, inspecting him as one did a leak under a sink. "Everyone was right about *that*, at least."

"You don't hold back what you think, do you?" Kevin asked boldly.

"Not a day in my life, especially not when it comes to my friends. So, where're we going?"

"The babies," Viper said, and quickened her pace towards a door on their right. Above it read the label *TODDLER STUDY*.

It was a small, sterile room with an inground pool in the middle. Around the walls were those strange heater tanks and hanging wetsuits, along with cabinets filled with either medical or cleaning supplies.

They walked to the edge of the pool. Kevin stared down at his reflection. "Where does this one lead?"

"Shh!" Tokala shook him and brought him back, but it was too late.

The bubbles came first. Excited bursts that rippled the water and masked what was breaching.

Two heads popped out. Gummy smiles and dangerous eyes, and chubby arms that splashed half the water onto the floor. The two kids looked like the same breed and age and were so delighted to see Kevin that they nipped at his fingers once they got him. All little kids did this, regardless of breed. It was their nature to bite. Even Kevin remembered being nippy up until age six.

These kids' teeth were sharper than most, and Kevin had to keep from shouting so he didn't startle the girls.

"They're still teething," Viper explained. "Their teeth are sharper than dogs."

"I-I can tell."

"And they can't control themselves, can they?" Tokala cradled the tiniest one. "Can you, you little snaggletooth?"

Kevin watched the other baby swim effortlessly in the water. It kicked its feet and used its arms better than Kevin could at that age. It felt weird to see one swim without an adult in the water. It got his heart racing.

Viper let her legs swing over the edge. Tokala did the same. Kevin, not wanting to feel left out, tucked his skirt around his hips and dunked his legs in. The water was astonishingly warm. He didn't think it was from the little ones.

A third child came up to them, curious of the noise they must've heard. She was the smallest of the three, not even a year old. Wagging their tail, she shot up from the water and jumped into Viper's arms.

Kevin knew the baby. It was the one Marcos had been play-ing with before Mikhail had died.

"This's Alexi," Viper said, trying to hold the struggling worm. "She's one of the most social babies born to us this gen-eration. She's a shark—" She laughed suddenly, as Alexi had found her cheeks and began pulling on them.

Kevin's heart lodged into his throat. He'd never heard a laugh so light, like it could brighten all darkness in a room. And holding a baby while she did it, it was a double gut punch.

He analyzed the baby's fins and tail and contrasted them with Viper's and Tokala's. They all looked different, but he didn't know how different they truly were.

Licking his lips, Kevin asked the question in his head before speaking it aloud. "You're really taken by her. Is she...yours?"

Viper's smile fell.

And he hated himself for that. He'd gone too far, it wasn't his business. He guessed he'd been around Maïmoú for too long and expected people to tell him everything about their personal lives.

Viper rubbed Alexi's back beneath her back fin. "No, she's not mine."

Tokala nudged up to her friend and put a hand on her shoulder.

"I'm sorry," Kevin said, unsure what he was apologizing for but knowing he had to say it. "I shouldn't have asked."

"It's okay," Viper said, but her voice said otherwise.

"You don't know," Tokala said.

"And I don't need to," he said. "Forget I asked."

"You...can," Viper said. "You can know. Down here, our populations are scarily low. Some of us are the last of our kinds. The Líders have done their best to keep us alive, but we're very weak. Our bones are brittle and our skin and lungs are fragile to the open air."

At that, Tokala stepped into the pool to be with the babies.

"Because of that," she continued, "we...sometimes... are asked to help keep our number up."

"*Asked*?" Tokala repeated, and Viper hid her eyes.

"Oh." Kevin's wings went limp. "Oh, Above, I'm so sorry."

"I've tried with a few boys like me," Viper said, "but it doesn't work. They did tests and surgeries on me, but nothing helps. They say I'm infertile."

Tokala hugged Viper's leg from the water, showing her support that no one else in the room could give.

"I've always wanted to have a baby," Viper said. "I don't know if it's because I've been told since birth that I need to keep my population alive, but when I see babies like this..." She cuddled Alexi. "I want one for myself, but with my progress so far, I don't think I'll ever be able to have one."

"You're not obligated," Tokala told her. "I always tell her this, but it doesn't get through. It's not right. You're *not* obligated to bear children. I won't," she told Kevin. "I've told them that I have no interest in being with men and threaten to bite off their cocks if they get close to me, and they listen."

Kevin knew she was trying to make a joke and laughed too hard. "Really?"

"I will *never* let a man get close to me. I'll snap his jaw."

"Woah." He pretended to back up. "I'll keep *that* in mind, too."

Viper forced a smile, but she couldn't keep it for long. "She's more...headstrong than I am."

Kevin's heart was breaking. He wanted to cuddle up against her like Tokala and Alexi and show that he was there for her. He could've explained the process of adopting a child to her and how it could've helped ease her pain, but this world...

It wasn't his. To some, happiness meant bearing life to a child with their own bodies.

He had to say something soon, but what could someone like him say? This wasn't his world. He didn't share her pain.

But he wanted to, because he wanted to show that he cared. He'd just met her, but he felt a deep-rooted connection to her full heart.

Instincts took hold, and he held her free hand. "I'm really sorry. I'm not sure what I can say that'll help because I don't want to hurt you, but I can't imagine how hard this must be. I'm sorry you're going through this."

"Thank you. I know it's selfish—"

"No, it's not!" said Kevin and Tokala at the same time.

"It's definitely not, not at all," Kevin added. "You want kids. You should be able to have them. Two kids, even, three. Six."

"Six? I don't know if I can handle six."

"Maybe you can. My parents had three. I have a twin named Derek and a sister who was adopted into my family. Her name's Nikki. They had us two and still decided to have a third. She's a rat."

"Wait, so did your parents nab her off the streets?" Tokala asked. "What did her parents think about that?"

"She didn't have any. She was what we called homeless, someone who doesn't have a home, who lives abandoned. My parents decided they didn't want any more biological children, but they still had that parental ache, so they decided to take her in."

"So...she's just like me." Tokala's sharp tail began to wag. "Is she pretty?"

"She is, and I have a twin, but he went missing...kind of. It's a long story I'm still having trouble talking about."

"Well, I'm not done talking about this girl. What does she smell like? Who does she like?"

When Kevin withheld that private information from her, Viper held his hand more securely. "Thank you for listening to me ramble."

"It's not ramble. You don't deserve that kind of grief. I really hope you get to have a child. I hope you can be a mom. You'll be great at it."

Viper kicked her little feet in the water at the thought of achieving her dreams.

And Kevin would've done anything to help her achieve them.

The door behind them opened. The little children, surprised by everything, looked up to the newcomer.

Once the door closed, all the children but Alexi dove back into the water and disappeared down hidden paths.

Marcos' hair was more unkempt than usual. Tiny wisps were falling into his face, and his collar was unbuttoned. If he could breathe, he probably would've been panting.

Viper squeezed Kevin's hand harder. Tokala bubbled her rage beneath the water. Alexi was the only one excited to see him. She giggled for a new embrace.

Marcos took a step forward, then looked down at Kevin and Viper being so close. He stepped back. "What're you doing?"

Kevin tried reading the room as quickly as possible. He knew not a lot of people liked Marcos, but he didn't know how the waterborne thought of him. "We're just hanging out."

"Where is she?"

Kevin's heart thudded. It was like his brain had been trying to make him forget his reality.

He thought he'd seen wrong, back when he'd first met Viper and Tokala in the tank, but Maïmoú had told him otherwise. When Mikhail had died, while Nadia and the guards had been searching for the murderer, Marcos and Zantl, they'd been staring directly at Maïmoú.

He thought he could free himself from soulmates and Deities for an afternoon, but that would never be the case. For the rest of his life, he'd be tethered to her and the life into which she'd sewn him.

Marcos could see Deities.

Marcos knew about Maïmoú.

Marcos, like Kevin, was a soulmate.

Kevin sat up with his wings. "Mar—"

Marcos' wrist blade shot out, and he defended himself like he'd done weeks ago when they'd first been introduced.

As if Kevin was someone to be feared.

Alexi wiggled out of Viper's arms and dove into the water to get closer to Marcos.

Marcos kept rigid as he knelt down and scooped Alexi up. He cradled her against his chest and neck as he lowered his knife at Kevin's head.

"I'm...unable to tell you what you need to do or where you should go," Marcos said. "My programming has been updated that bars me from doing so. But I strongly suggest that you waterborne go back to your pods, and you go back to your room.

We are in a state of mourning and it's not wise to be roaming unsupervised."

Kevin kept staring at the tip of Marcos' blade. He hadn't done anything to warrant this aggression. It was all Maïmoú's doing.

He got up properly, taking Viper with him. "Marcos, I don't know what you're thinking, but I wasn't in control of what happened to Mikhail."

"I...know," he said. "Zantl told me everything."

"Zantl?" They *were* part of this strange connection with the Deities, but Maïmoú had only mentioned it once. "How much do they know?"

The harrowing look in Marcos' eyes made them appear alive. "No. I don't want you conjuring her up again due to whatever anger you might be feeling."

"I'm not angry."

"So I strongly suggest that you return to your room. Please," he begged, more sincerely this time. "I don't want any harm coming to anyone else. Please."

Kevin felt like he'd just been accosted for yet another crime he hadn't committed. His defense was already forming, how he couldn't control Maïmoú and how none of this was his fault. He hadn't hurt any of the guards. He hadn't pushed Derek off the Muralha.

He wanted to ask Marcos how he was connected to the Deities and if he, too, had a Deity who spoke to him via dreams. He could've warned him ahead of time.

But Viper was trembling, and Marcos was scared, and Kevin didn't want to be the conductor of such negativity. He left the room without another spoken word.

23
Nikki

Trying to juggle school and work in the fallout shelter wasn't conducive to a healthy sleep schedule. Nikki hadn't had one in years, but she needed Vanna to have one.

After getting nowhere with one of the Drill's failing generators, Nikki pulled Vanna aside and told him they were leaving.

"Where?"

"I don't know. Let's play hooky."

"From the fallout shelter? No. My moms still need help with the Drill, and I offered to make them dinner tonight."

"You need to take a break from this place. It smells like a car manufacturer down here."

"I told you." He checked down the hall, then pulled on his scarf. "Fine. Let me make a quick call upstairs, then we can leave."

"Who do you need to call?"

He gave her a shy look. "I want you to meet somebody."

"You...used to need codes or passwords to open these up." Vanna grunted as he pushed open the circular door. "Nowadays, all you need is a little push."

"*A little push*" became both of them using all their strength to move the door a foot. It was down another abandoned hall not often used by Morgan's rebels. The exit was dirty and the door grated the concrete floor. It became so hard that they stopped pushing and squeezed through a tight sliver before plugging the hole back up.

It let them out to a grassy embankment and a dried-up stream. They were near a stone bridge just outside the purebred district. To an untrained eye, this exit would've been seen as an uninteresting sewer grate.

The season had cooled the world into a dark grey, signaling a rainstorm. It rarely dipped beneath fifty degrees, but today, Nikki needed to zip up her jacket and flip her hoodie over her rat ears. Vanna cuddled up in his scarf, about which Nikki teased him.

Vanna pushed her back with a cracking smile.

"There you are, you piece of shit," Nikki said, and lightly kicked his bike wheel to make him lose balance. "I missed that smile."

"Yeah, well, I've had a lot on my mind."

"Lucky you have me now. Who're we meeting, anyway?"

He biked up to Main Street.

"Excuse me. You know I can catch up with you."

He tested that theory and pedalled faster, which triggered her competitive spirit. Laughing, she broke into a sprint, bypassing him and hooking around the building.

This side of Raeleen had its perks. Her side was more un-tamed, with overgrown weeds and ferns growing from the pavement. Down Vanna's block were bookstores, cake shops, and pricey boutiques that grew into tall skyscrapers. Rottweilers combed out their styled hair and poodles jostled one another around a crystal fountain. Guards with their ties off had quick lunch breaks on reserved patios with family. Dozens of puppies chased one another in yips.

She couldn't see the Asilo from here, but she knew that up ahead, the complex holding her brother and multiple people hostage loomed above them.

She felt terrible for taking the time to play hooky. They deserved to be happy, but there was so much poison in the air. She should've been putting 110 percent into bettering the lives of those in need.

Vanna pulled back and biked beside her. "You okay?"

"Have you ever thought about telling anybody about what your moms do?"

"Uh, no. We'd be executed."

"But doesn't it weigh on you? All these people are living blind to what the Asilo is doing, and if those documents Morg showed me are true, then there's a whole other world we need to be focusing on."

"If you focus on the world's mistakes for the rest of your life, every little gain you make will be drowned in misery. I want to save Kevin. I want to help those in the Asilo. I want to reform the Guard and solve poverty and blast the Muralha apart, but I can't do that by myself. I'm too much a coward."

"You're not—"

"I am. I'm not like you or my moms or your parents. I'm not even like Derek and Kev. I can only do what I'm capable of. And now..." He turned the corner to a plaza. "I want to try finding happiness for myself."

Sitting on the edge of a bubbling fountain, tail tucked, waited Pippa. She was dressed out of her guard uniform and was wearing cute shorts and a top that showed off her belly.

Vanna sped up as Nikki came to a stop. He almost fell off his bike to embrace her in a half-circle turn. She lifted him off the ground to kiss him properly.

"I'm glad you're here," she said. "Did they give you any grief?"

"No. Nikki got me to play hooky." He turned to address Nikki, the extreme third wheel on this obvious date. "Nikki, this's Pippa. I know you've already met, but this can be your first official introduction. She's..." He took Pippa's hand. "She's my lover."

Nikki reined herself in from teasing him too harshly. He was, in every manner of speaking, way out of her league. "Hey. Sorry for the rude introduction back at the bunks. I swear I'm not that violent. Anymore."

"No worries!" she said. "Above, it's nice to finally get to, like, *talk* to you. I've heard *so* much about you from Vanna."

"Name's Nikki," she said, and shook Pippa's hand. Her grip was strong given her bubbly energy, but Nikki guessed she shouldn't judge by appearance. She was a spy working against the Asilo for a rebellious coffeehouse owner.

"I was thinking," Vanna said, "since we can't really hang out at my place, that we all hang out together."

"You're gonna make her be the third wheel?" Pippa asked. "Vanna, that's so mean. He's been dying to introduce me to you. '*Oh, I want you to make a good first impression*'. Just rattling on about it."

"Did you think I'd object?" Nikki asked. "I've endorsed *Derek's* lovers, and some of them had criminal records."

"Well, we all do now." Vanna got back on his bike and patted the back seat connected to the wheel. Pippa eagerly got on, making sure her tail didn't get run over, and enjoyed the free ride into town. Nikki walked behind them, completing her role as a third wheel.

"Hey, Nikki," Pippa said, crossing her long legs so they didn't drag. "I want to say sorry about the whole situation with Derek and Kevin. I should've never asked to go on patrol that evening. I should've asked for a different position."

"You couldn't have told the future," Nikki said. "If I'd known, things would've been a lot different, too."

She nodded solemnly. "And Vanna's told me all about you. All good, and most surprising. I feel like I've known you for so long, yet I never got to *know* you."

"I'm not a big people-person." She lowered her voice and ears. "How's, uh, Kevin doing?"

"He's...okay. Mikhail's gone missing."

"What?"

She pressed a finger to her lips. "It's confidential, but I've been trying to ask around about it. Apparently, nobody's seen him for days. Nadia's been a mess about it."

"Where do you think he went?"

"I'm not sure, but ever since it happened, Kevin's been given special treatment. I think his disappearance has something to do with him. All the other guards are super on edge about it. Morg's been hounding me day and night to snoop out intel, but so far, I've found none. I've tried cornering Kevin about it, but he's been, well, preoccupied."

"With what? What're they doing to him?"

"Oh, it's nothing bad!" Pippa said. "He's been talking with a girl."

Nikki stopped walking. "What."

"Her name's Viper. They've been inseparable lately, always running off together. Can't imagine someone doing *that*." She nudged Vanna's butt with hers. Vanna nearly crashed into a trolley.

"Christ," Nikki cursed. "Now *he's* hanging out with a girl, too?"

"I'll keep an eye on him," Pippa promised.

"You better."

As they entered a new part of the district, Nikki watched her reflection through the storefront glass. She slumped more into her shoulders, fixed her hair that was frizzing due to the inbound storm. She felt extremely self-conscious around this older girl who had everything figured out. She knew more about the Asilo, the fallout shelter. She knew more about Nikki's own family than she did.

Nikki fell behind with her worries. Vanna was up ahead, looking into a bookstore front with the intent to buy a box set. Pippa pointed out one wrapped in red silk.

Nikki looked in. She didn't fancy herself a reader, but maybe she'd start for the new year.

Lí was staring back at her. He was dressed the same as her but wearing darker clothes, fingerless gloves. He had the same nose as her but with different eyes, same fleshy ears but no rat ears. Same height, some facial hair around a similar jawline. He even had a similar face tattoo underneath the same eye.

They were one and the same, sharing the same body.

Nikki stumbled back. Lí did the same, mirroring her and the bewildered look on her face. The scene behind Lí wasn't Raeleen, but it was too blurry to tell where exactly he was. A city, but bigger, grander, like the one she'd seen in that dream.

With Shào.

Lí's reflection reached out to her. He palmed the glass with a mournful look.

Nikki's hand itched forwards to meet his when a hand rounded around his neck. It was small, but it was enough to make him flinch.

Behind him, floating in a black and red robe, was Shào.

And he was staring directly at their reflection.

At Nikki.

"Nikki?"

She jumped a foot into the air. Vanna had snuck up behind her.

"What's wrong?" he asked.

She looked for their reflections. It was only for a moment, but she swore she saw two other people. Instead of Vanna and Pippa, two others...

"Nikki!"

The sound of a trolley passed, bells and whistles warning her to get off the road. While looking for others that didn't exist, Nikki had walked backwards into traffic.

"What in the Above's name is going on with you?" Vanna asked. "Are you even listening?"

Nikki looked back at the mirror. Both she, Vanna, and Pippa were back to their regular selves.

"*Hello*?" Vanna snapped in front of her face.

"Sorry," she said. "Spaced out."

"Are you sure?"

"Do you need to go to the hospital?" Pippa asked, fishing something out of her pocket. "I have medicine, sleeping pills. I have muscle relaxants. They practically give this stuff away in the Asilo."

"I'm fine."

"Yeah, neither of us believe that," Vanna said. "Let's get you something to eat."

The grocery store Vanna had chosen welcomed them with real automatic doors and an air-conditioned breeze. Customers—mostly canines—shopped in spacious aisles. Some chatted with neighbors and the cashiers about their day. Specialty chefs chopped up samples for customers to try as employees restocked colorful, bulky shelves.

Vanna and Pippa searched for something to feed Nikki. Nikki, giving them their space, travelled down the opposite way.

She bit the inside of her cheek until she tasted blood. It was getting worse. These visions, which were once just nightmares, were now bleeding over into her real life. If she wasn't careful, would he take over, replacing her? She didn't know what was impossible when it came to impossibility.

At the end of each aisle was a sampling basket of free bread. After checking for guards, Nikki jammed her cheeks with free food. It was a free lunch that someone would've killed to have. A few crumbs could've fed so many mouths.

She wondered if Lí had worried about such things. He'd mentioned something about refugees, and for that brief moment in his head, she felt him fear for their safety, their hunger, the "lepers," whoever they were. If only she could bring some food back to them. To where, she didn't know. She needed to spend more time in Lí's head.

Her tail hit the basket of food and tipped it over. She dove for it and stopped it with her shoe, then lifted it back up.

She was wearing fingerless gloves. Her nails had been bitten down and were caked with dirt and something else, blood or grime.

She touched her face, feeling the stubble now growing over her jaw. Panicking, she ran out of the aisle to the closest mirror she could find. Her body, lighter. Her balance, off without her tail. She felt something in-between her legs.

"Shit," she said under her breath. "Shit, shit, shit."

"Nikki?"

She touched the mirror. Herself, her real self, was staring back at her, looking as confused and scared as she was feeling in Lí's body.

"*Shit.*"

"Nikki?" Vanna was walking towards her. "What's wrong?"

No. He couldn't touch her. She'd get him infected from her skin. His skin. *Their* skin. Their brains, they were merging as one.

Vanna held out two hands. "...*Nikki*?" he asked too slowly. "Nikki, did you take something? Are you on anything?"

Tripping on feet that weren't hers, Nikki left the store and bolted down the street. *This* was why she couldn't be open with him. He was too much of a realist. How could she describe what was happening to her? Not even she knew.

"Nikki!"

A trolley honked at her. She spun around it and jumped over the rails to the other side of the street. She heard her heart beat through her body like she was underwater. How was she to fix this? Could anyone see her like this?

Could he save every refugee? Every last one? Time was running out, and he was the only person who could do it. Lazy was what he was, and selfish. He wasn't putting 110 percent into saving humanity.

She hit her head, trying to stop herself from thinking his thoughts. How was she not able to keep him out? It was what she prided herself on. She was the level-headed sister.

She turned and was faced with the front side of the Asilo. Its dark walls disappeared into the fog settling over the city.

She had to save Kevin.

He had to save the infected.

She needed to keep her family safe.

He needed to contact Alliroue.

They were all depending on them.

She ran into an alley. Jumping over a puddle, she pressed her back into the cold stone and caught her breath. She could outline the shape of Li's nose in her peripheral vision.

She pressed the balls of her hands into her eye until she saw nothing but stars. Sky dots. Li's thoughts had monopolized hers. She had no idea which country she lived in or what language she spoke. Giving up, she slid to the ground and held down her head.

In, out. In, out.

"You're okay," she whispered to herself. "It's fine. You're okay."

"I'm not okay. I haven't had a healthy sleep schedule in years."

"That makes two of us." She clasped her hands together in a firm handshake. "We're okay, you and I. We're okay."

In the shadows of the alley, a dark figure approached her. "Excuse me," they asked, "are you alright?"

Nikki readied herself for Lí. He was an explorer, he must've found a way to Raeleen under the cover of night.

Marcos stood in Nikki's light. She blinked up at him—Lí's eyes were less advanced than hers—to make sure she wasn't hallucinating. A few more blinks, a rubbing of the eyes, and soon, her vision went back to normal. Lí's clothes oozed away and returned her to her own outfit.

She looked over her body. She was back to herself. It was all an illusion made up by her own distrustful eyes.

"How did you do that?" Marcos asked.

"Do...what?"

"You were..." He gestured to her. "Someone else."

Nikki picked herself up with both hands on the brick wall. "You saw that?"

"I don't know what I saw. You weren't anyone I recognized in Raeleen, but you were...familiar, somehow. How did you do it?"

"*Lí* was familiar to you?"

Her ears perked seconds after Marcos'. Far off into the city, a siren went off. It was drawn-out like wails, growing louder until she couldn't hear herself talk. They echoed towards the Asilo.

Marcos looked off into nothing. His eyes moved like he was speedreading something in front of them.

"What is it?" Nikki asked. "What's that mean?"

"I—I need to go. I need to find Zantl. And you. You need to go to...34th Avenue and 8th Street. Nadia wants...an assembly?"

"An assembly?"

"Yes, but this wasn't planned. I—" He left the alleyway. "I need to go. I'm sorry."

"Wait, what do you mean? What's going on?" she asked, but Marcos, against his will, ran towards the sirens.

24

Derek

Fuck snow. Fuck its beauty and fuck its atmosphere. The flakes could turn to ash for all he cared, burning away everything they touched until nothing remained.

He coughed into the open air. It was freezing out, but he couldn't rub his hands warm because his fingers would snap. He'd already lost their sensation from the blustering winds, so who cared if he broke bones? At least he'd be warmer.

He'd struggled out of Oliver's arms. While he was grateful for being saved from the sadistic torture humankind relished in, he couldn't be near anyone right now. Shoving out of his arms, Derek took to the gray skies and flew into oblivion.

"Derek, wait."

He soared upwards as fast as he could. He had no destination in mind. He had no plan. The air up here burned every one of his feathers, but he kept going. Faster. Faster. The streaks of tears turned to fire down his cheeks.

He saw Keva, the woman who'd been hung for his crime of being alive. He saw that girl from his visions, whoever she'd been. No, she'd had a name. Hadiya, a girl guilty, too, of being alive.

His heart panged, and he hoped it'd be enough to kill him. Everything had happened so quickly, he couldn't make sense of any of it. Maybe flying into oblivion would help. It felt safe, nothingness. Maybe he'd call the Moon his home.

He slammed into a warm, heart-beating chest, and two arms that wrapped around him. So strong yet so careful not to crush him, he could fall asleep in this embrace, if he wasn't seconds away from shattering.

"Please," Oliver begged, squeezing him tight. "It's okay."

"Let me *go*," Derek argued.

"Fifty feet more and you would've hit the Barrier. I don't want you getting hurt."

Who cared if he got hurt? Physical hurt would've been a blessing.

Fighting his own safety, Derek was brought back to Earth, and the two of them fell into forest depths below.

Winter in a forest was another plane of existence. It smelled like a new world, clean and crisp and colder than in the village. It sounded like it was raining, when really it was the weighed-down trees shifting the icy snow atop their branches. The dirty snow wet his body and stung to touch. He gathered handfuls of it and crushed it in his gloved hands.

His mind snapped. Before he knew it, he was hyperventilating, crying at nothing. He was in hysterics and knew he was being too dramatic, but that only made him cry more.

Oliver sat up with Derek in his arms. "Derek, I'm so sorry." His voice wavered in honesty. "I should've taken you away sooner. I should've intervened. I'm sorry you had to witness that. I'm so sorry."

He didn't listen to the rest. Curling up into a ball, Derek sobbed into a man he hardly knew.

Oliver whispered soft nothings in his ear, telling him it'd be alright and that everything was fine, but it wasn't and wouldn't be. A woman and her child were dead because of him. He'd broken a family.

Oliver sniffled and wiped his face with the cuff of his sleeve. "I'm here for you. Everything's going to be—"

"*Stop* it," Derek said. "Stop saying everything's going to be okay. I'm not. I can't stop shaking and crying. I'm allowed to be upset right now."

Oliver let go of him. "I didn't mean to."

"I know, but you need to let me fucking cry right now. Like, why do you think you know how I feel? Because we're mates? Because you're mated with me? The *fuck* does that have to do with anything? I don't even *know* you!"

Oliver's breath came out in slow, shallow puffs of white smoke. His fingers curled within the snowy grass as he looked off to the side.

Derek's lungs hurt from shouting. He coughed to get it out, but it still clung to him like the icicles dangling above.

The first sniffle from Oliver hurt the most. It was one thing to argue while you were crying, but the moment your words pierced another person, you were no longer the only victim.

"Shit," Derek cursed. "Oliver, I'm sorry."

A simple sorry wasn't enough to stop Oliver's tears. He hid it with a hand over his eyes, but Derek saw it, felt it—the regret, building.

"I-I didn't mean to...to minimize your feelings," he cried. "You're allowed to cry. I just don't know h-how to make you feel better, and it's killing me to see you like this. It hurts."

Fuck. Right. Their bond, or Oliver's bond with him. If he had a good sense of how demonkind and mating worked, then whatever Derek was feeling, Oliver must've been feeling it, too.

Derek gave him a hug, wrapping his wings around him to keep the snow away. "I'm sorry. I know you're trying to help. I shouldn't have yelled."

Oliver gingerly wrapped his arms around Derek's waist.

"I'm scared," Derek confessed. "Something's happening to me and my head. I think I'm speaking with our God, or an angel." He kissed the top of Oliver's head, right between his horns. His lips got lost in the thicket of black curls. "I'm sorry."

Oliver massaged his lower back. "It's okay. I know I don't know everything about you. I know I don't say the right things at the right time. I'll do better."

"No, you're doing fine. I'm the one who should be better. Thanks for saving me, by the way. I feel like that'll come to bite us in the ass soon."

"Maybe, but I couldn't stand by when I felt your heart racing so hard back there. I needed to save you."

"Consider me safe." He peeled himself up. "What're we going to do now?"

Oliver cleared his face with his sleeve. Derek helped to push back the wet curls around his eyes. "My home is a few more miles east of here. I can take you there for the time being, if you'd like."

A chilling wind crossed through the forest, sending a shiver down Derek's back. If he went with him, everything would change, and his bond with the humans would have an everlasting tear in it.

As if they hadn't torn his mind to shreds already.

"I'd like that a lot, actually." He helped Oliver up. As he dusted off his ass of snow, he realized where they'd landed.

It was a gravesite. Fifty or so tombstones jutted out from the snow, encaged by an iron gate. Most of them were leaning and faded by dead moss.

"Woah," Derek said.

"I'm sorry," Oliver explained. "It's hard to not bump into one around these parts."

Derek turned, and through birch branches and evergreens, he saw more ghostly outlines of gravesites. A hundred tombs over here, another dozen there. They were walking in fields of death.

"These aren't for humans, are they?" he asked.

"No," Oliver said, "they aren't."

Their "manor," in all honesty, looked more like an abandoned, haunted castle. When they teleported back to solid ground, Derek was facing an iron-clad gate and a dilapidated, three-story farmhouse. It had termite-ridden doors, tilting pillars supporting the porch, and chimneys that were missing brick. Derek could smell the mildew from the lawn.

A steaming pond encircled the home as a type of moat. Lily pads floated atop the frothy water. Chickens cheeped near the edge despite the snow coating the ground, and Derek swore he heard a neigh from the backyard.

"I know it's nothing compared to the Wueng Castle," Oliver said, "but this's all we have."

"Did you use to have other houses?"

"Yes, but they've either been burned down or ransacked by the humans. This's one of the last homes we have left."

Without any bridges, Oliver held Derek and levitated him over the water. "The humans think a sea serpent lives in these waters. It keeps most of them from antagonizing us."

"Is there?"

"Of sorts. Maxwell," he called out. "I'm home."

Something waded in the misty waters. Through the steam swam a boy with a slithery snake by his side. He must've been a demon, with his dark grey skin and nubby horns. Both he and the snake fixed their red, half-submerged eyes on Derek as he passed. It sounded like the boy said something in mild surprise, but the water bubbled his words.

"This's Maxwell," Oliver told Derek. "He's our own sea serpent."

Maxwell shot an annoyed glare at Oliver as he perched atop a stone protruding from his pond. Derek noticed that he had slits around his neck that he kept hidden with a scarf. They moved with his breathing, opening and closing for air. "Did you actually steal him away from the humans? You know I was kidding about that idea."

"I didn't. The king just executed a woman in Devnya Town."

Maxwell, who seemed disinterested in Derek's overall situation, suddenly became as tense as his little rock. His red eyes went wide, and his hair turned white. Like literally, starting from the roots and working down, his dark, wavy hair turned as white as snow. "What? I-I knew he was nervous, but— What happened? Is—"

"He's okay," Oliver said. "Relax. Nothing happened to him or Cellena."

"Oh." Maxwell's hair returned to its naturally dark tone. He got comfortable back on his smooth stone, his snake slithering up beside him. "Good."

Nothing was "good" about it, but Derek figured that's how demonkind acted, when it regarded their mates. As long as they were safe, nothing else mattered.

He could totally see how he and Jabel were a thing. It just worked.

The manor opened up to a wide living room and crackling fireplace. Similarly with the castle library, this place had been carved out of wood instead of stone. Wooden tables and walls, candelabras heating up nearby bookcases. The cedar floorboards creaked when Derek closed the door.

Nearest the fire sat three demons, all his age. The girl looked like Oliver's breed, with white skin and short, black hair. She was freckled with a million dark spots and wore a skirt that looked stitched by a child. The two others had dark skin with bright red hair, and one had *wings*. Giant wings like Derek's but unfeathered. They were fleshy and scaled with points spreading out at the joints: a bat.

"I'm home," Oliver said.

The freckled girl floated up in surprise. "Oh, my golly, you're actually here. Shimah, Kumo, make way!"

The winged boy hooted with approval and became airborne. He climbed to the ceiling and hung backwards from the rafters by way of his thick, strong tail. "Lookit that. Never woulda thought he'd actually come 'ere. Kumo, that's the angel, or whatever he is nowadays."

The other redhead looked over in wonderment. She was sitting in a chair built with two big wheels for mobility. She wheeled it around to better see him. "Wow, he's much taller than I imagined."

"What happened?" the freckled girl asked.

"An incident happened in town," Oliver said, and brought Derek to the fireplace. "Derek, this's Rosaline, and the one up there is Shimah, and this's his sister, Kumo."

"A pleasure." Rosaline floated above Derek and kissed each of his cheeks. "It's so nice to see you. Gosh, you're freezing. Are you okay? Do you need anything?"

Oliver nervously rubbed down his hands. "I'll, uh, make some tea."

"He's shiverin'," Shimah noted. "Oliver, make it two cups. Kumo, hand me your blanket. Wait, can I use my fire? Are we using our powers near him now?"

"That wasn't a problem in the first place," Rosaline said. "That's for humans."

"Right, right." Shimah flew back down, and from his hands, he produced a ball of flames. Derek flinched at the instant creation of light, but Shimah lowered it into the fireplace and threw it in. "That fire will keep you warm. It'll flame for hours without going out. Perks of being us. Man, you're really shiverin'. Are you good?"

"Shimah, give him some space. Goodness." She brought the blanket over Derek's wings. Her feet never touched the ground. "You alright, lad?"

"Peachy." He stripped himself of his jacket and gloves and rubbed his raw hands over the flames. He still couldn't feel them. He couldn't feel anything but uncomfortable itchiness.

Rosaline took his boots and jacket and hung them up by the front door.

Shimah hopped from rafter to rafter. "It looks like you've seen a ghost. Wait, can you see ghosts? Are ghosts even real, because I know I've seen one 'fore, and I know Maxwell reads books with ghost lovers in 'em."

"Shimah, hush," Rosaline said. "Go get Yomi and Brennen already."

"*Aye,*" he said, and flew up a tight stairwell to the second floor.

Demonkind's energy was nothing like that of humankind's. This place smelled of nature and herbs and they were so loud and clustered. Not that he hated any of that. He just needed space to decompress and he wasn't getting that here. He felt himself breathing harder.

"I'm sorry about him," Rosaline said. "He gets excited very easily around people."

"And we don't normally have guests," Kumo said. "Sometimes, he goes into town to get a rise out of the humans. One time, we caught him sleeping in a barn with cows. Nearly scared the old woman to death."

Down the stairs came two new demons and a baby. They looked the most human if you excluded the horns curving around their ears. They came to Derek like sophisticated angels, graceful in movement.

"Hello," the woman said. Her words were like honey in his ears. "My name is Yomi. It's nice to finally meet you. This's my mate, Brennen, and our child, Noemi."

"They're our doctors!" Shimah flew back in and lounged across his rafters. "Helped me more than once with scorch marks."

The man gave a low bow with the baby tucked against his chest. Derek didn't know where to look at him—it looked like someone had gone to his face with a sword and won. Deep scars were slashed across his cheeks and eyes, misshaping his natural bone structure. His nose was permanently fixed to one side like it was broken, and one eye was clouded over.

Derek gave him a short bow in return.

Yomi sat on one of the floor pillows, fanning out her long skirt like a queen. "It seems like you've been outside for a long time. I'd like to make sure you're alright and that you don't have any frostbite. Is that alright with you?"

Without speaking, Derek showed the woman his hurting fingers. She exhaled slowly as she studied his pores.

"May I?" Brennen examined them next, then pulled out a corked vial from his pocket. Baby Noemi tried reaching for them, to which he skillfully evaded.

"We specialize in healing the body and mind," Yomi explained.

Brennen took the cork to his mouth and opened wide. His canine teeth were twice as long as his other teeth and were dyed black at the tips. They sank into the cork with little effort. Droplets of black began dripping into the glass like sludge.

"We ran out of elixir," Yomi told her friends, "but it'll be fresher this way, more potent. Kumo, do you need any more tonight?"

"I'm okay," the girl in the wheelchair said, and flexed her arm muscles. She was skin and bones. "I get stronger every day."

Yomi smiled at the lie and turned back to Derek. "Our breed possesses the ability to heal. Females are able to heal the body while males are able to heal the mind and spirit using venom. We can't work miracles."

"Obviously," the man said around the cork, and motioned to his fucked-up face.

"But it can provide aid."

"Shoulda seen 'em when he first took a blade to the face," Shimah said. "What was it, two centuries ago? Knights got him in a corner. Broke his leg to carve him out."

"Shimah, hush," Rosaline said.

"But it was so long ago!"

"Still, Shimah, be kind! Read the room."

"You know I can't!"

Brennen extracted his sharp tooth from the vial's cork and handed it to Yomi. She began adding her own venom to the mix.

"It's actually very sanitary," Brennen told him. "It tastes like metal, but it's warm going down."

"Like vodka," Derek murmured.

"Easier to take than that."

They were right. As Derek drank the elixir, it warmed his throat and melted into his body like warm candy. He kept lapping his tongue inside his mouth. Tacky candy.

"What did they do to ya?" Shimah asked. "Did you run away from 'em?"

"He couldn't have," Kumo said, rolling her chair over. "There's no way."

"We shouldn't be asking him so many questions," said Rosaline. "He seems beat. You sure you're good, Derek?"

"I-I'm fine," he said. "Really, I just need a minute."

"I'm sorry, lad. You don't have to talk about it if you don't want to. We all know the humans' wrath one way or another. We can only imagine what happened to make you run out into the cold like this."

Derek rubbed his neck. Even with the fireplace's warmth, it was hurting to breathe. He couldn't swallow because everything inside him hurt from the cold. He couldn't heal. He couldn't fix himself.

"Derek?"

Every single demon was looking down at him, judging him like some pet in a cage, waiting to see what stupid move he'd make next.

Oliver walked into the room with two cups of tea. He was so tall, blocking the only exit Derek saw.

Derek got up. "I-I need to go," he said, and shrugged off everyone's care for him. "I need to—I need to leave." He escaped for the staircase and crawled up the steps.

"Derek?"

"Derek, where're you going?"

Holly was crouched at the top of the staircase, listening in on their conversation while playing with her dolly.

"Fuck." Derek spun around her and continued running. He didn't want her to think he was avoiding her. He wasn't avoiding anyone. How long until that venom worked?

He ran into the first bedroom he found and locked the door. He fell into a king-sized bed. Blankets of what smelled like animal fur soaked up his cold and replaced it with heat.

The house went still. Outside, the cold winds howled. Inside, this room's fireplace, crackling with embers. That was all he needed. That, and concentration.

The animal blankets covered his new bout of tears. In what vague memories he had, he wasn't a crybaby. He had to be cooler than that, yet there he lay, sobbing about something that wasn't his fault in a bed that didn't belong to him owned by a family his previous caretakers hated.

Keva had been right. He was a fraud.

He passed out. Maybe for an hour, maybe ten. When he came back to the real world, it was dark outside, and he was shivering.

Someone was adding logs to the fireplace. Sparks spit up and disappeared into smoke.

The logs fell. "I'm sorry," Oliver said. "Did I wake you?"

"Probably not."

"I'm sorry. I was worried you might've been cold with your wings."

"They don't normally get too cold," he said, but didn't disclose the fact that his toes were ice cubes. He burritoed them underneath the fur.

"Oh. Good. I'll see myself out now."

Derek watched him cross the bedroom. "Wait."

And he did, just like the humans, waiting on his every beck and call.

"I'm sorry for bailing on your family tonight," Derek said. "I hope they don't hate me."

"Oh, no. They understand. They were just really excited to see you. I've been... speaking very highly of you."

Derek looked for a grandfather clock. "What time is it?"

"About two. I'll head out. Again, I'm sorry for disturbing you."

Now that his eyes had adjusted, Derek took a better look around the room. The bed was wide and made of oak. A writing desk held a stack of parchment and a feathered quill soaking up ink. In the closet were dark sweaters and vests that looked handmade, and above the fireplace were paintings of demon folk Derek didn't recognize. Past friends or family.

"This's your room," he said, "isn't it?"

Oliver paused at the door. "It's okay. I'm taking up one of the couches downstairs. Maxwell's nocturnal, so he's been keeping me company."

"Sorry." He slumped back into his warm spot. "Sorry I've fucked up your schedule and bashed my way through your home."

"It's okay."

"And I'm sorry you fell in love with me. Sorry you got stuck with me."

Oliver came up to Derek and the fire.

"You don't have control of it, right? You could've ended up falling for a normal demon girl and had normal demon babies, but instead, you got stuck with me."

Oliver sat on the edge of his bed. "I'm not sure I've properly explained how mating works to you. I didn't fall in love with you and work my personality around you. All my life, ever since I gained consciousness in this world, I've been waiting for someone like you to complete me. I've been waiting for a patient, friendly, loving person to show me the kinder side to this awful world. You've seen me—I'm a wreck of nerves, always thinking the worst and stuttering over myself. You were the only person who could better me."

Derek hid half of his face in his blankets. This was sounding too heavy to hear after the day he had. "What if you never found me?"

"Some demons never find them. Back in the day, we used to hold festivals for neighboring villages to come and mingle with ours. Out of hundreds, two or three might find their mated pair. It's how Brennen and Yomi met. It was a beautiful ceremony."

"Well, what if your brain is wrong?" he scrounged up. "What if it's someone who looks like me, or acts like me? What if..."

Oliver leaned over him. His hand traced Derek's jawline until he found his cheek.

Derek melted into his palm. He smelled so good, his hand was so big.

"It's not wrong," he promised. "You're the only person I'll ever love." His thumb kissed over Derek's lower lip. On instinct, Derek opened his mouth to taste him.

"Are your feelings for me wavering?" Oliver asked.

If Oliver could've read minds, he would've gotten his answer weeks ago. "They've...doubled."

"That's good. There was a high chance you wouldn't be interested in me." His thumb rolled over his lower lip again. "You don't know how happy I was when you kissed me."

The memory that'd once been so painful refilled Derek's heart with desire. "I just...thought you were really hot and shot my shot. I didn't think it'd turn out like this."

"I'm glad it did. To think it might've not worked out would've been devastating. And you're..." He laughed to himself.

Derek pulled back. "I'm what?"

"It's embarrassing."

Derek gained back the slightest bit of confidence against him. That hand, it almost felt like dominance. "You're gonna have to stop acting like this, otherwise I won't be able to control myself. What's embarrassing now?"

He covered his face with both hands. "That you're a really kind and handsome...person...so I'm glad that whatever happens next, I'm glad I got to meet you."

Derek didn't know how good Oliver's eyesight was. He'd learned that the humans could hardly see in the dark, meanwhile, he could see Oliver's face and blush clearly.

So he wondered if Oliver could see him now, slowly hiding his reddening face underneath the blankets. He felt his ears heating up, his heart thumping so hard, he thought he'd throw up. "T-that so," he said. "Well, uh, thanks. I'd like to get to know you a bit more, too, before I, you know, make out with you again."

"Me, too." He played with something on his neck. "I'm not upset that I mated with you. I can tell you're a very loving person, and I can sense that you've been having trouble with your identity. Just know that whoever you are, whoever you choose to be, I'll be there to support you." He got up and walked to the door. "Do you need anything else before I go? Are you hungry? Thirsty?"

"I think I'm good," he said. "Think you covered everything I needed tonight."

He caught a smile rising on Oliver's face. "Alright. Goodnight, then, Derek."

"Night," he said, but he couldn't fall back asleep. He couldn't even jerk off or cry or do anything else embarrassing in this bed.

He was, for the first time since arriving in the Drail Kingdom, happy to be alive.

25

Kevin

Kevin considered himself to have a rather adept pair of lungs. Airborne crossbreeds needed to have them to keep them flying long distances.

With Viper and Tokala, he realized how terrible they really were, especially when underwater.

He was currently headfirst in lukewarm water, dunked like a cookie in milk. He was sitting at the top of one of the larger tanks in the building. There were walkways built up here for the waterborne and guards to enter and exit the water safely. He had his fingers curled in the perforated, metal grilles so he didn't fall in.

He'd lost count of how many seconds he'd been holding his breath, but he guessed it had to be over a minute. That was pretty good, wasn't it?

He peeked open one eye. Tokala was floating in the water, watching him with her arms crossed and a brow arched. She tapped her wrist to signal—tease him about—his time.

He used his wings to keep him better balanced over the edge. She'd bragged about how long she could hold her breath, and it'd childishly gotten to him, especially in front of Viper. He'd wanted to prove that he could live in their world.

He focused on something else. At the bottom of the tank grew special water grasses and "coral" that helped keep the water clean. Some fish used them as homes and hid around the branches. On the ground floor, through the glass, guards were eyeing him and his weird behavior.

Viper, who was swimming behind Tokala, was also watching him. Her hair, floating around her pretty eyes, her cute, innocent eyes blinking up at him. Her soft, kissable lips, *right* there, begging him to...

Choking on an intake of horny water, Kevin conceded and resurfaced.

Viper surfaced next to him. "Sorry. Did I do something wrong?"

"No, I just can't hold my breath like you can."

"You did really well, though. I was counting. It was almost two minutes."

Tokala surfaced beside her. "That's nothing. Viper can stay under for as long as she wants because of her gills, and I can hold my breath for almost two hours."

Kevin scooted up to the walkway's edge. He dangled his foot to be closer to Viper. "So you can't breathe in the water, but you need to be in it? How do you speak?"

To demonstrate, Tokala dunked her head back into the water. "Like this. We talk in this way that lets little air actually leave our mouth. It kinda tickles our throat."

Viper climbed up next to Kevin. Their clothes must've been made with a special material—they were already dry, as were her skin and hair. He felt so bad for staring, but he couldn't help himself.

"Viper, you need to get back into the water," Tokala said. "I know you like walking around, but you've been out of water for too long this week."

Viper rubbed a hand down her arm. The skin around her elbows and upper arms was a bit flaky.

"You should come back in," Tokala said. "Kevin, how bad is her skin?"

"It's not bad," Viper said. "I'm fine, Kala, it's okay."

She pouted. "Kevin, tell me."

To explain how a girl's skin looked was a test he wasn't ready to take. "I don't know."

"I'll go in soon," Viper told her. "One minute."

"Do you not like being in the water?" he asked her.

"It's not that. I just like being...up here. It's nicer right here."

Kevin's dangly foot unconsciously did the doggy paddle. He was becoming closer to these people—these friends—but there was definitely something between him and Viper. The way she looked at him and, subsequently, the way he looked at her. She'd steal glances at him and he'd follow the trail of blue dots from the nape of her neck down her tail. Not only did he want to hold her hands and listen to her talk, he wanted to *be* more to her.

But Tokala, through no fault of her own, was always around. Either her or that little baby Viper admired. He guessed it'd take time to gain her trust so they could finally be alone together. It might never happen.

He shook the thought away. "I don't mind if you need to get into the water," he told her. "I'll still be here. Your health is more important."

Viper filled her mouth with air, a challenge daring to be formed. Then she slowly dipped her toes back into the water and plopped back in.

She looked more natural in the water, like she was truly meant to live there. But not in these tanks, somewhere else. He didn't know where he was seeing this, but somewhere, he saw an entire world of water that stretched on for miles. It didn't hit any buildings or trees or Muralha, but the skyline, so they could swim—live—forever.

His fingers found their way into the water. He stirred it, creating ripples that tickled the underneath of Viper's nose. She watched him with her mouth submerged.

"Hi," he said.

"Hello. How do you do that, with your hair?"

He looked over at the small braid he'd done up that day. "It's pretty easy to learn. Do you want me to teach you when your hair dries?"

"I like how it looks on you. It's pretty."

He tried swallowing down his heart so he could hear his thoughts again. "Your hair is longer...prettier, so it'll be easy to braid."

Overcome, Viper hid herself and swam down to the coral. She sat with her knees up to her chin. A line of bubbles escaped from her mouth.

Kevin's hands shook at the blatant attempt at flirting with a girl who was leagues above him in every regard. Looks, personality, brain, heart. She was so kind and normal and he was bumbly. Maybe that's why they connected so easily: They were opposites.

Tokala, who'd been watching all this time, waited for Viper to sink before speaking. "I've never seen her like this before."

"Is she okay?" Kevin asked. "Did I embarrass her?"

"Don't act coy. You know what you're doing. Let me tell you something, *Kevin*. I've known that girl since she was a baby, and I've never seen her so interested in another person before. She has a knack for that, reading people, and for some reason, you're sounding off alarm bells in her brain."

"I-I think it's because I have wings. She said she's never met someone with wings before."

"Oh, that's bullshit and you know it." She spat out water between her two front teeth, streaming it back into the water. "If you're going for her, I won't stop you, but I'll kill you if you break her heart, and if you lay a little feathered finger on her the wrong way, I'll snap your neck faster than you can fall out of the sky."

Kevin picked a piece of skin from off of his thumb. "Got it. I'll try my best. But, Tokala, in all honesty, I haven't done this sort of thing before. I'm nervous I'll do something weird."

"Well, she hasn't done this, either, Kevin. She's *fucked* before, but she's never had a lover."

Kevin cringed. He didn't want to talk about this behind her back.

"Both of you are walking into new territory," she continued, "and I don't think that's a bad thing. You can go for her, just treat her like she's the most important person in your world."

That wouldn't have been hard for him to do, if she liked him back, but something was keeping him from wholeheartedly believing that.

Maïmoú, she was still connected to him. He hadn't heard a word from her ever since they talked in her Void over a week ago. He was glad she'd taken his advice to heal herself, but could he ever live a normal life with her involvement? How would he explain his predicament to Viper, a girl who'd never taken a step outside?

"Tricky business, isn't it?" Tokala asked. "You'll get used to it. Falling in love is the easiest, hardest thing you can do."

"You have a lot of experience with dating girls?" he asked.

"Oh, no. Not many girls can meet my standards. Most of them find me too...blunt, and hostile. I'll find one, one day. I won't give up."

Kevin looked back down into the rippling water. "I won't give up, either."

He wasn't a very brave person. He likely wouldn't be and had accepted that about himself long ago. Accepting this, though, had blocked him from experiencing the world the way it was intended to be experienced. Being scared shouldn't have impeded him from enjoying life. It began and ended with him, and he had to be the one to take the first step into it.

Standing up, Kevin took the ladder down to the first floor, where Viper was. She had her back to him, but once he knocked on the glass, she turned around and smiled.

He waved. "Can you hear me?"

She nodded and looked back up to Tokala kicking her feet in the water. She said something to her friend, and Tokala, taking the hint, swam away, maybe to try her own luck with courting a girl.

Kevin freed one of his hands and touched where Viper's face was. He didn't know if this was infatuation or the fact that he hadn't seen a waterborne before this year, but she had a face he couldn't look away from. Trying to gain that bravery deep inside him, he touched where her lips were.

And Viper, digging deep to find her own nerves, leaned in closer and closer, until her lips were kissing the glass near his forehead. She studied his face, tracing his features with half-lidded eyes. The tiniest of bubbles escaped from the corners of her wet lips.

"I...really want to be with you," he explained, words slipping out before registering in his brain. "I hope that's not too weird to say, but I do...really like you."

The bubbles stopped.

He pushed himself to keep going. "I know my life is chaotic and wild and I'm not too confident with my emotions, but I don't want to lose this chance with you. I wanna learn more about you, and not what you are, but what you like. What your favorite food is. How I can make you happy. I like when you smile, and I like looking at you. Sorry if that's weird to say, again, but that's what I feel. Sorry."

So close, with being confident, only to fall on his face with an apology. Being brave took time, he assumed, even if he did just confess.

Viper's tail and fins stopped moving in the water. She began to sink, tilting to the side like a statue thrown into a river. When she came back to the world of the living, her blush colored her ears, collarbone, upper chest and shoulders. Her eyes went wide as if he'd said something unbelievable. As if she didn't live in glass tanks where she could always see her reflection. How could she *not* see her beauty?

Looking for a place to hide, Viper darted down an escape route.

Kevin laughed out his nerves as he watched her flee.

"You coward!" he heard Tokala shout from somewhere in the tank. "Kevin, chase her!"

"I-I don't want to freak her out?" he said in a question.

"She's a fish! She *likes* to be chased!"

He didn't know what that meant, but his feet were already moving. Passing through the group of guards watching them, he took down a hall and gave chase.

He caught her swimming through different rooms and halls. Almost all the tanks down here were connected in some way, which made sense. Hallways were made the same way, same with streets. He ran in on families playing with young water-borne and couples playing with each other's hair. Viper expertly swam around them to evade Kevin and his feelings.

He used his wings to catch up with her, taking flight and dragging his hand down the glass. "Hey!"

She laughed, bubbles escaping out of her nose. "Tokala made you say those things!"

"No, she didn't! She just gave me the go-ahead to say them!"

"Why'd you say them?"

"Because I like you!"

Viper yelped in happy fear and pivoted left, down a tank he couldn't trail.

"Wait!" He found a door that led to where she went and pushed it.

He came to the open atrium that spiraled up a dozen floors. Balconies and hallways were tiered above him, holding hospital wings and meeting rooms for Asilo workers. In the center was a large, thick tank that grew up like a tree trunk and spread out towards the ceiling with branches. Waterborne lounged in the open water while guards watched over them with lazy cups of coffee.

Viper swam straight up into the tank, flapping her tail like a propeller.

Opening up his wings, Kevin took a running start into the atrium and flew.

It was so long since he'd actually taken to the sky. Defying gravity and soaring upwards, the refreshing wind blowing through his hair and in-between his flight feathers. He was rusty and hit the tank as he flew around it like a top.

Viper gasped at his extended wingspan. Kevin copied her as she swam to meet his pace. Around and around they went, sharing the spaces meant for them and making them their own.

He'd find a way to blend their worlds together. He'd learn to hold his breath and take the dive with her. His feathers were waterproof for a reason.

Maïmoú had called him her soulmate, two people bonded by fate who'd always cherish each other. He didn't know if it affected normal people like Viper, but he hoped it did. He wanted to be with her forever.

A fuzziness tickled the back of his brain. It started off slow, like an incoming sneeze. Then his hands tingled. It travelled from his head through every hollow bone of his wings.

Viper paused their dance. "Kevin?"

His wings stopped flapping. Something was wrong. He had to fix it. Save it. Save whatever was wrong with her. Save her.

A screech cried out through his head. It shook his eyes and dropped his body. The sense of death, of dying in somebody's arms and not being able to stave off the inevitable sense of nothingness.

He crashed into the tank, falling several flights and landing against a potted plant, cracking it.

The world rumbled without warning. The tank spilled out gallons of water from the top.

Viper quickly swam to the bottom. "What's going on?" she asked. "Are you okay?"

Kevin reached out in front of him, through the chaos. "Maïmoú?" he whispered.

Something—someone—groaned in his mind. It sounded animalistic, the snarl of a beast.

"I'm back," Maïmoú announced, and all the lights in the fallout shelter shut off.

26

Nikki

Nobody her age really knew what was happening, but the adults sure did.

She'd only been to one mandatory assembly. Usually, they were planned days, if not weeks, in advance. The last time it happened, her parents hadn't been in bed due to an emergency call from Morgan's. Now that she knew their secrets, it was probably something to do with the Drill. They thought that was more important than staying at home with their own kids.

Derek had refused to get up, staying in his pajamas and only being hauled out of the house after Nikki ripped out half of his feathers. With Kevin's and Vanna's help, they'd gotten to the city center amongst a crowd of strangers. She'd been too small to see the Líders give their speech about an increase in Guard-related attacks. She'd been too on-edge about so many people around her loved ones.

The other times occurred when she was homeless and too young to grasp the seriousness of assemblies. No warning until the sirens spooked her out of her canal. She'd watched as lines of people scuttled over her bridges. They looked like they were being mind-controlled, but she knew it was from fear of stepping out of line.

It was surreal, seeing it unfurl as a young adult. Guards, families, students, the elderly. Children as young as two were being carried by restless parents. The homeless watched on from the shadows, unsure if this assembly affected them.

Bodies were already funneling into the Asilo plaza. It was a public, open space, dotted with fountains and benches and crossed by tram rails. Groups were forming small pockets of questions with no answers. Nikki tried to gain higher ground to spot Vanna or Pippa, even her parents or Morgan and Del, but she didn't see any of them.

"What do you think this's about?"

"What happened?"

"Last time this happened, they killed somebody."

"How long is this gonna take?"

"I'm scared."

Her foot began tapping. This was anarchy—they needed someone to guide them. Where were the Líders?

Where was Kevin? He was somewhere here, beneath her feet, being held illegally by tyrants. She wondered how far down he was. If she tapped hard enough, would they reconnect? She should've started digging.

She looked down at her hands. She still felt like she was in Lí's body. Anxiety about this plague and someone named Alliroue and his survival, it was all paralyzingly hers.

And *Marcos*. He'd been the only one to see her for what she was. Did that mean he was involved in this? She wondered what demonic Deity he was connected to.

Demonic. Another word from Lí's word bank: the opposite of heavenly, something bright and good. A terror to beingkind.

Nikki broke through the crowd to gather more information. She couldn't stand by like this. She needed to move before she spiralled.

Some people acted like they knew what was going on. She heard everything from a tax increase to an execution to news

326

about the Muralha. She stopped listening when a guard said that a new breed was about to be unveiled. Hearsay thrived in a crowd.

When the Sun should've been in the center of the sky, the main doors to the Asilo slid open.

The people nearest the stage went silent immediately. Then the guards stood up straighter. People began hushing one another and pointing to the Asilo stairs. Atop the steps stood three idols.

Nikki squatted down and slipped through stunned Raeleenians to get a closer look. Nadia, Zantl, and Marcos. She'd never been so close to a Líder before. Only in pictures and hearing their voices on the radio. From this vantage point, she saw the white tufts inside Nadia's ears, the length of her nails.

She looked awful. Bobbed hair a mess, makeup smudged. And Mikhail was missing, just like Pippa had said. You didn't see one and not the other. They were a packaged set of authority.

Zantl stood off to the side wearing a large coat that made them look younger than they were. They looked as bad as their mother and couldn't take their eyes off the cloudy sky, which had grown heavier with rain in the past hour.

Marcos was staring into the crowd like he was still going over the revelations he and Nikki had shared together. She hadn't explained herself well during then, and she'd never speak to him again. Had he told the Líders about her body swap? Was *that* what this assembly was for?

Nikki stopped hunting for a better vantage point and tried becoming as inconspicuous as possible.

Nadia spoke into a microphone hidden in her coat hood. There was a delay before Nikki actually heard her voice:

"People of Raeleen, thank you for, uh, coming out here on short notice. I can see all of you are here today, and I appreciate your...cooperation."

Nikki didn't believe that, but from her stuttering, she didn't think Nadia did either, or cared.

"We...I...come to you today..." She held up a pad of paper to read off. "First and foremost, I'm here to give you the unfortunate and saddening news that our beloved Líder, my lover, and Zantl's father, Mikhail Farja, passed away this week."

A collective gasp. Whispers, concerns, theories already going too far on newborn news. Nikki didn't speak, but she, too, couldn't stop her mind. It wasn't saddening news, but this would change the world, probably for the worst. Nothing good came from a dictator's death.

"He, uh, died peacefully in his sleep," Nadia continued, louder, more unstable. Her hands were shaking. "We... we accept all condolences, my child and I, as we grieve Mikhail's loss. He was a beloved and intelligent lover and father, and the world is a worse place without him in it."

Thunder rumbled over the Muralha. Everyone turned to find where it was coming from before Nadia continued.

"We will be having his funeral this Monday. All postal and academic services will be postponed henceforth to prepare for the service. Thank you for your upcoming cooperation."

She flipped over her notes. "I...also come to you today with an announcement regarding the fate of Raeleen. You're all aware that we do everything we can to protect you. We need to protect each other, and we cannot do that when we're divided by defiance."

Nikki's instincts told her to look away, but it'd only make her look more guilty. That sounded like Nadia knew everything about the rebellion and was toying with them like a cat with a cornered mouse.

"We will not tolerate any forms of sabotage or distrust within our walls," Nadia continued, "and as such, we ask that if anyone has any information about distrustful individuals, including our Guard, I want you to report them to the Asilo immediately. No longer will secrecy devalue our city's protection."

The crowds murmured in a collective blur of voices. Nikki lowered her ears. She had to get out of here, but where? Back home? Back to Vanna's? If they knew about her involvement with the rebellion, how could she go back to her parents' place? She'd destroy everything, her family.

Her brain fuzzed up, tickling the hair at the top of her head. She felt lightheaded. Not like when she'd become Lí, but similar, like she was touching another person's soul in this ocean of thousands.

A louder voice spoke above Nadia's booming voice.

"Nicole."

She started walking. Step by step, against her will. A force had, again, overtaken her body.

"Shào?" she asked, breathless, but her feet kept moving her to the front. She couldn't control herself. People were staring, whispering. She brushed between two guards who went to grab her. As soon as they touched her, an invisible barrier threw them back into the unsuspecting crowd.

Nikki's legs went numb. Her body walked her straight into an empty space between the closest group of people and the Líder. Nadia was glaring at her. The guards had their guns up. Whatever was controlling her body was sentencing her to death and she couldn't do anything but stand and wait for an undeserved punishment.

Zantl's tail tucked between their legs. They whispered a warning to their mother. It was lost to the storm.

Nikki tried finding her own voice. A lie, even if it was a bad one. Something to say to Shào who was clearly puppeting her for God knew what reason. To say something to save her family

329

from being found out, or from her dying. Either one, whatever made her brain work, act. Say *something*.

Her lower half lifted upwards, magnetized to the rain. Her feet floated away from concrete. She'd become weightless, like Shào, and levitated a foot off the ground.

She couldn't speak; her teeth were chattering too much. Everyone was looking at her. Her name was whispered by strangers. Nearest the Líder, four guarddogs aimed their guns at her head. Others keeping the crowds back had hands ready on their pistols.

"What...is this?" Nadia asked. "Is this her? Maïmoú," she called out, "is this you?"

"Nicole?"

"Shào," Nikki whispered to herself. "What's going on?"

"One moment," he said in her head. *"I'm almost there."*

"What're you doing?"

"I can reach you. I'm almost there. Almost..."

The guards took knees for better shots.

"Shào," Nikki stressed. "Please."

"Almost..."

Unable to get to him, Nikki whispered his name in prayer.

A stray gunshot fired into the plaza.

She awoke as if she were still dreaming. Darkness, but not blackness. A quiet pool of nothingness, infinity on all sides, and floating.

An ocean, according to Lí's memories.

A bright star shone above her. With some fight still left in her, Nikki swam up, a hand out towards freedom.

"You have more fight in you than I did at this age," someone said. *"Thank God for that. Hopefully, you'll live longer this time around."*

"Huh?" Nikki asked the voice. She almost didn't answer. The voice sounded like hers.

It must've been, for she didn't receive an answer.

She awoke on the ground, blinking away raindrops. It'd begun raining, a split in the sky letting out sharp sunbeams.

Her mother was above her, along with her father and aunts. Her father was pointing his finger at people and yelling through tears. Her mother was hugging her body.

She didn't know why. She was feeling fine, better than ever. The ringing in her ears was even going away.

She sat up without using her arms or legs. Floating like she was underwater, she got up and levitated over her parents.

She looked over her hands, her feet, tail. She was still herself, only touched by magic, or divinity. Another word Lí knew, something to describe a Deity's powers.

She tried moving her eyes and couldn't. She tried her mouth but couldn't. She was no longer in control.

Her hands touched her front, and they slowly lifted up her sweater and hoodie to reveal an injury the size of her thumb right through her abdomen. It was red and dark and was bleeding into her belly button. It was as if she was watching herself from a dream. It didn't hurt.

"I-I have you," Shào said through her mind. "I got to you in time."

Her stomach growled like she was hungry, and the injury began healing itself. The skin grafted over the hole and filled itself back in. From her body popped out a shiny bullet. It clattered to the plaza ground.

"I have you," Shào promised.

Nikki tried to look for her family's reaction, but she was no longer in control of her own head. Shào was more interested in looking at the Líder.

In her peripheral vision, she saw Raeleenians on their knees, holding their heads and moaning in pain. Something like a mental bomb had dropped on all of them. Even Nadia had been affected by it. Marcos looked fine as he helped Zantl to their feet.

"What is happening?" Shào whispered. "Tell me, through thoughts."

No wonder—Nikki couldn't move her mouth. She thought, "What happened to me?"

"I believe you got shot, but I was able to get to you in time. I felt your heart. You're scared. Why is everyone gathered like this?"

What else could Nikki say but the truth? "The Líder's holding an assembly. She knows about my family and Maïmoú. My parents and friends, they're all gonna be found out and killed. You have to save them."

"What about Maïmoú?"

"Shào, my family," she stressed. "You need to save them. Forget about me."

"Oh, I won't forget about you." He made her look around Raeleen. "What has your family done?"

"They were trying to rebel, and then the Líder was talking about Maïmoú. I don't know how they know, but you have to save them, please."

Shào made her place her hand to her lips. "Of course. She did have a habit of introducing herself to world leaders. Even when she's so inept. She's here, isn't she? I can sense her."

"Shào?"

He looked to Marcos and Zantl as if he'd caught them whispering about him. She felt her body go rigid. "There're two more here?"

"What?"

Shào made Nikki smirk. "*What luck,*" he said, "*for me to find their soulmates.* What luck!" he said aloud in her voice. "These *are* your soulmates, are they not? Unathi, Sabah, Tsvetan? You must be so *keen* on protecting *your* soulmates this time around! You give them another chance to live yet let my soulmate suffer without me?"

Fighting through her inner pain, Nadia raised her hand, and the guards fired another round.

Shào raised her arms. The bullets ricocheted off them and back at the men and women who'd fired.

Dozens of guards fell like rag dolls. Blood splattered and bodies crumpled. People screamed as a forming stampede escaped the city.

Nikki didn't know how she could feel without the control of her body. The smell hit her, and she heard the officers and innocent crowdspeople scream and scatter. She'd just been shot and her stomach was twisting from a stronger, more unbridled agony. "*Shào—*"

He turned her body to her family cowering beneath her. They looked so small from so high up.

He looked to Vanna, to Pippa holding him. He lifted one arm.

Nikki screamed. Using her all to bring Shào's hand down, she redirected him from shedding any more blood. "*That's my family!*" she shouted in her head. "*What's wrong with you?*"

"Oh. My apologies," he said in her voice. "I hadn't realized. What a patchwork you have."

He was talking so casually for a kid with a kill count, as if he'd killed like this before. He wasn't even fazed.

"Which Deity are you?" Nadia yelled into her microphone. "Who *are* you?"

Shào turned. "Are *you* the one in charge?" he questioned. "You must've learned more in those abandoned fallout shelters than those humans ever did. What is this, an authoritarian regime? How *primeval*." He laughed. "You ask which Deity I am? Have you beings truly forgotten which Deity can do *this*?" He threw out his hand over the city. The buildings rumbled like they were in a rare earthquake. Trash cans fell. Windows cracked and littered the ground with shards of glass.

"Shào, stop!" Nikki yelled.

Shào, laughing with Nikki's voice, floated her higher. "I forgot this *rush*! The *feeling* of the world changing by your hand. What a feeling, Nicole! I can see why you detest this world!"

"This isn't what I meant!"

"*Saaaabah*," Shào called out, like an adult calling for a mischievous child. "I know you're watching me. Do you think you can get away from me? You have the power to kill me, yet you put me in a purgatory for 500 years? How *dare* you? I knew you were as cruel as the humans you hate so much, but this torture is unlike anything I've ever lived through."

"Shào!" Nikki tried regaining control of her own body. The bodies on the ground began bleeding out into the canals. *"Shào, stop it! You're making things worse! Stop!"*

"Nikki!" Her mother flew up to her and grabbed her ankle, but Shào wouldn't allow it. Holding out his hand, he manually moved her mother away, not hurting her, but causing her to scream as to what her daughter was doing to her.

"Shào, that's my mom!"

Shào eyed the sky above. "What, can you not push through your own barriers to save your own soulmates? Are you *afraid* of me?" He raised his arm at Marcos, who was trying to push Zantl through the doors, but they'd gone catatonic. "Then let me start my 500-years' worth of payback!"

Bombs detonated off in the Asilo buildings. One by one, each floor exploding in fire and balls of smoke. Those who were still left in the plaza were now running for their lives.

Nikki watched as the main Asilo building, the one Kevin was in, fall into itself. Multiple stories, gone in plumes of flames.

"*Shào!*" Nikki palmed the inner walls of her mind. Even if he killed the Líders, what would that do for them? Hundreds of people lived in the Asilo that needed help. Kevin was in there. And the rest of the guards would see Nikki, this unstoppable force that could kill them, and come after her family anyway regardless of the Líder's fate.

She didn't want this kind of blood on her hands, but they were painted forever red by his doing.

"You can't have it both ways, Nicole," Shào said. "To end cruelty is to kill those who think they can torment you."

Nikki had only meant Shào once. She didn't know his history and couldn't remember his last name, but from this, along with the combination of Lí's traumatic memories, made them feel like childhood friends who'd grown apart.

Whatever they had together, it was tarnished today by his— her—hands.

She pulled harder on whatever essence or soul she could grab on to. She thought she'd understood the value of being a soulmate, this consuming feeling of being adored. This wasn't adoration. This was blinded infatuation that'd been placed unto her without her consent, and Shào was abusing it without care.

"Nicole—"

She kept fighting.

"Nicole, wait!" Shào held her body in a hug. "I don't want to leave you like this. I can help you!"

She kept pushing. She would *not* let her story end like this. She would save Kevin and Derek and all of her family because they were all she had left, and she wasn't going to lose them to divinity. They *were* her divinity.

"Wait, what?" Shào asked. "Derek...Derek Harrow? He's your...he's your sibling?"

One last push and she felt her body freefall, pulled out of Shào's stranglehold. His voice echoed through the collapse, and she felt herself fall into someone's arms before losing consciousness.

27

Derek

Waking up sucked. First off, he didn't want to, and when his brain forced him to open his eyes, he was pissed, then depressed, then angry at himself for being pissed and depressed.

He awoke in Oliver's room, still smelling like him, still unsure if he was supposed to be here. He'd kick the poor guy out of his own room to cry. Cry about Keva and her death, about the humans' treatment of him, of that vision he had of Hadiya.

He pulled himself up with his wings. He didn't know how much he'd slept, but he couldn't imagine being any more awake than he was now.

Someone else yawned in the room, and Derek nearly shit himself.

Holly had found her way into his locked bedroom. She had a stick from outside and was poking the warm ashes of his fireplace.

"Uh, hey," Derek said.

Holly got up and rummaged through her many pockets. She pulled out a pink flower and placed it on top of Derek's buried foot. Then she bowed and ran out of the room. He should've expected it at this point, but he was still curious about the way her brain functioned. Childlike, but in an adult body, with something to say behind those wide eyes.

He couldn't even tell if Holly liked him, but today wasn't the day to dissect that. After stealing one of Oliver's oversized sweaters and placing the flower behind his ear, Derek went downstairs and faced the shitty day.

The smell of a hearty, warm breakfast warmed up the house. Syrup, maple bacon, and buttered toast. Sausages from meat he didn't know, with the smell of pepper that tickled his nose hairs. From the windows he passed, he saw morning birds chirping from snow-covered pine. It must've snowed last night.

All the demons were eating around a large dinner table stacked with food. Pancakes and tea and cut fruit and hash-browns. Someone had cut up rosemary and sprinkled it over a slab of juicy meat. It still had eyeballs. Derek couldn't look away.

Yomi was busy cleaning the kitchen while Shimah helped serve Kumo in her wheelchair. Rosaline was floating near the stove, watching a pot of rice to stop cooking. Holly, she now had a baby in her arms. Not her dolly, but that real, breathing baby he'd seen yesterday. Noemi? She was babbling through a mouthful of smashed peas as she tried to get Maxwell's attention from the table. He was reading a worn book around his plate of eggs. Seemed like he didn't always need to be in water to be alive. Must've been a snake thing. Or a demon thing. Snake demon.

"Oh, good morning, Derek!" Rosaline handed him an empty plate. "If you're hungry, help yourself to whatever's still left. I made sure Shimah saved you some food, and Oliver and Brennen said to eat without them."

"It was really hard," Shimah said. "Could barely stop my hand from stealin' all the fish." He snickered and helped Kumo take a biteful of hashbrowns.

"I can eat by myself," Kumo said. "My arms aren't that weak yet."

"How about *now*?" he asked, and kicked Kumo's wheel-chair, making her spin around.

"Hey!"

"And I'm making more eggs, if you'd like any," Yomi said.

Derek kept going back to the eyeball/creature dish. "What's this?"

"Oh, it's fish!" Rosaline said. "We didn't know if you'd like it because the royals don't like eating it, but if you're a bird, it kinda made sense to have some."

Derek sniffed it cautiously. It smelled like the ocean, but that didn't deter him from trying it. In fact, it smelled good, almost mouth-watering.

"Go on," Rosaline said. "I know you had a stressful day, and I don't think you ate dinner. Speaking of," she said, floating over to Maxwell. "I see you haven't touched *your* food yet. What's up?" She played with his nubby horns.

He shooed her away like a bug. "The humans have been in a swell of emotions since yesterday. *He's* been in a rut all night. He didn't get any sleep." He yawned, then ducked. The baby had thrown her baby spoon at him. "*Yomi*, can you *please* take her?"

"I don't think Holly will let me." Yomi tried for her own child, but Holly protected her with both arms. "Noemi is quite a handful, Derek. I'm sorry for any trouble she may cause. For being a baby for 500 years, she won't know any better than this."

Derek gave the kid a wave. Holly returned it.

"Good thing this snowstorm hit," Shimah said. "Any minute now, I suspect the humans to be bargin' in and demandin' if we've seen Derek. When they find out we're housin' him—"

"Hush, now," Yomi said. "The humans don't come out during snowstorms. If they didn't come for him last night, they won't be coming today. It's a Sunday, after all. They wouldn't visit demons on their holy day."

"They would for their angel," Maxwell said under his breath.

Ignoring them, Derek took his first bite of fish.

Then the second. Then third.

And then it was gone.

Fish had to be one of the best blessings from God, tailor-made for him and him alone. The meat was so juicy and mouth-wateringly *good*. It melted between his teeth and packed into the corners of his mouth so perfectly. He ate it, bone and all, and went for seconds without question.

"He has an appetite!" Rosaline announced with clapping. "Hurrah!"

"It's so *good*," he moaned.

"It's free meat that's easier to cook than deer or wildcat," Shimah said. "Also, where's Oliver and Brennen?"

"They just left a few hours ago," Yomi said. "Have patience."

As Derek dined on his most favorite thing in the world, he watched Maxwell out of the corner of his eye. Every now and again, he'd flinch or twitch his nose. At one point, he jerked forward only to shake it off and flip the page like it was nothing.

"Can I help you?" he asked, not looking at Derek.

"No." Derek slurped up the fin of his fish and crunched on the bones.

"You're not supposed to eat the bones," Maxwell reminded him.

He swallowed said bones. God, it totally made the most sense that he was mated to Jabel. "How does it work again? The mating business? Can you, like, see into his eyes?"

"No."

"Can you hear his thoughts?"

"No." He flipped the next page. "Not...really," he added.

"How's it like?"

Maxwell set down his book. Rosaline looked up, ready to intervene.

"It's different because he's not a demon," he explained. "I don't see through his eyes. Rather, I can sense what he's feeling. It's why Oliver knows when you're about to fall out of the sky. Or it's because he's always following you."

"You're one to talk, Maxy," Rosaline said. "How many times a week do you lurk in those rose bushes for Jabel?"

"That's because we have a system where we meet in secret every Sunday when his father normally goes to bed early and Nero watches over him. We also send letters, not that it's any of your business what we do."

"Hey, it's not like you keep it secret. You tell us every time you leave. And why tell him? I thought you didn't want him knowing for Jabel's sake."

"This's the most I've ever heard you talk about it," Yomi said.

"You're so *secretive*," Shimah teased.

"I have to be," Maxwell said. "Our relationship would get both of us hanged. And he wrote to me last night. I know Derek already knows."

"I won't spill," Derek told him. "Like I'm one to talk."

The demons turned to him. Yomi stopped pouring herself a cup of tea. Kumo sipped her bowl of soup.

"How do you feel about him?" Shimah dared to ask.

"He said you kissed him," Rosaline went on further. "Do you love him?"

He weighed the option in his mind. It wasn't like he hated him or even disliked him, but love? Did he love Oliver?

Everyone turned to the windows. Most of them had some type of pointed ears—Holly had an extra set—that probably made their hearing better than his. Fish in mouth, he sat up and looked through the pine for whatever they saw.

Oliver and Brennen were walking out of the woods. Oliver was backpacking an entire dead deer over his shoulders. Brennen helped carry its hind legs and their hunting equipment to a shed in the back of the manor.

"That's a good deer," Shimah commented on. "Should last us at least a week, maybe two."

"And it's a buck, too," Rosaline said. "Yomi and I can fashion those horns into a new cooking spoon. And you needed more fishing hooks, right, Maxwell?"

"And we can use the hide for another jacket for Kumo," Maxwell said.

"Hey, it wasn't my fault we blew a hole through the first one," Shimah explained, hanging down from the rafters. He flicked his finger to produce a tiny yellow flame. "We just burn too easily."

Derek took his plate of fish closer to the window. He watched Oliver drag the deer into the shed and pat himself of dried blood. He and Brennen had a talk as they washed up at a well. Oliver laughed at something Brennen said.

"They're tired," Yomi said. "They didn't even travel with dark matter."

"What's that mean?" Derek asked.

"When we're too tired or injured, we can't use our powers properly. Sometimes we can't even levitate."

"A real tragedy," Rosaline said, now as close to the ceiling as Shimah was.

"Yeah, and my fire don't work good when I'm beat," Shimah said. "And Maxwell can't sneak into Jabel's bedroom for a good time."

Maxwell threw his fork at him. Baby Noemi clapped at flying projectiles.

"And our elixirs are less efficient," Yomi finished. "They must've hunted that buck for hours."

Oliver's pointed ears pricked up, and he looked over to the window, to Derek.

Derek crouched down and shielded himself with his wings.

Rosaline laughed. "He caught you. Can't hide from your mate, Derek. They got echolocation on you."

"How do you deal with it? Have you ever mated?"

"My mate was killed centuries ago. You still feel them even when they're dead." She smiled fondly as she created a handful of dark matter to play with. She kissed it before it dissipated. "That's what makes us soulmates. Even after death, we're always connected."

Something touched the top of his head. Holly, resting her chin on him. She watched Oliver work, cradling the baby against her chest.

After cleaning up out back, Oliver came in with a light dusting of snow over his curls. He took off his coat and boots near the door and properly shook out.

"Good haul," Shimah said, and a chorus of praise hit Oliver in a way he wasn't prepared for.

He turned red as he bowed to his own family. "Thank you. Brennen spent the majority of the hunt tracking it."

"But Oliver took the shot," Brennen said, and immediately went to his mate's side for kisses. "You know I'm not good with this eye."

"You're still the best hunter I know," Yomi said, and kissed his scars.

Derek, instead of ogling two lovers, looked up to Oliver.

Oliver glanced at him twice, like he was pretending not to see him until he was caught in the act. "G-good morning," he said. "Did you sleep well?"

"Yeah," Derek lied, and he didn't know why, but something about seeing Oliver's big snow boots, the pink in his cheeks from being outside for so long, and the idea that he could hunt and kill and gut a deer, it got him going. Something primal, like knowing Oliver could provide for him. He was proud of him.

He set his plate aside. "Can I, uh, talk to you for a minute? Nothing bad," he added. "Just wanted to talk."

"Of course." He spruced up his hair that was beyond help. It was so curly, it was like a bird's nest Derek couldn't wait to wring his hands through.

They walked off to a new side of the house Derek had yet to see. It was a tiny reading nook, like a miniature library with windows overlooking the forest. It had two rocking chairs with blankets thrown across the backs of them, and around them were books, paintings, and unused candlesticks ready to be lit. Oliver lit two and set them on the small table against the window.

Derek admired the paintings. They were portraits of demons he'd yet to see. He spotted two with white hair like him, two women in love.

"Who're they?" Derek asked.

"Demons who've passed. These two, their names were Relic and Ramira. They were mates who were murdered about five years ago. Then these two, they were Monty and Jake. They were twins."

Hearing that made Derek's stomach clench, but he figured it was from breakfast. "Was there ever a demon named Shào that you knew of? He has black hair, stubby horns like Maxwell, a long, red tail with yellow fur at the end."

Oliver thought really hard, eyes almost crossing. "No, I don't believe so."

Derek clicked his tongue. "Right. What about Maïmoú?"

He looked up, ears sticking out to hear better. "Excuse me?"

"Maïmoú?" he repeated. "Is she a demon? Do you know her? It's only because I've had weird encounters with people named Shào and Maïmoú. They both talk, like, in my head or something. I thought it had something to do with demonkind."

"None of us have that kind of telepathic power. Perhaps they're angels guiding you."

"Yeah, I don't think either of them are angels."

Oliver pressed his fingers in-between his tight knees. "You feel better," he said. "I mean, your heart feels better. You're calmer. I'm sorry, I'd turn this off if I could."

"It's okay. It's nice that you're looking out for me. I'm still processing yesterday. I kind of don't want to talk about it."

"That's understandable." He played with a string around his neck. On the end of it was the inverted cross.

Derek played with his own. He wanted to ask him why he wore it if he was the creature the inverted cross damned, but that wasn't his business. Maybe it gave him comfort to know there was a God that supposedly loved all life, even his.

To save them from awkwardness, Holly popped up out of nowhere. She hid around Oliver's chair and pressed her chin into the armrest. Oliver gave her his hand, to which she teethed on like a toddler.

"That a normal thing with her?" Derek asked.

"Yes. She's overly attached to me. I can't remember when I was born, but when my memories start, she was by my side. Then I found Rosaline, who's my breed, then Shimah caring for Kumo. Yomi came in after, and then she found Brennen during one of our mating ceremonies, and then Maxwell came down from the mountains. His breed tends to be solitary, but when our numbers became so low, we had no choice but to group up. That's when we found out we were special."

"All of you were, not just every demon?"

He nodded. "We're immortal. We can't die by conventional means. Brennen got stabbed straight through the skull and didn't die. Kumo had her legs broken and she didn't bleed out." He petted Holly's hair. She nuzzled into him like a true cat. "Now, we're all that's left."

"Sorry," Derek said, though no apology could help at this point.

Oliver still acknowledged it. "Thank you."

"What's her breed?" he then asked. "Is she some sort of cat demon?"

"Oh, no. Holly isn't a demon."

"Huh?"

"All demons have that dark matter I spoke about." He created a cloud of the dark stuff. "Some of us have wings and can breathe fire. Some can breathe underwater or disappear and reappear at will, but all of us have this power. Holly doesn't have dark matter."

"So she's like me," Derek said. "Hey, Oliver, can I be honest with you? I don't think I'm an angel. Like, I don't get it at all. I don't know nothing about humans or the afterlife, and I know I don't have my memories, but I'm probably a bird, aren't I? Like, why is that a weird thing to bring up to the humans?"

"Do you feel more like a bird or an angel?"

"I don't know. I don't like labels. I just want to be me."

"Well, you're allowed to be whatever you wish to be here. We aren't holding you to any high expectations to be someone you aren't."

"Thanks. You know, you always make me feel better. Must be that mated energy flowing into me."

"I-I know that's not how it works."

Derek leaned forwards in his rocking chair, meeting Oliver's eyes. "I guess that just means I'm falling for you."

Oliver wilted and covered his large nose with his hand. "Ah, please. You're embarrassing me again."

"What? I'm only telling you—"

Holly stood up and knocked into Oliver's rocking chair. Her eyes turned to slits as she locked on to movement near the tree line.

A dollop of snow fell. Two squirrels chased each other around the bend before jumping back into the brush.

"It's alright," Oliver said. "She's just like a cat. She thinks she sees something in the air and goes into hunting mode. We haven't been able to teach her that nothing's going to hurt her."

Derek doubletook the area Holly was looking at, then, realizing what he was waiting for, got up and stretched. "*Fuck me!*" he moaned. "God, I hate this. I hate royal duties and I hate labels and I hate all this divine *bullshit* I'm forced to care about. I'm just one person, and I can't—Do you wanna fly?"

"Pardon me?"

"Yeah, just...*fly*. Get away from all this bullshit. I don't wanna be tied down anymore. I wanna be free, with you," he added. "If you'd like."

Oliver licked his lips, then looked outside. "I didn't see any humans in the forest."

Derek smirked and took his hands. "Then get your pretty ass dressed. We're going on a date."

"I don't remember inviting you," Derek said as they walked through the heavy snow.

Holly just stared off into the forest, clinging hard to Oliver's arm.

"I did warn you about her clinginess," Oliver said.

"Is she really coming with us?"

"I'm not sure. Holly, dear, we're going to go flying. Flying, you know?" He levitated a bit. She clung harder.

"Can you even fly with her?"

"Oh, yes. She likes being high." He motioned for her to climb onto his back. With how tall she was, Derek thought Oliver would have a harder time lifting her, but he picked her up like nothing.

Derek cracked his knuckles and flapped his wings.

"Do you need a running start?" Oliver asked.

"Is that a challenge?" He kicked his feet in the dirt like a horse. "Stand back."

He shouldn't have talked shit. He had to find the densest snow on the most leveled ground of the backyard to even try to get airborne. His eyes targeted a clear path through two trees. His wings flapped on instinct, but the cold air had turned them to icicles.

The higher they flew, the more colors they saw. The clouds were pastel pink this morning and curved with the horizon, the valleys and forests locking together like earthen puzzle pieces. A flock of geese flew with them towards the north. The sea enveloped this world like a mother's hand.

Oliver flew beside Derek, watching him with the cutest smile.

"Something on your mind?" Derek called out through the wind.

"You look beautiful up here. I can see why you like flying. Your heart is singing."

"I don't know if hearts sing."

"Trust me, yours does."

They flew in tandem through the mountains. They stirred up goats that were scaling the cliffs and a family of black bears hunting for their own meal. He even saw wolves, a pack of them, a mile uphill.

"There's so much wildlife out here," Derek said.

"Most humans don't travel this far out. They're afraid of my family, and the Barrier."

"The Barrier?"

Oliver pointed ahead of them. Within the mountains, Derek saw blurry snow between trees and stone. He thought some snow had gotten into his eye, but after rubbing it out, he saw it: the start of the Barrier.

It was like magic. This invisible Barrier cocooned the entire world, but he often forgot it was there until someone pointed it out. Where it touched the land, it was entirely opaque. Dark in color, with some type of goo swirling through it, almost like where the ocean met the shoreline.

"That's what you can't cross, right?" Derek asked.

"Yes, no matter how many times we or the humans try to break it."

Derek banked his wings and flew closer.

"Be careful," Oliver warned.

"I will," he said, but he flew right up against its curve, flying up and down the hills to follow its magical properties like a map. If he could only *touch* it. Something about the Barrier was calling him, like he had to make contact with it, or else...

Slowly, he reached out his hand and poked through it.

"*Derek!*"

Two hands gripped his neck in a chokehold, and he was pressed into a little boy's body aiming to kill him.

Shào brought Derek back into Drail and down the mountain.

"Where is she!?" Shào shouted. "I know you know where she is!"

Derek screamed. He saw the mountains, sky, tumbling in circles until they blended as one. He saw Oliver.

"Derek!" he shouted.

Shào kicked Oliver back. "Away with you!"

Oliver grunted as both he and Holly cratered the snow.

"Oliver!"

Shào crashed Derek several feet away. His tail slashed across the snow as he climbed atop Derek and pinned him down. "Where is she, fledgling? You must bring her to me right now, or else I am going to strike down—"

Derek's vision was spotting green. He couldn't breathe. He was suffocating. "I don't know who you're talking about! What do you want from me?"

"Nicole Lenore, your sister! You must find a way to connect with Maïmoú and get me to her! I *need* her!"

Oliver coughed and held his side in pain. Blood was dripping down his lips and jaw. "D-Derek?"

"Oliver, get away from here! It's Shào! He's—"

"Focus, fledgling!" Shào shouted. "Concentrate. Bring Maïmoú to me. If she so much as touches a hair on Nicole's perfect head, I will kill you in a million ways. Bring her to me now!"

Tears rolled down Derek's cheeks. "I-I don't know what you're talking about. Please."

A shadow hovered over them. Holly, stick in hand, used her weapon as a sword and thwacked Shào in the back.

Shào turned to a girl who could never speak. "Holly Bennett," he breathed. "We meet again."

Holly hissed as she continued hitting him.

"Don't make me hurt you. You *were* the most favorable soul-mate in the timeline."

Shào's grip was lessening, and Derek's body moved on its own. Thanking God for his flexibility, he wriggled his legs in front of him and kicked Shào hard in his face.

Shào's head whipped back. What Derek thought to be blood splattered out between his teeth, but it was darker and thicker like mud.

Shào fell and coughed up more and more darkness. His body suddenly glitched to the left, then right, like he couldn't control his teleportation. He appeared as a ghost at one point, the mountains visible through his clothes.

Oliver watched not Shào himself but the footprints he was making in the snow. He looked like he was trying to sit up, but whatever was wrong with his side kept him from moving, teleporting.

Shào cursed something in a foreign language, and the last glitch he made slammed him into both Holly and Derek.

Derek's vision went black. They were falling, tumbling into darkness with the sound of rushing wind. With every blink, the world changed. They were falling down the mountain, then through the Temno Forest, and then off of the ocean cliffs. Then nothing but ocean, endless from sky to floor. Holly was grabbing hold of him. Shào was in front of him. The three of them were free-falling like lead bags to the sea.

They dropped through the clouds Derek once fancied. Holly separated from them and began spinning on her own. Her screams hurt to hear. It was the first time Derek had heard her voice. It was light, like a mother's.

"*Fuck*!" Shào reached out for Derek. "Come here!"

"No, you're crazy!" Derek tried flapping his wings. He had to save Holly. She couldn't fly, but he couldn't, either, not like this. She'd die. *He'd* die.

It reminded him of something in his past, of falling to his death.

Seconds before he and Holly splatted like berries, something...happened. He couldn't say for sure, but something or someone touched them. Their fall ended too soon without pain, and they were teleported somewhere cold, dark, and smelling of pure saltwater.

He face-planted, and counted the seconds of quiet, making sure he hadn't just died, before peeling himself off the salty sand. He was in a dark, dingy cave that smelled of algae. Outside, he heard the waves pulling in and out of the cove, but their only light was a human-sized hole a hundred feet above them.

The room had been carved out of cement, a substance he hadn't seen since arriving in Drail. It had the same gritty texture, same drab color. Sea snails were living inside the pressure cracks made from years past.

Holly was staring up at a circular door carved out of metal. It wasn't the type of metal the humans used. It looked sleeker.

Someone had etched words along the door's curve:

EST. 2022
SECOND BEINGS' CONGREGATION
(SBC)
FALLOUT SHELTER

28

Kevin

Kevin screamed Maïmoú's name as an air raid siren blared through the fallout shelter.

He was knocked off his feet from the earthquake aftershocks. Glass fell like raindrops. The floor, solid concrete, cracked around the heavier tanks.

"Kevin!" Viper hit the glass tank. "Kevin, what's happening?"

He held his head, trying to get his answer. "*Maïmoú?*" he thought.

"*Where* are *you?*" she asked through his mind. It sounded like she was snarling through the words, ready to hit the closest thing next to her. "*Shào...Shào...*"

"*I don't know where I am. I'm in the center of W4, I think?*"

"*I know you're up there!*" Maïmoú snapped, voice echoing like she was running in and out of his ears. "*I can sense you, you creature!*"

The lights flickered, and an echo of cries carried through the building like the moans of the dead.

Viper sank deeper into the tank, watching her world shake.

"I-I'm here," he told her, stuttering as he crossed a crack. "It's okay."

"Is this one of the things that happen to you?" she asked. "The invisible person who hurts you?"

Kevin swallowed hard. "Yeah, but I'm here. It's okay."

"But it's not." She watched a piece of the ceiling fall near the stairs and winced when it crashed on the floor. "You're going to get hurt. Can you see?"

"A little. Can you?"

"I can see in the dark, but Kala can't. She doesn't know. S-she doesn't..." Exasperated bubbles left the corners of her mouth. "I need to find her."

Kevin dug his nails into the glass, trying to get past the barrier keeping them apart. He didn't doubt her abilities to swim back to Tokala in complete darkness, he just didn't want her to leave where he couldn't follow. He *could* see in the dark, but not as well as Nikki or Viper or most crossbreeds. He'd literally be in the dark, alone with Maïmoú's rage.

Better him than her. "Go find her. I'll..." He looked at the entrance he'd come through to chase her. An unstable walkway was teetering over it. He stepped back. "I'll go back to my room. It'll be safer there than being out in the open. I think that's how earthquakes work."

"What's an earthquake?"

"I can't be visible right now," Maïmoú said, so close to his ear, it made him shiver. *"I'm holding up parts of the building and I know, I* know *he's near. He's—Shào, I'm here! Look at me! Look—"*

She was gone from his mind.

Kevin, shaking, gave Viper an affirming nod. "Go. It'll be okay."

"You'll be okay?" she restated, and Kevin nodded to hide the waver in his voice.

He waited until she swam out of view, which took a few seconds due to her constantly looking back at him. When she was gone, Kevin took a breath and turned to find his way back to safety. His eyes stayed on the ceiling. Dust was now puffing out with every shake.

Many of the waterborne had left the safety of their tanks in search of answers. The rules down here were thrown to the wayside since the guards were as confused as they were. They were all grouped in comfort circles, asking questions and waddling in place.

"Maïmoú," he said under his breath. "Maïmoú, what's going on? What're you doing? Are you okay?"

He felt bad, insinuating that she was the one responsible for this, but who else had these abilities? Earthquakes didn't happen that often in Raeleen, and it was too in-time with her return. Why she was doing it, if she was okay, he needed these answers immediately. He doubted that Maïmoú cared, if she was calling out the name of another Deity, her oldest friend turned enemy.

Now, every hall he turned into, every corner he slipped around, he was looking for both Maïmoú and what this Shào person might've looked like. It didn't help that everyone down here was floating in water.

He came up to dead end after dead end. Some doors were too heavy for him to move on his own. Other entryways were barricaded by fallen debris. Sparks lit up the floors as crossbreeds tried finding their own ways to safety. Some gave him nasty looks, as if *he* was the reason this was happening. He was eighty percent sure it wasn't.

"Maïmoú, where are you?"

He stopped running. He had no idea what room he'd ended up in. To his back were tanks making up most of the wall. One had completely splintered and was spilling gallons of water across the grated floor. Light fixtures sparked in what little water was left.

A cry. A whimper from a child. Someone had entered the room behind him.

Illuminated by a flickering hall light stood a man carrying a baby. He was nothing but a black silhouette, but from his voice and his hunched-over appearance, he sounded in need of help.

"Are you alright?" Kevin asked. He was a middle-aged man with no discernible ears or tails. Salt-and-pepper ponytail and unkempt beard, short in stature, suffering with some kind of fungal infection. Dark marks splotched his face and exposed forearms.

The little baby he was holding was Alexi. It looked like she'd been bawling for over an hour. Her eyes were bloodshot as she hid into the man's fancy shirt.

"Oh, thank All I found you," said the man. "I need you to take her. I can't leave her here, but I can't bring her with me." He flinched from hearing something on the floor above them. Kevin heard nothing but the delayed sirens and rumbles.

"I can take her," Kevin said, because how could he not, "but I don't know where she needs to go. What tank did she come from?"

"She doesn't need water right now, she—" He flinched again. "I can't be here. I shouldn't be here."

"Do you want to stay with me?" Kevin offered. "I'm trying to find my way back to my room."

"No," he said. "I'll be back for her in an hour. Or less. I need to...I-I need to find Sabah. I need to stop them from meeting."

His ramblings were as incoherent and flighty as he was acting. He was wringing his hands together and shifting his weight from foot to foot.

Which is what it looked like, to Kevin. His eyes had yet to adjust to the real world.

The man was missing a leg. It ended at the knee, letting him levitate in thin air while he tried holding a normal conversation with Kevin.

Kevin's lips puckered, trying to find a way to speak casually. In his head, he was quickly compiling all the names Maïmoú had once dropped on him. While he'd only been told the name of every Deity once, he'd made sure to memorize them for later use.

Not Sabah—he was looking for her.

Not Unathi—Kevin had already seen them.

Neither Fate nor Ataleah—they were accordingly missing.

And not Shào—he wasn't young.

"You're...Tsvetan," Kevin guessed. "You're the Deity in charge of the Earth."

Tsvetan lifted his head. The strands off his ponytail stuck out and fell over his eyes. Unblinking, not breathing, for why would a God pretend to be alive?

"She's been in contact with you," Tsvetan said, almost as a question but already knowing the answer.

The room rumbled again.

Kevin took a much-needed inhale. "What's going on? Is this because of Maïmoú? Are *you* doing this?"

"I'm right, aren't I?" Tsvetan asked instead. "She's been in contact with both of you. She's doing all this because of *you*."

"*Kevin...*"

The ground crumbled. Like a serpent slithering through sand, the tiles beneath their feet broke apart, and Kevin fell backwards into a dark chasm.

It strangely didn't hurt, falling to his death. Tsvetan must've pillowed his fall. He heard tiles crack against his head and he tasted metal in his mouth, but other than that, he was fine.

Then he tried to turn and screamed.

Pain radiated down his back through his twisted left wing. It was bent in a crooked way with some of the flight feathers permanently snapped. It'd take months, maybe even a year for them to grow back.

A year to fly properly again. A year to be free again.

He bit back his tears. Nothing else hurt except his back, but he was lying atop debris and twisted pipes and water, at least two inches of it.

Tsvetan looked down from the hole, checking to see if Kevin was still alive.

Kevin lifted up his head only to drop it back down. He was going to fall asleep like this. He couldn't keep his eyes open, as if giving up now was his final option.

He forced his eyes open. He'd fallen into a deeper part of Asilo. None of the lights were on, but he still could still see the tanks around him.

Beasts. Giant, floating animals without arms or legs, with heads and tails larger than trucks, were locked stationary in the waters. They were teardrop-shaped and floated like sky dots in the blackened sky, their titanic eyes on the girl floating amidst their gathering.

Darkness had drenched Maïmoú's dress completely black. It was coming out of her mouth, nose, eyes. She'd given up wiping it away.

"Maïmoú—"

"*No!*" Maïmoú held her shoulders with both hands, crossing them over her chest as if she herself was feeling Kevin's pain. "Shào!" she screamed. "Fix him! Fix his wing! You have to!"

Kevin dragged himself along the floor. The glass tanks were beginning to crack. "Maïmoú, I'm alright!"

"Why!?" Maïmoú screamed at the room. "This isn't *fair*! *What* did I do wrong this time? Even though I'm doing my best, even though I'm trying to save everyone, *every single time*, I'm the one punished!"

A pipe burst and spewed hot steam into the room.

"Why can't I have one good thing? Why can't I ever—I can sense you, you know!" she yelled at the ceiling. "I can feel you watching me!"

From the ceiling hole, Kevin saw Tsvetan disappear with Alexi.

"Tsvetan!" Maïmoú tried floating up to him, but the powers that be brought her down. She stumbled, blackness spilling out from her mouth. "You watched as my Hadiya and Hassan were murdered in front of me, you watched Shào die in my arms, you sat back and watched all seven billion of my humans get vaporized by *your* own hands!"

She laughed dementedly. "You always said that humanity was the worst thing to happen to the world, but it's always, *always* been you three! You don't care about the world! You're weak. You're *cowards*!"

She pointed at the skylight. "You want me to fail, but you forget who I am. I am Maïmoú of Athens, Deity of humankind and the world's biggest bastard, and I will not give up on what I deserve to have!"

Kevin kept calling out for her. It was all he could do. He pleaded to whoever was listening that he make it to Maïmoú and tell her that this wasn't the way to fall. She was stronger than this, better than this. She didn't have to hurt for his sake.

The tanks cracked from her pressure. Water rushed over his body. He saw Maïmoú through heated bubbles, Tsvetan, suddenly, touching his soul. When he did, Kevin's head filled with a drugged sleep, sedated. No longer could he keep his eyes open, and he fell.

29

Marcos

"Tell me what's going on," Marcos demanded, "and tell me what your family's been hiding from me."

"You...you don't know what you're talking about," Zantl said, but Marcos knew they'd cornered them on the truth. This small, unbelievable piece of technology clenched in his fist held a world veiled by lies, decades of history erased by Zantl's family.

He let Zantl redress. He assumed that, based on the empty bottles and snack wrappers around their stained mattress, they must've been living here after disappearing. Their naked body made Marcos cringe. Whoever they'd been with, whoever had vanished like a ghost, had looked so much older than they were, and they'd been intimate together. All of Marcos' hypotheses that Zantl was seeing someone in the Asilo, and they'd actually been with...

Something other than this world, an unknown entity named Unathi.

Once Zantl was decent, they tried for the door. Marcos blocked them with his body.

"Move," Zantl said.

"No. Tell me what's going on. Who are these people? Why can I see them while nobody else can? What"—he lifted up the thumb drive—"is on this?"

Zantl's ears pointed back. "I'm guessing you were able to switch on the computers to see what was on them."

Computers. Marcos knew that word, but he didn't know how. "What room was that?"

"A storage closet, like this. That one happened to have old tech in it. Old tech that was harboring you."

"Then who built me? Who really built me? Was it that girl, Alliroue?"

"Dunno."

"Stop fucking with me!"

"Don't yell at me!"

"No! I saw myself in those memories. I saw myself well-cared for and loved. That world looked nothing like Raeleen, and that girl..."

He touched his heart, remembering the feelings she made him feel, how precious her smile was in the sunlight. "She smiled at me. Do you know how long it's been since someone actually smiled at me like that? Without the look of disgust? She loved me, and you took her away."

"Uh, no, I didn't," Zantl said. "I was, like, a baby when my parents finally got you to turn on. I didn't have a say in what they did with you after that, nor did I care."

Marcos backpedalled. At this rate, he was only going to get sass from them that'd lead into another lash out and disappearance. "Tell me about who that person was. The person who disappeared. Unathi. What's really going on?"

Zantl looked ready to either be sick or to bite. "You won't get it."

"Yes, I won't, so any type of information would be helpful to someone who's literally been in the dark for decades."

The corner of Zantl's lip curled upwards, a smile. "More like centuries."

The word didn't register in his brain. Centuries? What could that mean? 100 years? 500? 1,000?

Zantl sat on the mattress with a creak. "You asked a bunch of questions in the past five minutes. What do you wanna know first?"

Everything. He wanted to know about the mysterious, disappearing people, the violence they carried, what this had to do with him and Kevin and anyone else who might've been involved. He wanted to know about the girl on the screen and the futuristic world she lived in. He wanted to know who'd built him.

"What...are we?" his mouth ended up saying, "and why can we see invisible people?"

HUMANOID MODEL r51: MARCOS AMIR
Copyright © 2100
...
Humanoid r51 did not start up correctly.
Running all diagnostics. Please wait...
98% complete.
Rebooting main control systems.

Marcos, feeling lifeless, awoke in nothing but code. No color, no senses—his brain was shut off. This was his stasis, his own version of sleep. He liked to believe nothing segregated him from normal lifeforms, but this was his reality: advanced, artificial intelligence able to link up to a robotic body.

Usually, this lasted only a second, like waking from a dreamless sleep. Had he powered off accidentally? Was he hurt? Was this his version of death?

"You're not dead. Not yet."

Unknown application error found.
Information: unknown.
Restarting...

His memory bank reopened and filled in the missing details: Zantl and their upheaval of information; Marcos, walking aimlessly through the streets of Raeleen, knowing everything about Deities and not knowing what to do; Shào and Maïmoú and their hatred for one another. Each one had their own "soulmate," a person who was intimately connected to them. Familial, romantic, friendly, it all depended on the person and their unfortunate circumstances.

He remembered seeing Nicole Lenore levitate during the assembly. Her eyes had been glowing with bloodthirsty animosity. Those guards, perishing with a wave of her hand. She'd toppled the Asilo like a tower of playing cards.

He'd rushed to save Zantl. Say it internal programming, say it his own innate need to save children. They'd frozen in fear from their home crumbling above them, and Marcos had dove through fire to protect them.

Unknown application error found.
Restarting...

Someone clicked their tongue. "Can you stay still? Even when your main systems are shut off, your brain is still so... active."

Marcos couldn't speak. He could only listen and wait. The voice belonged to an older woman.

"I never understood that about robotic life," she said. "How you could turn on and off, be saved from death just to be re-placed with a new body. No other species can do that, not even the most resilient flower. You were always such an interesting...species, in that way. Divergent from beings and their primitive instincts, from animals and their self-preservation. You could've been a great successor to their failures."

Marcos had never heard this woman's voice before. She sounded so mournful.

He willed his voice to start. "Who...are you?"

She ignored him. "How's this?"

**All systems repaired.
Rebooting...**

Marcos blinked, eyes ablur. A sprinkle of water was hitting his cheek like he was beside a waterfall. Birds chirped on branches. Summertime, a tropical vacation.

"Wait, don't wake up so soon. Wake up in the real world. Wake—"

His vision refocused, and his brain whirled on.

He was lying on his back, staring up at a mosaic ceiling. Blue and silver and gold, swirling into flowery patterns as natural artwork. Waterfalls gently flowed from the walls into manmade rivers that ran along the room.

"Elegant" wasn't the right word to describe this place. It wasn't beautiful or magnificent or grand or rich.

It was dreamlike, a phenomenon he'd never experienced before. Crystal curtains swept around open arches and white pillars. Gold flecks in the walls made them appear bejeweled. There were floor pillows around him, lacy and looking more expensive and softer than the richest beds. The water looked too good to drink, the air felt too crisp to breathe.

And above him, staring down at him, was the woman who owned the mature voice. She had deep, dark skin with dreadlocks tied up in a bun. Beads dangled from the ends, etched in ancient letters. She wore a beautiful gown made of silky blue styled with working pants and combat boots.

Her wrinkled face contorted as she looked down at Marcos, like she didn't know what to do with him now that he was awake. He'd been asleep on her knee.

He got up. The room he was in was encircled by a small moat, and outside, through the arches, were towering spires. They twisted high into the sky, a bright, blue sky twinkling with millions of stars. Everything looked like a reflection in a crystal pond. Breathtaking.

The woman scooted back like he was an infection. From Zantl's rushed explanation of Deities and soulmates, Marcos guessed that this water-based, blue-wearing Deity was none other than Sabah, Deity to all weather and water.

She shooed him away with her hand. "Go, then. Do whatever you soulmates do and get out of my head."

"I'm...in your head?"

"Not exactly. You're in the Gardens, so you..." She sighed and fixed a loc behind her ear. "You don't remember this place, do you? You don't remember anything about me."

Marcos hesitated before answering. "I...used to," he said, working out that truth Zantl had explained to him. "I used to know you, before I woke up in Raeleen. You're my...soulmate, the Deity who's connected to me."

Sabah sighed again, continuously upset by truths she already knew. "Of course. You—" She got up like she had severe back problems. She groaned as she straightened up. "You need to get out of here. A few hours here can last days in the real world. Nothing's wrong with your system update, is it?"

Marcos got up with her. She was over six feet tall, with wide hips and muscular curves. "Did you fix me?"

"I saved you from being buried. You're welcome. Now, get out. I'm not used to beings meddling in here."

"Your name's Sabah, right?"

She looked down at him. "Did Unathi's soulmate tell you about me, or...Maïmoú's?" She said her name like a curse.

"Zantl did."

"Right. I can't keep track of your numbers anymore. You lot just *had* to be born at the same time. It'd been so easy with just one or two, but now, *seven*."

"There're *seven* of us?" he asked. Seven of him, of Zantl and Nicole. Kevin? "Who're the rest?"

"I don't care to remember their names," she said dismissively, "All, it's hard to talk about this, knowing you don't remember who you are."

"My memories were taken from me. I just found out about all this today. The leaders of my world found me in a fallout shelter and were only able to restart me by taking my memories out."

"Like giving a child the manual for a car," Sabah said under her breath.

"But I did find a few memories," he added. "I think it was my old home. I saw a girl, Alliroue, and saw the world from a balcony. Do you know her? Zantl said they didn't know much about her because she spoke in a different language, but..."

He looked out to the fantasy world outside her room. "It didn't look like this."

"This world doesn't exist," Sabah explained. "This's a place only for Deities and soulmates. We call it the Gardens. After the world got...*infested* with beings, we created our own world, away from their civilizations. You've been here before."

"I don't recall," he said. "Where did I come from? Zantl was vague on the details. They talked more about you Deities."

"What did they say to you?"

He told her what he knew. Deities, their powers, their names. Shào and Maïmoú and their destructive personalities, and how they had to be separated by barriers and miles. Other people lived somewhere, beings called humans, and how people could live multiple lives after they died. The process was called being "reincarnated."

It felt like he was telling a teacher how to teach.

"I've been having trouble understanding," he finished. "Maïmoú is angry with someone named Shào. She's angry at all of you for trapping her."

Sabah scoffed. "I'd like to find one atom on this Godforsaken Earth that she *isn't* angered by. She's just like her humans. They're so selfish. Same with crossbreeds, same as Shào. Parasites."

Marcos could feel the indignation she felt towards these two. He understood her viewpoint—after coming in such close contact with both Shào and Maïmoú, he couldn't imagine loving them or the creatures they governed, their "Domains."

"Why did she try ruining the world?" Marcos asked.

"Because she's the Deity to humanity. They were vile insects that plagued the world with every advancement they made."

"What *are* humans? Are they like crossbreeds, only without animal features?"

"Well, they look exactly like you and me, but they were all awful. The only good they ever created were you robots, and you were only able to live for a few years before—"

"Wait, there were more?" Marcos asked. "More people like me? More robots?"

"Yes, yes, there were millions of robots on Earth before...everything went wrong."

More robots like him. People he could connect to. People who knew what it felt like to feel without a heart.

More people who could talk to Deities.

"Maïmoú and Shào needed to be separated," she continued. "They could no longer live on Earth. They were destroying everything, so we had to do what needed to be done."

"What did you do?" Marcos asked again. "How did you...punish them?"

"You think I *punished* them? Is that how we're spinning the narrative nowadays? I *saved* the Earth from them. I take no shame in that."

"But what did you do? How come the Earth doesn't look like what it looked like in my memories? What's on the other side of the Muralha? Where're the other—"

"It doesn't matter," Sabah said, cutting off his curiosity. "You need to get out of here. I need to find Unathi and Tsvetan and get in contact with them, figure out our next steps."

Marcos felt the conversation ending when it should've been beginning. He was speaking to a God, a magical being able to control water. All weather, all rivers. "Oceans," whatever they were. Zantl had said they were important. He wanted to know more about them and her and listen to her talk. What was their relationship? Did he love her? Was she like a mother? She sounded like one.

Sabah's gaze snapped back to him, brows knitted. "I am *not* your mother," she stated, and raised her hand at him.

He flinched as if she'd strike him, but she instead shielded his eyes with her whole hand. She pushed him back. "Now get out of here," she said, "and let me work."

He fell for a fraction of a second before landing on his back and breaking a table.

"Woah!"

He rolled to his side. He'd dropped right into the middle of a meeting between Nicole's and Kevin's family. They were all standing around the circular table he'd just broken, having a heated discussion.

Morgan Owens, standing alongside her partner and friends, dropped her hand. She'd been pointing at a diagram of the Asilo she'd drawn on a chalkboard. She looked at the ceiling where Marcos had fallen through. There was no hole.

"*O...kay*," she said slowly. "You know what, definitely not the weirdest thing that's happened in the past twenty-four hours." She snapped her fingers, and two dogs got up. "Tie him up with the other one."

30

Derek

Derek gasped for air that wouldn't go down his throat. Honestly, if God hated him so much, He should've just let Shào have his way. Let him strangle him to death or toss him into the sky high enough to kill him. Whatever He wanted, let Him have it. At least then Derek wouldn't have to die trapped in some hole.

He scaled the cave wall again, reaching for loose stone while pretending that everything behind him, above him, and in front of him didn't exist. He didn't have enough space to take flight, and he wasn't strong enough to climb up by himself. He was gonna die. The walls, closing in on him.

His grip slipped and he fell backwards on his ass. The walls were too slick with algae to climb. "Holly," he said, "what're we gonna do?"

Holly was still trembling, face going pale with every second they stayed down here. She had a hand to her heart as she stared up at the giant, circular door. It had etchings describing this place as a "fallout shelter."

That phrase sparked something in Derek's brain. It felt like home, a safe place he wanted to be in.

He was fucking losing it. "What's wrong?" he asked her.

She shook her head and didn't stop. She kept scanning the walls, the dirt, the handlebar carved into the metal door.

"Hey, Holly?"

She looked back at him with tears in her eyes.

"Are you okay? Are you hurt? *'Ow'*, you know? Are you hurting anywhere?"

Hand still on her heart, she nodded.

"Okay, where? Can you show me?"

She went for the door handle.

"Hello?"

The underside of her wrist glowed white, something in the door beeped, and with a thick *pop*, the door opened. Wet, metallic air poofed in their faces. Through the crack was nothing but pitch darkness—not even Derek could see through it.

Holly must've, because as soon as it opened, she wedged her arm through the gap. The underbelly of the door dug through ancient sand as she forced it open with her bare hands.

"H-hold on." Derek tried to help her, but she was taller and more determined than he was. With just enough space for her agile body, she slipped through.

"Hey!" Derek cast a needy look back at the ceiling hole. Leaving out that way would've been so much *easier*.

His eyes adjusted, and he gasped. On the other side of the door was a metal stairway spiraling even deeper into the Earth. It had no railing and was missing steps from erosion. The faint sound of footsteps tapped down the stairs.

"God damn it, Holly," he cursed, and brought his wings in close for the trip down. Sure, he didn't know if he was going to be trapping himself underground forever, slowly suffocating on his own breath before sea worms ate away his body, but he couldn't let Holly die like that, either. She didn't know better.

It felt like summertime down here, hot and congested with the smell of metal hurting his lungs. Halfway down the steps,

Derek took off his jacket and wrapped it around his waist. Every minute got hotter and hotter.

Down, down. The only inkling he had of there being more stairs was Holly's footsteps. When they stopped, Derek, scared shitless at being alone, jumped the remaining flights.

He landed on more concrete. He'd come to another basement level with another circular door. This one was already cracked open, but he didn't know how Holly was doing it. Her wrist had glowed, like something in her body was the key to unlocking the secrets of this place.

The door opened to a packed, cluttered hallway that looked like it'd survived an earthquake. Beams and wires were hanging from the low ceiling. Half of the walls were either blown out or crumbling from the weight of the mountain above them. Stubborn beams of sunlight found their ways through, lighting up bags of garbage, broken pipes, and more dilapidated stairwells. Everything smelled of decay.

He followed the wires as a sort of map. This place had *electricity*, or once had it. He spotted electrical boxes at four-way intersections and even a rotary phone. No wonder the Drail Kingdom had felt backwards when he'd first woken up. This place, weirdly enough, made more sense than horse-drawn carriages and royal castles.

A shiver ran up his spine. Did the humans know about this place? If they did, why were they living so far back in the past? The tech was right under their noses. Feet. If they didn't, then how the fuck did the world get so backwards without them?

Holly screeched and pulled Derek away from thinking. It came down a hall you needed three staircases to get to. They were cramped like everything else here and cut in-between rooms, privacy abandoned. He passed through lounge areas with couches slumped against the walls into bathrooms without stalls, the porcelain stained yellow.

It was like this place was made with either extreme budget issues, or small people. At points, his head hit the support beams.

He pushed through a wall of garbage bags to a new hall. The doors here were left ajar, hinges rusted. He saw bunk beds taking up all four corners of the rooms and rugs chewed up by rats. Some had desks or chairs, but there wasn't much room for activities. It was like a group of people had hurriedly packed their lives into burrows and bounced.

One of the doors had been thrown open, letting go a single stream of light into the hall.

Derek came up to it carefully. Holly was on her knees, crying into the bedroom's cot. It had that, a baby carriage, and a small bedside desk. That was it. The whole space was smaller than Derek's old closet back at the castle. Dead roses were strung up on the walls as decorations and someone had drawn doodles on the wall with crayon, but they'd all faded from time.

Derek waddled off to the side, giving her her space, and came around to the bedside table. It was stuffed with letters and pieces of paper. Atop it was a stuffed monkey with pink blush marks. When Holly noticed it, she stuffed it between her boobs to protect it.

Derek knelt down. "Holly, can you tell me what's going on? Are there people down here? You seem to know your way around. Did you...used to live here?"

A whimper escaped her lips, and she turned on her hands and knees towards the drawers.

He helped her open one, but it was stuck on the lower drawer. He gave it a stronger tug.

Papers flew out about the room. Pieces of torn sheets, pamphlets, papers stapled together that now tore apart from being uncovered. One paper caught Holly's eye and she snatched it out of the air like a cat with a fly.

It was a folded piece of paper with a child's doodles on it. Two people stood side by side, one of which was clearly Holly— her orange hair and cat ears were dead giveaways. There was even an arrow pointing to her head that read "me," indicating that she'd been the one to draw this. She was holding a baby in the drawing named Baby, fittingly. Around her were other stick figures of smiling, colorful people. Derek didn't know their names or how to pronounce them, aside from one.

A tall, black-haired boy with horns and a tail, drawn with a long nose and cute, awkward smile.

"Oliver."

Holly's hands shook as she cried into the picture. Her tears smudged the antique art.

"When did you draw these?" Derek asked.

She shook her head, repressing her past.

Letting her feel, Derek flipped over more papers. He found more drawings: castles in bright skies, girls in dresses, rain-bowed and pretty.

Some were pages of writing. A lot of it was heavily-worded and smudged. He couldn't follow much of it—stuff about being careful about air quality and going outside for long periods of time, stuff about scheduling. One page had a long list of chores to do like sweeping and laundry with check marks beside each task. Above it was a date: 22/07.

He flipped the paper over and nearly dropped it.

It was a photograph of Holly. Colored, perfectly preserved like it'd been a snapshot of real life. She was smiling and had the life she was currently missing in her eyes. The background was of this place, this "Second Beings' Congregation," but it looked cleaner. Well-lived in, the walls intact for suitable living. Baby was reaching for her cheek as the photo was taken, making her laugh unexpectedly.

And next to her, one arm wrapped around her, was Oliver.

Derek's skin went clammy. It was like seeing a doppelgänger of the man he'd gotten to know. He had the same face and eyes and hair, but he was wearing clothes that Derek hadn't seen in the kingdom. His jacket was more modern, the fabric cut tight to his body, and his hair had this kind of gel in it that accentuated his curls.

"Holly, is this where you came from?" He began picking up more of the scattered pieces of history. "Is this how the world looked before? This's...tech, right?" he asked, guessing at a word he'd known all this time. Pieces were fitting into place, he was beginning to remember sights, sounds, the smell of metal and oil. "Tech, like technology? Lights and wires and stuff. You *know* about all that?"

She gulped. "This..."

Derek stood back. Her voice, it was so light.

"This." She held her head again. Remembering seemed to hurt too much. "I'm sorry, I think my brain is filled with worms at the moment. They make it hard to think."

Derek held back what first came to mind. "Oh," he then said. "Uh, that's okay. You're alright."

"But I'm not. I don't think I ever was." She pulled up her sleeves to scratch her arms. "I don't think I was born right."

Derek squatted down to her level. He didn't think he'd ever get on her "level"—the way she thought, how she spoke—but he was going to try. If he was honest with himself, they were a lot alike: People expected a lot from them, but they couldn't meet their expectations. "Sure you were," he said. "No one's born wrong."

"I believe I was. I've been told this several times."

Derek helped her settle. "Do you know where we are right now?"

She doubletook the room they'd been in for the past ten minutes. "This was my bedroom. Oliver and I, we were born here. This was our home."

"When?"

"A long time ago. Hundreds and hundreds, before everything changed. We lived here with the Minister—" She covered her mouth as if she'd be sick. Something gurgled in her throat. It took her a minute before she swallowed it back down and continued. "He...we all lived down here with him. He said the world was too cruel to live in. He said that down here, we'd be protected."

"From what?"

"I was one of the only people in the world who wasn't affected by it, because I talked to Deities. They said I was special, but I never understood it. They tried testing me." She was breathing harder now. "But they didn't know why I wasn't affected by their radiation."

"Radiation?"

"The poison in the air, from what Shào and Maïmoú did." Her eyes were desperate, pleading for something he couldn't give her. "I only wanted to leave. I'm only twenty-one years old, I didn't know. Leah, she didn't know. We couldn't stop them from doing what they did."

"Wait, what?" he asked. "I'm so lost. So people *knew* you talked to Deities? This was, like, a known thing?"

"Yes," she said, hurried now, as if she were on borrowed time. "Yes, they knew. Everyone did. So many cameras and news people. Oliver and I, we weren't used to it. We grew up here, sheltered. We didn't know."

"So what did Shào and Maïmoú do? Did *they* make the world like this?"

"They ended the world with their fights. They hated each other, yet they could never stay apart." She reached into her sweater for her monkey. She gnawed on its head. "I-I don't want to see them fighting anymore, Oliver. I don't want any more people to die. I wanna go back home. I'm scared."

Derek pressed a hand into his forehead. So much information was piling on top of itself, he'd need a solid day to wrap his brain around it. He still didn't know why seeing Deities was so important, other than it made your life suck. "Holly, Oliver isn't here. It's me. Can you tell me again what—"

Dust and parchment pushed out behind him. A door opened, announcing new arrivals.

Two people had followed them into the fallout shelter. The man was small and looked in need of a shower. He had oily, greasy hair pulled back into a long ponytail with some type of fungus growing on his face. He floated a foot off the ground like a demon, but it might've been due to the fact he was missing a whole leg.

The woman was tall, with dreadlocks pulled up in a messy bun and stress marks around her eyes. Her eyes almost glowed blue in the dark.

Gods, he figured.

"What the *fuck*," the woman said, "are you doing here?"

31

Derek

Derek quickly gathered up the old papers and photographs and shuffled them together. "We didn't mean to break in."

The two strangers exchanged worried glances. The man seemed to warn the woman not to do something. They spoke in a language Derek wouldn't understand in a thousand lifetimes. It wasn't Drailian, wasn't even close to it. The woman answered with coughing, wet and sickening like the ocean itself.

Holly's eyes had turned back to slits as goosebumps travelled down her arms. The strange man, noticing this, faked a smile at them. "You must be, uhm, Derek. And you're Holly Bennett, of course. It's nice to meet you again. My name is Tsvetan, and this is Sabah."

Derek backed up more. He didn't mean to stare, but not even Shào looked as weird as these people. Their clothes were *glittering*. "You're a Deity, right?"

Tsvetan strained to keep his smile. He started nervously rubbing his hands together. "H-how did you know that?"

Sabah said something snotty. Tsvetan politely hushed her up.

"Well, uh, Derek, Holly," he said. "I think it's time you two head off, away from...this place. It's not safe, you know.

Wouldn't want to be buried down here for eternity." He chuckled. It didn't reach his eyes. "Right?"

"*Right*." Derek brought Holly backwards with him. "So are you two one of the humans' God, or are you some type of other—"

"Of course we're not the humans' *God*," Sabah said. She had a low, commanding voice that bullied Tsvetan's meek one. "Who do you take us for?"

Derek thought it best that he didn't answer that. Tsvetan must've known to, for he butted in swiftly.

"O-okay now." He placed himself between Derek and Sabah. "It'd be wise not to get heated down here, *Sabah*. Let's just take these two back to the surface and work things out topside."

Derek, patience fading, noticed another piece of paper near his foot. He reached down for it.

Tsvetan and Sabah jerked back at the same time. Their hands tensed as if they had claws ready to be retracted.

Derek carefully stuffed the paper into his butt pocket. "Did we do something wrong? Why're you so afraid of us? This's Holly's home. Well, old home, I think. She's allowed to be here."

"You didn't...do anything *wrong*," Tsvetan said, to which Sabah cast him a "what-the-fuck-are-you-talking-about" look. "Back before...this was...her home."

He said that so weirdly, Derek had half a mind to call him out on being so vague. They were in an underground "fallout shelter," from memories a cat girl had trouble placing.

"Before all that," Tsvetan added, "I need to ask you one question. Have you been in contact with anyone who looks like us? Someone who's about your age, or a little younger. A boy with—"

"Yeah, Shào. He tried killing us, like, ten minutes ago. He hates me because I...know someone..."

He stopped talking. The two Deities looked as if he'd said something unspeakable, like he'd said he liked boys as well as girls.

He hid in his wings. "I don't know much about this stuff. Shào's been telling me I'm a soulmate and I can see you people because of it. Holly can see you, obviously." She still hadn't blinked. "All's we did was get thrown down here and find this room."

He took out the papers and started filing through them. "The humans think I'm some kind of angel, which's sort of like a human with wings, but I have a tail. Anyway, it's someone who can talk to one singular God they call their God, but I don't think I've ever met Him before. I've only met you two and Shào. I don't know what that means. Is Holly an angel, too? Is this where angels come from, because this feels creepily like the Underground, not the Heavens."

Tsvetan ran a hand through his greasy hair. Sabah looked ready to crack a tooth by how hard she was clenching her jaw.

"What about the other one?" Tsvetan asked. "Has she been in contact with you?"

"Who?"

"Maïmoú."

That name again. It was like a promise Derek had been holding onto ever since arriving to the Drail Kingdom. Spoken by Gods, lingering in his head, that girl's name was delivering him to the truth locked away.

When he didn't answer straight away, when he was lost in thought over a girl he didn't know, Sabah sighed tiredly, letting her head fall, loose braids dangling. She muttered something in her language.

Tsvetan winced. "Sabah, stop. Remember what happened the last time she lost her soulmates. If she finds out we hurt him—"

"She won't know."

"Of course she will! Look at his face." He motioned to Derek, who was still lost in a daydream. Maïmoú. Maïmoú. "He's clearly been in some sort of contact with her. Shào likely explained everything to him. Let's pretend—"

"No." Sabah jabbed a finger into Tsvetan's chest hard enough to push him back. "You and Unathi *promised* me. We *all* swore we would spend as little time as possible with these people, yet I know you've been visiting your soulmate across the ocean. Unathi's in a *relationship* with their soulmate, Tsvetan. You think I didn't know?"

Tsvetan's jaw locked. "What about *you*?" he dared to ask.

Sabah's eye twitched. "I haven't visited him *once*. You know my stance on these beings. They're parasites."

Holly tugged on Derek's jacket. She was mumbling a phrase over and over again. "This's bad, this's bad, this's bad, this's bad."

Derek held her hand. "Holly?"

"It's not a bad thing to be affected by your soulmate," Tsvetan told her. "They're tied to us. We can't change that. What we can do is help them by explaining their circumstances to us."

"Which is?" Derek asked.

Tsvetan cast a brief glance at him before going back to Sabah. "Your heart and mind is connected to the humans' Deity, but unlike the ones the humans created, this Deity is alive. Her name is Maïmoú, and she's a very catalytic young girl who is not yet in control of her Domain. It's why humanity keeps suffering."

"So it's not because of the demons?"

"No, it's because of her."

"*Everything* is because of her!" Sabah yelled. "The world ended because of her, because of her attachments to these *animals*." She glared at Derek like a wolf with its prey. "We're taking care of this before it gets out of hand again."

Derek wanted to get another word or two in. This incredibly one-sided conversation he was getting lost in kept bringing up his name, but why? He hadn't met these people before, but they'd already had such strong emotions tied to him. It was like the royals all over again.

His vision blotted out. His feet left the metal ground. Gone was the sound of emptiness and Holly's hands on him. He was transported away like a demon had taken him.

He squinted away frigid air. He and Holly were now outside, hanging hundreds of feet above the ocean. To their left were the cliffs that hugged the coastline, where he could see a tiny hole, no doubt the hole he'd failed to climb out of.

He looked down and wished he hadn't. Waves were crashing into each other, foaming mouths chomping, tongues lapping at the chance to drown two innocent victims.

Sabah floated in front of them. She had her hands out, keeping them immobile.

Derek choked. Holly hissed and clawed at the invisible hand around her neck.

Tsvetan appeared seconds later. The wind was whipping his ponytail like a flag. "Sabah, what're you doing!?"

"I'm *sick* of these people ruling our lives. This one"—she nodded at Derek—"is more trouble than he's worth, and this one"—to Holly—"is a reminder of what we lost. You ask me to remember what happened last time to Maïmoú's soulmates. I do. Her tantrum cratered northern India."

Derek's heart thudded. India. He knew that word, too. All these new terms were sparks trying to light a match inside him. Maïmoú. India. Soulmates. Past mixing with future. A time long ago, back with...

"You can't fault her for that, Sabah," Tsvetan said. "*She* is a child. *We* are adults. She lost what were essentially her parents, can you imagine—"

"I cannot, nor can you."

"Yes, you can!" A blood vessel burst in Tsvetan's eye, and a single flower bloomed behind his ear. "*I* can! We *did* lose our child! I lost *my* soulmate! How dare you say that to me—what is wrong with you!?"

Derek would've liked to know. He had no idea what the fuck they were talking about.

The grip Sabah had on Derek lessened. He felt himself fall and tried flapping his wings to save himself. Could he take flight in midair like this?

"These creatures have desecrated your forests and my oceans," Sabah said. "Nothing is wrong with me. I am simply taking care of what needs to be done. These creatures cannot live on our—" She coughed wetly. "I can't stand being around these creatures and talking to them like they're...*us*. If Maïmoú finds out about this, then fine. If she can hear me"—she looked at Derek—"then this's for your own good."

"Wait, wait!" Derek kicked his useless feet. "I don't understand! Why do *I* have to die?"

"The longer you live, the quicker Maïmoú will resurface. We've all felt her presence emerging back into the world. You've felt her, haven't you?"

"I—"

"*Don't* lie to a Deity," she warned. "I've been alive for 2.5 billion years, I can smell a lie forming before you even think it. I am the patron of all water. Every storm across any sea, every drip of water left on this dying planet, belongs to me."

Beneath them, the ocean roared. Tsvetan cowered. "Sabah..."

"No. Any more time wasted and these new soulmates will conjure those two out of their Voids. Then this planet's doomed all over again, and I will *not* let us live through another extinction. I *won't*."

"Knowing Maïmoú, she'll likely be here very soon. She must've brought this boy over due to her Barrier's deterioration and is scared. Sabah, *please*, talk this over with Unathi. They'll level your head."

"My head doesn't *need* leveling by them!"

"I won't let you do this!" Tsvetan grabbed her. "You swore you'd never kill *anyone* without reason after the Separation. That's what you promised us. Remember how awful you felt after doing this to the world. It was only 500 years ago. I know how fresh it is in your mind. What if he was *your* soulmate?"

Her face hardened like she'd been backstabbed.

"Think about Marcos. I know you see him as your own child. You *care* for him. You're *allowed* to care for him."

Sabah battled that in her eyes, trying to refute him.

"Uh, please let us go," Derek begged. "Let Holly go, at least. She has nothing to do with this."

Tsvetan looked close to tears as he shook his head. "Holly has everything to do with this. She's the reason the Earth has become what it is now."

"*What?*"

Holly cried and covered her eyes. She didn't want to hear this.

"Her strings of fate are broken in half, just like the bond you and your brother share with Maïmoú. Holly is connected to *two* Deities, two of the strongest known to All. They'd once been stronger than Shào and Maïmoú combined. Holly is bonded to both Fate...*and* Ataleah."

They said their names like human prayers. Holly's eyes swirled with mixed emotions, knowing their names the same way Derek knew Maïmoú's.

But that wasn't what Derek's mind clung to. "Wait, I have a brother?" he asked.

Something caught the Deities' attention across the sea, and their animated, spiteful argument came to a grinding halt. Their shoulders dropped, Tsvetan looked up at the sky. The waves ate one another below.

"Shit," Sabah cursed.

"Shit," Tsvetan agreed, and the two of them, along with Sabah's hold on Derek and Holly, disappeared.

"Fuck!" Derek flapped his wings, but he was falling backwards. He, like with everything he did, failed.

With his pendant close to his heart, Derek clasped his hands together and said every prayer he knew to any of the Deities who'd answer.

The shock immobilized him. The water wasn't icy or freezing, but fiery. His heart was being stabbed relentlessly by below-zero icicles.

He inhaled a mouthful of ice water. He couldn't swim in these temperatures. He kicked with numb legs as he followed sunbeams. Another mouthful, then back underwater, dragged deeper down. Holly...

Cartwheeling through a high wave, Derek's boot touched the melting sand underwater. He pushed himself forwards. His knees scraped glass. The waves licked his exposed skin, hungry to take him back.

"*Derek!*"

Two arms dragged him ashore. He couldn't see who or what; his neck was frozen, locked in place so his head didn't roll out to sea.

"Holly! Yomi, get Holly before—!"

"I have her. Holly, please stop biting me."

Oliver pushed back Derek's damp hair. His breath came out in cold puffs. "Are you okay? Oh, thank our God I found you. I couldn't sense you anywhere. My brain kept bringing me to the cliffside, but I searched everywhere and couldn't find you. Then I felt you above the ocean and heard something splash. I thought it was a seal."

Teeth clattering uncontrollably, Derek brought one hand to his face and tried making a fist. He couldn't. "Oliver."

He clamshelled his hands and brought them to his lips. "Don't talk. I have you."

"I-I can't feel my hands. I can't—Help me."

Yomi came into view. She was kneeling beside Holly as Holly threw up seawater. "We need to get them out of these clothes. They'll freeze to death."

At the mention of "death," Oliver buckled and sobbed uncontrollably over Derek. "I'm so sorry. I should've been more alert. I don't know what hit me. Something struck my chest. I thought I was having some type of heart attack. Then I couldn't find you and Holly, she'd sounded so scared. I'm so sorry."

"Oliver, we need to get them back home," Yomi said. "Now."

"Okay. Okay." He hugged Derek as he lifted him into the air. "I got you. You're safe."

"Brennen, my love, restart the fire!"

Startled, Brennen fell off the manor couch and went for more firewood.

Shimah jumped down from the rafters. "Oh, shit. Where'd you find them?"

"At the coastline," Yomi said. "They were in the water."

Oliver helped Derek undress and sat both him and Holly by the fireplace. Shimah draped a quilt over Derek's shoulders and hunted for a second one for Holly. Brennen ran upstairs and came back with his darkest vial of venom. Derek didn't question its powers this time and downed it in one shot. Holly refused hers.

"Holly, please," Brennen said. "You know it's not going to hurt you. It'll make you feel better."

Against the fire, Derek's red, oily fingers burned three times hotter. He wanted to pull away, but Oliver held him firm like he wanted him to burn.

Yomi examined his skin. "We need to bring them to a hospital. You need to put aside your feelings and think about their safety. The humans can treat them far better than Brennen and I can."

"You've treated far worse with much less."

"Under the direst circumstances with our own kind. You know Holly won't take our medicine. The humans will take him back in this condition and treat him, and we can treat Holly."

The front door slammed shut and Maxwell stormed into the kitchen. The snow on his hair steamed away with his elevated body heat. "I'm gonna lose it. No, I'm really gonna lose it."

Rosaline floated in behind him. "Maxwell, it'll be okay."

"No, it won't be, Rose! We're *fucked*."

As she tried helping her friend, Rosaline looked up. "Oh, Derek. Holly." She floated to Holly's side and nuzzled her head. "I'm glad you're both safe."

"I'm not!" Maxwell shouted. "I just came back from Jabel's. There's something wrong with the humans, they've been in fits all day. And a riot almost broke out tonight. They were deciding on whether or not to storm the Temno Forest to get Derek."

Derek stood up and covered his naked body with the quilt.

"Where're you going?" Oliver asked.

He didn't know. He was out of the water, but he was still suffocating. It was too hot here. Why was it so hot?

He dragged himself and his quilt up the stairs. Before he could close Oliver's door, he collapsed to the floor and cried. Giant heaps of sobs ran down his cheeks as he relived the day in full. Those Deities, weren't they supposed to make them feel wanted and loved? Not only did he feel so utterly hated, the realness of his death from that height, of hitting the water any harder than he had...

"Derek?"

Derek covered his head. He couldn't save his voice from drowning in his throat.

Oliver knelt beside him and hugged him. He pushed up his feathers and massaged his back. He smelled so good, like home.

"I-it's okay," Oliver said. "You're safe."

But he wasn't, knowing those freaks were flying around the world searching for him.

Being his disgusting, hated, sinful self, Derek brought Oliver into bed.

Their chests pressed together. Oliver tried taking off his shoes as Derek pillowed himself underneath dead animal pelts. Their hands couldn't stay off each other.

Oliver placed his arm underneath Derek's pillow and massaged the back of his head. "I'm sorry."

"It's not your fault."

"Is this okay?"

"Who cares anymore."

"I do. I don't want you to be uncomfortable." He nestled in closer. "Do you know what happened back there? On the cliffs? You were talking to someone."

Where could he have possibly started? "You wouldn't believe me if I told you."

"If it's something related to our God, I'll understand."

A smile cracked his lips. "I hate this."

"Hate what?"

"Being fawned over. It's like there's a reason people should care about me."

Oliver pulled back.

"I mean, why should they? All I do is fuck everything up and make things worse." He buried himself until his toes touched Oliver's. "I don't get it."

"Derek, I know you're dealing with a lot, but I need you to know how relieved I am that you're back. I was so sure I wouldn't see you again and that I'd have to deal with this alone. I thank our God every day that you've come into my life and made me understand so much more about myself that I never knew." He kissed the top of Derek's head. "I love you."

Derek didn't get that phrase. He loved *things*, like fish and alcohol and masturbation and good times. He loved Cellena and his friends, this so-called "brother" Sabah told him he had. Hadn't Shào said that he also had a sister? He guessed he loved all those things.

But his person? A man who cherished every part of him, even the weird parts, the sinful parts? What other word could describe such a bond other than love?

He let himself cry. Because he was allowed to cry. And he was allowed to feel. And Oliver didn't make fun of him or make him feel like less of a person for doing so. In fact, he held him tighter, because he loved him, and the humans couldn't do a damn thing to stop that from being true.

Derek wrapped an arm and wing over Oliver. "You're dumb. You're so dumb."

Oliver smiled. "*You're*...dumb."

Derek gasped dramatically. "How dare you? *You're* the dumb one here, obviously."

"I'm sure that you're dumber."

"Who says it like that? That automatically makes you more dumber."

Oliver's high-pitched laugh brought them, if at all possible, closer together.

Derek rocked on Oliver's bed at two in the morning. He'd neither gone to bed nor gotten up in fear of waking Oliver. He tried ignoring the guilt he was feeling over not being able to tell him what'd happened. Every time he tried, he felt like vomiting. All they'd done was snuggle all day. He felt like a terrible lover, a terrible person.

The bedroom door creaked open.

He grabbed Oliver through the sheets. He wasn't ready. He didn't want to die at the hands of Deities or soulmates. He wanted more time.

Holly stood in the crack of the door, her amber eyes glowing. She waited until Derek noticed her before creeping in. She'd changed into warmer clothes, but she still looked frozen.

Without speaking, she crawled into Oliver's bed and curled up inside an animal pelt.

Neither of them slept for the rest of the night.

32

Nikki

Nikki awoke stubbornly inside a room that smelled like home, but to which, who was to say?

She sat upright, her left side numb. She'd fallen asleep on a grey couch in a warm-colored living room. Bookshelves were stocked with books and glass figurines, and the walls held up paintings of pretty sunsets. The windows behind her let in the scent and sound of waves. It was eerily quiet like nobody was home, but she had no clue who *owned* this home. She couldn't remember how she'd gotten here in the first place or who'd brought her here.

She made fists on the couch. She was dreaming. Had to be. There was this sense that nothing existed behind these walls until she conjured it up. Everything was too pristine. She needed to wake up. Someone important was awaiting her in the real world.

Someone walked up a creaky staircase, and the door to this dream room opened.

Lí came in holding two cups of coffee. "Oh, you're awake," he said. "I was wondering when you'd come to."

Nikki sat up straighter. She'd seen Lí through dreams and mirrors, but never before had she been face to face with him, talking to him without the use of her own mouth. He was a real *person*, who smelled like this room and also aftershave. She didn't know why that startled her. She couldn't imagine herself shaving.

"Don't freak," Lí said, and sat both cups on the coffee table. He sat beside her with a long exhale from a hard day's work. "It's only us."

Nikki scooted back.

Lí noticed and half-smirked. "I know you have trouble trusting people, but I'm *you*, remember? And you're in a dream. I literally can't hurt you here."

Nikki inspected the room again. "I almost died when Shào and Maïmoú blew up that building you were sleeping on. Pangea or something? So I think I can get hurt in a dream."

Lí's smirk fell. "Right. Well, they won't be coming here. I don't think," he added. "This world is ours."

"And where exactly is our world?"

"Well, right now, we're at my mom's place, back before everything went wrong in the world. She lived in a city called Tianjin, just outside of Beijing, but you knew that already, didn't you?"

She *did*. This room, is she focused hard enough, wasn't as new as before. She knew the layout of the first floor and this mother she didn't know the name of. How his—her?—mother was born in China, and her father was Mongolian. Two places—countries—from a time far ago.

She didn't know what any of it meant, but she knew it all the same.

She spaced out. Memories began trickling in like she was reading a memoir about Lí's life. They were in his mother's study. His grandmother had knitted that quilt. He was twenty-three, human, gay, married, and allergic to bees. But as every fact came in, they slipped out just as readily. She didn't know his middle name or what he liked to do in his free time. She didn't know his birthday. She couldn't hold on to a new thought to save her life.

No, she did know his birthday. April 30th. Same as hers.

"It's okay," Lí said. "Don't think about it too hard. Please, have some coffee. It'll calm you down."

Nikki eyed the cup, then gave up reasoning and took a sip.

"Iced mocha," he said as she licked her lips. "Our favorite."

Nikki lowered the cup. "Why am I here?"

"Not sure. Shào once told me that beings can tap into their past lives during traumatic events, like a mental, go-to therapist. I guess you needed to talk to somebody, and I was the closest somebody to you."

"That doesn't sound like me."

"I know, and I won't force you to talk. I know how hard it is to talk about your feelings, even to yourself."

"Something with Shào..." She held her head. She couldn't think straight in a dream.

Lí watched her above the lip of his cup. He kept looking at her like he wanted to say something.

She broke her concentration. "Were you ever actually a real person," she asked, "or have I just been going crazy this year?"

"I was real, or used to be. I've been dead for 500 years, but I was very much alive at one point."

"Oh. Sorry. So, your heart, or brain—soul—became mine?"

"Correct."

"Weird."

"Very." He smiled again. "Is it weird to say it's nice to finally meet you? I've always wondered who I'd become after I died. It's nice to know I got to live again."

Something with Shào, something about the Líders. She took another sip. "Are you even 'living' again, if it's me who's living your life?"

"You're only another version of me, as I'm another version of you. Do you still like baseball?"

"Yeah."

"That's good. And Vitaliya's still with you?"

"Vitaliya?"

"I guess you call her Vanna this time around. I'm getting glimpses of your life like I'm watching a recap episode of a TV show. She's your cousin now? Funny. She was my childhood friend. I guess that never changed."

Nikki took another sip, finally enjoying the present from her past self. She felt herself sinking into a deeper layer of subconsciousness. The waves outside grew louder.

"It's nice, isn't it?" Lí asked.

"What is?"

"To not have to worry about anyone for five minutes."

She didn't believe that. She was always worrying about someone. About her siblings, her family. Lí, the Líders, Shào, Maïmoú. Everyone was worth worrying about, and she had to be the one to glue them together. That was her purpose, both in this life and the last.

But none of those feelings came with her into the dream. Nobody was outside these walls. The doors were locked. For once in her life, she was free to live for her own sake.

And that made her feel incredibly, devastatingly lonely. She was free of worry, but what was the point of living if you couldn't help other people?

She set the cup down.

"I know it's hard," Lí said. "Trust me. I know you feel like you have to try to solve Shào's problems, but that's not your burden to bear. You're allowed to choose your own path away from him. I know he's hurt you," he continued. "I see it in the way you hold yourself. He's...controlled you, hasn't he?"

Nikki tried remembering. She'd been in the city center. There'd been an assembly.

"That was a terrible thing he did to you, and I know you want to try to find a way to justify his actions, but you're allowed to be angry with him."

The Asilo. Her parents, crying as she rose above them. The crowds, slaughtered by a wave of her own hand.

She held her stomach, then wrapped her other arm around herself. She'd been *shot* at. She'd felt the bullet enter her stomach, but Shào had found a way inside her brain and saved her. But by doing so, all those guards, those innocent people trapped in the Asilo. Kevin…

Lí touched the cushion separating them. "You probably haven't cried in a long time, yeah? When I was your age, I didn't even laugh too hard in fear of someone noticing me. But you're here now. You're free to express yourself. Ourself. I'm not sure how this exactly works. I never was one to follow my own advice." He took a long sip of coffee. "You're allowed to let go here."

How impractical. Letting go of oneself left you vulnerable to attack, and she wasn't about to do that again.

Her nose stung. She swiped at it. It still stung, messing up her face, so she kept it down. Her body hurt. Her eyes welled. Something was wrong.

Lí broke the distance and hugged her.

She didn't pull away. Or maybe her subconscious didn't want her to. Burying her head into Lí's hoodie, Nikki went against all who she was and let herself go. Everything that'd been piling up against her let go through swelling emotions. Crying, that didn't come naturally to her. She wanted to be strong and defend both herself and now her family, who'd selflessly taken her in. She couldn't let herself break down so easily in front of them.

This.

This was nice. Therapeutic, finally allowing herself to be herself: an eighteen-year-old, crybaby rat who was afraid of her own shadow at times, who just wanted to be held by safe arms without cringing at herself for thinking that that was weak.

"You'll be okay," Lí said.

She snuffled through her composure. "Did Shào do this to you, too?"

"Unfortunately, yes."

"Did he love you, too?"

"He did. Poor kid. I felt so bad."

"Was it weird for you, too? He acts all weird with me. I don't like it."

"I know. I was an adult when he found me, and he was still a perpetual thirteen-year-old. I felt so bad for him, but he tried respecting my boundaries. Besides..." He pulled off the fingerless glove on his left hand to reveal a silver ring on his second-to-last finger. "I'm already spoken for."

Nikki drew back. "What does that mean? I know that you're...married, and gay, and I think those two things are connected, but I don't know what any of it means."

"It means I'm tied to a person. His name is Tai."

"Does that mean you're in love with him?"

"Very much so. Does marriage not exist in your world?"

"I don't think so. People just get together or break up." She valued the ring. "Does that mean I'm going to meet Tai? That they'll be my...lover?"

"I really hope you do. Some souls are destined to meet in every timeline." He tapped something that was connected to his ear. While Nikki didn't know all parts of his life, she knew it was called a "cell phone," a device people could attach to themselves that could communicate with others instantly.

He brought up a holographic picture of a boy smiling at the camera. He was a "human" like Lí, but had pure white hair with a dyed strip of pink near his eyes. They were so blue, his eyes. They matched the sky.

"He's pretty," Nikki said.

"I know. Have you met anyone who looks like this? He might find you again. He was quite forwards when we met. He literally backed me into a corner, pinning me against the wall." He smiled at the memory. "He was so gentle with me."

"Well, will he be a boy when I meet him? I only like girls."

He laughed. "That, I'm not sure. How funny is it that we both happen to be queer. What's your sexuality, if you don't mind me asking?"

"I...don't know," she said. "I don't know what that word means."

"Oh. That's incredible. What a world you must live in."

"It's not all that great."

"Is any world?"

She played with her ringless hand, then looked out the window. "What's that noise? The swishing. Do you live near a river?"

"It's the ocean. I can't wait for you to see it, Nikki. I hope it changes your life as much as it changed mine."

"What is it?"

"You'll see soon." He closed his tired eyes. "It feels like you're going to wake up soon. Say hi to Marcos for me, will you? I miss that little guy."

"Wait, what?"

It was like waking up through a hangover. Never did she pick up the bottle—she only drank coffee as a means to energize herself. But she'd seen the aftereffects on Derek. She was groggy with a headache that only grew with clarity. She wondered if Lí liked to drink. No, right, given that they were the same person?

She couldn't fully wake up until she forcibly opened one eyelid at a time. Slowly, she blinked up to fluorescent lighting and the smell of the fallout shelter. She was in those bunk beds again. She'd been stripped of her hoodie and shoes to her thin tank top and sweats. A useless bandage covered the healed bullet wound in her abdomen.

Vanna was waiting on the other bunk bed, rocking to keep himself calm. When she began stirring, his ears pricked and he turned to her with tears in his eyes.

"Hey." She coughed, voice dry. "What's wrong?"

Hiding his face, Vanna knelt over Nikki and hugged her.

She offered him a literal shoulder to cry on. "What happened?" she asked in a softer tone.

"Do you remember anything?"

"Yes, up until I passed out." She forced herself out of bed. "Where's my mom and dad?"

"Let me, uh, get my mom to explain it."

"But what about the Asilo?"

He left her unanswered and slipped out of the room.

"*Vanna.*" She checked around the bunk bed for her hoodie and pulled it back on. Attached to her bed frame were two shackles someone had undone.

Rubbing her free hands, Nikki ran out for her best friend. "Vanna!"

Dozens of people were running down the shelter halls. They were carrying packages and talking frantically with one another. Most ignored her, but those who saw her stopped what they were doing to glower at her. A few covered their mouths and stepped back, whispering secrets.

Throwing her hoodie over her ears, Nikki ran for the Drill.

The people doubled, tripled. Hundreds of bodies were now filling the shelter with noise. Everyone was moving or talking or both. She couldn't find her way through.

"Okay, everyone, back it up!"

Nikki locked on to Morgan's voice. More and more people were looking at her now—the new psychopath of Raeleen was now awake. "Morg."

Morgan always held a certain type of respect in Nikki's eyes. She'd built up this coffee house and rebellion with her own two hands. She always had a smile on her face. She wasn't perfect and held biases Nikki didn't agree with, but she had a different type of strength Nikki revered.

Now, looking down at her, Morgan regarded Nikki as a threat, just like the Líders.

She backed away from her niece. A space bubbled out around them. More people watched and waited for Nikki to detonate again.

She held her stomach. "Morgan?"

Morgan grabbed Nikki by the arm. "Come with me," she said too loudly.

She followed, trying to think up an excuse for what they'd witnessed. Would they excommunicate her from the family? Was she even a crossbreed in their eyes? She'd floated like a bird.

Morgan led her to a hall she hadn't fully explored. It led to the infirmary, a place they didn't have to use that often. She noticed guards wearing oversized masks and gloves like impromptu doctors. She spied through the doors they passed and saw crossbreeds sitting on operating tables.

But they didn't look like crossbreeds. She saw pointed tails and fins, giant gashes on their necks and infections on their skin. Had Nikki been responsible for that, too? Some were gasping for breath. Were they having panic attacks?

As she strained her neck to see, Morgan threw her into a conference room with a big, circular table and rolling chairs stacked in the corner.

Her family was discussing something important. Her mother was making a case to Nikki's father and Vanna. She stopped once Nikki entered.

Her mother stormed over to her, and between Shào and Maïmoú, Marcos, and the Líders, Nikki only expected to be hit or face some type of punishment she hadn't meant to receive.

Falling to her knees, her mother fell into Nikki for a warm hug.

Nikki didn't know where to place her hands. Her parents didn't hug her, mostly because she didn't like it. They were too warm for her.

She couldn't remember the last time she'd hugged her mother.

"I'm so glad you're still here," her mother said.

Her father came over and hugged both of them. His cologne and shadow overpowered Nikki's senses. She gripped a fistful of their feathers and brought them closer.

"We saw you during the assembly," her father explained. "We heard the Líder address you by name and started running up to the front."

"And then we heard the gunshot."

"We thought you died."

"You're not hurting anymore, are you?"

"We couldn't find the bullet."

"I'm okay," Nikki said, and wished so badly that the conversation could end there. They could start working on the Drill again. They'd find Kevin and then drill to Derek and then they'd be a family again.

Her mother pulled back. "Nikki, what happened to you?"

Sweat dripped down Nikki's pits. Shào first? What about Maïmoú? And Lí, how was she going to explain *him* to them? She was still having trouble mapping out his timeline. A world outside Raeleen that once held a big building complex named Pangea and some plague that'd infected people. China.

She was tempted to contact Shào and just have him explain himself through her mouth, but she couldn't speak to him. She didn't know if she ever wanted to see him again. Seeing him made her happy, but the thought of him made her sick.

She bit her inner cheek. "I—"

"Morg!"

She almost punched the concrete wall. The voice had come from a walkie-talkie connected to Morgan's coveralls.

Without taking her eyes off Nikki, Morgan clicked the radio and held it up to her ear. "Was that you, Del?" she said loudly. "Speak up, baby. Ears're still fuzzy due to the whole lost-hearing-aid thing."

The connection crackled with Del's rambles, then cut off.

"Okay, wonderful." Morgan went for the door. "Iysra, Marshall, come with me. Nikki, we're putting a pin in you for now, but we are *not* letting this go. You floated. We all saw that. And the Asilo is—"

The radio screeched for Morgan again, and Morgan went to her loved one.

Nikki and Vanna waited for their parents to leave before following. Dozens of people were waiting outside the hall, pretending they weren't eavesdropping on a family's conversation.

"What's going on with Del?" Nikki asked as they ran. "Do you know?"

"Uh, yeah."

"Do you mind *telling* me?" She looked down the hall to another group of those strange crossbreeds. She wanted to ask them what was going on and if she could help gather them. Clustered panic made her anxious, like it was her fault the world wasn't in alignment.

"Those are people my moms found wandering outside the Asilo," Vanna explained. "They don't have a place to go, so my moms' people have been bringing them here. They're the people who've been living down in the Asilo. The waterborne. They breathe in water."

Nikki watched the tiled floors appear and disappear beneath her. It was wet in places like someone had just gotten out of the shower. People who breathed underwater...

She knew of them, but *she* didn't. Lí did, in his timeline.

Vanna led her down a spiral staircase and through a corridor. Three guards were patrolling this area, but they didn't have their guns or badges. Dirt was caked to their uniforms. They gave Nikki space when she came near.

Survivors of her murder spree.

Vanna held up his wrist to the door. It slid open upon his command.

"How did you do that?" Nikki asked.

"My moms figured it out from old tech down here. It's like a key they implant in your wrist. They only turn it on for lockdown scenarios."

She went to ask how that was possible, but as she did, she went for a weapon.

Marcos was restrained to a support beam in the center of the room. He'd kicked out a rolling chair, demanding to be heard. Del, covered in grease and cuts, must've been trying her best to keep him calm.

"Please, I don't wish to hurt you," Marcos said, "but I need to get back to the Asilo. There're hundreds of people who need me."

"Just settle down." Morgan reached for something behind her back. All the adults had him cornered. Her parents' wings were spreading open.

"There are 2,100 people living in the Asilo!" Marcos argued. "I need to go save them. I know where to go."

"Ugh, can't you just shut him down?" Morgan asked someone in the shadows. "He's yours, yeah? Tell him to cool his processors."

Nikki looked around Vanna for the source of this mysterious person.

Her tail fell, flopping to the floor in disbelief.

Zantl, future leader of the world, came out of the shadows. It looked like they'd just scarcely survived the collapse of the Asilo, covered in ash, the ends of their long hair frayed like they'd been electrocuted. It looked like a bruise was forming over half of their face, but it was just soot.

"Holy shit," Nikki cursed, not knowing what the curse even meant. A relic from Lí's past. "What's going on?"

"I'd like to know the same thing," Morgan said. "They just dropped down from the sky like baby birds kicked out of the nest an hour ago. This one is mute—can't get a word out of them that isn't hostile, and this Unit hasn't been—calm down!" she yelled at Marcos, but he wasn't listening.

He struggled more against his restraints. "Please, let me go! I need to save Alexi. I need to. I can't—" He shut his eyes. "Sabah, help me!"

Both Zantl and Nikki looked up like trained dogs to a whistle. Nikki knew that name, somehow.

The lights flickered above them. The adults looked up, ready, waiting. Zantl fell to their knees with their hands over their head.

Morgan watched the room with bated breath. "We need to turn him off," she decided.

"*What*?" Marcos asked. "Are you that cruel? The Asilo is still coming down!"

"The Asilo's been down for two hours, and I'm at my wit's end trying to save all these waterborne from dehydrating. It's my retribution for ignoring them, I understand, but I'm just one person."

"Amidst hundreds, and it's still not enough. They need to be in specialized water containers in order to breathe. And there're files in the Asilo relating to my past that are extremely important. I need to recover them before—"

"Don't get smart with me, Unit. You're not even real. You're a dog who joyfully follows the orders of two—"

"Shut *up!*" he screamed, and startled back the adults in the room. "You have *no* idea what you're talking about. Not once in my eighteen years of living have I ever had a choice in anything in my life. I am a *robot*. I'm given orders I cannot disobey. You have no idea how it feels to do half of the instructions I've been forced to carry out. Do *not* say I have joyfully done anything in my life, because I can count the number of times I've been happy on my *hand*."

Nikki stepped back. That feeling of not having control over your body, being dictated without your consent, she related to that now. She understood the feeling of being used.

She stepped between them. "Morg, leave him alone."

"Nikki, get away from him," Morgan said.

"No. You have no right to yell at him like this when the world's turned upside down. Everyone's nervous, and yelling isn't helping."

"Yelling is actually the perfect way to take care of this. I have a million things falling apart that I have to deal with with only one working ear, not to mention my own *niece*, who floated above our heads and murdered every guard around the Líder with a *whoosh* of her hand before murdering her in cold blood, the same Líder who somehow snooped out that I'm planning a rebellion right under their nose. Nadia's dead, by the way. She died trying to get back into the Asilo."

Nikki grimaced. "Morg, I'm sorry. I don't...know how to explain myself."

"Do you *know* what happened?" her mother asked.

"When you floated," her father added, "how was that even possible?"

She did, but her explanation would've sent her to a ward.

"Can't you tell them already?"

Everyone turned to Marcos, who was looking at Zantl, who looked like they would've rather been anywhere other than here. They cringed at being acknowledged.

"Tell them," Marcos urged. "You know about this more than anyone else."

"And why should I?" Zantl asked.

"So they can stop thinking I'm crazy."

"I'm able to stop that?"

"What're you talking about?" Morgan asked. "Is this about Nikki's situation?"

"I believe so," Marcos said.

"What on Earth can possibly link you three together?"

A spark. A bubble of energy that blinded Nikki. The musty air popped from hundreds of feet underground and ended their forming madness.

Four people fell into the fallout shelter. Three waterborne people, one of whom was holding a baby. She and the baby looked similar, with cuts in their necks and long tails able to cut through the water. The other girl had pure white hair and pink eyes.

The last one was a boy, who always looked tall to Nikki but was of average height. A crybaby, a shy, little bird with broken wings.

Kevin was barely standing by himself. His left wing had been broken, missing feathers and bent in an uncomfortable way. His eyes were bloodshot. His skin was pale.

He squinted at Nikki, then smiled a little when he realized who he'd finally found.

Then his eyes rolled back into his head and he fell into her arms, senseless.

33
Nikki

"Kevin!"

Nikki dropped to her knees to catch Kevin's inert body in time. He was still breathing but weakly. His wing was broken. She pushed back his hair to feel that the texture had changed. Broken blood vessels now crossed his closed eyes like worm trails, and his finger beds had been picked to death.

All of them huddled around him. Their mother touched his face. Their father tried controlling his crying hiccups as he checked for a pulse. Vanna, still unable to come to terms with any of it, stood back with his moms.

Zantl broke the silence. "Can I *ever* get away from you people?"

It must've been rhetorical, because they threw up their hands and went to sulk in the corner of the room, away from everyone they deemed unimportant.

"H-how?" her mother asked Zantl. "How is this happening?"

Zantl crossed their arms and legs and fell to the ground like a child.

"Tell us," her father urged. "If you know what's going on, you need to tell us."

"I don't need to do anything other than wait for my lover to give me the all-clear that I can leave this hellhole. It stinks worse than W4 down here."

Drowning all of them out, Nikki focused her attention on who mattered. She leaned her head against Kevin and heard his heartbeat, telling her that yes, this was real and yes, he'd come back alive. Somehow, through some type of divine intervention, he'd been returned to them.

One of the girls who'd entered the shelter with Kevin sneezed. She was tall like Vanna, and her tail was thick and pointy, almost scaly, though Nikki couldn't tell what her breed was. And not only would that come off as rude, it wasn't like Nikki could talk to girls like her. Tall, big, unafraid of where she was. Was she a Deity?

The other girl, the shorter one holding the baby, took a step back.

"What happened to him?" Nikki asked them.

"I...don't know," the shorter girl said. Her voice was softer than Kevin's, like she was afraid of existing. "Is he alright? Is he...i-is he dead?"

"Do you know him?"

"Yes. We got separated when the Asilo was coming down. I thought Tokala and I would get crushed, but then some-one...or something...saved us. And then Alexi was handed to me by—Tokala, you're alright, aren't you?"

She asked this of the tall, white-haired girl.

"Yeah, I think," Tokala said, "but, uh, where are we?"

"I don't know. Kevin's hurt. He said he'd be alright." Tears welled up in her bright blue eyes. "What's wrong with his wing?"

Marcos, who hadn't taken his eyes off the shorter girl, twisted his body and broke his chains in half.

The girl looked around the suddenly cramped room and blew up her cheeks in nervousness. The frilly thing on her back unfurled as she went for the door.

"Wait," Marcos said. "Viper, I need her. Please, give her to me, right now."

The girl—Viper—did as told. After handing the robot the child, she slunk back towards the door. "I'm sorry," she said, "I can't—this's too much." Giving one last look at Kevin, she darted off into the hallway.

"Viper, wait!" Tokala said. "Did she just leave? Are there too many people in this room? She doesn't do well in rooms. Vipes, wait!"

She bumped shoulders with Nikki on her way out. She somewhat looked her way. "My bad."

Marcos snuggled the baby close, holding the back of her head as her cries were muffled into whimpers. He whispered a lullaby to her to calm her down. It seemed to work. He knew how the baby worked.

Nikki didn't peg him as someone good with kids, but she guessed today was the day for miracles.

"Prayers being answered," Lí would've said.

"Okay," Morgan said, clapping her hands. "I *cannot* concentrate in a room of misfits. First, we work on what's in front of us. Del, go."

"His radius is broken," she said instantly. "He looks malnourished. His blood was taken recently. There're bruises up and down his arm, likely from his blood being taken over multiple days."

"Okay. At least he didn't break a bigger bone. Remember when you broke your humerus down here?"

"Morg."

"Right." She wiped her face of sweat. "Marshall, Del, get one of the stretchers from the medical ward closets. Vanna, medical kit, whatever you have available. Iysra, bleach down an operating table for us to use. Not that we're doing surgery, I just don't know what our boy's gone through and want all our bases covered. Nikki."

Nikki tensed up.

"Stay...with Kev," she decided, and Nikki had absolutely no problem with that. She had no handle on medical procedures or what needed to be done at this stage. Plus, having a passive role in helping Kevin might've deterred her family from asking about her kill count. Perfect all around.

She squatted beside her older brother as her family dispersed. She tried holding his hand. His fingers lay limp beneath hers, unable to tell her he was alright. She watched his chest move up and down.

"He's not gonna die."

Nikki turned. Zantl was hiding behind the pillar Marcos had been chained to. They were peeping out like a child. "He won't die, so I don't know why you're all freaking out."

"What happened to him?"

"Dunno. I was busy not being killed by *you*."

Nikki hung her head. No matter who spoke to her, their words still hurt because she knew it was true. She was the villain here.

Her parents came back with a stretcher and eased their boy onto the white burlap. He moaned, but he neither opened his eyes nor shed any tears. It was strange, seeing this complete other version of Kevin. Where had her eldest brother gone, her crybaby? What a change these months had made on him.

Morgan rolled him out. Nikki followed a foot behind.

"I'll get him ready," Morgan said as they walked. "These bird bones are some of the most fragile bones in the crossbreed texts. I think I have a splint and wrap I can make up for him. He'll have to let it heal for a few weeks."

"Is there anything else we can do?" Vanna asked.

"We'll have to wait until he wakes up. Then we'll take care of what we understand."

That throwaway line stabbed Nikki harder than she thought it would. She hated that they didn't have the full context of a secret she'd been keeping from them. Out of everyone down here, Marcos was the only person she could confide in.

And Zantl, if they, too, were part of this.

She and Vanna waited outside the hospital room. Her mother and father along with Vanna's moms and a few of Morgan's helpers were in the medical ward. They prioritized Kevin, but there were so many waterborne in need of help as well. People were having trouble breathing, they were in shock, they also had broken bones. All from Shào's doing. Because Nikki couldn't control her Deity.

Her tail flicked behind her, hitting the wall like a grandfather clock. "Vanna."

He turned to her, halfway. He looked like he was about to throw up.

She let go a shaky breath. No more secrets. No more lying. "I didn't...mean to do it," she said honestly. "I had no control over my body. It wasn't me."

He slipped to the floor and hugged his knees. "I watched you die today."

She steeled herself.

"When we found you on the ground, you were bleeding out from a bullet wound. I checked just before you woke up. There's no wound. I thought I was going crazy. I think I still am."

"I can't explain it without *sounding* crazy," she said earnestly. "What else can I say?"

He ran an agitated hand through his stiff hair. "I just have the feeling that you're *lying* to us, that you've *always* been lying to us and that there was always something you were keeping us from. I didn't have any sane justification for these feelings and chalked it up to me being anxious, but we've been asking you what's wrong for weeks. You're not a good liar, Nikki. You have a tell."

He looked at her, tears forming in his eyes. "I kept Kev and the fallout shelter a secret because I thought it'd endanger you if you knew too much. Is this the same problem? Are you dealing with something bigger than what we know, and you're trying to protect us by keeping your distance?"

She guessed that'd be the easiest question to answer. "Yes," she said. "I am, or have tried to. Didn't do a good job at it."

"Above." His foot began tapping. "This's like Zantl, isn't it? All those rumors about them being special and having powers. You have them, too, don't you?"

"I don't know. I need to talk to them. I'm still figuring it out."

"Figuring *what* out? That you can murder people by looking at them?"

"No, that I can talk to people who aren't there, that there's a kid in my head who keeps whispering to me, that I see people in mirrors and reflections that used to be. Christ, Vitaliya, I'm sorry I'm scaring you, but I can't give you direct answers about this because I don't know what the hell's going on anymore myself."

Vanna unballed himself, splaying out his legs to push himself farther away from her. "Who's Vitaliya?"

She rubbed her eyes. "No one. It's just...you."

He got up. "I'm not mentally prepared for this, so I'm going to go throw up." He pointed towards the bathrooms. "When I get back, maybe Kev will be up and we can talk about this properly."

"Vanna, I'm sorry."

"Vanna!" Pippa ran down the hallway. She was covered in soot that she'd tried her best to scrub off. Upon seeing her, Vanna melted.

"Are you alright?" she asked. "How's he doing? I just heard." Her eyes kept darting back to Nikki. Vanna answered her with a needy kiss.

Rubbing his back, Pippa led Vanna to the nearest bathrooms.

Nikki let them go.

The worst feeling in the world was feeling unneeded.

With her leg propped up against the operation door, Nikki watched the world continue on without her. These waterborne people had found their way into the fallout shelter like homeless into a newly opened shelter. One even came up to Nikki and asked where the nearest guard was. She tried explaining that the guards here weren't the guards they likely knew and that she didn't know if any of them could help them. She said it kindly, as she knew these people had just survived something traumatic.

The person had burst into tears and fled down the hall.

Nikki turned up her hoodie. Lí had told her it was good to focus on yourself rather than others once in a while, but he was a shitty liar. She knew he'd run himself ragged for a stranger. He'd saved people from a plague, he cared more about Vitaliya and his lover than himself. It was how they—their soul—operated.

But she didn't know these people, didn't know their needs or what water they needed to be in. Marcos had said it was special water. Did she need to raid Morgan's pantry cabinets for salt?

She slapped her cheek, pulled on her hoodie strings, and faced the world. She had to try.

A sizable number of waterborne were congregating near the cafeteria, the hub for gossip. Some of the guards working for Morgan had fired up the stoves to cook up quick, bland meals: stew, beans, cups of watered-down coffee. It smelled like her school's cafeteria, like pizza and peanut butter and jelly sandwiches. It made her feel self-conscious that someone from her grade would see her down here.

She heard survivors sharing their experiences. They explained their escapes naturally, while others spoke about being floated away and landing in this shelter, separated from loved ones. Deities, no doubt, but who? Shào? He'd been busy controlling Nikki.

There was a line for the water fountains. Some people were pushing their way to the front for a drink.

"Stop pushing!" a guard shouted. "These are freshwater fountains only! Freshwater only!"

The dejected "saltwater-borne" cast desperate looks at those who could stay in line. Instead of drinking, the "freshwater-borne" splashed their faces and neck injuries. They must've been painful. Nikki saw the redness inside of them.

"How do we make it saltwater?" Nikki asked a nearby guard. "My aunt mentioned a faulty water system that she didn't use. Have we tried using that?"

The guard tucked their tail between their legs and fled. More and more people were noticing her and hiding their own tails, and children, from her.

Before another onslaught of rumors spread, Nikki ran out of the cafeteria and down a hall she didn't know well. She kept her hoodie over her eyes so she didn't upset anyone else. She wasn't being helpful. She wasn't needed. She was becoming a *burden*.

She found a ladder nailed into a wall and climbed it. It led her to a loft that overlooked the hallway, which had only a railing, an L-shaped couch, and a radio tucked into the corner. It wasn't plugged in, and she didn't need it to be. Curling up on the dusty couch, she hid away from the world and pretended that everything was okay.

She was a terrible liar, even to herself.

"Shào," she whispered to herself. "Why did you do that? You ruined so much, and for what? What were you hoping to gain from hurting so many people?"

Her head was as dark and empty as it had been that morning. Yesterday morning? She didn't know what time it was down here. She didn't even know if she could ever talk to Shào again. What if she'd forced him out so strongly that he couldn't return? Would that've been a blessing? It would've solved some of her problems, but knowing he could always come back created a thousand more.

She felt sick, infected from the inside. She wanted it scraped clean, but her hands were too dirty.

Someone hit the bottom of the ladder. "Ow. Who decides to put a ladder in the most stupidest place possible? I can't even..."

Nikki saw her tuft of hair first. A ball of soft, white curls, flecked with black spots like an ice cream swirl. The rest of her came up in annoyed grunts and heaves. It was the girl that'd travelled with Kevin, the tall one with the scaly tail.

Tokala put her hand out in front of her, feeling for the railing and then the floor. "Why do I have a shitty feeling that there's nothing but ground in front of me?" she asked herself. "You'd think a tank would be up here. Everything down here smells like an old mop bucket, I can't tell. Hey, is anyone here? Can someone tell me if I'm about to fall to my death?"

Nikki licked her lips to get them to work. "Um, no," she stammered. "You aren't going to die. I don't think."

Tokala lifted her head towards Nikki, but her eyes didn't land on hers. She did smile, though. It was nothing but fangs. "I know that voice. You're the first person I heard down here."

She ambled her way over. Nikki could only assume she couldn't see due to either an injury or birth defect. She helped her find the couch.

Tokala tripped and landed most of her weight against Nikki's hip. And lap. She was too heavy and knocked the wind out of her, but Nikki didn't care about breathing. She couldn't.

Her lips were inches from Tokala's neck. She'd never been so close to a girl like this before. It was why she didn't venture close to them, because like this, face to face, chests pressing together for a breath, her brain stopped working. No thoughts. Just the feeling of someone touching her skin and sharing her breath.

"Sorry about that." Tokala got herself together and sat a cushion away. Surprised by the feeling, she bounced a bit, making everything she had bounce as well. "What is this, a couch?"

Nikki felt terrible for looking, but she honestly couldn't have pulled her attention away if she tried. Tokala had black freckles all across her body like the rest of Nikki's avian family, but she had pink eyes. *Pink.* Nikki almost fainted.

"You're still here, right?"

Physically, she was. "Yeah," Nikki said. "Sorry."

"Don't be. I was the one who fell on you. I'm Tokala. Blind. Mostly. Also albino. Got one cool attribute in exchange for a shitty one. The shitty one being the blindness, not the albinism." She snorted. "Anyway, who are you, and where the fuck am I?"

Nikki looked down at how close their hands were. "Um. The fallout shelter. Morgan's. My aunt's. The Asilo...collapsed, and you were brought here."

"It collapsed? Fully? What happened to it?"

"I—"

"And may I congratulate whoever did it."

Nikki choked, actually choked on her own spit, and hit her chest to get it down. "What?"

"Did it explode naturally, because there've been people down there who've wanted to blow it up for generations and couldn't find a way to do it."

"I...don't know," she said, because of course she knew who'd done it, but she didn't know what to say to her. She wanted to *congratulate* Nikki? For killing so many people? For millions in property damage? For being a *criminal*?

"I...did it," Nikki confessed, "but it wasn't my fault. I couldn't control my body. Someone else was—"

"*You* did it?" Tokala lowered her excited voice and grabbed hold of Nikki's elbow. She shook it like a child. "*Good* on you! Good riddance to that place. If everyone got out okay, then nix to all of them!"

"But you don't understand. I don't think a lot of people got out."

Tokala frowned. "I smell a lot of waterborne down here. I just wound up here, somehow. One minute I was swimming for Viper, the next, *blip*, here I am." She smiled a smile that looked all too right on her. She could've torn Nikki in two. "We must've all come here for a purpose. Maybe it was fate that we met?"

Nikki's brain broke. Physically, mentally. Nothing was working between her eyes.

She blushed so deeply, she felt the heat cap at her rat ears. A fated meeting? With a girl? She wasn't that lucky. No girls liked her. She was too stubborn and hard-headed. She got angry easily, she didn't listen. And was there really such a thing about fated pairs? Lí had mentioned it, but was that really true? A perfect match, threaded through multiple lives?

Lí had had Vitaliya—Vanna—and she got that much. Their opposite personalities balanced each other out. And Lí had Tai, his husband, but Nikki wasn't meant to have a forever lover, either. Just the thought of it...

It made her feel...

She gulped down her feelings, but they wouldn't stay down. She always saw Derek as the lovey-dovey sibling who took in lovers like his heart depended on them, and Kevin was so in-tune with his feelings, she was jealous of his heart.

And now the opportunity had literally landed in front of her. What did one do in this kind of situation? How fast could she run away from Tokala?

Tokala giggled. "Aw, are you stunned silent? Did I embarrass you? How cute."

Nikki's heart skipped. Her chest hurt. Did she need to turn herself into the medical ward?

"What's your name?" Tokala then asked. "I've been asking around for help, and you're the first person to actually take the time to hear me."

Nikki pretended she didn't hear that. Or anything she was saying. Her voice was so calming. "My name's Nicole. Nikki," she corrected. "Nobody really calls me Nicole—Nikki's fine."

Tokala's tail wagged. "You're Kevin's little sister! I've heard all about you. We're a lot alike, you know."

"Well, I'm not that little. We're only two years apart, and all rats are small, so..." She stopped before she embarrassed herself any further. "How do you know Kevin?"

"We met in the Asilo. He was seducing my best friend."

"What."

"I know! I'm still mad at him for not asking me permission first. That's, like, the biggest rule when it comes to fucking someone's best friend. You need my seal of approval first. But what can you do? Viper's happy. She's the friend, by the way. My best friend. They met a while ago and Viper was head over fin for him. Have you seen her around? Small, petite, blue eyes, spiky fins."

"Uh, the one holding the baby?" She and Kevin were *together*? In what timeline did Kevin date?

"Yeah, and she ran off without me! She knows better than to leave me out of water. I can't find my way anywhere on land. She must've been scared shitless to run away like that."

"Well, she did look scared. Everyone is." She brought her knees to her chest, tail over feet. "Sorry about burning down your home."

"Why'd you do it? Was it a mistake?"

"It was! Someone else...was controlling me. I couldn't stop it until it was too late."

"Then why're you beating yourself up about it? You did everything you could, didn't you?"

"I guess, but—"

"Then quit it. You're fine, and everything's going to be fine."

"It won't be. Everyone hates me. They're too afraid to look at me."

Tokala tried to. She looked at her forehead instead of her eyes. "I'm not. People are scared of me, too. *Look* at me. Sharp and fanged, with a shitty personality not a lot of people can get around. People might think badly about you, but that's because they're stupid, and you shouldn't pay stupid people any mind. They're stupid."

Her hand found the top of Nikki's head, and she petted her between the ears. "The world's on fire. Don't worry about things you can't control. Just take deep breaths and you'll be fine. When's the last time you took a breath?"

She had no idea. She only realized then that she'd been holding it while Tokala spoke, taking in her every word. She exhaled quickly. "I'm breathing."

"*Are* you?" she teased. "Come on. Take deep breaths with me. In."

Nikki stared at her open mouth. Her lips were so pink.

Tokala waited.

"Oh." She did. Held it.

"Now out," Tokala breathed out.

And she did.

"Again."

She did.

"Again."

Nikki chuckled, then did. "Okay, okay, I get it."

"Do you? Remember, you gotta breathe when things get too serious. If you can't control anything in your life, remember that you can always breathe."

"Unless...I'm underwater. I don't know how to swim. I'd die in seconds."

"Well, I'm a fabulous swimmer. If you ever go swimming, I'll come save you, okay? I'll help you breathe." She leaned in, leaning Nikki backwards. "Or I'll kiss you back to life. Is that an option you'd be interested in?"

Nikki didn't trust her mouth for what it'd say, so she clapped a hand over it to keep from answering. Even though she felt safe around her presence, even though she was nice and beautiful and smiled at her like she was worth a smile, she couldn't let herself fall so utterly.

If she did, she'd have to buy a ring that rivaled Li's.

34
Kevin

Kevin knew where he was. It hurt to be alive and he couldn't open his eyes, but he'd come to know that musty basement smell anywhere.

He awoke on his belly, neck and shoulders numb. He was in Morgan's fallout shelter, in one of the bedrooms where Vanna liked doing his homework. He'd only spent a few evenings here, but the first impression had stuck. It was the biggest secret his family had kept from the government. They were all criminals, and he assessed that he'd done a fair job at keeping that fact away from the Líders.

Blinking away eye crust, he got up to find said family.

He bit back a scream. Pain twisted his fragile bones into carnival pretzels. Something was broken: his back or one of his wings. Someone had placed the left one in a sling, curling the feathers into a natural position for the bones to heal.

He paced himself getting up. He held his head in place. He leaned on the metal bars of the bunk bed for support. His legs shook but he shook them out. He needed to find Morgan.

The halls down here were identical to the ones he and Viper had run through. He didn't smell saltwater, but he did see the people that carried the smell with them.

Dozens of waterborne were wandering through the halls like lost convention-goers. He'd never seen the shelter so crowded before. For a second, he thought he was still in the Asilo, before he saw the Raeleenian flags tarnished with graffitied spray paint.

His hall emptied into the lobby that acted as the central hub of the fallout shelter. It overlooked the Drill so it was always in view and gave workers a place to take their breaks. A circle of couches, a coffee table.

Mom and Dad, arguing about something silly. Morgan and Del, switching between those conversations and giving orders from their walkie-talkies. Vanna was sitting on one of the couches with Nikki hovering over him. On the floor, sitting in their own circle, was Tokala, and Viper, with Marcos, Alexi, and even Zantl.

Kevin teetered into the hall. Most of them had their backs to him. Zantl's sensitive ears flicked at the sound of his footsteps, and once their eyes met, they yipped and dashed into the fallout shelter, afraid of Maïmoú's unlucky soulmate. It took a few more steps before Mom noticed him.

He was swarmed with love. Faces crashed into his as they hugged and kissed and welcomed him back. He hugged and kissed each of them back a hundred times. He might've given Mom one too many kisses. And loving Vanna never felt like enough. After learning about his depression and anxiety, he wanted to sit down with him and make sure he was okay in every sense. He even patted Marcos on the back, as a hug felt too intimate and a nod didn't feel like enough.

"I didn't think you'd come back to us," Dad said, fighting back tears. "You were out for hours. We thought you wouldn't—"

"Don't say that," Mom said. "He's back. That's all that matters. Del, for All That's Above, get him something to drink. Kev, baby, are you hungry? Thirsty? Do you need anything?"

"How's your wing?" Del asked. "Make sure not to move it around. It came to us broken."

"And that entrance!" Morgan said. "Tell us what happened to you there. I need something to go on, and the robot gives me nothing that makes sense."

"Excuse me—"

"Don't overwhelm him," Nikki said. She'd fallen back as their family barraged him. "Let him wake up and get his bearings before you start asking him questions."

Kevin smiled. Raising his arms, he signalled for his little sister to meet him halfway.

She walked over hesitantly. How he missed her, with her short stature, her wildly curly hair, her little buck teeth that made her smile all the more cuter. He was transported to the first day they met, when she'd officially been welcomed under their family's wings.

She plunged her face into his chest, and he embraced her in a late hug. He couldn't remember the last time she'd voluntarily given him so much affection. She even allowed him to kiss the top of her head, pass the curls and right between her little ears.

Wriggling her face free, Nikki touched Kevin's face, making sure she had the right boy. Then she stormed towards the kitchen. "Do we have any chocolate? He needs some sugar. He looks sick. And something cold! It's a million degrees down here. He's going to catch a fever."

Mom and Dad laughed at her. Kevin had never seen them laugh together.

"Hi, Kevin," Tokala said from the floor. "How's your wing?"

"Oh, uh, fine. How're you here?"

"Still don't know. Me and Viper just poofed here."

At the end of the couch waited Viper. She'd changed into an oversized sweater and short shorts likely borrowed from one of his family member's closets. She was shying away from his family.

Tearing up, she came over to Kevin and gave him one of the gentlest hugs he'd ever received.

He cradled the back of her head. He didn't know how much she could take, but she didn't pull away. She even mimicked his touchy hands, holding his face, curling her fingers around his neck.

"Are you alright?" she asked.

"Yeah, you?"

"Yeah."

He pulled back to look at her closely. He didn't know if he'd ever see her again after the collapse, and now here she was, alive and touching him and mingling with his family. It was like a nightmare with a sudden happy end.

Mom cleared her throat. "Kev?"

He expected them to be angry with him. Or Viper. All of them. Too suited to Asilo culture, he thought he'd done something wrong and was going to be reprimanded for it.

He separated from Viper, blushing furiously.

"What's going on?" Mom asked slyly.

"Uhm..."

"Is this your person?" Morgan asked. "I never thought I'd see the day. Del, we should've placed bets. I know those longing stares into each other's eyes from our school days. Remember that?"

"You never did that to me," Del said.

"You're such a liar. I was the first one to come on to you." Morgan whined. "What am I *saying*? My brain's been fried for the past twenty-four hours. Does anyone know what time it is? Midnight? Morning?"

"Whatever's going on, Kev," Dad said, "I don't care. I'm just glad you're with us again."

"But what happened to you?" Vanna finally asked. "What happened to Derek, and the Asilo, and these people? What happened to you?"

"We should have everyone here," Mom said, then looked for Nikki. "Nikki, where are you?"

She came out opening the kitchen's double doors with her butt. She looked to be holding the fallout shelter's entire supply of dark chocolate in her hands, Kevin's favorite snack.

They moved into one of the conference rooms that wasn't overtaken by lost waterborne. Morgan had ordered someone to bring in drinks and cookies to accompany Kevin's chocolate. Kevin went to sit off to the side when Morgan rolled out a chair for him in the front.

He drank a full cup of lemon tea and finished two bars of chocolate before speaking. It was hard to condense months of one's life into a cohesive storyline. What should he leave out? Where should he start? Usually, these types of talks were saved for Derek and the many shenanigans he needed to talk his way out of.

Sitting oddly on the couch so he didn't agitate his wing, Kevin told his family everything that'd happened to him that season. He jumped around, as he wasn't ready to talk about Derek, and he didn't know how to bring up Maïmoú's name. He held Viper's hand so he didn't lose focus. She kept quiet as he spoke, and soon her curiosity about chocolate got the better of her. The smile she made while eating helped him power through.

He left out parts he knew Nikki could handle but Mom couldn't. In his story, Maïmoú didn't exist. Instead of being a cog in Zantl's plans, Marcos became a sympathetic person who'd been strung along against his will.

Marcos helped highlight the Líders' rise into madness since he knew them better than most. He talked about their experiments on waterborne and how they'd been in the works for generations. He told them that Mikhail was dead.

After giving Kevin a side-eye, he also opted to not bring up Maïmoú directly. Hearing a government-owned robot talk about semi-invisible thirteen-year-olds would've made his family even more suspicious of him. Kevin saw the way Morgan watched him.

He instead tried bringing up memory chips and secret rooms, a girl from a forgotten time. He was very passionate about this part, the most animated Kevin had ever seen him, but Morgan dismissed it, as it didn't pertain to Kevin's side of the story.

"But it *is* very important."

"We'll talk about it later," Morgan said. "We need to know what happened to Kevin first."

"You're only saying that because you don't trust me."

"Oh, *no*. I trust you wholeheartedly. It's why I had you chained up when we first met."

"Morg." Del brought her lover's scattered attention back on Kevin.

After mentally preparing himself, Kevin finally got to the Muralha, and he told them what'd happened. He knew they wouldn't completely believe him—hearing voices didn't make a story sound credible. Maybe they wouldn't believe any of it and call him crazy. Maybe they'd laugh. But he loved and trusted them enough to speak the truth.

Nikki listened to every word without interruption. The more he delved into his story, the more her eyes widened. It surprised him that she hadn't asked him any questions about this part. She took it all without blinking, collecting facts and ruling out suspicions.

After Kevin finished, Morgan slapped her knee. "But how? That last part doesn't make sense. You said someone tried hauling you and Derek over?"

"And you don't think you hallucinated it, right?" Dad asked.

"It was real," Kevin said. "I felt their hands on me."

Morgan rubbed her glasses off her face. "How was Mikhail dead all this time? None of my guards even knew, or if they did, they didn't tell me."

"It sounds like only a few lived to tell the tale," Del said.

"How were they able to do this?" Dad asked. "It's like torture."

"It's what they do best, I'm afraid," Morgan said, "but if— I mean, *since*—there's something over the Muralha, there's a chance Derek's still on the other side."

"But Kev said he couldn't see anything on the other side," Mom said. "You said it was like molten rock, right?"

"I'd take molten rock over sky and nothingness," Morgan said. "But before any of that—"

"W-we need to focus on the people still in the Asilo," Nikki stuttered. "That's what we need to do, yeah? Marcos said there's thousands of people down there. We need to save them, yeah? With the Drill?"

"I don't think you can," Kevin said. "The roof was collapsing when we left."

"Which means our chances of getting in are slim," Morgan said, "and with the threat of guards and waterborne running amuck puts us in worse conditions."

"This isn't a hard decision," Nikki said.

"We have to be rational."

"I *am* being rational."

"How about this?" Morgan said. "We get the Drill ready by next Thursday to plow through the Muralha. Líders are all dead, yeah, so we'd only have to deal with packs of guards who don't have any alphas. In the meantime, I'll send my people into the Asilo to scavenge for survivors and intel. If I find any of these waterborne people, I'll bring them here or work out a better refuge center than what we currently have. I still don't understand how or why all of them magically came down here, but maybe it's a sign we're doing some good down here."

Her ideas relaxed a twitching muscle in Nikki's cheek. "Fine."

"Fine," Morgan repeated. "Everyone okay with that? If everyone's set, and before any of us process all of...*this*." She gestured to Kevin and his friends. "We need to talk about *you*."

Nikki's ears went up.

"What happened?" Kevin asked. "Is this about the chocolates?"

"No." Morgan, along with the rest of their family, converged on the youngest member.

"I...There's more important things going on," Nikki said.

"More important? You destroyed the Asilo!" Morgan said it in a tone that might've been anger but was actually sheer bafflement. "How do you explain that?"

"I don't know."

"From the beginning's a good place to start."

"Wait, what?" Kevin asked. "Nikki didn't destroy the Asilo."

"You don't understand," Morgan said. "You weren't there."

"There'd been an assembly outside the Asilo," Del explained. "Nadia came out with Zantl and the Marcos Unit."

"So you know it was important," Mom commented on.

"But besides that," Morgan said, "which I can't even believe I'm saying, when it was going on, Nikki...*floated*."

Kevin looked at Nikki. She wasn't meeting anyone's eyes.

"And you survived being shot at," Vanna said. "It healed like nothing."

"And you killed—"

"Stop it," Nikki said. "Look, I know it looks bad, but trust me, I can't..." She turned to Kevin. "I can't explain it clearly to you, because none of you here would understand."

Kevin's hand slipped from Viper's only to realize he couldn't let her go in fear of slipping away himself. He recognized that resistance in telling the truth. Keeping earth-shattering secrets from your close ones for their own good.

Unlike Derek, Nikki couldn't lie. The more time she spent holding something in, the more she broke. Surprise parties were always a struggle for her.

She looked ready to faint from holding in such a long-kept secret.

Finally snagging Kevin's eyes, Nikki grabbed and pulled him out of his seat. "I need to talk with Kev privately," she said, and dragged him away from Viper, much to his dismay.

"Nikki, wait."

She brought him into one of the worst places in the fallout shelter: the crematorium. He'd only been here once with Derek on a dare. With all the lights off and something creaking in the corner, the two of them had run away and never came back.

Nikki made sure the door was locked and backed him up near an operating table. Her hands were shaking. "Okay, first off: Are you okay? Like, actually okay?"

"Not really, but I'm here."

"Okay." She looked around the empty room. "Kev, I need to ask you an important question, and I need you to not lie to me, okay?"

"Okay."

"Okay." She exhaled. "Do you know who pushed Derek off the Muralha?"

Kevin picked at his cuticles. How could he explain someone like Maïmoú to Nikki?

Nikki stared into the cracked tiles. "Another question, one that'll probably be easier to answer: Do you know...who Maïmoú is?"

The silence between them should've been enough, but to be polite, Kevin confessed. "Yes."

Her face dropped. "So you've seen her?"

"Yes."

"You've talked with her?"

"Yes."

"Has she tried to kill you, too?"

"What?"

"I'm sorry," she said, pained. "I should've been there to protect you."

"What? No, Nikki, you got it wrong. Maïmoú's my friend." He pulled back his messy hair. He'd lost his hair tie between the fallout shelter and here. "How do you know about her?"

"She tried to kill me. She strangled me. She's worse than the Líders. She's not even a crossbreed."

"No, no." Even though he himself had been indecisive about Maïmoú's morality, he still needed to prove to everyone that she had a good heart. "Maïmoú's the only reason I'm alive right now. Ever since the beginning, she's been helping me escape. Nikki, are you like me? Are you a...a soulmate, too?"

Nikki's face had gone yellow and sickly. Looking like she might throw up, she nodded once.

Kevin held his breath until it hurt. His little sister, all this time, she'd been battling this same war. "For how long?" he asked.

"I don't know. I guess since birth, but I only found out a few months ago, right after you and Derek..." She backtracked. "How long have *you* known?"

"Right when I got on the Muralha. The voice told me her name was Maïmoú, and then everything spun out of control. Which one is yours?"

"Shào."

"*Shào?*" He remembered that name spat in hatred from Maïmoú. "Above, Nikki."

"I can't believe this. So Maïmoú hasn't threatened you?"

"No. Has Shào—?"

"No, Shào is..." She paused. "Well, he isn't good, but Maïmoú is crazy."

"Maïmoú isn't..." He paused. "Well, I don't know exactly how *well* she is, but she hasn't threatened me."

"Was she the one to break your wing?"

"No. The ground caved in around her and I fell, but she was sorry about it, I think. Nikki, she's the one who's been holding up the Muralha. Without her, we'd all be dead. What did she do to you?"

Nikki rubbed her belly. "I don't know how to explain it. I haven't told anyone until now."

"Me neither. I thought I'd gone crazy."

"Same here. I didn't think anyone would be able to understand. Have you met Shào? He was Maïmoú's friend, once, I think."

"He's the crossbreed Deity, the one who went crazy and betrayed her."

"What? No, *she's* the one who's crazy." She sat up on the operating table. "I can't believe this."

He couldn't, either. He was so caught off guard by this conversation, he laughed. Finally, he could share his experiences with someone who understood. "I'm glad I'm not the only one in on this."

"I think Marcos' in on it."

"Yeah, and Zantl. And that baby."

"The *baby*? The one Marcos was holding? Why? With who?"

"Some old man, I think. I saw him in the Asilo before my wing broke."

"Jesus," she said, which Kevin understood, somehow. "Something bad must've happened to them in their pasts. I think Maïmoú did something, because she's imprisoned here while Shào's somewhere else. Do you also have a person connected to you, like someone from a past life?"

"Yeah! His name's Hassan."

"Mine's Lí!" She finally shared his bemused expression. "I wish you could've met him. I think you and him would get along."

"Same with you and Hassan. He's just like me. Nikki, Derek's in on this, too. He's soulmated with Maïmoú like me. She was the one who pushed him off the Muralha. To help him," he clarified when Nikki went wide-eyed. "She was trying to get us out before the wall broke. She said he's alive on the other side."

"He's really alive?" With confirmation that she hadn't lost either sibling, Nikki sighed in relief. "Thank God. Or the Above. Whatever. So, does every Deity have a soulmate? You and Derek have Maïmoú, I have Shào. Marcos' got one, I think her name was Sabah—he was yelling her name when he first got here—that baby has one. Zantl must have one, too, yeah? It'd explain why weird stuff always happens around them. Do you know which one?"

"I think their name is Unathi."

"Jeez." Nikki leaned on the crematorium machine. "So she hasn't tried to kill you, yeah? Has she tried to control you, manipulate you?"

"In what way?" he asked, which was probably the wrong way to ask that. She hadn't manipulated him, right? She was trying to help him.

Nikki rubbed down the top of her hands. A frightened, guilty look washed over her, the kind you pulled after listening to a horror show on the radio late at night when you weren't sup-posed to. "Shào...took over my body during the assembly. He used me to kill a bunch of guards."

"What?"

"He was angry. He kept yelling out the names of the other Deities, I think, who'd wronged him, and he kept thinking about Maïmoú. It was scary, Kev. I've never been more scared."

"I'm so sorry."

431

"I've seen them fight," she continued. "When they're together, they're ruthless. They were throwing each other into buildings and cratering the ground with their bodies. She tried to kill me."

"Are you sure? I know she's a little headstrong, and she doesn't think things through."

"Shào did everything to protect me, but Maïmoú still got to me." She touched her throat, remembering something painful. "She choked me, Kev."

Kevin refused to believe her, but then again, she couldn't lie. Her stony eyes told him not to believe her but to understand a different part of Maïmoú he'd tried evading.

"Kev, I don't think you know the real Maïmoú," Nikki said. "Even *I'm* afraid of her."

He didn't want to hear any more. Maybe later when he didn't have so much adrenaline shaking his hands.

"I...think I know how you feel," Nikki continued. "My feelings about Shào are so messed up. I've been remembering things from Lí's time where he admired him, and it screws up my brain. I don't think we should be this close to Deities. It's gonna kill us."

The door Kevin thought Nikki had locked burst opened, restarting his heart. He readied himself for Maïmoú and to defend her again. It'd become in his nature, and Nikki had been the first person to tell him that this way of thinking might've been wrong.

Morgan came in instead. The rest of his family clustered around the gap in the door. "Uh, hello? We were just having a conversation about powers that may or may not be magical?"

Nikki pulled her Lying Face again, which looked like she was struggling with stomach problems and made her look so guilty. Kevin had a couple years on her to perfect the perfect poker face, but tonight wasn't the night for any more secrets.

So, taking Nikki's hand, Kevin told his family the truth.

35
Kevin

His family took the news as well as he expected them to.

Mom was close to tears. Dad didn't believe them. Morgan and Del had a question for every sentence Kevin got out, and Nikki tried to help by adding in her side of the story. Surprisingly, talking about trading bodies with past reincarnations from a future that was still in the past didn't help them sound sane.

It also didn't help that Marcos kept interrupting with his own opinions and instances with Deities. Nikki had been right—his Deity was the one in control of all water, Sabah. Why was the robot connected to the Deity who could drown his circuits? It sounded too comical.

After giving up all that he knew and answering every question he could, Morgan sat down, then sat up, took a breath, and left without a word. When she came back, she stuck him with a pile of documents. "So this's all true."

She said it as a statement, but Kevin humored her and took the questionable papers. He saw Maïmoú's name, her picture blurred in the skyline and her debating some man in a suit.

"This must've been her from before," he said, flipping through the ancient texts. "That's her, with the long hair."

Morgan looked over his shoulder. "That's a picture of the sky, Kev. There's no girl there."

Figured. If she could only be seen by soulmates, then cameras probably couldn't capture her. Deities were only meant for his eyes, and Nikki's.

And Marcos'. If he could get sick, it showed in his face. He shifted his robotic weight awkwardly from foot to foot before finding a chance to break in with his thoughts. When it didn't come, Kevin nodded his way.

"Let me find Zantl," Marcos said. "They'll know more about this. I'll make them tell us. We're done with keeping secrets."

Morgan waited for him to leave before speaking. "So he's in on this, too? And that baby he's carrying around? And Derek?"

"I believe so, yes," Kevin said.

"I probably shouldn't say this, but can you...do it now? Float and explode things with your minds?"

Kevin looked over to Nikki, who was chewing on her lip.

"I don't think so," he said honestly. "Since waking up, I haven't heard anything from Maïmoú."

"Neither have I with Shào," Nikki said. "They might be too far away from us, or their brains might be damaged."

"Brats in control of the world can get brain damage?" Morgan asked indignantly. "Great. Makes perfect sense."

"They're only kids," Kevin defended.

"They're monsters."

"That girl is the reason Derek's gone," Mom said coldly. "She's the source of all our pain these last few months. It's all *their* fault."

Morgan left the hall again, but instead of bringing back secret documents or more clues about Maïmoú's past, she came back with five bottles of cabinet liquor. "Rest up, everyone. We aren't touching any of this until we level out our brains, and I don't know about you, but a good bottle and a night's rest will do all of us good. If anyone needs me, I'll be in the galley, hopefully passed out on the floor."

Without a more practical guide into the realm of Deities, his family deflated. Morgan and Del went to drink away their feelings. Mom needed a minute by herself. Dad helped Vanna into the cafeteria for coffee, which was filling quickly with hungry waterborne. This left Kevin, Nikki, Viper, and Tokala alone.

Within the awkward quietness, Viper sniffled back tears.

Kevin's heart broke in two. "What's wrong?" he asked, as if anything had gone right yet.

"I just...it's a lot to take in?" she struggled to say. "I don't know what any of this means. I knew about Zantl's powers and what they could do, but this is...this...."

Tokala's ears twitched in alarm. "Hey."

Viper touched her gills. She was gasping like she was drowning.

"She needs to get into water," Tokala said sternly. "She needs brackish water, now. She'll faint."

"There were fountains in the kitchen," Nikki said, "but I think they said it's only for freshwater-borne. Are *you* okay?"

"Yeah, I'll be fine. And freshwater's not good enough for her. If she gets put into that, she'll drown herself. But thanks for thinking about me. That's sweet."

Nikki blushed. "W-well, there're other showers down here, but I don't know if they'll work."

"We'll make 'em work. Come on." Tokala grabbed hold of Nikki's hand. She missed several times before latching on. "Show me. Viper, follow us."

"There're other showers across the shelter," Kevin added, pointing behind them.

"Then go bring her there first. Nikki and I will go together." Pulling Nikki's shoulder from her socket, Tokala left with her through the crowds.

Kevin helped Viper stand upright with both hands. "I didn't know they were so close."

Viper coughed. "Nikki's...very much her type. They've been talking for hours. Well, Tokala's been. Your sister's just been staring at her."

"Oh." He'd have to ask her how she felt about that. It'd be her first love.

No other bathrooms looked quite like the bathrooms Morgan had down here. She'd said the pipes would burst upon spurting, so she'd kept her rebels from using them.

But Derek had been curious one night, as he often was, and dragged Kevin into one of his shenanigans. With Kevin acting as his wingman by the entry door, Derek had turned on one of the jets and tasted the water. It'd tasted like blood and rust and made a horrible sound when coming out. They'd run away before being caught by Morgan or worse, their parents.

Kevin thought back on the taste now. Aside from the rotten taste from unused pipes, the water tasted like W4. It tasted like Viper.

Not many waterborne had found their way to this side of the fallout shelter. Some were inside the bathroom, trying out the open showerheads and toilets. It was a communal bathroom that held twenty or so toilets, showerheads, and open bathtubs that reminded him of a pool. A few of the people had worked around the faucets and buttons and were now bathing in four feet of water.

Kevin led Viper to an unoccupied corner of the bath. He saw a crossbreed that looked like her. He asked, "Is this water for brackish-borne?"

"It is," Viper wheezed, and stooped to get in. Kevin helped strip her down to a baggy t-shirt and short shorts.

It was strange to see a bath without any bubbles in it. All the people had sunk to the bottoms of the shallow baths, some hunching over and drinking in the needed water through their gills. Bubbles left Viper's lips until she stopped breathing altogether, like she could've stayed underwater for years and been completely content.

Kevin sat cross-legged on the wet tiles and stayed with her for about an hour. He found it extremely easy to calm down when he was with her. The world had been thrown off-balance, he'd returned to his awaiting family only to cast distrust over them, and staying with her was enough. He liked watching her swim or bob up and down as she stayed in one place, close to him. His hands made ripples in the water. She swam closer to him when he did that.

She held his hand, when they were close enough, and he became an anchor for her. He thought he was rather good at it; he guessed that, after this, he wasn't going anywhere without her. She'd tethered herself so tightly around his heart that she'd made grooves around it. Even if they were to separate again, he wouldn't be able to stray far.

It sounded too much like they were soulmates, and that made him blush like Nikki. It felt too intimate of a connection with someone he'd only met that year, but he supposed he liked Maïmoú just as much.

Comparing his bond with Maïmoú to his crush on Viper was and would never be a fair comparison to make.

News must've spread about the baths. Every ten or so minutes, a new crowd of waterborne would find their way into the showers. Soon, Viper was bumping shoulders with strangers and stepping over tails.

Kevin tapped her shoulder. "Do you want to get out?"

After thinking about it, she nodded, cheeks puffed, and the two escaped back into the hall.

"I'm surprised they still work," he told her. "Do you want to try the other bathroom? I can take you there."

She shook her head. She still didn't look well even after being in water.

He looked away. He felt so awkward asking her what was wrong because he knew. She was terrified, probably hungry, and maybe even homesick for the Asilo. He couldn't do anything to help her with a lot of those factors other than food, but she was so skinny. Did she have a diet she needed to follow? What were her favorite foods?

He looked up to the ceiling, an idea forming. "You haven't been outside before, right? You haven't walked the streets or gone shopping?"

She said nothing.

"Then I have an idea. Let me bring you upstairs to my aunts' coffeehouse. It's really pretty and cozy. They sell pastries, which are like sugary desserts you can eat for any meal, and coffee, and more chocolate. You tried dark chocolate, but there's also milk chocolate, white chocolate, chocolate with berries mushed in. It's all good."

The way Viper fluttered her tired eyes at him made his brain drop to his crotch. "Can we—"

A pair of heavy footsteps ran up to them. It was Pippa, one of Viper's guards, holding on to Vanna like Kevin was doing with Viper. When Viper saw her, she hid behind Kevin's wing.

"There you are," Pippa said. "I was looking for you. I'm trying to get a headcount of every waterborne to make sure they're getting hydrated. Viper, you found the bathrooms, right? Now all that's left is that baby shark, Alexi. I cannot for the life of me find her or Marcos. Vanna said he ran after Zantl, and now it's like they both disappeared."

Kevin looked over to Vanna. "What's going on?"

Vanna smiled nervously. "We...I mean, you know my moms. They saw the opportunity to bring in guards for her mission to build the Drill. We met and, well..." He shrugged, like it was just fated to be. "She kept good tabs on you when you were in the Asilo."

Kevin reexamined Pippa, this bubbly, energetic girl just out of the academy. "You've been working for my family this whole time. And you're dating my cousin?"

"Yeah. Guess I don't need to hide it anymore, now that the Líders are allegedly kaput. Do you know where Zantl is? I feel like if I find one of these—what're they called—*soulmates*, I'll be able to find the other. Ya'll seem to cluster together."

"I haven't seen either of them," Kevin said.

"Then we'll keep looking. I'm sorry to cut it short, but knowing these people can shrivel up after an hour without water's making me jumpy." She turned, spinning Vanna around. Vanna gave Kevin an almost sorrowful wave, like he wished he could've stayed longer but couldn't, and left with his supposed lover.

How much had his family changed since Derek's disappearance? First Mom and Dad laughing with each other, then Nikki making moves on a girl she just met. Now Vanna had a lover, a *guard*, a profession and class his mothers didn't favor. He'd have to catch up with them and their growth.

But he had other people to worry about first. He pulled Viper back into the present and down a new hall. "I'm sorry, you got interrupted. What were you saying?"

"I...wanted to know if I could lay down somewhere," she said, "if there're no tanks. I want to rest my...everything."

Kevin mentally calmed himself down. There would be a time to show Viper the world. Tonight wasn't it.

He led her down a hall without many people. It was empty save for a few guards sitting on the floor. This was the other, lesser-known set of bedrooms that Morgan had let fall to the wayside. The rooms were smaller and were occupied with cleaning supplies rather than furniture and pillows. The room he chose was closet-sized with a cot pushed up into the corner, hooks coming loose on the walls, and a small table missing one of its legs. Viper flopped down rather dramatically in the bed-sheets.

Kevin closed the door on his tail feathers and turned on the fluorescent light above them. It sputtered out a faint, yellow hue.

Viper buried her face in the pillow, tucking in her knees and tail and making herself small. Kevin crossed his ankles, keeping to her boundaries.

"I've never slept in a bed like this before," she confessed. "I know the guards use them when they work night shifts, but waterborne usually sleep in our tanks, or rest in cots just outside of our tanks."

"Is it comfortable, sleeping in water?"

"It feels vulnerable. The guards can watch us sleep. But beds make me nervous, too. Everything does. I'm so tired, Kevin. All I wanna do is sleep."

"Do you want the lights on?"

Her toes curled into the blanket. "Do you want them on?"

"I don't mind either way."

"Okay, then," she said, and off the lights went, casting them in darkness. It felt more fitting for her.

But the silence was dragging, and his brain was begging him to fill it. He went to pick at his fingers. "I'm sorry," he said. "I don't know what to say."

She wiped her face on the pillow. "Who's Maïmoú?"

"She's the Deity girl linked to me from the past, a girl who can do unspeakable things to the world, but who can also save it." He stopped himself. He was doing it again. "Deities are... a difficult group of people to talk about. I've only met two, and I don't know them that well. At once they're very protective and kind, but at the same time, they can be...hostile."

"I'm sorry you have to go through that."

"Thank you."

440

The response came so naturally. It was normal to be thankful for someone worrying about you, but he hated that it was still tied to Maïmoú. He wondered how Hassan had done it. He'd been a father figure to her. When Kevin had dreamt of that little farm cottage, he'd cared for Maïmoú, like a true father with his young daughter.

Viper's fanned tail thumped on the bed sheets, and Kevin looked over to see her staring up at him.

His heart thumped with her tail.

"You wanna lay down?"

He nodded. Again, brain not where it was supposed to be. He just wanted to be closer to her, in any way. He needed that anchor.

He maneuvered his broken body onto the cot, letting his wings fall over the edge, and snuggled in against her.

They listened, the two of them in this space. They heard the hum of the machinery working overtime to accompany so many people. People walked by their room, ignoring their presence so it was only them. No more talk of Deities, no more threats. Only each other and their breaths warming up their pillows.

He snuck a glance at her. "You okay?"

"Yeah," she said. "Are you?"

"No."

She hid her face better. "I lied. I'm not okay. I don't think I can remember the last time I was. When I'm with Tokala, I guess it lessens, but sometimes, it's too much, you know? Sometimes, I feel so heavy, and I haven't done anything in hours."

"What can I do right now to make things better?" he asked.

"Hug me and tell me things will be okay."

He placed his pillow on the floor and scooted in. He didn't know how far she wanted him to go or how far one could take a hug, but he didn't care. She'd given him a chance to act on her needs and by any God's name, he'd set out to achieve them.

He didn't know what to do with his legs. He'd never held someone like this in a bed before. He'd hugged his parents' goodnight and given awkward, side-arm hugs to Nikki when she allowed it, but nothing like this. This hug held too much potential.

He palmed her shoulder blade, around the spiny frill connected to her back. His other hand, the one around her pillow, cupped the back of her head. He patted down her hair to dry it faster. "Everything will be okay," he promised. "I don't know how or when, but we'll get through this together and everything will get better soon."

"Will it?"

"Absolutely. There're so many things I want to show you when this's over. I want to take you to ice cream parlors and have dinner with my family. I want you to meet my twin, Derek. He's always so fun when meeting new people. I want to do so many things with you. And Tokala, too, of course." He swallowed back his mouth full of spit. "You're the exception."

A shy hand wrapped gingerly over his hip bone. "I am?"

He closed his eyes and smelled her hair. She smelled of summer, like rays of light hitting a puddle and reflecting the bright sky above.

"I never thought I'd be able to do this with someone," Viper whispered into him. "My past, it was...with boys, and with guards, sometimes, I was taken advantage of."

He pulled back. "What?"

"But it's different with you. I feel safe with you."

"Wait, what do you mean?"

She didn't answer. Her arms felt like dead weight over him now. "Men are...scary when they're with me. You've helped me overcome my anxieties. I really like that about you. You make me feel like I can fall asleep next to you, and nothing bad will ever happen to me again."

He stared past the curve of her head into the dark, shapeless wall behind her. He wasn't intimate with people, but he wasn't an idiot, either. He knew what she was implying.

His stomach melted into the pit of his gut as he tried processing what to say and how he was feeling. He now understood how easily Maïmoú jumped from one emotion to the next. This heat inside him, it wasn't from fear or love but *hatred*. Intense, acute hatred for vile men who deserved to die. It frightened him how ready he was to hurt someone, and how, at first, he didn't think that was wrong.

He still didn't think it was. He wanted to hunt those men down like animals and make them suffer.

To combat these new feelings rushing inside him, Kevin held Viper tighter. "I'm sorry," he said, trying to control himself.

"Now we both have painful secrets that're impossible to bring up to people."

He hugged her more, burying her, hoping to bury that secret in her memories, but that wasn't how this worked. Pain like that wouldn't fade without scars. They were emotions you had to live through and hopefully find someone to share with. Their traumas weren't the same—they'd never live each other's lives—but this breakthrough in trust was a starting point.

He pressed his lips against the top of Viper's head. She hadn't come up for air, was only breathing in the clothes Morgan had lent them from upstairs.

She wiggled her feet again.

"You okay?" he asked.

She nodded. "Mhm."

"Mhm?"

"Did you just kiss me?"

"Yeah. I think," he added, because he honestly couldn't remember.

She pulled up, hiding her thin lips behind a sheet. "I didn't really feel it," she whispered. "Can you maybe try again? Somewhere I can feel it?"

Funny how quickly bloodthirst could dissolve and boil down into a stronger kind of animalistic drive. He felt his impassioned heart beat through his body into every feathered nerve.

Leaning down, Kevin brought Viper up for air and kissed her right.

36

Derek

"Derek, are you sure you're alright?" Oliver asked through the door.

"Yeah, totally. Totally fine. I just need a few more minutes with Holly. Again, totally fine. Nothing's wrong."

"Are you lying?"

"Yeah, sure." He looked over the notes he'd scrawled on the back of his hand. "I just need a word with her."

Oliver paused, panicking Derek's heart, before his footsteps creaked the floorboards. "Okay. I'll be downstairs getting ready. I'll be waiting for you both, okay?"

After the door closed, Derek sighed and squatted down to collect himself. Both he and Holly hadn't gotten any sleep that night and, similarly, had both locked themselves away so they didn't go insane.

Derek started pacing the perimeter of the rug. He was in some type of writing room or tea parlor on the third floor, one fancy enough for only couches and bookshelves and windows of snow-capped pine. He couldn't stop moving here, as his brain wouldn't stop overthinking.

"So, today's a No-Talking day, right?" he asked Holly. She was currently spinning in a chair, kicking off the ground to keep her momentum going. She nodded.

"Okay." He wiped his face of sweat, then cursed when he saw that he'd smudged his hand notes. "Here's what I have so far. We need to figure out a way to tell Oliver about, lemme see...

"The existence of Deities and how most of them are batshit crazy, what soulmates are and how both of us are one, whatever that means, what was in that basement, the existence *of* that basement, the pictures we found down there that you once drew but don't remember drawing, and how all of this is connected to us and invisible people only we can see. Shouldn't be hard at all. So, firstly, does he know *anything* about that underground fallout shelter place?"

Holly chewed on her cheek, then shook her head.

"Do you know for sure?"

She shrugged.

"*Holly.*"

She grabbed for Derek's quill to write something down in her notebook. As she wrote down her thoughts, Derek wasted time by over-analyzing how many ways this conversation with Oliver could've gone south. *"Hey, Oliver, turns out I'm connected to a Deity who I've never met before and other Deities wanna kill me for it for some reason because they hate* her, *not me, so if you stay with me, you'll be in constant danger and I'll likely die early because some girl with a weirdo name used to know me from my past. Your best friend's also in on it. Also, I used to be a girl."*

He felt sick.

Holly gave him her notebook.

I haven't any idea what happened underground.
Memories are coming back to me, but when I think about it,
I get dizzy.

"You don't think that's because you're spinning?"

She motioned for him to continue as she spun.

I did recognize the two people we met down there. I don't know why. It's like my memories have been jumbled up into a salad.

"That's like me. I had amnesia when I first came here, and still do, sort of. You think they're related? Some Deity is taking away our memories?"

She wrote down more thoughts.

I think this amnesia might be the same for Oliver and the other demons. He's never brought this up to me before, and many of us don't remember how we came to be 500 years ago. Before today, I had no idea that place existed. I didn't even know about ~~Baby~~
~~The child~~
~~The infant~~
The little boy who looked like me.

Derek studied how furiously she'd scribbled out those words. "That was your old home, right? You and him and that...baby used to live there together."

She took back the notebook, and Derek walked towards the window to let his thoughts escape easier. "Shào and those other Deities said I had a brother *and* a sister. That's, like, really fucked up that I don't remember them and they do, or they know about them. Somewhere, I have this entire other life I don't remember having."

A dollop of snow fell from the trees. Hyper-aware of everything always, Derek scanned the forest, the sky, anywhere a floating person could be hiding.

He didn't find any floating person, but he did see someone just as deranged.

"Woah!" He pressed his face into the cold window, then tried opening it. "Hey!"

Riding towards the demons' manor, dressed in haughty winter clothes and jewels, was none other than Jabel, followed shortly by Cellena on her own white horse.

Derek banged on the window. Neither of them looked up. Jabel kept checking down their path before ending his journey at the moat encircling the manor.

"It's Jabel and Cellena," Derek told Holly, and went for the door. Holly had already left, leaving the door swinging behind her.

Derek flew down the stairs into the main living room area. Every demon was too preoccupied to notice him. Shimah and Kumo were digging through wooden boxes and pulling out gold jewelry. Rosaline and Maxwell were beading identical bracelets on each other's horns. Yomi and Brennen were in the kitchen, cleaning up a bigger mess than usual.

"Welcome back to the world of the living," Rosaline said. "We saved you some breakfast, or as much as Shimah would let us."

"You missed this whole bit where we light Rosot berries on fire and everyone tries tossin' 'em in my mouth," Shimah said. "I saved a few for you to try."

Derek walked over an emptied box of mothball clothes. "What's going on?"

"We're celebrating the turn of the new year. We dress up, dance, sing, and drink. There used to be more of us to make it an all-week celebration, but..."

Oliver floated back to the first floor. He'd been nailing up strings with paper stars dangling from them. "Good morning," he said. "Is everything okay?"

Derek tried on a smile, but it didn't fit. To feel better, he walked over to his man and let himself be eaten up by a hug. It was becoming the only way he could relax, being with him.

Too bad the laws of this world forbade his body from merging with Oliver's. They could've become one and would never have to separate. The closest he could get away with that was sex, but he didn't think he'd ever fuck someone so wholesome.

"Get a room," Maxwell called out.

"Maxwell, be nice," Rosaline said. "Derek, you okay? Do you need anything?"

"Just this," he said, and hugged Oliver tighter.

"Here, my dear." Yomi came in with a vial of fang venom. "This's from Brennen, for your nerves."

"Thanks." That metallic taste hurt good going down. "Also, uh, Jabel and Cellena are outside."

"*What?*" Maxwell sat up too suddenly, clipping the bracelet—hornlet?—Rosaline was creating on him and scattering the beads on the floor. "I told him he wasn't obligated to come today. We wrote letters."

He disappeared in a cloud of dark matter to go outside. Derek snuck over to the windows and saw him helping both Jabel and Cellena off their horses. Jabel was much taller than Maxwell. He had to lean down to hug him properly, snuggling into the crook of his shoulder as a gentle snow fell around them.

"Get a *room*," Derek called out.

Maxwell stuck out his forked tongue, then brought the royal heirs over the moat into the manor one at a time, puffs of black smoke trailing from side to side. Jabel dusted off his jacket before Maxwell jumped back and helped take it off for him.

"Derek!" Cellena ran up and smushed her face into his chest. "How I've missed you."

"Hey, there." He scooped her up and hugged her right. He'd missed their scents, expensive perfumes that tingled his nose. "I missed you, too."

"I've missed *you*! You've not written to us once! Are you alright?"

"Hey, I was only gone a few days, right?"

"It was too long. I'm so sorry about what happened to you in town. I'm sorry that our parents did that in front of you. You don't hate us, do you?"

"Course not. You're okay."

"See, Cellena?" Jabel said. "I told her you wouldn't hate us, but she didn't believe me." Unable to help himself in a safe space, Jabel leaned down and kissed Maxwell. "It's nice to see you again."

Maxwell burned up. Literally. A puff of smoke left his color-changing hair, turning it from its natural black to stark white. His face turned a deeper shade of red like an apple as he waved the smoke away. "R-right. Yup. Same."

Derek mockingly laughed at them. The hypocrite. "Ew, two people loving each other in earnest? How *dare* you. Off into the ocean, both of you."

"Don't joke," Jabel scolded.

"Hey, you didn't answer my question," Cellena said to Derek. "Are you alright?"

"...Yeah." He wiped his hand notes off on his pants. "I'm just...ready to hang out today. You're here for this party thingy, right? Were you invited?"

"This's the first time I get to experience it," Jabel explained, trying to stay regal-looking with Maxwell clinging to him like a schoolgirl, "and Cellena's been pestering me to bring her this year."

"Your parents allowed it? Won't they, like, kill you for coming here?"

"Our father went into town for a quarterly meeting with his landowners. Left our mother in the castle. I hardly suspect she'll notice our absence, but to be sure, I had Nero tell her that Runa will be teaching us the important skill of categorizing scrolls." He rolled his eyes. "She shan't come looking for us."

"*Shan't*," Derek said with a snort. "Fuck, I missed you two."

"And I you!" Cellena hugged him again and didn't let go.

After the demons and heirs introduced themselves and everyone was given tea and cookies to dine on, they all relocated into the lounge.

And drank. Derek got to savor in his vodka again and tried mixing it with a new drink to gain a deeper high. Two bottles in and he became warm and stupid. Everything to do with Deities smoldered in the fireplace. He didn't even feel bad about his lost memories anymore. If Holly could find them, he'd find his eventually, and then he'd reunite with his alleged brother and sister and everything would be fine again. Were they birds, too, or did they have bat wings like Shimah? He couldn't wait to find out.

He got off seeing Jabel act like a real teenager out here. Without his father breathing down his neck, he let himself slouch on the couch with his lover. They shared a cup of hot chocolate, courtesy of Cellena stealing it from the castle kitchens, and they stayed glued to each other's sides for the whole afternoon. Thighs touching, heads leaning against the other's as drowsiness stole them away from the festivities.

Jabel had been so uptight when Derek had first met him. Now, he had his shoes off and was trying hard to make Maxwell laugh. It took Derek's all not to grill him on it—he was mirroring their touches with Oliver.

As the afternoon rolled into night, Brennen and Yomi brought out pipes that smelled of herbs and berries. Smoking it made their eyes glossy with delirious delight. Shimah took one to smoke while Rosaline tossed lit berries into his mouth. Jabel was nervous about them getting too high, but after drinking a thick ale that made him cough, he settled down. He took to stroking Maxwell's curly hair, making it turn white and grey and then black.

"Y'all are so *handsy*," Derek slurred, passing them his half-finished drink. "Couple of lovebirds, huh?"

Maxwell took the bottle. "*You* try keeping away from your mate for weeks at a time. Our meetings are precious. When we meet, we don't take our hands off each other."

"Precious?" Derek teased, but neither of them disregarded their feelings as anything less.

"And you've been with Oliver," Jabel said. "How has that been for you?"

Derek watched said man throw another log on the fire. "Good? What's it supposed to feel like?"

"I haven't known another non-demon/demon relationship. It was rare in my grandfather's time, and now, it's nearly extinct. How does it feel?"

"Just, like...I dunno," he said. "It feels like a crush." He dropped to a whisper. "He's, like, *really* devoted to me."

Jabel snuggled into Maxwell's side. "Their love is some of the strongest known in the world. They'll do anything for you, even sacrifice themselves for you. It's something to ease into."

"I don't mind it now."

"Nor do I. Once you find your rhythm, every day with them is a gift."

"Okay, too much info."

"*You're* the lovebird here," Maxwell said, and Derek didn't disagree.

Nothing was really scheduled during this festival. The demons switched from indulgences to singing and dancing without notice. Rosaline and Shimah took to battling each other for the worst dance moves. Cellena danced with Kumo, who had to keep in her wheelchair but wanted to learn ballroom dancing. Yomi and Brennen helped cook the deer Oliver had hunted and brought out samples for everyone to try. Derek devoured all the fish dishes while he persuaded Holly to try some. She'd finally come down but kept back from the horny drunkenness. She chose to people-watch from the banisters, her eyes on Derek.

Everything tasted familiar, like remembering a home-cooked meal. He forgot about Sabah and Tsvetan, the fallout shelter, Keva. While he dozed off on the couch, Oliver and Brennen brought out carved instruments to sink him even deeper into his high. Kumo played a flute with flowers and ravens etched into it. Shimah, a guitar made from horsehair. Rosaline danced to the rafters.

Oliver threw another log on the fire. He was wearing pretty necklaces and a headpiece that left his horns sparkly.

Derek opened up his legs to air things out. Oliver's eyes were half-lidded with a smile Derek didn't often see. With the number of bodies in one area, things had become hotter. Oliver had peeled off one of his layers, revealing a loose shirt that showed off his biceps.

"This's nice," Derek told everyone. "Like, really nice. I needed this."

"I'm happy you're enjoying it," Oliver said.

Smirking, Derek opened one wing and motioned him in.

He came. "Hello."

"Hey."

"Are you okay?"

"Dance with me."

"I don't really dance."

"Does anyone? Cellena, you stay there with your pretty self. Shimah, Kumo, move."

"Bah!" Shimah blurted out, and hung from the ceiling with drool dripping off his nose.

"Just so *you* know," Derek warned Oliver, "I'm an *amazing* dancer."

"You'll be much better than I. I have two left feet." He danced Derek towards the foyer, away from everyone else. He didn't want an audience. "I love days like this. Living the way we do, we never know if today's going to be our last. This festival's becoming more of a celebration to memorialize the

453

fact we've lived another year, not to celebrate our God giving us a new year to live."

"Is that what this's for?"

"It used to be. It's alright. I know you don't believe in it as strongly as I do."

Derek's heart turned. "It's just that so much has happened to me. I've seen a lot of stuff that doesn't make sense. I don't want to add to the list, especially if it's a tricky subject that needs a mature mind to talk about. I'm trying not to think at all anymore."

"About everything, or about what happened yesterday?"

Derek answered by dancing around him, walking over his tail and rubbing up against him.

Oliver half-heartedly danced with him. "I feel like my world has shifted this season. I can't even think without panicking. I didn't even greet their highnesses correctly."

"Dance to forget."

"But I don't want to forget. You make me hopeful for brighter tomorrows."

"Now, is that a good thing or a bad thing?"

Oliver's hand snuck past Derek's waist. "Good thing."

Grinning, Derek embraced this new side of Oliver, shutting his eyes and hearing him breathe.

Then a hand slipped into his pants.

In a turn of events, Derek was the one to stop Oliver's wandering hand. He checked the redness in his eyes to make sure he hadn't lost it.

"...Yes?" Oliver asked.

Feeling like he wasn't in on some joke, Derek hid him around the corner into the kitchen.

"Did you do that on purpose?" he whispered, sensing where that hand would've travelled if he hadn't stopped it. "Do you know what you just did?"

Oliver bit his grey lip, then nodded. "Was that okay?"

"Oliver, I'm in a very fragile state right now."

He futzed with his hands. "Do you...want me to take care of it for you?"

He could've screamed. He probably had, he couldn't remember. All he remembered was hauling Oliver up the stairs and trying to rip off his clothes without tripping over Holly. Fuck dancing and drinking. Fuck procrastinating and pretending he was chill with partying. *This* is what he needed right now. To feel like Derek Harrow, to be normal again, he needed to turn off his brain and let his dick decide his future.

"Do you think it was obvious asking Shimah to boil some water for our impromptu night bath, or do you think it went over his head?"

Oliver sat at the edge of his bed. His hands were threading through his wire-thin tail. "Do you remember if you've ever done this before?"

Derek outlined Oliver's chest with a free hand. The other rubbed down his thick thigh.

Oliver bit his lip.

"You okay?"

"I haven't done this before, you know."

"I haven't done it with you either, in this timeline."

"Huh?"

He straddled Oliver with the slowest of movements, grinding his hips against his to make him blush. When he got comfortable, he tore open the condom he'd stolen from Yomi's and Brennen's room. "You gotta say in this, you know. If I'm going too fast, we can stop. I'm good with cuddles."

"But you want more than that."

"I want *you*." Derek knew some people were like this, that not many people were so drunkenly in lust with sex as he was.

Oliver was filled with love, yeah, but it could've been on different levels than Derek.

Derek pulled back his ready hands. "Tell me when, love."

Oliver gulped one last time and looked him in the eyes. "When."

He was falling again. For a winged kid, you'd think he'd be better at taking to the sky and not plunging to his death. Maybe he was ready to die and his brain was telling him that was okay.

Shades of blues were flying by. He was falling alongside a dark, crumbling wall, and something behind him was roaring, like a motor or a waterfall. Water droplets were soaking his wings.

The fall lasted seconds. He half-expected himself not to die, to victoriously grab onto the wall at the last minute, but no. He just fell into the sky, waiting for a queer death.

He closed his eyes. That would be nice, if life would ever allow such a peaceful end.

An energy bloomed behind his wings, like a gust of wind had blown him sideways and stopped him in midair. He felt himself slip into someone's arms.

Tsvetan, that meek, one-legged Deity from the fallout shelter, was looking down at him. He looked scared, as if wondering how Derek had managed to fall from the tallest structure on Earth and not die.

"Can you understand me?" he asked hurriedly.

All the blood in Derek's body began filling his ears. His head fell back. He saw sky dots. He saw water.

Tsvetan looked up to the sky for someone to help. "Did she push you out? Oh, All, I can't bring you back to her now. She'll know I was involved. But she'll only get angrier if you're taken from her. Oh, what do I do?"

How was Derek supposed to know? He wasn't one to meddle in divine affairs.

An idea dawned across Tsvetan's green eyes. "I'll send you away, then. It's the only way. I'm so sorry. This's for your own good...and for *her* own good."

For whom? Nikki, his sister? Cellena, his friend? Holly, the other soulmate connected to these beasts?

Still unsure of his decision, Tsvetan touched Derek's forehead, and Derek disappeared from the world, his memories spilling from his head as the sound of waves saw him off.

Derek rolled out of his warm blankets and dropped to Oliver's floor. Confused from his dream, he stared out the snowy window.

Confused from his last memory in Raeleen, Derek Jada Harrow, age twenty, an osprey crossbreed who lived on 201 Newbridge Lane in Raeleen, who'd once played a part in an underground operation to drill through the Muralha and save their country from corrupt rulers, whose memories had been wiped by a shit Deity, stared out a window to a world that, to his knowledge, shouldn't have existed.

Derek Jada Harrow needed to get the fuck out of this backwards country and get home.

37
Nikki

Nikki expected Morgan to get them out of the fallout shelter by next morn. She pictured her family rampaging through the streets in the Drill with Morgan's packs of guards, busting through the Muralha for good.

That night, Morgan ordered her family to stay in the fallout shelter. When morning came, Del found her passed out in the kitchen with enough empty beer bottles around her to tranquilize a horse. Whatever a horse was. The thought of its existence made Nikki queasy.

"Nikki?"

Kevin was a whole other issue. With their adult family inebriated, Nikki had thought her older brother would help her get a grip on this situation they'd become entangled in.

They'd met up for five seconds, then *gone*, poof, off with that girl he was allegedly involved with for the night. She'd guessed they'd found a bedroom to cuddle in, or do whatever people in love did behind closed doors.

First Vanna, now Kevin. Did *Derek* now have a lover wherever he was on the other side of the world? Probably, who was she kidding?

"Nikki, are you okay?"

Those lovey-dovey thoughts weren't helping her right now. Or the thousands of waterborne lost down here. Guards under Morgan's command had come back from recon that night. The Asilo was in piles of ash—the packs had come back coated in it. The casualties were anywhere from 500 to 750, most of which were waterborne.

"Hey."

She needed to be doing more. Sure, she was only eighteen, but she could've been volunteering in the kitchens or babysitting parentless children. She could've been out on the streets helping survivors. She'd have to pull all-nighters, hold a meeting with her parents to buy more provisions...

"Nicole, *look* at me!"

Nikki's sneakers skidded on the tiles, and she was backed into the wall by Tokala. They'd been walking down the hall between the cafeteria and the workout gym, searching for her parents and failing to spot a feather.

Since yesterday, they'd stayed within arm's reach of each other. They walked together, ate together, all the while Nikki saying absolutely nothing of import to her. A lot of it boiled down to their shared interest in finding their loved ones and so they kept close, but Nikki couldn't ask her why they were sticking together.

Maybe Nikki had wanted to keep her distance from her, keep from getting distracted. She wanted to be helpful, but when Tokala was near, all her attention went to her. She wanted to stare at her and have a reason to help *her* alone. Was it infatuation? Maybe. She'd never felt it before, she didn't know what it felt like. A distraction from people dying and hating her? Surely. Something more?

Tokala's breath hit Nikki's face. Nikki held hers, hoping it didn't stink.

"You're acting so jumpy," Tokala said. "What's going on?"

"Nothing."

"Uh, *this* is not nothing. We've been walking around forever and you don't seem to know what you're doing."

A string in Nikki's heart got plucked. "Well, I'm a bit stressed right now. I can't find Kevin or your friend, I want to find my parents—"

"And do what?"

"Huh?"

"When you find them, what're you planning next?"

"I don't know. Talk with them? It's been a minute since I had a meeting with them."

"And what is it that you want to know?"

Nikki gave her a look that might've gotten through her clouded vision. "Why're you asking me? I'm still struggling to figure out what I want."

"I know. That's why I'm trying to hone you in on what you want. You're getting all scatterbrained on me and it's freaking me out. I'm guessing you work better when you're clear-headed."

"That's the thing. I don't know what I'm getting into any-more. I found out that there're all these soulmates and Deities I didn't know about. Kev's involved with the most dangerous one but only wants to hang out with your friend. My parents and aunts are getting drunk. Vanna's off with his girl, not even talking to me anymore. I'm lost," she declared.

Her feet lifted off the ground. Two large hands cupped un-derneath her armpits and, like a child, Tokala lifted and pinned Nikki up against the wall.

Nikki's feet dangled, helpless. Her tail twitched an inch from the floor. Tokala's cold body warmed her up as her chest crushed her. From this angle, Nikki could see the wetness on her lips. They could've kissed, they were so close.

Her brain emptied to the floor like spilled marbles, the last of her coherent thoughts tumbling away. She hadn't pegged

Tokala as someone physically strong, just mentally, but her arms, they had no waver. Her gaze was intense.

"Focus," Tokala said, and Nikki snapped back to her eyes. God, they were so pink, pink as the morning sky. She was cross-eyed and it only added to her beauty.

"What is the one thing you want to know right now?" Tokala asked her.

Was that a trick question? What did Nikki want to know *now*? Where to start: Why was Tokala teasing her? Why did Nikki feel so weird when she was around her? Did it have something to do from Lí's timeline, or was she putting false hope into someone who only looked like Tai? If she was her past self's lover, what was Nikki doing wrong? She felt like she was fumbling her heart before a girl who had hers all put together. Did they get married now, or did they have to wait?

Tokala cocked a brow. "*Hello?*"

Nikki blinked. "Hi."

The bad-cop persona slipped, and Tokala smiled. "Fuck, you're cute. Okay, how about this: What information are you missing? This whole Deity thing, you're befuddled by it. Who seems to know more about this than anyone else? Who was the first person who got involved?"

Her? Kevin? Marcos was new to this, so she guessed...

"Zantl."

"They were the first," Tokala agreed. "They've been showing these signs of Deity junk since they were a baby. Now we gotta name to it, and they're cooped up somewhere down here."

"I'll...find Zantl, then," Nikki decided. "I'll ask them about what they know."

"That's a good girl." She set Nikki down. "Above, that took a while. You're so cute when you're jazzed up."

Nikki's mouth wouldn't work, so with a goal in mind, she took Tokala's hand and started their hunt for Zantl.

She tried wiping her free hand of sweat on her sweatpants. She didn't know if this nervousness was a result of yesterday, the last few months, or Tokala herself, but this wasn't her.

But as much as this wasn't her, this whole year had been a whirlwind that'd swept her off her feet without direction. She'd been in freefall for days. With Vanna's and her family's distance and the loss of her two older siblings, she'd taken to figuring everything out herself.

So it was nice that Tokala had come into her life. She'd shaken it up, fried it thoroughly from her brazen touches and declarations of attraction, but now Nikki had a goal, and she hadn't had one of those in many moons.

She just wished she knew how to thank her without using words. She didn't want a timid squeak to pop out and regret ever getting to know her.

She tried clearing her throat naturally. It sounded like she was coughing up a hairball. "Thanks for helping me think straight."

"Course. I hate seeing people freak out. I felt like I had no choice but to help. Plus, I do really think you're cute."

Nikki crumbled. "Stop it," she said, but *did* she want it to stop? She wanted to stop from stopping *herself*—her brain was protecting her.

"Do you want me to stop?" Tokala asked.

"No, I'm...embarrassed. You can't even see me."

"Just because I'm legally blind doesn't mean I'm sightless. I have a blurry idea of what you look like. Black hair, dark skin, small face, big eyes. You're a rat."

That wasn't making her feel any better about this. "We just met."

"How do you go about flirting with people you just met? From the sidelines? They won't know you like them until you tell them, and I don't like pussyfooting around. I know what I like, and I like you."

"*Like me.*" She said it like a joke because it was one. She wondered, for a second, if Tokala was teasing her to humiliate her.

"*Do* you like me?" Tokala asked.

Thinking about it too long would've gotten her the wrong answer, but Nikki didn't want to finalize something she was still working out. "I like being around you, I guess. I like the way you speak to me. But I'm not as forward as you are. I like being in the shadows. I appreciate the gestures, I do. I'm just..."

"Uncomfortable," Tokala filled in.

"Wobbly," Nikki rephrased, "but, to answer your question, kinda."

Tokala smirked. "I asked you multiple questions."

"And the answer is...kinda."

Despite the vagueness, Tokala grinned and brushed her arm. "That works for me. You're really easy to talk to, too, you know. I don't talk to just anybody. I'm very picky with my people, and you're one of the good ones."

"I don't try to do anything special. That's why I think you'd have better luck pitching for another girl."

"You're special enough for me."

Overwhelmed with the idea of being known, Nikki barreled ahead to keep from looking at her. She said she could only see things up close. Hopefully, she couldn't see Nikki's uncontainable smile reaching from ear to ear. *You're special enough for me.*

They investigated the more obvious hiding places first: the cafeteria, the bedroom halls, the bathrooms, the lounges. When those didn't yield any results, they took to hunting in tighter corners. You would've thought that the next leader of the world would've been easier to find, but they were elusive. No sightings, no rumors apart from ones that led to dead ends. Options dwindling, Nikki beelined for her aunt's office to see if she had any better leads.

She walked in on a laboratory setup. Around Morgan were lab trays and medical equipment alongside machines and wire cutters. She had Marcos sitting on her desk as she worked her pudgy fingers into an open compartment in the back of his brain. She studied his inner workings like a surgeon. Alexi watched patiently from Marcos' arms, nibbling on his fingers as she babbled in baby talk.

Nikki barred Tokala from entering, unsure of what she was stepping into. "Uh, what's going on?"

"Oh, good, you're awake," Morgan said. "Not burning down buildings with your mind powers, yeah? Close the door, please. Don't need any more of those guards poking their noses in."

Marcos jerked. "Hey, watch it!"

Morgan retracted her screwdriver. "Can you *please* stop squirming?"

"Can you *please* watch what you're doing? I have the sneaking suspicion that you have no idea what wires you're snipping back there."

"*Oh*, how I wish you were still tied to Nadia's programming. This backtalking is grating on my ears. And this would be easier on *everyone* if you didn't insist on holding that baby 24/7. My Drill is set to be finished any day now. I should be working on it instead of you."

"Oh, I'm *sorry*, was I supposed to feel secure leaving her unattended around power drills? I'll pass. She's not leaving my side."

"I *did* offer to hold her," Del said from across the room. She was toiling with a machine Morgan was connecting to Marcos' skull.

"Absolutely not."

"Uh, again, what's going on here?" Nikki asked.

Morgan went back to work inside Marcos' head. "I'm trying to find the chip the Líders implanted in him that gave them the ability to control his line of thinking. Since their deaths, it's been deactivated, and I want to see what tech they used to make it. As you can see, I've already disabled the very needed chip of polite hospitality."

"You're extracting the chip so I don't have it in my *brain* anymore," Marcos corrected. "That's what we agreed upon. You get to play with the tech, I get to be myself."

"Yes, yes, one in the same. Now stop moving."

Marcos grumbled but tried following instructions.

Nikki tried not looking inside his head's compartment. It felt like she'd walked in on him undressing. This whole vibe was off and she wanted out. "I won't take up much of your time, then. Marcos, do you know where Zantl is?"

"They were in the air-purifying station last time I saw them, though they might've run off by now. They've been trying to find a way out of this place since arriving."

"I'm not letting them leave," Morgan said as she worked. "Until I get this sorted, Zantl is not stepping foot outside this place. I still need to speak to them, once my guards find them."

"I'll help you look for them," Marcos offered, then grimaced—Morgan had hit another nerve, or whatever he had in his brain. "Once *this* is taken care of."

Nikki left them be and went to find the air-purifying station herself. She remembered walking by it on her ventures. Upper right-hand corner of the map, next to the water filtration and backup generators. Whoever had made this bunker made it abundantly clear that its inhabitants could live down here for years, perhaps generations, if maintenance had been upkept.

Guards were stationed around the filtration room's door, but they weren't protecting it so much as they were lounging near it. They were playing cards on the floor. They seemed without purpose now that their job titles had been buried. Nikki walked Tokala around them and opened the suspicious door.

"No!"

The noise came from down the hall. A few guards lifted their tired heads, but most kept to themselves, uncaring.

"That was Zantl's voice," Tokala said.

Three guards were down the hall, talking down to someone half their height. Despite their size, Zantl held themselves up like a true Líder. Or a teenager used to getting things done their way.

"Stop ignoring me!" they shouted. "I need to leave!"

"It's not safe," a guard said. "You can't return to the Asilo."

"Who'd want to return to that sty? I want to get out of here! It smells like fish."

"Morgan said—"

Zantl stomped their boots. "I don't care! Let me out! I'll blow this place apart, I swear I will!"

"They're lying," Tokala whispered, spying on them around the corner. "I've seen what they can do. If they could leave, they would've done it by now."

"They can't get a hold of Unathi," Nikki said, and remembered the last time she'd talked to Shào. Were all the Deities too far away to assist them? Were they being ignored?

When Zantl saw her, their ears flattened. They scanned the hall for a new escape route.

"I'm not going to hurt you," Nikki said. "I want to talk."

"Like I'll ever talk to you. I heard what you said to your parents. You let out *all* our baggage like it's nothing."

"I don't know what *baggage* we share."

"Can you not keep her in the dark about this stuff?" Tokala asked. "What good is it to keep her out?"

Zantl's upper lip curled in a growl. "Don't talk to your Líder like that."

Tokala snorted. She towered over the kid, yet their confidence was equally matched. Zantl took a step towards her, a fight bristling.

Someone behind them stumbled on their feet. Nikki didn't want to break the gaze she had on the skittish wolf, but when Zantl got the look of death in their eyes, she caved.

Kevin was standing at the hallway corner, holding Viper's hand. Viper, too afraid to look them in the eyes, hid behind Kevin's wing.

"I heard you from down the hall," he said. "We were going to the showers. Is everything alright?"

Zantl went to move, but Tokala, trained with excellent hearing, blocked them from escaping.

Nikki counted each head. Too many chefs in the kitchen. They'd get nowhere like this. "Tokala, can you take Viper to the showers? Or Viper, you take her. Whichever's easiest." She grabbed Zantl's sleeve. "Kev and I need to have a word with the new *Líder*."

Something about Kevin's presence earned Nikki some of Zantl's cooperation. With a simple ask, they followed Nikki and Kevin to the loft where Nikki had properly met Tokala. Zantl even sat down on the couch, tail tucked and arms crossed.

Kevin sat next to Nikki, and the two awkwardly waited for the other to speak. Zantl clicked their tongue in wait.

"We don't want to make this a bigger deal than it already is," Nikki said. "We just want to know more about these circumstances with the Deities."

"I'm not their messenger," Zantl said.

Nikki gave Kevin a look saying, *"How* aren't *we their messengers?"*

Giving the look back, Kevin asked Zantl, "First, how're you feeling? I can't imagine what you're going through."

They shrugged, indifferent to losing their home and parents at the same time.

"Do you feel uncomfortable talking to us?"

They fake-laughed. "Oh, yeah. The soulmates to Shào and Maïmoú corner me and ask if *I'm* comfortable. Don't act coy. You know what your Deities can do. One whimper will bring them out of hiding and murder everyone in a five-mile radius. You're ticking time bombs."

"But Shào hasn't spoken to me since the collapse," Nikki said.

"Same with me and Maïmoú."

"Even worse."

Nikki backtracked. "Which Deity are you connected to again?"

Zantl pouted deeper into the couch. For a second, she thought they were going to give them the silent treatment for the rest of this conversation. Then they mumbled, "Unathi."

"That's the life and death one, I think, the one in charge of the cycle," Kevin said. "That's what Maïmoú told me, anyway."

"And how many are there again?" Nikki asked. "Sorry, Shào never told me any of this, and Lí's memories are blurry."

Kevin listed them. "Shào, Maïmoú, *Unathi*," he said, motioning to Zantl, "then Tsvetan, he controls the Earth, I think Sabah controls water, and then..." He subconsciously picked at his fingers. Nikki took his hand to help him stop.

"You're making this more difficult than it actually is," Zantl grumbled. "Ataleah and Fate, animal and destiny. Those're the two you're missing. But you don't have to remember their names. They've been dormant for billions of years. Something about being too weak to stay visible, I don't know. Unathi doesn't talk about them, and I don't pry into people's business like *other* soulmates tend to do."

"Does Unathi talk about these things often with you?" Kevin asked.

"They've told me everything."

"I don't know about any of this," Nikki said. "So there're one, two, three...*seven* Deities in control of the world?"

"I guess," Zantl said.

"Can you please stop playing with us?"

"We just want to get to know you better," Kevin said. "We understand what you're going through. It's like we're part of a secret club."

"Oh, *God*." Zantl looked at a light fixture. "Unathi, *please* come out. I don't want to be the one to talk to them about this. It's weird."

Nikki eyed where Zantl was looking. Nothing flickered. Nothing happened.

Zantl sighed and unfolded themselves, kicking out their boots and huffing. "Fuck me."

"No one home?" Kevin asked.

"Fuck off. You can pretend you're some goody two-shoes with a heart of gold, but Deities influence us, and I know you're just like her. You go around helping people when you only fuck things up more for us. That's Maïmoú in a nutshell. And this *rat*, feeling inclined to put her nose into everyone's business yet offering nothing in terms of actual help. Shào to a Fucking T."

"Excuse me, I'm right here," Nikki said.

"I know. And I know both of you can be confrontational, childish, and evil if you're pushed to the edge, so I don't wanna be anywhere near you two. I'm impartial like Unathi. They taught me how not to give a shit."

Kevin went to disagree, then closed his mouth in a tough line. "I saw you with your Deity once," he said. "Can you tell us a little bit about them? I noticed you use they/them pronouns for them, same as you. What a lovely coincidence."

Zantl disregarded the similarity that probably meant more to them than they led on. "What's there to say? They keep the cycle going, like a placeholder to make sure nothing lives forever or nothing dies off unexpectedly. Not even *they* are immortal. One asteroid can kill them all."

"When did you meet them?"

"When I was a baby, they found me almost immediately, same with how Maïmoú found you and Derek. The orphanage I was at knew about Unathi's powers around me and brought it to the Líders' attention. Idiots thought *I* was a Deity and took me without question. They have this rudimentary understanding of what Deities actually are based on what they found in their fallout shelters. Had," they corrected, frowning. "I tried keeping them in the dark as everyone ought to be, but they kept digging, finding secret documents about the past."

"Why do the fallout shelters have so much info on the Deities?" Nikki asked.

"It was secret info buried deep enough to survive the tests of time. Why do you think these fallout shelters were built in the first place?"

Nikki recalled the way Shào and Maïmoú had fought in Lí's dream, how many buildings they toppled without care. "Because of them?"

"Duh. They're licking their wounds now, but if they find a way out of their cages, we're fucked."

"Is that why your parents kept me in the Asilo?" Kevin asked. "Because they knew I was a soulmate?"

"God, you're slow. Right when you said Maïmoú's name, they knew. They wanted to experiment on you rather than execute you, find out how you and I were alike. I told them not to. I told them to keep away from you, your sister, everyone."

"So you knew?" Nikki asked.

"Not until the First told me."

"The First?"

Zantl sighed again. "The first Deities? Everyone other than Shào and Maïmoú? Sabah, Tsvetan, Unathi, and Ataleah and Fate. They were the adults that took care of the world first. For billions of years, it was just them. But then Ataleah died and Fate disappeared, and then beingkind were born."

"Beingkind?"

"Us. Crossbreeds. And humans. You should know about them from your memories. Both of you were humans in your past lives."

"Did you have a past life?" Kevin asked.

"Uh, most people have several."

"Were you a human?"

"...No."

"Who were you?"

"Some kid named Salem. Worked for the government on some special operation with the Moon."

"Your past life worked with the *Moon*?" Nikki asked.

"Dunno. Unathi said it's bad to tap into your past lives. They said it makes you go crazy."

Nikki scratched her belly.

"What happened to the world after Shào and Maïmoú were introduced as Deities?" Kevin asked.

"They *fucked* it. The brats couldn't handle the responsibilities. They fought each other constantly. They couldn't resolve their problems with each other. Their Domains grew out of hand, and their baby minds couldn't catch up."

"Maïmoú said that she and Shào were friends once," Kevin said.

"Maybe for, like, a few centuries, but Maïmoú was a bastard and Shào was an asshole. Can you see them having a happy ending?"

"How do you know for sure?"

"Uh, because Unathi told me? They watched them grow up from the sidelines. Sabah and Tsvetan babied them more. Well, Tsvetan did, but he babies everyone, obviously."

"Obviously," Nikki said sarcastically.

"Okay," Kevin said, "but Maïmoú said that the Others didn't treat either of them very nicely. She said they were like a broken family."

"Well, if you lived with monsters for children, how would you handle them? You hit kids if they don't behave."

"No, you don't," Nikki said.

"Yeah, you do. Unathi and their friends did what they could, but Shào and Maïmoú were beasts cut from a different cloth."

Kevin readjusted his broken wing over the couch. "So what happened to break the world? Maïmoú said she was trapped here."

"Same with Shào, somewhere else," Nikki added. "The world used to look completely different in Lí's memories."

"Shào and Maïmoú got into a fight that almost extincted their Domains. To stop it, the First separated them from their Domains. Maïmoú and crossbreeds in Raeleen, Shào and humans on the other side of the world."

"Across the world?" Kevin asked.

"So, what, they were put in *timeout*?" Nikki asked.

"Act like kids, get treated like kids. The First had planned for us to evolve separated across the sea, but then you got born and they got awakened like farmers to a chicken's call. Maïmoú's now close to breaking the Barrier keeping all of us in. The First are trying to keep her subdued, but even at her weakest, she's still insanely overpowered."

"Maïmoú said the Muralha is breaking by itself," Kevin said. "She's been awake trying to keep it up."

"It wouldn't be falling if she hadn't tried breaking it."

"Well, she wants to get back to her humans."

"The ones she almost killed. The First know what they're doing. They—*most* of them—survived loads of mass extinctions."

Kevin fiddled with his scarred fingertips. "What's your relationship with Unathi?" he asked. "You seem to be rather close."

Zantl smirked, then held up their left hand. On their third finger was a beautiful ring of onyx.

Nikki counted which finger they wore it on, then gasped.

"We're lovers," Zantl said, "matched forever under the stars, destined to be together forever."

"Oh," Kevin said. "I...didn't expect that."

"Of course *you* wouldn't have. Your love for Maïmoú is familial, and Lí never loved Shào correctly."

"Shào was a child," Nikki said, "and Lí was already with someone."

"Whatever. It was still a selfish thing to do to your Deity. Unathi met me when I was a baby, but I knew we were always meant to be together like this."

Both Nikki and Kevin cast skeptical glances at each other.

"You were with them as a *child*?" Nikki clarified.

"Ew. No, not like *that*. We waited until I was an adult to... do stuff." Their ears flicked. "They wouldn't hurt me on purpose. They aren't weird like that."

But the whole thing felt too weird for Nikki to write off. If she had her facts straight, Zantl had only turned eighteen that year. If Unathi had been with them since they were a baby, feeding them these biases and waiting for them to turn of age...

"Above," Kevin said. "I'm so sorry."

"Uh, for what? That I have an insanely hot and powerful Deity in my head? That I have the sanest Deity on my side?"

Someone creaked the ladder steps. Marcos had come to join them. He repositioned baby Alexi in his hands, making sure her fin didn't clip his shirt. "That you were groomed," he concluded. "You were groomed by a God."

Zantl moved away from Marcos, then from Nikki and Kevin when they caught them staring. They sank deeper down. "What is this, some kind of intervention? Don't act like you suddenly get this. You don't get their world like I do."

"You shouldn't have gone through that with Unathi," Kevin told them. "All that pressure on your shoulders must've been tremendous to carry alone."

"If I'd known, I could've helped," Marcos said. "I was always right outside your door, and you never told me about this."

"I didn't *need* your help with anything. Unathi said it's not wise to interfere. Bringing people in—"

"I've known about this for weeks and I'm still having trouble," Kevin said.

"And I've been around it all my life," Marcos said.

Nikki realized what both boys were trying to do and added fuel to the fire. "It's terrifying to be alone in this. I wish we could've helped you."

"Stop it," Zantl said. "The First aren't the bad ones here. Unathi isn't a bad person."

"I get where you're coming from," Kevin said. "I've had this warped idea of Maïmoú from the start. I still want to defend her and love her. I can't help it. I understand the threads that bond you to your Deity."

"No, you don't!"

"But what they did to you was wrong," Nikki said.

"No!" Zantl got up. "Unathi warned me about this. They said not to get close to other soulmates, that you'll peer-pressure me with lies spun by Shào and Maïmoú to get what you want."

"What about me?" Marcos said. "My Deity is Sabah, Unathi's friend. What motives do I have in telling you that an adult sleeping with a child is wrong?"

"It's not!" Zantl tripped moving away from the couch, from them. "Unathi *loves* me. They've never done anything to hurt me. They were there for me, they taught me everything I know."

"And I wasn't?" Marcos asked. "I always tried to be there for you, but you shut me out. You shut your *parents* out."

"They *weren't* my parents! Unathi—" They faltered. "Unathi is my everything. They're my whole world, they wouldn't..."

They caught their reflection in the metal plating of a fan unit. Unable to look at themselves, they decided to run. They shoved Marcos aside, took to the ladder, and fled from the truth.

"Hey!" Nikki chased after them. She couldn't leave them alone like this. That way of thinking, the way they'd been bottle-fed one side of the story by their Deity, it wasn't right. They needed the whole story.

She ran hard. Zantl was pushing aside anyone who was in their way, stepping on toes and knocking over kids younger than them. Nikki zigzagged around them.

"Quit following me!" Zantl yelled.

"We want to help!" Nikki said, hearing Marcos and Kevin keeping up behind her.

"You don't get Divine love like I do," Zantl said. "I couldn't help it. Their love is too good not to reciprocate."

"You shouldn't have been forced to believe that," Nikki said. "You should've been allowed to think for yourself. You were a child."

Sound travelled in the fallout shelter. Between their back and forth, Nikki heard metal clangs, generators, hammers, radio static. The additional anarchists and waterborne also built on the thrumming. It wasn't quiet here.

When she turned the last corner, all of the noise disappeared, drowned out by a loud, dying scream that reverberated in Nikki's brain.

Then she was thrown off her feet.

An explosion detonated somewhere behind her. The whole of the hall shook. People dropped to their knees, covering their face. The walls didn't shake, they vibrated.

Nikki picked herself up, ears ringing. Smoke was filling the hall from the west where the Drill was, where her family was working.

She went for Kevin, but he was already up. He was mumbling something under his breath as he looked for Marcos, then their parents. Nikki, not wasting time, ran for the Drill. "Mom!" she shouted. "Dad!"

People were scrambling, yelling out questions and fleeing the scene. Their mother and father had fallen while Del was holding back Morgan. She was crying out painfully for the Drill before her.

It was on fire, flames reaching the roof and spreading. The engine was leaking flammable oil around its flattened tires and crushed bumper. Vanna worked between watching his mother weep and trying to break the glass to the emergency fire extinguisher.

Maïmoú, blond hair twirling through the smoke, her hands stained black, floated above it all. Specks of red flames danced across her dress like morbid confetti.

Morgan pried herself out of Del's arms only to fall into a workbench. All of her hard work, her plans to try and give them a better life...

"Maïmoú!" Kevin called out. "What're you doing!?"

She looked behind her. Her eyes were bleeding black. The darkness leaving her mouth muffled her words.

Kevin went for her, but Nikki kicked out his knees and got on top of him. Protecting him with her own body, she glared up at evil incarnate.

Maïmoú wiped her lips. "I can't...let you leave...this way." Her voice was so hoarse. It was like a corpse trying to speak. "I don't have time...for this."

"What?"

"There's no more...time to..."

Her broken, inaudible voice was failing her. To fix it, she punched herself in the stomach. It didn't work. She tried scratching at her throat, which also failed. In a final attempt to communicate, she puked up a gallon of blackness before glitching away, leaving them in a burning world.

38
Derek

As Derek got dressed without trying to wake up Oliver, he came to the stupid conclusion that Raeleen was shitty. The derelict and vacant buildings, the insufferable humidity, the Guard, the Líders. It wasn't a good place to live.

But it'd been his home. When he thought of home, he saw his apartment above the clothing store, the yellowed grass, the Sun setting over the Muralha on a roof he wasn't allowed on.

He saw Kevin. Nikki. Mom and Dad. Vanna and Morgan and Del, and their hidden fallout shelter. His love of alcohol and the insecurities that'd followed him across the ocean. Everything was coming to light like developing photographs, all of which had a blurry Raeleen in the background.

Now he was here, somewhere that definitely wasn't Raeleen, and he was freaked.

His wing hit the bedside, and Oliver inhaled loudly and rolled over in bed. He covered his hickeyed chest with one of the animal pelts to keep his modesty. "Is everything alright?"

Derek haphazardly put on one of Oliver's sweaters, not caring if it was two sizes too big. Where on Earth *was* he? How far had he fallen from the Muralha? Had he fallen down? Up? Was he on the other side?

He dry-heaved. His chest hurt. What'd happened to Nikki after he'd run away from the guards? He'd wanted to keep them away from his family. Had Kevin made it over, too? Had that girl thrown him off? She must've been Maïmoú.

"Derek, wait."

Derek ran down the stairs into the living room. Someone had done a pisspoor job of cleaning up—tinsel was scattered across the floor and plates of deer were left on the couches. Shimah and Yomi had divided up breakfast duties of washing dishes and reheating leftovers in the kitchen. Brennen bottle-fed baby Noemi with an ice pack between his horns. Rosaline battled her hangover with lemon tea.

Holly was underneath the kitchen table, rocking. Her eyes had gone to slits again.

Holly was a serval. He hadn't recognized her breed, but everything from her hair to her ears screamed serval, a wildcat breed found in Raeleen.

Derek's stomach growled. His dad always cooked for them on his days off. He made the best bacon. Sliced fruits for Nikki and frosted pastries for Kevin. Whenever Derek woke up late, he'd get the scraps, but his dad would save him the fattiest bacon slices and the most frosted pastries.

They didn't eat deer in Raeleen, or fish. He hadn't known the latter existed until coming here.

Yomi went to greet Derek, but she found him jogging in place in the hallway, shaking out his hands like he had something sticky on them.

"Yes?" she asked.

"I just got my memories back and I don't know what to do and I'm really, *really* freaking out right now."

Yomi calmly put a warm drink in his hand. He couldn't keep it from spilling.

"What'd you say?" Rosaline slurred. "Speak slowly. I can't—"

"I got my memories back," he interrupted. "I remember everything."

"How?" Shimah asked. "Did they just pop up?"

"I don't know. I had a dream I was falling and then I was saved. I must've landed here by mistake, or was it on purpose?"

"Okay," Yomi said. "Sit down. You're alright."

"I'm not."

Oliver floated down the staircase. He'd gotten dressed, but his hair was still sticking up from their night together. "Is something the matter?"

Too afraid to be alone, Derek flew over and hugged his man.

"Oh." Oliver tried looking down at him, but Derek buried deeper into his chest, not ready to come out.

"Derek got back his memories," Yomi explained.

"Oh, dear." He walked himself and Derek over to the couches, pushing aside plates to make room. He rubbed his back in gentle circles. "Are you okay?"

"I don't know. I'm seeing everything at once."

"Would writing things down help? Holly, can you bring over your notebook?"

Holly didn't move from the kitchen.

"I came from a place called Raeleen," Derek said. "It's like here but hotter. I think I'm in trouble. I'm not supposed to be here and they wanna kill me for it."

"Who?"

"Deities?" he guessed.

Yomi motioned for her mate. He was already uncorking a vial.

"I don't need it," Derek lied. He really wanted it down his throat bad, but, "I'm afraid I'll lose everything the second I calm down. I don't wanna forget again."

"Like a dream ya woke up from," Shimah said. "Ya wanna write it out 'fore ya forget."

But how could he really forget Raeleen, the weather, his siblings, the school from which he narrowly graduated, and the architecture. Fuck, not even ten minutes have gone by and he was afraid of forgetting about *architecture*.

"It's too early for shouting," said a sleepy voice from the stairs. Plodding out of bed came Maxwell, shirtless and hair wet from a morning bath. Next came Jabel, still dressed for bed with crust in his eyes. They held hands as they helped one another down the stairs. "What's going on?"

"Derek got his memories back," Yomi said.

"All of them?" Jabel asked. "Do you remember the Heavens?"

"Not...really." Drinking down Yomi's offered cup, Derek tried explaining everything that was flashing through his mind. He told them about the Guard, the Líders, the Muralha and Barreira and how they resembled the Barrier. He went down the list of his family members and outlined each of their breeds, then described Morgan's secret operation in detail. He didn't care if they knew. The fuck did it matter? The more he divulged, the more he remembered, like he was down a dark path lit only by the occasional firefly.

When he was only halfway through the story—where was half of the story?—Shimah raised his hand.

"Shimah, not now," Rosaline said.

"I gotta question," he said.

"Go ahead," Yomi said.

"Okay, uh, what the *fuck* are ya talking about?"

The question birthed a series of others from the crowd.

"*Where* is this place?"

"What do you mean when you say they're like humans?"

"So is Holly a crossbreed?"

"How tall was the wall?"

"How did you survive?"

"How many Gods are there?" Oliver asked. He'd started holding Derek's hand and hadn't let go. His grip was cutting off blood circulation.

"I don't know. Four? Six? I've only met a few."

"It sounds like you're makin' it up," Shimah said. "*Are* ya makin' it up?"

"Shimah, be kind," Rosaline said. "Why would he be lying?"

"I'm not lying. I just don't know all the details. It doesn't make sense." This was the last thing he needed, to be told that all of this was a hangover dream. He tried to finger his necklace to calm down but found it missing. It must've fallen off in the sea.

"This must be why you had such a challenging time fitting into our ways," Brennen said. "To think they don't have marriage there..."

"It's incredible," Yomi said.

"And same-sex couples," Jabel added. "You had two aunts who were married to each other and nobody cared? They weren't even married, you don't have a word for that. They're able to live together—a-a bird and a monkey, you said—" He held his head. Maxwell rubbed his back in support.

"You said someone pushed you off the wall that surrounds your world?" Oliver asked. "They were...another God?"

"Was it the Shào boy you keep mentioning?" Yomi asked.

"I think it was Maïmoú," Derek said, and as he said that, he got seriously pissed at how little he understood about either world. Everything seemed to be smushed together by a child's impatient hands.

"This doesn't make any sense," Jabel said.

"Which part?" Brennen asked.

"All of it. You mean to tell me that there's this entire underground dungeon that not even my father knows about? I've been at his side for years. Nothing about an underground—what did you call it—fallout shelter, was ever brought up to me."

"That's not all," Derek said, and went for his discarded jacket hanging up near the door. "When Holly and I got trapped down there, we found photos from her past. I grabbed a few before Sabah and Tsvetan dropped me."

"What are photos?" Oliver asked.

"Like paintings from the past. They're taken on cameras. We had them in Raeleen."

He peeled back every jacket pocket, then checked his pants to make sure he wasn't going crazy. "I *did* bring them, didn't I?"

"Can we possibly go back and search the area?" Jabel asked.

"If they were paintings, they might be at the bottom of the ocean," Brennen said. "We should start looking now."

"Uh, no, we can't," Maxwell said. "Jabel and Cellena are still here. We need to get them home before their cover gets blown. It's almost eleven."

"But we should continue talking about this, love," Jabel insisted. "If this's true, my father needs to know posthaste."

Derek tried the insides of his boots, patted down his ass. "No, *no*. I just had them."

"What were the paintings of?" Oliver pressed.

"They aren't actually paintings, they're more like pages...from a notebook..."

Derek's head turned to Holly. How often did she blend in with the background? Without giving out much input, she was easy to lose in an empty room.

She walked into the living room with timid steps. In her hands was her notebook. She'd added to it since Derek had last seen it. It was now bloated with extra pages tucked in safely to preserve lost memories.

She handed the notebook to Oliver without a word, and the book sprung open with secrets. The first page was that drawing Derek had found, which Oliver acknowledged but put off to the side, knowing it wasn't as important as the rest.

The photograph of him and Holly holding her baby, them smiling in the past, hooked him like a fish. It had water damage, but Holly had dried it well, preserving it.

Oliver covered his mouth as he examined it in detail. Jabel and Maxwell came over to see, as did the rest of demons, too curious about technology none of them had seen before.

Oliver wiped his eyes and placed the photograph on the table. He held both wrists to keep from falling apart mentally, emotionally. Brennen offered him a vial. He didn't take it.

"H-Holly," he stuttered, "what is this?"

She bit the head of her dolly as a coping mechanism.

Oliver got up. "Holly, what *is* this? When was this painted?"

"We found it in the fallout shelter," Derek explained. "She said she used to live there...with you."

"But I don't remember living underground. All my memories start in Drail. I've lived in houses and shacks, never..." He looked back at the photo. "What am I *wearing*?"

"You look so..." Shimah said but didn't finish.

"Futuristic," Maxwell ended.

"Is this the Underground?" Oliver asked. "Is this where all demonkind comes from?"

"I don't think so," Derek said. "I learned in church that the Underground is supposed to be a thousand miles underground. There was light coming through the walls when Holly and I went down, though I think that's because the walls were old. It was deep, but not that deep."

Oliver looked ready to throw up. His white skin had gone green as he shivered in mental sickness.

"Do you remember anything?" Derek asked. "Holly got some memories back when she went down. The place was called the Second...fuck, I don't remember. The Second Church? The Second, Second—"

"The Second Beings' Congregation." Oliver, shocked at his own guess, covered his mouth again. "How?" he asked himself. "I've never been there."

"You're remembering." Derek massaged his lower back. "You're okay."

Oliver finally acknowledged the others in the room and held Derek back. He was seconds away from crumbling and Derek had to keep him together.

"What if these Deities erased *all* our memories?" Yomi asked. "We linked our lost memories to the natural passage of time, the way a person can't recall infancy, but this theory makes sense."

"*I* haven't seen this place 'fore," Shimah said.

"Nor have I," Brennen said.

"Maybe only Holly and Oliver came from there?"

"Then where did *we* come from?" Maxwell asked.

"Maybe another one?"

"It might be the Underground," Jabel said. "Does our God know about this?"

"I don't think your religion is connected," Derek said. "The Deity who saved me from the Muralha was missing a leg. Sabah had this nasty cough before she drowned us."

"Why did one try to kill you if one wanted to save you?" Rosaline asked.

"Fuck if I know. They're weirdos working on their own agendas. They got distracted by something across the ocean and disappeared. They disappear like you, by the way, like with the dark matter."

"They saw something across the ocean?" Yomi asked. "Based on what you told us, can we assume they were looking towards the country you come from? Perhaps you didn't come from the sky. Perhaps there's land across the ocean?"

"Don't be nutty," Shimah said.

"It's not nutty enough to disregard, lad," Rosaline said. "I really want to know what a radio is. Sounds cool."

"So there's *more* than one God in this," Jabel clarified, "and some are *children*? Isn't that dangerous?"

"It's unfair," Yomi said, "for a child to have that much power."

"Unfair."

Derek looked up. Had Cellena woken up? That voice...

"It's unfair."

The front door cracked open, letting in a chilling air.

Derek shivered, but not from the wind. His brain felt like it was oozing out the back of his skull. The lightheadedness returned. He slipped down on the couch.

Jabel jerked forwards. His hand went straight into his eye socket as he doubled over to suppress a scream. In pain, he fell into Maxwell.

"Shit—" Maxwell held his own heart, feeling half of the pain Jabel was enduring. Grimacing, he got up and gave his prince room to lie down. "Fuck, fuck, fuck."

"Another attack?" Brennen jumped to his feet with his baby.

"It's never been so strong before," Yomi said. "Brennen—"

A rumbling came from upstairs. It was Kumo in her wheelchair. "Everyone!" she shouted from the banisters. "Everyone, come upstairs, please!"

Maxwell and Brennen stayed with Jabel. The rest of them ran, flew, and teleported upstairs. Kumo rolled out of Rosaline's room, which Derek only knew from how everything smelled like her. Cellena was in her bed, gripping the sheets like she was being tortured. A sweat had started on her forehead. Her screams were too painful to hear.

"Something's happening," Kumo said. "She started banging her head on the headboard. I heard it from my room."

Yomi steadied her to keep her from hurting herself.

485

Derek felt it himself, the way his stomach twisted and turned. Something was off about not only himself but the air around them. Something was coming.

Yomi fumbled with a vial from her pocket, but Cellena flung out her hand in a spasm and cracked it to the floor. "We need to get her to a doctor."

"We can't," Oliver said. "They're going to think it's us again. They're going to kill us."

"Where..."

Derek stopped searching for the invisible girl calling out his name. Invisible, *dying* girl. She sounded straight-up deceased, groggily like a monster impersonating a kid. Behind him? Above? She was now speaking into his ear.

"I'll take her." Rosaline carefully scooped Cellena up. Her back was arched like a parasite was trying to tear out of her body.

"L-let me carry her," Oliver offered. "I can help."

"You should go with her," Yomi said. "Brennen and Maxwell will bring His Highness. If they show up alone, they won't be able to defend themselves if knights come. Brennen and I will start making vials."

Holly. Derek needed to go back and find Holly. Was she feeling the same way? Was someone else talking to her? Where was she?

"Hello?"

"Take Derek with you," Yomi said. "It'll only be as a safety precaution in case the humans do decide to come here after their attack."

Off, off, something needed to be fixed. He felt it underneath his nails, in the depths of his ears.

"Derek?"

Unexpected tears dropped from Derek's eyes. Loss, the sense of forgetting someone important, it dragged him down into the farthest pits of the Earth. He was losing her. He needed to go find this girl, this child, *his* child.

Tired footsteps trudged down the hall. A shadow emerged from the right, coming in closer.

A black, bleeding hand clung to the side of the door frame. Pulling himself up, Shào, snarling, glared into the bedroom for Derek. "Why the *fuck*," he asked, "is Maïmoú *so* dead-set on fucking over this world?"

Derek stumbled back. Shào was bleeding black from his mouth as darkness twinkled from his eyes. He held one of his arms as he limped inside.

"She's killing me," he continued. "Did you know? All Deities are connected telepathically. The transference...when they're in pain..." He glitched five feet left, then five right. He vomited up darkness. "We all suffer together."

Derek hit Oliver harder. "Go," he ordered. "Take all of us. Right now."

"What—"

"Go!" he ordered, and Oliver, like a trained dog, teleported Derek away before he got killed or worse.

He got swept up in darkness, momentary and empty, then fell to pristine tiles. Oliver had brought him back into the royal castle, what looked to be the main foyer that led out to the front yard. Maxwell and Brennen were already there with Jabel, along with Holly, and one by one came the rest, dropping down in clouds of darkness.

There were maids and servants in the foyer, but nobody bided demonkind any mind. They, too, had collapsed and were writhing in pain, fighting off the connection they shared. Maids had fallen down the stairs, knights into the curtains, clutching them to stay upright.

Derek turned in circles. He needed to save them, but Jabel, Cellena. And Holly. He needed to protect her from Shào.

"Excuse me!"

Shào appeared seconds later in a pool of dark matter. Both Derek and Holly jumped while the others, unbeknownst to them, worked on the royal heirs.

"I was *talking* to you," Shào said. "How impertinent. What happened to the days peasants bowed to Divinity? You used to fight wars to be acknowledged by us. I used to be *strong*. I used to be *feared*." He pulled a face, then puked again. "*Stop it!*" he yelled to the ceiling. There were either tears in his eyes or that sparkling sludge was beginning to trickle into his eye sockets. "Sabah. Tsvetan, Unathi, Ataleah, Fate, *anyone*! For the love of All, stop her. I know you're feeling this, too, this—"

He looked to Derek and Holly. "Curse this connection we share. If we survive whatever Maïmoú is plotting, I pray you find every way to cut the threads that bind us. This bond, it's too harrowing."

Holly grabbed Derek and ran him outside.

"Holly?"

"Holly!" cried out Oliver.

She pushed open the door leading out of the castle. The wind was clattering against the window shutters. Something cracked, like a tree or some part of the castle. The demons looked up to watch dirt and debris vortex in the sky.

A broken piece of wood spun out and cracked feet from Derek's head. The wind was picking up in a violent fury. Wispy clouds were crossing the sky too fast. They covered up the dawning Sun in patchwork.

He doubletook the sky. Through the snowy clouds was a streak. It was like an eye floater that drifted in your vision, invisible if not directly looking at it. But this wasn't a blob of cells in his eyes. This crack in the sky had to be seventy or eighty miles long, cutting across the clouds in a curved line. More cracks built from the main one, then more and more, a lightning bolt frozen in time.

"What is that?" he asked the Gods.

The crack shifted in slow motion. Giant pieces of glass the size of valleys separated and came falling down. Derek didn't think they were moving at all, but as he watched, he realized the pieces were growing in size, coming down at speeds his brain couldn't fathom.

He dropped to his knees, wings splayed out, and watched the sky break into pieces.

Shào teleported back between them and the sky. He looked up, keeled over as he held his splitting stomach. "Who's doing this?" he muttered to himself. "Who's powerful enough to break a Barrier?"

"Shào," Derek warned, but Shào knew. He, too, was watching the end.

But then Shào looked to his left, then right, a child lost in a snowstorm.

Then he sighed and, as if caught for his crimes, lifted both arms above his head. His long sleeves danced in the wind. "Whichever Deity thought it a good idea to break this damned Barrier, allow me to tell you this—"

The ground cratered beneath him. A pressure too immeasurable weighed down on his hands. He grunted, struggling to hold up nothing other than the sky itself.

"You shan't...be killing me...so easily...*this time!*" he screamed, and upheaved the invisible weight.

The wind knocked Derek forwards, face-planting him into the snow. When he got back up, he saw the pieces of glass turn to the west. The larger pieces moved in slow motion, pieces that shouldn't have been able to move through the power of one small boy. They hardly turned, but it was enough to send them off course and away from the last human settlement on Earth.

Derek watched in baffled awe, the power of a God. The Barrier shards glittered like shooting stars as they crossed the morning sky, landing in the ocean and valleys and away from civilization. Shào had saved them.

Shào took in the aftermath of his accomplishment, like he himself hadn't realized his own strength. He wobbled forwards as he watched his work fall.

He collapsed, arms useless at his sides. The darkness dribbled out of his mouth as he cracked a smile. "Place a sportive bet with me, fledgling, for I don't believe we have much time left in this world." He pointed a weak hand to the dazzling sky. "This time around, how badly will Maïmoú of Athens scar the Earth?"

39
Nikki

"Everyone, out!" Nikki yelled. "Now!"

Nobody needed to hear it from her. The amount of fire in the fallout shelter was enough to get people trampling. Once the smoke hit the ceiling sensors, red lights started flashing. People who hadn't run from the initial explosion were booking it now, preserving their livelihood in a place that should've protected them. The sprinkler system had come on, but it hadn't been worked on in generations. The water stained the floor like ink from Maïmoú's mouth.

Nikki, heart still racing from seeing that devil so close to her family, began counting heads. Nobody had been taken. Nobody had died.

Vanna came over with a fire extinguisher. He fumbled with the hose and tank. His eyes were drenched in tears and sweat and something else Nikki didn't know. His bony hands couldn't stop shaking against the pin.

"Here." Nikki offered to help.

"Let me," said a voice. Marcos had come up with Zantl, who was watching the smoke fill up the space in dread. "I know how to use an extinguisher. Nicole, hold Alexi."

"Uh, what?" she asked, but Marcos was already giving the baby to her. It smelled so weird. It weighed so much. She held it at arm's length, unsure of what to do with it, as Marcos worked the extinguisher over the flames.

"Fuck this," Zantl said. "If Unathi isn't coming, I'm leaving. I'm not dying in one of these places. Marcos, come."

Marcos did not. After using up the fire extinguisher, he firmly planted himself between Nikki and Kevin, choosing his side without words.

Zantl's ear flicked. "Marcos, I said come."

"No," he said. "I'm staying with the people who value being around me. If you see me as nothing more than a tool to help you escape life, then go."

"What?"

"You are free of me," he said simply. "You are no longer forced to be around me."

"What the fuck does that mean?" Zantl asked. "Did you not hear me back then? I said I didn't want you *involved* in this. *None* of you should be digging into this. Why do you think I kept closing the door on you? Did you ever think that maybe, I might've been trying to *protect* you?"

"Protect me?"

"Yes! God, you're all so daft. Look, have you ever wondered why you've never heard from Sabah up until now? She wanted nothing to do with you *specifically* because she didn't want to get involved in your life. You should be grateful to me for keeping you out!"

They sniffled back emotion Nikki had yet to see in them. "I was trying to protect you," they said, and ran off to find their own way.

Marcos watched them go, letting his master's words repeat in his mind.

But they didn't have time to reminisce over lost connections. "We need to evacuate," Nikki said. The flames were doubling, tripling. It was burning the side of her face. "It's gone on for too long. We need to leave."

"But my moms—"

"We can handle it." Del came over, struggling to pry Morgan's attention away from the burning Drill. "You kids need to get out now."

"But we can help," Nikki pressed.

Their mother came over, covering her face with her wings. Their father was tying a bandana around his mouth to keep from suffocating.

"You need to get out of this," their mother said.

"We shouldn't have gotten you kids involved," Del continued. "It was too dangerous. I'm sorry. We're sorry."

"I'm sorry, too," Kevin said. "I should've told you everything about what happened at the Muralha."

"Kev, you were traumatized, and you're just a kid."

"I'm twenty."

Their mother kissed him and Nikki on their foreheads. "Out."

"Are you sure you're good?" Nikki asked them but mostly Morgan. Years of work only to be blown up in her face by an invisible being.

Morgan bit her trembling lower lip. "I've lost one child tonight, I'm not losing another. Vanna, go. We'll deal with this."

Vanna gave each of his mothers a hug before running Nikki and their group towards the escape exit.

Hundreds of bodies were trying to climb up one metal ladder. Nikki stepped back immediately, as she didn't want her presence to get her special privilege up the ladder. There were too many children down here.

"I can make a path for you," Marcos said.

"No path-making. Everyone deserves a way out."

"Every life is precious. However, given our circumstances—"

Before Marcos could finish, Nikki gave him back his baby and ran them elsewhere. "Vanna, can we use the doors that lead to the river?"

"What about Viper and Tokala?" Kevin asked.

Nikki's brain and heart battled her on what she needed to do. She needed her family to survive. She couldn't live with herself if her desires sent them to their graves. But the same applied to Tokala now. It was a different part in her brain, but they both held the same amount of value to her.

Giving in, she ran down the hall that held the special bathrooms. Only a few waterborne were left abandoned in the water—elderly and those unaware that anything was going on. Nikki pulled up her pantlegs to help each of them out while searching for that head of white curls.

"Maybe they're already outside," Kevin said, picking his fingers to death.

"Or maybe they're trapped," Vanna said. "Maybe Pippa got out, but not the blind girl."

"Vanna, hush." Nikki helped the last of the waterborne out of the shallow end. "We'll keep looking."

"We really need to leave," Marcos reminded them. "I don't need to breathe and can withstand temperatures up to 125 degrees, but you—"

"Then lead the way," Nikki said. It was getting harder to see through the smoke. "Hurry."

Slowing down to make sure he didn't outrun them, Marcos found the closest other exit outside, the circular door Nikki and Vanna had used to play hooky. With the strength of four, he easily pushed open the cement door, baby in hand.

They, excluding Marcos, gasped for fresh air only to intake more smoke. The Asilo a few streets down was still on fire. Heavy soot had colored the stormy sky even darker. A distant siren blared out a nameless emergency, pitch haunting.

People both in and out of Morgan's coup were out on the streets. The waterborne who'd made it out of the fallout shelter were hiding in empty canals, touching the stained walls and wondering where their water had gone. Those without gills were wandering, pointing up to the sky and cowering. Some were looting. Most were lost. Without leadership, the world was left to govern itself. It'd be wiped off the maps in days.

"What's going on?" Nikki asked. She saw some adults pointing to the north, but nothing was up there other than the Muralha.

Kevin scanned the crowds. "I need to find Viper. She couldn't have gone far, not with Tokala. She probably went up the ladder and is now in the coffeehouse."

"We should stick together," Nikki said. "I'm not losing you again."

"You're not going to lose me, but I'm not losing her. I... I think I love her."

Marcos gave him a weird look. "That's a strong word for someone you just met."

"Love can happen instantly," Vanna reminded him. "You wouldn't know it if it fell into your lap."

"Actually—"

"Enough," Nikki said. "Kev, get up this embankment. Marcos, help him. We'll help find everyone's lover before this's over."

"Oh, *everyone's?*" Vanna asked.

"Shove it," she said, and smacked his butt to get him up the hill quicker. "Kev, come on."

Kevin was staring down at the yellow grass, body rigid. He watched a bee flutter from a wilted flower.

"Kev?"

The bee's buzzing grew louder in her ears. She tried popping them to make it go away, but it grew louder. Her hair stood on end. She couldn't think.

She looked up, as did Kevin, as did Marcos and his child. The little one cried at something she did not understand.

"Nicole!"

Nikki looked directly into the cloudy Sun. "Shào?"

"Hey, what's going on down there?" Vanna asked.

"I don't know, but we need to—"

Nikki's hand slipped forwards, and she crashed her shoulder into the soggy soil. Her vision doubled. Her brain split in two. A rumbling shook her core and she did her best to keep from throwing up. It threw Kevin and Vanna to their hands and knees, it freaked out the baby in Marcos' arms. Marcos watched, staying upright but developing a twitch in his head like he was malfunctioning.

"Nicole, what is Maïmoú doing?"

Nikki turned to Kevin. "Kev, what's happening?"

"I...don't know," he struggled to say. "She's speaking to me, but it's sounds like she's dying."

The sky crackled with newborn thunder. Bright, static electricity zapped through the sky in unnatural natural zigzags. They created X marks and slashed through the smoke to reveal pockets of darkened sky.

Nikki headbutted the embankment and kept climbing. "Come on," she urged, to herself, her friends, the Deities above, and everyone on Earth. "Keep it together."

They halfway jogged, halfway struggled down the streets back towards Morgan's coffeehouse. Nikki's eyes kept catching on every person they passed. The public was suffering the same internal pain they were. Those with stronger fortitudes and builds were doubled over with stomach pains. The rest had collapsed, giving in to unknown powers.

Outside the coffeehouse were revolutionists looking for guidance between the pangs. Waterborne were on the ground, shaking. She saw fish and sharks and snakes, but no spiky tail, no beautiful, pink, optimistic eyes telling her everything would be alright.

Nikki covered her mouth with her hoodie as she watched the sky turn black. What a terrible first impression of the world: a dark, humid city on fire.

"Kevin?"

Both Nikki and Kevin turned, Kevin's wings unfurling, Nikki's hurting heart racing. Running up to them, hands out for balance and safety, was Tokala. She had a bruise on her cheek as people carelessly pushed her to find their own footings on land.

"Hey!" She got to her before anyone else tried putting their hands on her. She cupped her swollen cheek. "You good?"

"Oh, thank fuck," Tokala wheezed. "Finally. Where the fuck am I? Something's up with my body and I lost Viper in the crowds. I was pushed up a ladder and then someone took my hand and led me out here. Why does the air taste weird?"

"You're outside. The sky's on fire and it's about to rain. We need to get you out of here. Can we bring her upstairs to your room, Vanna?"

"I need to find Viper," Kevin said, and called out her name. When nobody answered, he tried flapping his wings to see up ahead. He cried and fell into Marcos.

"Are we fucked?" Tokala asked. "Like, actually, are we fucked? Is the world ending?"

"The world's not ending, and we're not...We're going to make it."

"I'm calculating a very low probability of that occurring," Marcos said, helping Kevin to his feet.

"Marcos, not helping."

"Calculate a brighter future," Vanna said. "One where the world doesn't catch fire."

Marcos looked up to the sky as if actually calculating such improbable odds. Nikki wondered if his programming could predict scenarios like that, and if he was optimistic enough to follow through with the code.

A crack of thunder split like a gunshot in Nikki's ears. It knocked her into Tokala, Tokala off her feet. It physically parted the clouds, revealing a clear view of the Muralha.

Large, angular chunks of the Muralha were gone, letting in tiny streams of yellow light like crooked window blinds. She counted ten, twenty, a dozen more cracks to the north. She watched Muralha pieces the size of houses come crumbling down the wall and booming into the forests below.

"Above, Vanna cursed.

"What?" Tokala asked. "What's going on?"

"Do you want those odds now?" Marcos asked, and Nikki almost strangled him if he was able to breathe.

Someone knocked into Nikki, pushing her into Tokala's chest again. They grabbed her shoulders and shook them.

"What the *fuck* are your Deities doing!?" Zantl screamed. "Tell them to stop! They're gonna kill us all!"

"You're back," Nikki said.

Zantl stomped hard on Nikki's foot. "Shut *up*! What're Shào and Maïmoú planning? If they think breaking Barriers is going to help anyone, they might as well start marking our graves early!"

"Are they the ones doing this?"

"Of *course*! Who else has the ability to do this?"

"I don't want to die," Vanna blubbered, and Nikki went to tell him that nobody was going to die with her around. She had a duty to be there for people, that was her purpose in life. In every life she'd become reincarnated in, that's what drove her soul into taking action, into living.

She surveyed what was before her. Marcos was staring intently at Zantl like they had a book on their face. Kevin, muttering to a God and Vanna rubbing down his wrists, Tokala, sniffing the air for a sign of normalcy...

And another. Someone so out of place had broken into their small group.

"Excuse me, rat, are you listening to me?" Zantl asked, unaware of the person standing behind them.

Nikki strained her neck to take them in. They were a tall, breedless, genderless being with long, dark hair like Zantl but shaved on one side, standing, *towering* behind them. Their natural beauty and fashion sense actually caught Nikki off guard, changing the composition in her heart. It was like seeing a model poised for the runway, complete with perfect jewelry and makeup.

Then the person looked at her with their bright yellow eyes, and the organs in Nikki's stomach dropped. Slight apprehension with this one. The energy was off, unsettling.

Noticing Nikki's reaction, Zantl turned to meet their God.

And took a step back. This was the unmistakable Unathi, so divine and strong in purpose, the God of life and death who was in love with Zantl. Flecks of memories came back to Nikki from Lí's time. He knew Unathi and was trying to forget.

Zantl talked with them. "Talked," but they only used their hands. They flipped and rolled their wrists and pointed at specific places on their body. Raeleen didn't have a word for this way of speech, but Lí had, in his time. Sign language, for those who couldn't hear, or speak, in Unathi's case.

Unathi took Zantl's tiny hands in theirs. They set them down, leaned forwards, and kissed their forehead, to which Zantl partly accepted with hesitantly parted lips.

They tried stepping back. "No," they said. "No, I don't want to."

But you couldn't say no to a God. Taking Zantl in their arms, Unathi kidnapped the little heir without another motioned word.

"Did...they just disappear?" Vanna asked. "They were right there, yeah? Was that a Deity? Was a Deity here?"

A new person popped up beside them. She was an older woman with thin dreads tied up in a messy bun. She looked strong, dressed like a general of all Gods.

Marcos cradled his child away from her. "Sabah?"

Sabah said nothing to him. With a complicated look, she yanked him by the shoulder and disappeared him away.

The child fell. Nikki, taken by surprise by these unceremonious abductions, dove for her too late. She wouldn't make it, Vanna was too far away...

Two arms wrapped around the baby girl. The man appeared from nowhere just like the Others had. He was another older Deity with a frail physique and missing leg. Some earthly, moss-like substance grew over his skinny body, but he was spry enough to catch the little girl in time.

Tsvetan cradled the baby to his chest. The poor girl was sobbing uncontrollably and reached up for his comfort. He smiled affectionately at her, wiped away her tears with a kiss, and stole her away.

Nikki's feet felt like they were slipping from Earth. All three of them, gone, just like that. She hadn't seen this happen from a watcher's perspective. She wasn't prepared for any more losses of life.

"What...just happened?" Vanna asked.

"I...don't know," Nikki said, "but we need to...we need to find shelter, yeah? We need to hide. Kev, is Maïmoú talking to you?"

She waited for his answer. Shào had gone radio silent, but Maïmoú might've had a clearer station with him.

Kevin, too, had vanished, leaving Nikki alone once again.

40

Kevin

"Kevin, listen to—"
"Run!"
"We—"
"Come on, go!"
"Now!"
"Now!"

Maïmoú's voice was making him delirious. It was unending, the warnings layering in his brain. He'd been trying to focus on Nikki's instructions on escaping the fallout shelter, keeping away from any puddles, searching for Viper, *and* getting a word in-between Maïmoú's hysterics, not to mention not passing out from continuously bumping his broken wing and inhaling toxic smoke.

Her voice was breaking like it had done on the Muralha. It was like she was drowning. Knowing he couldn't save her made him feel even worse. As a friend, a father, someone watching a stranger's house burn from the sidewalk.

"Come...to the Muralha," she ordered. *"It's the only way."*

"Why?" he thought. *"What's going on?"*

"The Muralha...the Muralha..."

He couldn't break it to her that that was impossible with a broken wing. He could start running the other way, away from his sister and friends, but he heard it, that sound indiscernible from thunder: the Muralha, cracking to pieces. He knew it from when he'd lost Derek over the ledge. If he *were* to magic himself up there, would he be safe?

"*Yes!*" Maïmoú screamed at him. "*I won't let you die here. I'm trying…I can't…*"

She was holding up the Muralha again, he guessed, but the pressure was finally taking its toll. After hundreds of years, she was finally giving up.

"*I'm not giving up!*" she yelled. "*I'm Maïmoú of Athens. I don't know what giving up means.*"

"Maïmoú—"

"*Stop it,*" she interrupted. "*You're distracting me. Come to the Muralha already. Now.*"

They were outside the coffeehouse. Nikki was urgently talking to the group as Vanna held back tears. Marcos was bouncing his baby to distract himself. Zantl was holding their head, overthinking something. Kevin wondered if they were speaking to their own Deities and if they were having the same freakout as he was.

He searched the street for Viper, trying to fly and remembering he couldn't due to the pain. It was a slap to the face. She was probably scared and alone, petrified of this new world in which she'd found herself. He shouldn't have let her go.

His feet left the Earth. He was hovering without the water, floating without the use of his wings. Only a few inches was all it took before a force lifted him away from Nikki.

He tried calling out for her. They all had their backs to him, as he'd lagged behind during the run. If any of them could've helped, it would've been her.

But he had no control over his voice. Maïmoú had taken it all away, and he'd become her puppet on tight strings.

"*Come…here!*"

Her invisible grip threw him on his heels and skipped him through puddles. He passed through the crowds of families and waterborne looking for a place to rest. They gave him bewildered looks as he came and went.

Their faces blurred together. Raeleen did. The nicer buildings turned to graffiti-stained ones. He flew through chain-linked backyards and across emptied riverbeds.

Stuck in his own body, Kevin watched the storm clouds swirl. They looked menacing—he wouldn't have been surprised if a tornado struck down.

"I'm saving you, I'm saving you," Maïmoú repeated to herself. *"I'm not losing you. Not again. This won't be like Papa and Mama. I'm going to save you."*

He wanted to ask what'd happened to his and Derek's past selves, but they'd been dead for generations, so he assumed it wasn't pleasant. *"I want you to save yourself, too,"* he thought back. *"You deserve to be saved."*

She laughed in his mind. *"You're probably the last person on the planet who wants that."*

"You're not going to die from this, are you?"

His foot snagged on a piece of broken asphalt. He tried another question. *"You said you're going to save me, right?"*

"Yes," she answered immediately. *"I'll always save you."*

"Then you're going to save everyone, aren't you? My sister's here. My parents and aunts are here. All my friends, they need to be saved, too."

Maïmoú said nothing.

"Maïmoú, Viper's still here. If you're saving anyone, it's gonna be them, right?"

The Muralha let out another thundering *crack*.

"Why?" she whispered to herself. *"Why does it always end up like this? Am I still not good enough?"*

"What do you mean?"

"I do my best," she continued. "I'm always here for you, yet when it comes to me and your loved ones, you always, always, always..."

Her "always" repeated like a drop in a well.

"Maïmoú?" he asked. Hurting a child's feelings with your own felt awful, but it was the truth. Between him and his loved ones, how could he choose himself?

His hip clipped against a parked car. The Muralha was coming in closer.

"Hey, Papa," Maïmoú said, "if I save all of them, will you like me more? Will you and Mama not hate me?"

"What're you talking about? I'm Kevin, and I don't hate you."

"I don't want you to hate me. I'm doing my best. I don't have anything left to give you."

She didn't have to give him anything. He liked her as a person who could change and as a child who desperately needed medication and therapy. A child didn't have to give anything to an adult.

Although, according to Mom, he, too, was just a child.

Maïmoú brought him to a bridge that led into a dead field. It was dilapidated and didn't look like it could survive a truck's weight. The stream was barely there, just a bit of green water fit for frogs.

Underneath it, using the shade and what little water there was, was a curled-up girl, spotted with blue freckles with her cheeks nervously puffed out.

"Viper."

Whether she was concentrating too hard or had lost her touch, when Kevin said her name, Maïmoú released her powers over him. He fumbled on the ground, feet skipping on land and water, and fell to his knees above Viper.

Viper shrieked and covered her head, but when she saw that it was Kevin, her back fin unfurled. "Kevin," she gasped.

Still finding his feet, Kevin fell down the embankment and into her. She'd been crying in the stagnant water. The tears fell without her being underwater.

"Oh, Kevin." Her hands found him. "I'm so sorry. I was with Tokala and lost her. The crowd and sirens were too much. When I came to, she was gone and there was a man trying to grab at me. He wasn't bad, but my brain told me he was, so I ran. I kept running and then fell—I didn't think I'd ever see you again. Are you alright? How's your wing?"

"It's okay. I think."

"I can do it," Maïmoú said in his head. *"I can save them, I can. For Papa and Mama's sake, I can do anything."*

"I think," he said, not remembering if he'd already said that. "What about you?"

"I don't know. What happened? I was in the bathroom with Tokala. I didn't know where she went. I smelled smoke."

"The Drill exploded. Maïmoú's doing. They're evacuating everyone now. Tokala got out."

Viper sighed in relief, then started coughing. The tank top she had on smelled of soot and was hanging limply off her shoulders. Kevin fixed it for her, letting his hands rest over her living, breathing body.

Viper cast a tearful look up to the houses around them, to the skyscrapers disappearing into fog or ash or something else of Maïmoú's doing. He wouldn't be able to tell her everything about this world. Cars parked in driveways, palm trees blowing in turbulent wind. Wind itself, not the congested, salty air she was used to. It played with her hair as she took in the new world.

She sniffled, a new kind of pain overtaking her.

He brushed away her tears. He wanted to kiss her again, but he didn't know all her boundaries and didn't want to cross one by mistake. They'd shared two more kisses since their first, half-asleep and in need of physical touch, but did that qualify as a relationship? They hadn't discussed it. Sometimes friends kissed.

"It's so overwhelming," she confessed. "I don't understand any of it."

He took her in his arms to warm her up. "That's okay. I don't know a lot of things."

"Are those sirens normal?"

Kevin listened to the cries of the air raid siren. "No. This's a...special occasion."

"The smoke isn't normal, is it?"

"No."

"Not the fires, either?"

"No, but sometimes things catch fire. It's part of nature."

She looked to the Muralha. "Is that normal, the sky, the way it's turning shades? That's not normal, is it?"

Betwixt the panicked commotion of Raeleen, the sunrise, unbothered, was painting the sky in soft oranges and lavenders. The Sun was still behind the Muralha, but in an hour or so, they'd be enveloped in warm light.

"Actually, it is," he told her. "Every morning and evening, the sky puts on a show for us. It can be any color imaginable, even green, sometimes, after a really bad storm."

"I never knew." She sniffled again. The tears didn't stop. "It's not fair," she whispered. "I never knew."

"I know," he said, but he didn't. He wouldn't understand being kept underground your entire life, to not know a sunrise or sunset, to never get to experience life the way it was intended to be lived. He just had to be there for her. It was the most he'd asked of her, and she'd delivered tenfold.

"KEVIN."

Kevin slapped a hand over his mouth. His body shivered. An unexpected tear rolled down his cheek as Maïmoú's scream ripped apart her throat. Her screams, these quakes ravishing his body, they were her. The lightning, the thunder, the shaking. All of it had been her.

He turned, holding onto Viper for dear life. He should've been allowed to have people in his life whom he valued equally. Some he'd gotten to know, some he'd been with for years. Lifetimes, according to the Gods. Maïmoú, she'd always been there, watching over him, protecting him, and yet still, was he not allowed to live?

He tried to get Viper to stand, but his balance was unstable. They fell back into lily pads.

"Kevin?"

Behind him, something 100,000 times louder continued on his daughter's screams.

Birds scattered from the Muralha, cawing for their brothers and sisters to follow. A strong wind brushed over the top and into the valleys of Raeleen.

Over the rooftops, the meadow, and the forest, the Muralha, which had kept watch over them for generations, which had kept them safe, split down the middle and ruptured.

Water, water Kevin had never imagined in such quantity, overflowed and spilled forth into Raeleen. It was an entire wall of cascading blues and whites, roaring like a beast finally unleashed from its cage. It ate the forest in one wave. It swallowed houses, streets, neighborhoods, gone. The raw strength broke the Muralha into large pieces and spat them out like meteors.

Kevin's mind stopped working. He couldn't hear Maïmoú anymore. He didn't know what to do. Where had the sky gone? Where did the sky meet the Earth?

The last thing he saw was a five-story-tall wave crashing through the streets and sweeping everything away in pieces, then Viper as he hugged her.

And then he was gone from the world.

41

Kevin, Nikki, & Derek

He didn't know where he was, *who* he was. His brain was floating in weightlessness, a blissful ignorance. Maïmoú said reincarnation existed in this world. He still had trouble processing that. If he had drowned and was now dead, would he simply come back as a baby in a new mother's arms? Was he about to start anew?

He didn't know if he wanted that. Some people might've, but he'd worked hard at his life as Kevin Harrow. He'd grown past 5'6" and kissed someone he loved. He used to be a pushover who hid behind Derek and Nikki at the slightest inconvenience. Knowing a simple mistake could reset everything, it made him want to fight to live.

That started with opening his eyes. His lids were the heaviest they'd been, held captive in a deep sleep. He grasped at the walls of his mind, pushing himself free.

He was lying on ice. Some type of bug buzzed past his ears. On instinct, he swatted at it, and landed his hand into a pile of mushy ice.

"Ah!" He sat up, suddenly very much awake. He'd awoken in a field covered in blue and white ice. The trees in the distance were frozen stiff. The mountains were tipped white. Even the sky was white, though he saw this dark cloud stretching across it. If he squinted, it looked like a crack in the sky.

It looked like Hassan's world, minus the temperature difference and ice: a wheat farm in a world he didn't recognize.

He didn't want to be in Hassan's world. He wanted his present back, his Raeleen.

Or what was left of it. No way was it salvageable after so much water.

Being careful of his hurt wing, Kevin got up and sneezed. "Viper?" he called out.

No one spoke up. No one came to him, except for a deer grazing near the trees. It hopped away when it caught him staring too long.

He touched his heart. Back in the dream he'd shared with Maïmoú, a red string had connected them. He'd felt the tug inside of him, a bond that couldn't be broken.

He felt nothing now. The string was now loose and knotted across this new Earth.

Without any strings to guide him, Kevin got up and searched for help on his own.

With her sensitive ears, it was hard not to notice what was happening. The sound of cracking, her friends' and family's anxiety. Whatever had happened to Kevin had escaped her notice, but she pinned that down on Maïmoú.

She heard the Muralha breaking now. Everyone had in some regard, some just chose to busy themselves with other endeavors. The evidence that the end was near was there, and they'd waited until the final minute of the final hour to do anything about it.

She didn't know who to reach for first. The largest crack had frozen her into malfunctioning like she was Marcos, wherever he was in the world. He, his baby, and Zantl had disappeared with their Deities, leaving her alone with Vanna and Tokala.

When she heard the final break, she grabbed Vanna by the wrist, Tokala by the arm, and ran them into the city. She needed to find them shelter. Bring them home, into Vanna's room, back into the fallout shelter for whatever was beyond the Muralha. She still didn't know. They said you fell into the sky if you crossed over. She imagined worse.

She got all but four steps before every single corner of the Muralha gave way, bursting like a beaver dam in a rainstorm, and water Nikki hadn't seen in this lifetime came through. Waterfalls of foamy white drowned everything in its path. She couldn't see it, but beyond the houses, she heard cracking, screeching, roaring of natural destruction. Onlookers turned to watch, unable to scream due to fear. It drowned out the sirens, her heartbeat. It was coming for them.

"Nikki?" Tokala asked.

Nikki answered her by hugging her. She brought Vanna down and covered them both with her body. It was the last thing she could do for them.

Whispering an apology to them, Nikki closed her eyes and awaited the end.

She was in darkness, not of death, but not of comfortable sleep, either. It was like she'd been erased from the world. All her senses faded and she was lost in a floating, dark abyss. She was an essence now. Was this death?

No way. She still needed to find Derek and Kevin, again. She had to find her parents and make sure they were okay. No way was her life going to end here. She wasn't going to allow it.

"I'm glad you have them in your life."

She turned around, two eyes without a body attached. There was a pinprick of light in front of her, her light, herself.

Lí was smiling down at her like a proud parent. "You're lucky you have so many siblings," he told her. "I was a single child. Growing up, I stayed close to myself. I had a harder time opening up. If I had someone like Derek and Kevin around, I think things would've ended differently with me."

The fog lifted. Nikki's body and legs came back to her. The space they were in looked like they were underwater at night, the reflections of the Moon shining down on them.

"I'm sorry," Nikki heard herself say, because the way he said it made her feel nostalgic for sadness. "Am I dead?"

"No. Not yet. I don't think it's your time. But I guess no one's ready for their time."

"Were you? Sorry," she said immediately. "You don't have to answer. I'm scatterbrained."

"It's okay." Without answering the true question, Lí floated over and took Nikki's hand. Tiny fish swam around their fingers. Beneath their feet, she saw more aquatic life swimming within a sea of stars, moons, planets bigger than life itself. Bubbles left Nikki's mouth, astonished.

"You're doing great," Lí told her. "Don't worry so much about me from now on. Live for yourself. Life is precious, even if it continues on. I hope that makes sense," he added with a laugh. "I'm not so good at this."

She didn't mind. Who knew how to give good advice without being practical? She didn't even know if this was real.

Before a word could come out, she sank into space.

The sound of water woke her. It was calming, the sway of coastal waves. She was going to wake up back in Lí's mom's house. Maybe she'd get another cup of coffee.

Ice water lapped at her ankles, and she was startled awake to the real world.

The minute she opened her eyes, she pinched her thigh. She *had* to have been dreaming still. There was no way what she was seeing was real.

It was morning. The Sun had travelled to a new part of the sky, and the ground before her was water. Everywhere, all at once. It moved not like a stream or lake but something more. The waves ebbed and flowed, washing up sand that clung to her clothes. It mirrored the color of the sky and sprinkled crystals atop the brightest waves. In the distance, it truly looked like that, like crystal mountains were jutting out from the horizon.

She didn't know if she was crying from the salinity or from the view. She wanted to jump into it, taste it, start swimming in it even though she didn't know how to swim, and let the current take her away on some new journey. It was breathtaking, so wide. It was an ocean.

She hiccupped and squatted down, covering her eyes to keep the Sun out. She had to get it together, but every sense was being bombarded by a natural beauty she hadn't known existed. The sound made her weep.

She slapped her cheek and shot back up, jumping in place to get her blood pumping again. She was going to freeze out here. Wishing she had one of Li's pairs of fingerless gloves, she blew into her reddening hands to keep warm.

Behind her were tall, white cliffs she'd have trouble climbing. It felt like a storm had blown through. She tasted water in the air and the trees farther up on the cliffs bent and swayed with delayed breezes.

To her right, she spotted a building. It had pointed spirals made of grey-white brick. It looked important, if a little silly in design.

Having it as her only marker, Nikki, taking one last look at the ocean, sailed forth to find her family.

—— —◇◇◇—— —

As soon as Shào saved humanity, he puked up all his guts, fainted, and evaporated into a cloud of darkness.

Derek exhaled a long cloud of white. The wind died out so unnaturally that it felt like he was waking from a dream. The Barrier had broken into those gigantic pieces of glass and floated away from Shào's doing—how was this *not* a fever dream? At least a hangover hallucination. It was just as imaginable.

"Derek!" Oliver ran out of the castle. Before reaching him, he looked up to the sky and his pointed ears fell. His eyes followed the crack in the sky from west to east.

"That wasn't me," Derek said, "though I think I had a part in it, somehow."

"That's..." He laughed and helped Derek back up. "Are you alright?"

"Fuck if I know."

The humans came to slowly. They held their heads and drunkenly found their feet. Cellena coughed as Rosaline and Yomi sat her up. Jabel was in Maxwell's arms, still overcome from being at death's door. Maxwell, red-faced, nursed him back to health.

Oliver's tail flicked. His enemies for five centuries were waking up to his trespassing. A flight response was building in his eyes.

"Derek," someone grunted out. Coming down the stairs was Nero and his wife, Runa, holding each other to balance one another out. The tension felt by demonkind lessened at the sight of friendly faces.

The two workers helped the royal heirs up. Other knights and maids came close but didn't make a move around the formidable demonkind, beings who'd just helped save their future leaders' asses.

Derek bit his lip. He felt the tension growing like wildfire. He had to step in. "The Barrier broke," he announced, entering back into the castle. "You're not trapped no more."

As soon as he said it, the humans able to stand looked out the windows and opened doors.

"How?" Nero asked.

"How, indeed." Runa's smile was infectious. She was at one of the windows, giddily balling up her hands as she studied the sky she loved. "This is *monumental*. Is it cracking? Does it have mass? Oh, all this time, we thought it to be invisible. How extraordinary. Did you see what happened, Derek? How did it happen?"

"Uh," Derek said, and hoped that was a good enough answer.

High heels clicked down the stairs. Down the carpeted steps came three knights, some type of church man, and then the queen, left behind by her own husband to wait out doomsday. The only inkling she was suffering like the rest was a hand to her temple, but she looked more pissed than anything.

Until she saw her children lying helplessly on the floor. Upon seeing them, she lifted her dress and ran down into the foyer. Nero and Runa bowed and gave the royal family space.

"Where have you two been?" the queen demanded. "I was looking everywhere for you. I just sent a letter to your father. I thought the worst had happened."

Cellena coughed to clear her throat. "The demons, Mother."

"Don't speak." The queen glared at Derek. "What have you done to our kingdom? We let you into our home, we fed you, taught you, revelled in you, and now it's one mistake and retribution after the other. You invade us and nearly kill my children. What have we done wrong to you?"

Derek already had a list forming in his head: Killing a mother in front of him, shaming him for his gender and sexuality, calling him the wrong name, forcing him into a religion he didn't agree with.

Cellena stopped him from ending an unlikely peace treaty. She took her mother's hand. "Mother, please stop. They didn't do anything wrong."

"It wasn't them," Jabel continued for her. "There's so much more that you don't understand."

"Derek got his memories back."

"He knows what he is."

"And where he's from."

"He's spoken with the Gods."

"They're to blame for the world."

Their mother looked back and forth between each of her kids. "What has happened to you two? You're speaking in tongues."

The front door creaked open again. Holly had come in, watching something behind her. Her tail was flared in alarm.

"Oh, Gods, what now?" Derek asked, and pushed open the door with his wing.

Nothing about the world had really changed. The grounds were still snowy and the Barrier still looked like *that*. The morning Sun was rising. Birds were chirping.

People were moving. Ambling out of the forest and tree line, walking up the cliffside and flying down to colder land. They popped out like dandelions. Azaleas? Whatever flowers grew in Drail, people were coming out of the woods in droves. Every animal, every kind of person. Dogs, mice, cats. Families of tigers and foxes and herds of horses. But they weren't animals, they were like him and Holly, humans with slight animal features that made them look cooler. Ears and tails and wings and fins. They came out like the blind, touching the trees and snow and sniffing the chilly air that smelled of salt.

Oliver came out beside him. He rubbed his eyes to see straight. "What on Earth?"

"They're like me," Derek said, "and Holly."

The queen came out covering her mouth. "What is this? Is this an invasion? Who are these people?"

Derek closed the door on her. "What the fuck did those Deities do?"

"Did the Gods do this?" Oliver asked. "Are they responsible for this?"

"They must be, but I don't know who. I don't know how."

Holly's ears were flicking back and forth like radio antennae trying for the perfect station.

"Holly, do you know what happened?" Derek asked.

She took the first steps out into this new world. She went up to groups of birds, then fish, then lions. She paid particular attention to the babies held by mothers and fathers. She almost picked one up, she was so interested in it.

"Please do not touch her," said a blond-haired boy.

"I'm freezing," said the long-haired kid beside him, visibly shivering from the cold. "Can we go into that building?"

Derek cursed under his breath. That was the Marcos Unit and *Zantl*. Out of all the fucking people to magically be brought here, it had to be two of the scariest people back in Raeleen who Holly found. Zantl had all these secrets surrounding them and their parents, and Marcos was something completely other than this world. Were *they* Deities? Zantl fit the bill. Shit, he'd have to tell someone about that. Maybe Morgan or...

Working quicker than an actual robot, Holly scooped up the baby in his arms and zoomed back to the castle. Marcos flinched at the brazen kidnapping attempt and chased after her. "Wait, give her back!"

"Hey!" Zantl plodded aggressively through the snow to catch up. They couldn't match the speeds of a determined cat mom and weird robot dad. "Don't leave me alone!"

Derek snorted, watching Holly steal a child from the Marcos Unit and the next heir to an entire fucking country. He choked into Oliver's arm, still wanting to hide but curious about what the fuck these Deities had done. He saw more people, more newcomers. They'd all come from his home country.

He stopped hiding, and breathing. He sniffed the air and froze. Hitching his breath, he spun around Oliver and locked eyes with a young girl in the middle of the lawn.

He walked forwards, letting Holly run past him with the baby and Marcos and Zantl coming up shortly after. They doubletook him, shocked at finding him alive. He couldn't be bothered. No one else in the crowd mattered other than the girl he saw walking up towards the castle.

She stopped walking. Her round ears flicked to Derek, who she'd just caught sight of. He couldn't hear her, but he saw her lips move. "*Derek?*"

Letting go an ugly cry, Derek jumped off the steps and took flight. His shadow crossed over crossbreeds and banks of snow.

He crashed on top of Nikki in a flutter of feathers, tackling her into the snow and kissing every inch of her face.

"H-hey!" She hugged him underneath his wings. "Are you *crying*? The Derek I know doesn't cry, yeah?"

"I-I can't *breathe*." He hugged her back as hard as he could and then some. Snot dribbled down his upper lip and onto her as he cried into her. "How the *fuck* are you here?"

"I honestly don't know. It's such a long story. I think I might've died for a second there. What about you?"

He laughed. "Who cares about me?"

"I do!" She hugged him once more, then shivered and pushed him and herself up. "This's snow, yeah?" she asked, dusting it off her bare shoulders. "I hate it."

"How do you know—Oh, fuck, who cares?" He kissed her forehead again. He'd only gotten his memories back this morning, but the missing feeling of his siblings had burned a hole in his heart. Her cute little cheeks and her bright red eyes. Her soft, calloused hands and the smell of her clothes. He felt his body patching itself together. "I'm never letting you go again. We're merging together forever. I love you."

"I love you, too," she said, softer now, and relished in their shared hug. He'd missed her strength. He missed everything about her. "Is this where you've been living? Have you seen anyone else? I found Marcos and Zantl quick. It's hard to miss them."

"You're *friends* with them?" he asked.

She shrugged, unsure of how to answer. "Again, *long* story."

"I bet I can top it."

"Bet you can't."

"Uh, I survived falling off the Muralha—"

Nikki started laughing, already knowing their stories couldn't be matched.

Derek continued. "Survived almost dying, lived with humankind, got *saved* by Deities. Wait until you hear about them."

"There're humans here?"

"What, like you know them?" he asked sarcastically. No one in Raeleen should've known anything about them. Derek hit her shoulder for lying.

But this was his sister, she who wore her heart on her hoodie sleeves. Her face was seriously playful, like she was too happy not to joke about this.

"Wait, *do* you know?"

A bird crossbreed crossed above them, and Derek and Nikki whipped their heads up, hoping to spot a familiar face. Their mother and father, their aunt, Kevin. God, Kevin. Where had he ended up on this divine voyage across the sea?

"Where is he?" Derek whispered.

"I don't know. I lost him right before I came over."

The queen, Cellena, and Jabel came outside to witness change come into their countryside. They were followed by their workforce of maids, gardeners, clergymen, and knights. The remnants of demonkind stood beside them. Marcos and Holly fought for the baby. All barriers were broken when it came to revelations.

"Where—"

"Where have you been?"

Derek gasped. His question was finished for him in his voice, his dialect. Turning around, he found his mirror image walking through the snow to meet up with them.

"Hey," Kevin said, tears already falling. "I've been searching everywhere for you."

Derek didn't know who moved first—he'd lost feeling in his legs—but they'd met, somehow. Plowing through the snow and taking flight halfway down the hill, Derek collided into his twin like a wave against the shore.

Kevin laughed a laugh Derek had missed. His hair was longer, and one of his wings was in a sling, but he was still his Kevin, his other half that completed him.

Kevin kissed the top of his head. "Finally."

Derek couldn't find his words, so he expressed himself through kisses. His face tasted like salt.

"Okay, ow. *Ow.*" Kevin cringed and held his broken wing. "I love you so much, but—"

Derek reluctantly got up but held his sweater to stay close to him. "How is this happening?"

Kevin sucked in his lips. "Uh, do you know a girl named Maïmoú?"

"Uh, kinda. Do you?"

"We all do." Nikki came over and helped them stand. "And Shào. And Sabah and Unathi and Tsvetan. We know about the Deities."

"Really? All of them?"

"More or less," Nikki said.

"Long story," Kevin added.

"Stupidly long."

"Any annoyingly indirect."

Derek smiled in delirium. "What the fuck are our lives?"

"Messy," Kevin said.

"And unfair," Nikki added.

"Derek?" Oliver floated over the hill. He looked at Kevin and blinked. Looked at Derek and blinked harder. "My goodness," he said, "you really *are* twins."

"Hello," Kevin said. "My name's Kevin. It's nice to meet you." He elbowed Derek. "Who is this?" he whispered.

"He's my..." He looked to Oliver for confirmation. "Lover," he said, the word perfect on his tongue.

"I knew it," Nikki said. "I was just thinking about this, too."

"About what?" Derek asked.

"About how you wouldn't last long without taking on a lover."

"And this isn't even the worst first impression I've had," Kevin joked, then called out, "It's nice to meet you!"

"Oh, uhm, it's nice to meet you, too." Oliver teleported down to meet them.

Kevin yelped and Nikki tripped over a snowbank.

Oliver yelped and tripped back. "I-I'm sorry!"

"No, no, you're good." Nikki caught and righted herself. "Just not used to people teleporting around me."

"I don't think we ever will," Kevin said. "Above, I'm *so* glad I don't have to search for you two anymore."

"None of us are going anywhere," Nikki promised.

Derek smiled at that. Patting both siblings down, he showed them to the castle. "Come on. You're all freezing."

"You are, too," Nikki said, not addressing the goosebumps forming on her skin. He noticed that Marcos' baby was using one of her hoodies as a baby wrap.

Cellena and Jabel left their mother's side and came out into the open. They took in the sight of their country, watching as dozens and dozens of new faces were drawing to the largest building in the area.

The queen began fanning herself in negative-degree weather.

"All these people are freezing," Jabel said.

"We must get them inside quickly," Cellena said. "Women and children first, but we should check on the injured and the elderly as well."

"And they're people like Maxwell," Jabel noted. "They have gills, do you see that?"

Maxwell had gotten close to him, keeping a hand out in case his prince fell. It was behind the queen's back, but Maxwell was still eyeing her with contempt.

"We must be reasonable about this," the queen said. "We don't know what these people want from us. We can't open our doors to strangers." She peered at the several demons and knights littering the foyer, then at the rat girl holding her fallen angel's hand and said fallen angel's look-alike hugging him.

Her shoulders sagged.

"They need our help," Cellena said, and gestured to the Marcos Unit now reunited with his baby. It looked like he was playing keep-away with it from Holly, who was innately interested in holding her.

"It doesn't matter what they look like or what threat they might pose to us," Cellena continued. "We know nothing about them, and right now, I see young children in the snow and crying. I cannot turn my back on them. Can you, Mother?"

"That is a question for your father. He should be here within the hour."

"Our duty is to protect our people," Jabel reminded her.

"And our people include demonkind."

The queen gawked at her youngest child.

Cellena didn't budge. "We are free, Mother. The Barrier has broken. I do not believe that demonkind has ever been out to hurt us. They're our friends."

"*We* were out to hurt them," Jabel said. "At least let us see what these people want from us."

"They're the same as us, are they not?"

"Aren't they?"

The queen backed up as more crossbreeds cornered her for help. The knights behind her awaited her orders.

Kevin elbowed Derek again.

"Oh, she's like the Líder of this country."

"*She's* in charge?" Zantl brushed past a knight and got up in the queen's personal bubble. "Are you the highest authority in charge? I'm the current Líder of my world and to the beings standing before you." They held out their hand, not to shake hers, but to get something from her. They were comically short beside the queen. "Take me to your hearing room so we can discuss things more privately."

The queen couldn't take her eyes off of Zantl's wolf ears, which were flicking rapidly to keep the snow out. Under her breath, she said a prayer to her God for things to be clearer in her mind. For her sake, Derek hoped Their God wasn't as nosy as the Gods who yearned for violence.

"If you need someone to explain things," Nikki said, "I know why we're here and what happened. Most of it, if that helps you. I can help."

"I can, too," Kevin said.

"I have information pertaining to this predicament as well," the Marcos Unit said, "but my processors aren't adapting well to this sudden temperature change. I'll have to be in a more stable work environment in order to function."

The queen gave up understanding and sighed. "If you can shed any amount of light on the current situation unfolding in my kingdom, I ask that you step inside and... help me learn, or understand. Please."

"We'll do our best," Nikki said, and took to Derek's side. "You okay?"

A shit-ton of answers came to him, ranging from reassuring positivity to overwrought negativity. The world was broken but repairable. He'd found his family but only half of it. He was tired. So, so tired, A lifetime of sleep wouldn't make a dent in it.

"I need a drink," Derek said, and he and his family, both new and old, took refuge in the humans' open home.

Maïmoú

Maïmoú of Athens, in all her spanning years stuck on Earth, hated the ocean. Ever since the Hellenistic Period, this'd been the case. She'd seen it up close when she was a kid and thought it her enemy. Little did she know she couldn't drown in it like a normal human.

Now, fully in the realm of her godhood, she hated it even more. She hated the Deity it was prescribed to and hated how it limited most of humanity's efforts into evolving. Shào had had no troubles cultivating the seas and the skies for his Domain— the waterborne and airborne had claimed it easily.

Nothing angered her more than defiable limitations.

She was floating it in now, arms and legs splayed out as she floated through the debris-ladened water. The Muralha had finally cracked and, per Kevin's dare, she'd abandoned it in lieu of saving the last crossbreeds. She'd been ready for it to give way for years, but out of sheer narcissism, something she'd built up in humanity quite well, she hadn't let the Muralha fall. She couldn't let the Others win in their efforts to kick her while she was down. And, against her better judgement, she couldn't let Shào's people die. Again.

She'd thought about it, deciding whether or not to save them. It was a dance she knew well. She hated him, loved him, couldn't stand being near him, needed to be within arm's reach of him at all times. Bonds were complicated between Deities. They, whether they admitted it or not, were the most loving beings on the planet.

At that last second, she was going to use her remaining strength to save Kevin. Only him. He was all she had left, after all. She'd figure out the rest later, if any of them survived. But then, of course, like *always*, he'd fallen in love, and his heart expanded to some mudskipper girl who was more spineless than the amphibious fish she was born as.

So, taking on the challenge she'd been chipping away at for over 500 years, she'd let go the pressure she'd been containing and let the Muralha fall. She'd planned on trying to mentally transfer the crossbreeds someplace safer when it happened, but as soon as the water burst forth, she'd been swept away by the current. Her mind shattered to pieces, and when she'd come to, she was floating somewhere down Main Street, unable to move, with not a single other body floating on the surface.

They hadn't died. They'd disappeared. They, she assumed, had lived.

Of that group, however, she hadn't accounted for the thousands of drowned pets or the billions of dollars' worth of property damage now worth nothing. The city was completely lost, submerged under a mile of water—its empty canals finally had enough water to replenish the old streets for the water-borne. She knew someone somewhere would judge her for that.

"You shouldn't have done that."

"You should've done this and that in these much better ways."

"Why did you endanger your soulmates again?"

"Why couldn't you save Derek from falling?

"Or break Kevin out of the Asilo?"

"Are you weak, Maïmoú?"

"Are you losing your touch, Maïmoú?"

As if she'd let anyone see her fail.

She just couldn't physically move right now. Water was trickling around the sides of her head and eyes, bobbing her in a sea of her own destruction. She only saw the tops of the tallest buildings now. Luckily that stupid Asilo building was now at the bottom of the freaking ocean. That reeked of Shào's doing with Nikki Lenore. Kevin would praise her for not murdering her.

She inhaled slowly. She hadn't felt pain like this before. It wasn't the nausea or dizziness she'd learned to deal with, or the immeasurable pain and body tremors she expected from stunts like this. This felt like she'd been impaled, the type of injury where you couldn't feel the effects at first but knew it'd kill you if you moved an inch. Pain she couldn't heal from lay dormant in her chest.

She couldn't deal with this now, not when she still needed to find where the crossbreeds had gone. She needed to be there with them. She needed. Wanted. *Deserved* her soulmates.

More.

She made her body move. She needed it to bend to her will. She needed to show the world that humans would once again reign as the most dominant creatures in this universe. Why couldn't she do it? Why couldn't she be stronger than what her mind was allowing her to be?

More.

She tried lifting her arm out of the water. She reached for the Moon, the brightest she'd ever seen it. Without any pollution muddying the view, without the Barrier, she could see its craters and lunar bases dotting its ground. The storm which had ravished the land had passed. It was a new day.

The veins keeping her alive twisted around indestructible bone. She'd been through pain most beings couldn't physically comprehend, but *this* was getting ridiculous.

She battled it out with gritted teeth. Pain would bring her closer to the things she cherished: Derek, Kevin's safety, the ruins of Greece and India, Shào. Shào. Shào.

MORE.

Her vision blurred, as did the world, and gravity, her biggest nemesis without a face, took hold of her. With her mind breaking in two, her body went limp, and she plunged down into darkness.

"No!"

She did cartwheels through emptiness. She was in a tunnel of wind and water without a way to stop herself. Like dropping from the ceiling, she landed hard in the ruins of her own mind, her prison.

Raeleen was gone. The water, the sky she'd broken. Replacing it was endless darkness, corroding columns and foundations of houses that would never be. It mirrored the state of her own mind like a magnifying glass in-between her ears: ruined potential of growth, stuck in dark and decaying limbo.

She should've been thankful. Her pain, her spasms, all of it was gone. She was allowed to heal in peace here, a coma-like state while the Earth kept spinning.

Maïmoú's eye twitched. She *detested* being here. She didn't have time to heal. She had ten million things to accomplish and being dormant wasn't one of them. She wasn't like Ataleah and Fate, hiding away due to whatever hang-ups they had. Being dead, injured, cowards. That wasn't her.

She utilized her stalling energy on breaking out of her own head. After being stripped of her powers and left to die, she had more trouble breaking free. She'd perfected it a thousand years ago, but comparing herself now to herself a thousand years ago was like comparing an infant lost at sea to an infant teething on an atomic bomb.

"Come *on*." She hit the ground with her fist, shaking the whole Void. "We're not doing this again. I'm not staying cooped up here. I'm fine."

The darkness growled like an animal, imploring that she stay for at least a few years. Upon Kevin's request, she'd caved and reentered for a few days, and she'd always regret it. That small amount of healing wouldn't amount to the pain he had to suffer in the Asilo.

"I'm getting out," she rephrased, and pushed her long hair out of her face. She was getting out. She would no longer be a prisoner.

She took a running start. The invisible walls screamed in protest as she climbed back into the world. She dug, scratched, plowed through. The stars above her crackled like sparklers.

She puked up dark matter. "Let me *out*!" she screamed.

Something in the back of her mind snapped. Her chains, her sanity. Tumbling forwards, she inhaled a mouthful of salty water up the nose.

Her senses returned to her. Coughing, she tried getting up and out of the ocean. She rarely used her powers to float, but she couldn't stay like this anymore. Kevin, Shào, Derek. The people she loved, she needed to get back to them now.

She cursed and slapped the water, seeing her reflection ripple. "Why?" she asked no one. "Why is it always me? You must *love* this, don't you? Just like how you love watching the planet die, you sit back and watch the only person trying to change this cursed timeline and laugh. You're all psychopaths."

As she expected, she got no answer. After 500 years of being trapped, not one of the Others, not even Tsvetan, had come to talk to her. Argue with her, battle her, hug her. Not like she expected the last part, but no one had even tried convincing her to calm down.

She didn't know what they'd exactly done to her 500 years ago, but she knew what they'd wanted: to kill her and Shào for good. Kill all the humans and crossbreeds who'd made the world better. They saw beingkind as parasites and wanted them exterminated for good.

What a selfish way to revert back to their good old days, all pinned on two thirteen-year-olds.

Looking back up into the clearest skies she could imagine, Maïmoú readied her broken mind and teleported herself to Shào. Usually, if a Deity was close to another, they'd feel a string in their heart get tugged. It was the string of fate that threaded them all together. When someone acted out or, say, massacred an entire village, the string would be yanked.

She sensed it—sensed *him*—like an internal radar had been switched on in her head. All this time she had no idea if he'd survived the Separation or not, but she knew him. She knew that, despite his fascination with martyrdom, Shào wouldn't walk into Hell without dragging Maïmoú down with him.

She disappeared and travelled across the world in an eye-blink. Her body was pulled against time and space. After breaking every law the Earth tried placing on her, she teleported from the Brazilian coastline Raeleen had been built upon and found herself a mile in the sky, looking down at England's southern coastline.

She breathed out a confused exhale. She saw farmlands and mountains and forests that'd overtaken the confined land. Raeleen had had enough materials to rebuild the Asilo, maintain a humanoid robot, keep most of its buildings and Old World's fallout shelters functional. This country had farmlands, a broken Barrier—who'd broken it?—and oceans.

Oceans. She cursed the Deities and their ways. *This* place had an ocean, and Raeleen didn't? They'd left the crossbreeds without access to the Atlantic, pushing them to rely on defective techniques to get them through life. What little lakes they'd provided for them had dried up in the 2150s, only fifty years after the Separation. That was the one good thing Zantl's family had done: preserve the waterborne species. When they'd started housing the water breathers in the Asilo, Maïmoú had regained a smidgen of faith in Shào's Domain.

But what their predecessors had ultimately done to them earned them a ticket to every permutation of Hell that existed. They'd experimented on their capabilities, expunged their existence from the public so nobody knew about the sadistic treatments being done to them. Thousands mutilated and diseased, and *she* had been penalized to watch it happen for centuries as a floating corpse.

She really hoped Unathi would end Zantl's life soon. Cut the cord and start over as a new reincarnation. She hated Unathi as much as the Others, but she remembered them as the smarter Deity of the group.

But she also knew how much Unathi must've loved Zantl. When she'd found out that Unathi had entered Raeleen to have sex with some sixteen-year-old, she understood what was happening. When Tsvetan had come out of the woodwork to pretend to be a dad to a baby shark—they were freaks, all of them—she wanted to strangle them both. Ignoring her was one thing, but coming into her prison to coo and gawk at their new-born soulmates *instead*? She'd tried so hard to become visible then just to tear them apart.

She pushed back her hair again. She focused on this coastal village. Beneath her, both humans *and* crossbreeds ambled around the coastline in disbelief. She watched them like a patron at a zoo. Waterborne from the forests found their way into the frigid oceans. Bird crossbreeds were high in the sky, looking for their separated loved ones. The air smelled different here. It smelled of pine trees and snow.

Her humans were alive.

And Derek and Kevin were near.

She could feel them. They were close. She floated towards their energy to a remodeled castle on the cliffside. It seemed like the humans had devolved to a freaking Renaissance era. Men were dressed as knights riding horseback. They were organizing crossbreeds into some semblance of order. How impossible it was to gather beings during an upheaval.

She paused over the castle. Betwixt the flyers and swimmers, there were a few who flew without wings, swam without fins.

Dragon crossbreeds, *real* dragon crossbreeds. She only counted a few, but she knew their breeds anywhere.

When the Separation had occurred, she'd assumed the Others had massacred the world's single magical species to teach her and Shào a lesson. Their breeds hadn't come over to Brazil with the crossbreeds, and she'd mourned them. Their species had been so domineering. They'd owned countries and controlled civilizations due to their semi-divine powers.

They must've only been uncoupled like a motherless child in a mall. Wandering around, she saw a Snow-Faced Hilltop dragon, Carnes Bat dragons, and Yokani Toxin dragons. She even spotted a South American Water dragon. She couldn't find any Greek Mavros or Chinese dragons, but she guessed that much. They had been dead for thousands of years, and the crossbreed variants had gone extinct after the 100s. Shào was the last Chinese dragon alive, unable to die by conventional means.

She looked above her. Like in Raeleen, this country's Barrier had been broken.

"What did Shào do here?" she asked herself. *She* had only broken the Muralha. *This*, this hadn't been her.

She teleported inside the royal home. The foyer and halls were cluttered with confused crossbreeds and humans trying to help them.

She left them all be. Up these stairs. Down these halls. She panted, following her parents' threads. They were entangled again.

She came to a locked door carved with dragons and wartime. She touched the handle, licking her lips. She must've looked a wreck. She hoped they wouldn't mind.

Sitting on couches was an upscale family who must've owned the castle, dressed regally and looking important, and in front of them, sitting together as they ought to have been, were Maïmoú's parents from another time. Derek and Kevin sat beside their sister and the other soulmates—Marcos, Zantl, the baby Alexi. There was another, one Maïmoú knew from the 22nd century. Holly, if she remembered correctly. She looked exactly the same, as if she hadn't died after 500 years.

None of them mattered. None of them would ever matter as much as her Hassan and Hadiya.

Maïmoú floated into the living room to meet her twins. "Hi," she said, smiling. "I'm back, so everything's going to be okay."

Kevin picked at his cuticles as he listened to the humans speak. Derek dropped his head on the shoulder of a Snow-Faced Hilltop dragon. They looked close. They looked mated.

Unable to be ignored, Maïmoú walked around the glass table to get their attention.

She walked through it, invisible.

Her dead heart panged. "No." She looked down at her hands. "No. No. No."

Neither twin noticed her. Desperate, she tried to touch Kevin. "Kevin?"

Her hand phased through him and into the couch.

She ripped her arm away. She began to shake. "Derek? Kevin?"

None of them looked up. None of them saw her. She was being ignored.

Her heart sped up, shaking her whole body. This couldn't be happening. Not again. Not after everything she'd accomplished for them. "Look at me!" she screamed. "Please! I'm here!"

Kevin sneezed. Nikki fixed his hair for him. Derek was smiling into that dragon's shoulder.

Maïmoú clutched her heart. Fine, then. No big deal. She'd just push herself even harder, that's all. In a few days, they'd be able to see her again. They had to. They would.

Saddened by their long-awaited reunion, Maïmoú floated through the castle's roof and over the sea.

Her humans, they felt okay here. The crossbreeds looked fine. The dragons she thought had gone extinct looked healthy, and the land, although primitive, sported enough materials to easily house Shào's 300,000 people. She saw plains, mountains, rivers, and forests.

Gentle winds carried the ocean breeze through her. It twirled her dress still stained by dark matter. It would've given her goosebumps if she could feel such a thing.

"What?" she whispered. "What're you all waiting for? I know you're all dying to see me. Well, here I am."

The clouds parted, revealing bright beams of sunlight through her. Her body didn't cast a shadow on the passing clouds.

She tore at her hair, begging for it to rip knowing it wouldn't. "I said I'm here!" she yelled. "Where are you? Why're you ignoring me?"

Holding her sides tight, so tight her nails dug into her stomach, she heaved over. Not to vomit. Her body just wasn't centered and she needed to fix that. That's what she did. She fixed things.

Spit dribbled from her mouth. "Kai!" she screamed. "Shào Kai, you come out right now and *look* at me!"

Nobody answered her.

And that was okay, too. They were just ignoring her. They did that. Soon, Tsvetan or maybe Unathi would come to her. Sabah would come next, silently judging everything they did and berating her for existing. Maybe Ataleah would be there, floating like a lifeless balloon without a thought in her head. Maybe she'd finally see Fate and he'd introduce himself to her as a long-lost uncle or something.

Shào, he was who she needed most. She wanted to hold him and taste his skin and kill him and revive him. Shào, her other half, her husband, her best friend and enemy, he was the reason she'd been fighting for so long. Even if the Others didn't like them, even if Shào refused her, he and she were destined to be intertwined forever. Their love exceeded all the stars and planets combined.

Whatever anyone said, she'd done it. Humans and crossbreeds were safe on an island not threatened by its own Barrier, Hassan and Hadiya got to live another lifetime, and Shào was alive somewhere in this Godforsaken world with his stupid soulmate and stupid crossbreeds. She'd saved everyone, and everyone was happy.

Her lower lip quivered.

She blinked back her emotions. She wanted to believe she had the willpower not to revert back to her old self, but she failed. Alone, Maïmoú cried by herself, to herself, and for herself as the world beneath her slowly rebuilt itself.

THANK YOU TO ALL MY KICKSTARTER BACKERS!

AJ Knight
ALE Cappacetti
Aaron Martinez
Abigail Spears
Akeea Fox
Alex
Alexis W
Alynne
Amara
Amaryllis Jeanne
    Quiliiou
Amelia
Amelia H
    bookcasequeen
Andrew C
    Stackhouse
Andromeda
    Taylor-Wallace
Anon. H
Ashley Kelly
Athens
Avery "AJ" Gragg
Azure
Bad Artist Bri
Baron
Briar N
Briseis
Brooks Moses
Calypso Rhyder
Celestine De La Tour
Chelsea Zajitz
Chelsey
Christian Blakes
    (@blwhere1)

Clara Luca
Connor Lee
Cristov Russell
Damadorias
Danielle
Darcy Coleman
Dawn
Deathgod_Shi
Demitri Beltran
Denver
Doc
Dr Serenity
    Serseción
ET Gilmore
Elizabeth J. Sargent
Em
Emily
Emily
Emily P.
Erisol
Fiz
Fright Moore
Gabriel Rivers
Gaku
Gryvon
Hannah Carter
Hikaru_wins
HippyeXD
I McClure
Iliana Nieves
illusivium
Iris Lynch
IronRequiem
Jenkins Blue

Jenna Wilhelmi
Jessica Graves
Jo Morelli
Joshua M Dreher
Julie Alviar
K Rainey
Kat
Katherine Long
Kemone Armstrong
Kit Farmer
Kosta
Kristineyancey
   @gmail.com
Kylie Weaver
Lane Lopez
Leishycat
LumineSomnium
Maia Ragna
Mari
Me_Culp_
Mia Tylia
Mikayla P.
Moona OM
MythSigh
Nadine K.
NanLia
Nanija
Nellie
Nicole Norrington
Niki Pentland
Nisha Hollis

OdinsSage
Olivia Montoya
Pate
Phillip A
Phoenix
Quartuusk
R. Joseph Snyder
RJ Hopkinson
Roaming Kitsune
Rotten Boi
Runo
Sam Vermillion
Sapphire
Sekinat Adekanbi
Shihachi
Shochu
Skywings14
Susan S.
Tanya and Scott
The Blerd Newsletter
The Selkie
   Delegation
The Wereable Squad
Tiaan Vermeulen
Tim Sauke
tower
V-Gin
Waffle
Wick P. Crow

Melissa Sweeney grew up in a small farm town in Connecticut and got her B.A. in English at Central Connecticut State University in 2017. Before, during, and after that time, she drew and wrote about her characters as a dubious coping mechanism for her anxiety. She currently lives with her girlfriend and their cats and continues battling on which story to write next. You can follow her on social media (@melissanovels) or on her website melissanovels.com.